M. K. Hume is a retired academic, who is married with two grown-up sons and lives in Queensland, Australia. Having completed an MA and Phd in Arthurian Literature many years ago, M. K. Hume has fulfilled a lifelong dream to walk in the footprints of the past by retelling the epic tale of Arthur in a magnificent trilogy. The first two novels in the Arthurian trilogy, *Dragon's Child* and *Warrior of the West*, are also available from Headline, as is the first novel in M. K. Hume's new trilogy about the life of Merlin, *Merlin: Demon's Gift*.

Praise for M. K. Hume's *King Arthur* trilogy:

'An altogether totally original version of the Arthur legend, owing more to Cornwell and Iggulden than to Malory, with a sense of reality pervading it that keeps you interested. It's a slice of history that's totally, utterly believable. Magnificent' www.booksmonthly.co.uk

'M. K. Hume fuses history and myth to offer an imaginative retelling of the latter years of Arthur's reign. This is historical fiction of the most bloodthirsty and roistering kind. Hume tells her story with such gusto that the pace never flags. Fans of Fiona McIntosh, David Gemmell's *Troy* and Manfredi's *Alexander* series will greedily devour this book' *Australian Bookseller & Publishers Magazine*

'It's always good to come across another great historical series and this new trilogy from M. K. Hume looks set to be one. Exciting, violent and bloody and full of historical facts to keep you gripped throughout. Up there with Conn Iggulden and Bernard Cornwell www.

KING ARTHUR:
THE
BLOODY CUP

M. K. Hume

HEADLINE PUBLISHING GROUP
An Hachette UK Company
338 Euston Road
London NW1 3BH

www.headline.co.uk
www.hachette.co.uk

First published in Great Britain in 2010
by HEADLINE REVIEW
An imprint of HEADLINE PUBLISHING GROUP

First published in paperback in Great Britain in 2010
by HEADLINE REVIEW

1

Cataloguing in Publication Data is available from the British Library

ISBN 978 0 7553 4873 2 (B format)
ISBN 978 0 7553 7415 1 (A format)

Typeset in Golden Cockerel by Avon DataSet Ltd,
Bidford on Avon, Warwickshire

Printed and bound in Great Britain by Clays Ltd, St Ives plc

Headline's policy is to use papers that are natural, renewable and recyclable
products and made from wood grown in sustainable forests.
The logging and manufacturing processes are expected to conform
to the environmental regulations of the country of origin.

Friends, real friends, are rare and special. We have family, built in, and whether we like them or not is immaterial. Mostly, we love them because we have shared history, memories and blood.

But friends are chosen because they fill the empty places in the heart. The best friends stand behind us, protecting our backs in times of trouble.

So Lynne Baker, Roger Hughes, Pauline Reckentin, Robyn Jones and Penny Steel, this book is for you. Pauline convinced me years ago that I would succeed in this endeavour; Roger is my mate, a fellow reader of odd, interesting ideas, and Robin and Lynne and Penny have stood 'in the trenches' with me when times were tough and I tried to slay the odd dragon.

Therefore it is fitting that Artor's most terrible blows and most difficult decisions are dedicated to you all. You've been with me on life's journey, and you have cared for me regardless of my manifold sins.

ACKNOWLEDGEMENTS

The Bloody Cup, Volume III of *The Chronicles of Arthur*, is the culmination of a perilous journey of self-discovery. Every adult person in the Western World knows that King Arthur dies at the conclusion of the Arthuriad, so how can an author find something unique to say of a man whose very existence is an inextricable part of the history of Britain?

Much of the credit for completing my task must be given to those friends and supporters who advised, encouraged and conspired to carry me over the line to complete my journey. My special thanks go to my super-agent, Dorie Simmonds, whose enthusiasm, expertise and confidence put the project together so professionally. My special gratitude goes to my partner, typist, editor, marketer and manipulator, Michael Hume, who helped me to see and understand the challenges that all men of action and ability (such as he) face as they reach the zenith of their lives and their futures begin to fade away into old age. The need to retain dignity and self-worth is important to all men, most of all those who have flown so very, very high as Arthur did during his forty years as Dux Bellorum of Britain.

To all those who helped me to try to bring Arthur back to life, may his gods walk with you through life and when you join him at last, may he recognize you – and offer you a beer! To you all, the good and the bad, my eternal thanks.

Myrddion's Chart of Pre-Arthurian Roman Britain

The Journey of the Bloody Cup

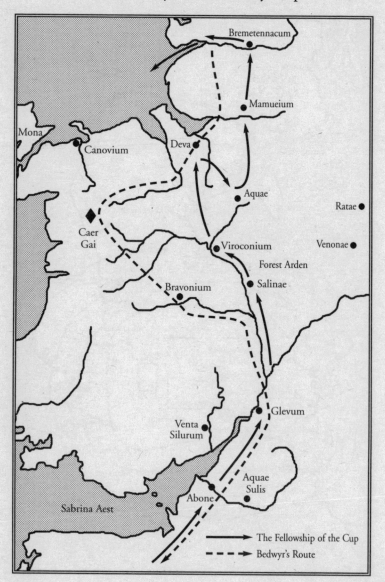

Bremetennacum

Mamueium

Mona

Canovium

Deva

Aquae

Ratae

Caer
Gai

Viroconium

Venonae

Forest Arden

Bravonium

Salinae

Glevum

Venta
Silurum

Aquae
Sulis

Abone

Sabrina Aest

→ The Fellowship of the Cup

-- → Bedwyr's Route

Site Plan of Cadbury and Cadbury Tor

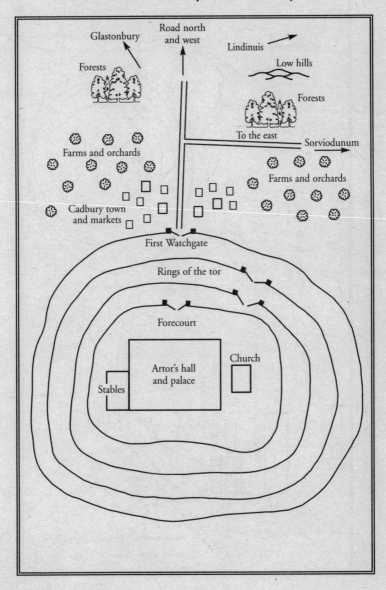

Glastonbury and Environs

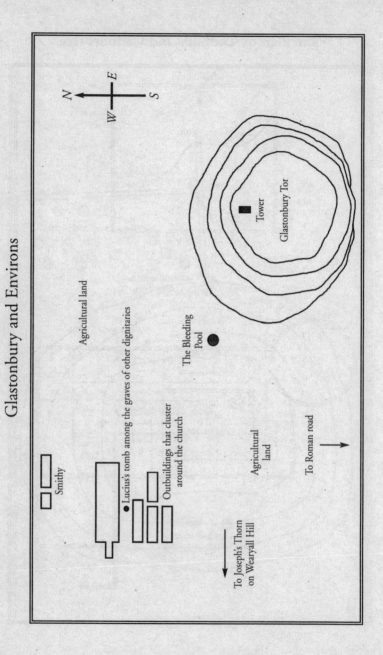

Floor Plan of the Villa at Salinae Minor

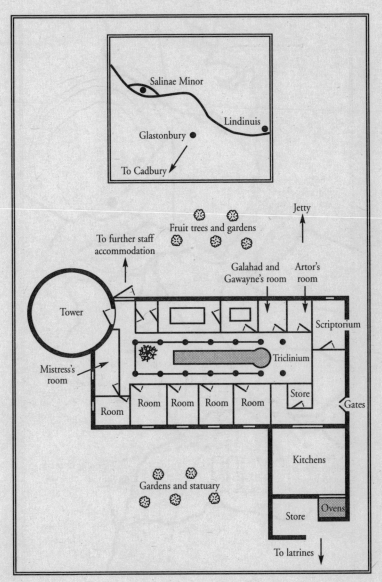

The Final Campaign between Artor and Modred

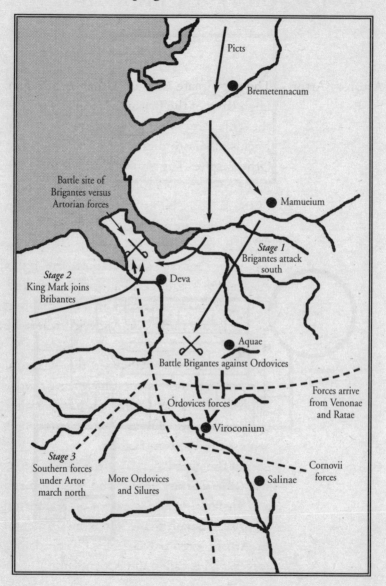

Picts

Bremetennacum

Mamueium

Battle site of
Brigantes versus
Artorian forces

Stage 1
Brigantes attack
south

Stage 2
King Mark joins
Bribantes

Deva

Aquae

Battle Brigantes against Ordovices

Forces arrive
from Venonae
and Ratae

Ordovices forces

Viroconium

Stage 3
Southern forces
under Artor
march north

More Ordovices
and Silures

Cornovii
forces

Salinae

DRAMATIS PERSONAE

Artorex/Artor:	The legitimate son of Uther Pendragon, High King of the Britons. Artorex is sent to the Villa Poppinidii as an infant by Bishop Lucius of Glastonbury to protect him from Uther's spite. The young man assumes the name of Artor when he is crowned as King of the Britons. He rules his kingdom from the unassailable fortress at Cadbury Tor.
Ban:	Named the Firebrand of the West, he is Uther Pendragon's champion. He fights Artorex in single combat and is defeated. Ban accompanies Artorex in a suicidal raid on the Saxon fortress at Anderida where he is killed.
Bandur:	Also known as Sea Changer, the Thane of Nidum. Bandur is an old warrior who chooses to die at Gawayne's hands rather than surrender during Artor's campaigns against the Western Saxons.
Bedwyr:	Son of the guardians of Arden Forest. He is from the Cornovii tribe, and was captured and enslaved by the warriors of Glamdring Ironfist, a Saxon thane. He is instrumental in Artor's eventual defeat of Glamdring's forces, and is called the Arden Knife.

Botha:
Captain of Uther Pendragon's Guard. He is ordered by Uther to kill Artorex's family and destroy the Villa Poppinidii.

Bregan:
A blacksmith in a village close to the Villa Poppinidii whose son, Brego, is saved by Artorex from the depravity of the Severinii family. In gratitude, Bregan makes Artorex a gift of the iron dragon knife.

Caius:
Son of Ector and Livinia, and foster-brother to Artorex. He later becomes Steward to King Artor. Over many years, Caius proves his perversity, although he is an excellent warrior, and is eventually caught in an attempt to rape and murder Nimue. Myrddion poisons him with lethal mushrooms when he becomes convinced that Caius will never change and might escape punishment for his crimes.

Cerdic ap
Cerdyn:
The flag-bearer of Artor's emissaries who were sent to negotiate with Glamdring Ironfist. The envoys are all slain.

Cletus:
An elderly steward at the Villa Poppinidii.

Ector:
The Celtic husband of Livinia. Ector is Master of the Villa Poppinidii near Aquae Sulis. He is the father of Caius, and the foster-father of Artorex. He acts as Pater Familias and, prior to his death, brokers the marriage of Artor's secret child, Licia, to Comac, Llanwith's son. When he dies, he is buried in Gallia's Garden.

Enid:
Wife of Gawayne. Enid is a quiet, gentle young aristocrat who loves her husband and is happy to bear Gawayne's child. Unfortunately, the birth is difficult, and Enid almost dies. Myrddion and Nimue intervene and their medical skills save her life.

Frith:
An elderly female slave in the Poppinidii household. She mothers Artorex during his childhood and is his confidante. She becomes maid to Artorex's wife, Gallia, and dies with her during an attack on the villa by renegade warriors sent by Uther Pendragon. Her ashes are mingled with those of her mistress in Gallia's Garden.

Gaheris:
Gawayne's younger brother and the youngest son of King Lot. He is also one of King Artor's emissaries who attempt to broker a truce with Glamdring Ironfist. He is murdered with the other envoys that undertake the mission, an act that precipitates a treaty between Lot and Artor.

Galahad:
The infant son of Gawayne.

Gallia:
The first wife of Artorex, daughter of a Roman trader from Aquae Sulis who has died in an epidemic of the plague. She is murdered on the orders of Uther Pendragon, along with her unborn child. Later, Artor orders a garden, called Gallia's Garden, to be built in her memory.

Gallwyn:	Mistress of the kitchens at Ratae. She is the foster-mother of Nimue.
Gareth:	Grandson of Frith, protector of Licia and, for a time, the Steward of the Villa Poppinidii. Gareth builds Gallia's Garden and cares for Licia until she marries. Freed from his oath, Gareth journeys to Cadbury Tor to hold Artor to his word that the young man may become a warrior and join his guard.
Gawayne:	The eldest son of King Lot and Queen Morgause of the Otadini tribe. Although a philanderer of note, he is one of King Artor's staunchest supporters. He is the brother of Gaheris. Foolishly, Gawayne is seduced by Wenhaver, an affair that continues through his marriage to Enid and the birth of his son, Galahad. It is only when Gawayne flees to the north that he manages to escape his libido and the amorous clutches of the queen.
Glamdring Ironfist:	Thane of the Western Saxons. Glamdring executes Artor's envoys who have been sent to the land of the Demetae to broker an honourable truce. During this treachery, Gaheris, the son of King Lot, is murdered because the boy will not forsake his oaths to King Artor. Artor defeats Glamdring during the battle of Mori Saxonicus where the Saxon is out-manoeuvred and outclassed by

	Artor. Later, because of the hatred and duplicity of the Cornovii slave, Bedwyr, Glamdring is trapped in his fortress of Caer Fyrddin and is executed.
Glaucus:	A sarcophagus merchant. Queen Wenhaver's maid, Myrnia, is ordered by the queen to find a bath and the confused maid enlists the help of Myrddion. The adviser purchases a sarcophagus in the form of the goddess Andromeda that is adapted to meet Wenhaver's requirements. Glaucus is instructed to destroy the lid of the coffin to ensure that Wenhaver does not become aware of Myrddion's practical joke.
Gruffydd:	One of Myrddion's most able spies. He saves an infant, Nimue, from freezing to death at Durobrivae after her Jute mother was raped and murdered. He becomes Artor's sword bearer. Later, after the death of Gallwyn, her nurse, Gruffydd takes Nimue to Cadbury where she is apprenticed to Myrddion.
Julanna:	Wife of Caius and mother of his daughter, Livinia Minor. She becomes the dowager of the Villa Poppinidii, with a number of daughters to Caius – she rules the villa in all but name.
Licia:	Daughter of Artorex and Gallia. Licia marries Comac, the youngest son of Llanwith pen Bryn, Artor's friend and one of the Three Travellers. Artor agrees, for he

honours Ector's decision and knows that Llanwith will keep Licia safe. She is required to change her name to the less Roman-sounding Anna. In time, she becomes queen of the Ordovice who believe she is the daughter of Uther Pendragon and, therefore, Artor's sister.

Livinia Major: Wife of Ector and the last of the Roman Poppinidii line. She is mother to Caius and foster-mother to Artorex. She is accident-ally slain by Caius during a domestic dispute. Artor swears to the dying woman that he will protect her son.

Livinia Minor: Eldest daughter of Caius and Julanna. Livinia Minor and Licia are good friends and she marries the son of the Magistrate of Aquae Sulis.

Lot: King of the Otadini tribe and a fierce enemy of King Artor. He is allied to the Eastern Saxons and only breaks his oath to them when the Thane of the Western Saxons kills Gaheris, his youngest son.

Lucius: Bishop and leader of the Christian community at Glastonbury. He is charged by Uther Pendragon with the task of killing the infant Artorex but, instead, sends the babe to Lord Ector of the Forest Sauvage to be fostered. Later, Lucius hides the sword and crown of Uther Pendragon to ensure that only the rightful claimant to the High

King's throne can find and recover them. Artorex succeeds in this task, and becomes High King as King Artor of the Britons.

Morgan: Eldest daughter of Gorlois and Ygerne. She is the sister of Morgause, the half-sister of Artorex and is a noted witch-woman. She meddles in Artor's marriage and offers de-stabilizing advice to the impressionable Wenhaver. She gradually isolates herself, and becomes a recluse north of the Wall.

Morgause: Second daughter of Gorlois and Ygerne. She is the half-sister of Artorex, and is married to King Lot of the Otadini tribe. She is the mother of Gaheris, whom she mourns insanely, and journeys with her husband to see justice done against the Western Saxons. She is reputed to have been seduced by the boy king of the Brigante and sends the resulting infant, Modred, back to his father to be raised.

Myrddion: Chief advisor to the High King. He finally leaves his master to wed Nimue, his apprentice. They make their home in distant Caer Gai, a ruined fortress in the mountains.

Myrnia: Maidservant of Wenhaver and scapegoat for the ills that assail Wenhaver's life. Artor is forced to intervene when an angry Wenhaver wounds the young girl with a sewing hook. The servant is blinded in one eye and is

	badly scarred. The girl is sent back to her village with a substantial dowry.
Nils Redbeard:	The Captain of Glamdring Ironfist's fortress at Caer Fyrddin.
Nimue:	An infant girl saved by Gruffydd. She is made a ward of Artorex when he is still Dux Bellorum. Later, she becomes Myrddion's apprentice and the love of his life. Because of her exceptional character, the people of Cadbury call her The Maid of Wind and Water. When Caius tries to butcher her, Myrddion steals her away and they flee Cadbury to settle at Caer Gai where they make a pleasant life for themselves and live happily.
Odin:	A Jutlander and member of the Scum, mercenaries who assist Artorex to capture the Saxon fortress of Anderida. He becomes Artorex's bodyguard.
Pelles (Pinhead):	A member of the Scum, and a talented bowman. He marries a local woman and becomes one of Artor's most trusted captains.
Perce (Percivale):	A kitchen boy at Ratae who aspires to become a warrior. He accompanies Gruffydd and Nimue to Cadbury Tor where he becomes Targo's bodyguard and servant. The aged mercenary tutors Perce and sees to his training, eventually arranging for Artor to make him a member of the king's guard.

After Targo's death, Artor takes Percivale into his bodyguard for love of the old Roman. Percivale is a Christian.

The Scum: A small group of some twenty mercenaries who are recruited by Artorex for the raid on the impregnable Saxon fortress at Anderida. Rufus, Pinhead and Odin are three notable members of the Scum.

The Severinii: A Roman family domiciled in a villa in Aquae Sulis. The family consists of Severinus (an epicure), Severina (his mother) and Antiochus (his catamite). The Severinii have been responsible for the rape and murder of at least eight children from the local villages. Severinus is a friend of Caius and is brought to justice by Artorex. The Severinii are executed and their villa is burned to the ground.

Simeon (Simon): A Jewish priest at Glastonbury. He is a master metal-smith who fashions Artor's crown and re-forges Caliburn, Artor's sword.

Simnel: The cousin of Luka, and responsible for the plot to assassinate the King of the Brigante and his heirs. Artor captures the murderers and tortures them until they implicate Simnel in the plot. Under threat of being cast out of the union of kings, the Brigante leaders hand Simnel over to Artor, who exacts revenge upon the traitor for the loss of his friend.

Targo:

A professional Roman soldier who is Ector's sword master at the Villa Poppinidii. On the instructions of the Three Travellers, he instructs Artorex in martial skills. Over time, Targo becomes Artor's most trusted and loved servant, fighting next to his lord in all of Artor's twelve campaigns, including the last battle at Mori Saxonicus.

Retired at last, he acts as an advisor to Artor and trains Percivale to become a warrior. Eventually, he develops a lung complaint during a time of plague and dies. During his illness, Nimue treats Targo at great cost to herself and wins approval when she speaks at Targo's funeral. Artor is bereft at the loss of his friend, the only man who had his complete trust. Targo leaves *Targo's Laws* behind as his legacy, and as a means of keeping his lord safe. He charges Odin to protect the High King until death.

Three Travellers:

(1) Myrddion Merlinus. Myrrdion is the chief advisor to both Uther Pendragon and King Artor. He is a healer, philosopher, architect, strategist and spymaster.

(2) Prince Llanwith pen Bryn. Llanwith eventually becomes king of the Ordovice tribe of Cymru. Before he dies, the king arranges the marriage of his youngest son, Comac, to Artor's daughter, Licia, thus

ensuring that Artor's daughter will receive life-long protection.

(3) Prince Luka. Luka eventually becomes king of the Brigante tribe of Cymru. In later life, Luka is assassinated by Simnel, a venal cousin who covets his throne. Luka's sons and grandsons are also killed in the plot. Artor takes a fearsome revenge upon Luka's murderers.

Ulf: One of the three Celtic warriors spared by Glamdring Ironfist specifically to return the heads of Artor's emissaries to the High King with an insulting message. Ulf vows to kill ten Saxons for every Celt killed at the execution site, or die in the process.

Uther Pendragon: The successor to Ambrosius as High King of the Britons. He is the father of Artorex.

Vortigern: The King of Cymru several generations before the time of Artor. He is remembered because he welcomed the Saxons into Dyfed to placate his Saxon queen, Rowena. He attempted to sacrifice Myrddion in a bid to build his fortress at Dinas Emrys.

Wenhaver: High Queen, great beauty and strumpet, Wenhaver has sulked, hindered and run roughshod over the court of the High King for decades. Even as she ages, her considerable vanity and self-satisfaction continue to plague Artor and his plans for the future.

Wyrr: Glamdring Ironfist's albino soothsayer and

the brains to Glamdring's brawn. This dangerous symbiosis is destroyed when Bedwyr kills him at the gates of the Caer Fyrddin, during Bedwyr's escape from captivity.

Ygerne: Originally the wife of Gorlois, the Boar of Cornwall. After his death, she married Uther Pendragon. She is the natural mother of Artorex.

PROLOGUE

It is always better
    to avenge dear ones than to indulge in
    mourning.
For every one of us, living in this world
    means waiting for our end.

Beowulf

Three furtive men made their separate ways to a lonely bothie north of Ratae. Summer was almost fled and the woods wore the first yellowing leaves of autumn. Although the night was still, the moon was obscured by cloud as if the last storms of the warm months were building around the mountain chain.

'Enter, traveller! You're late!'

The man who spoke was muffled in a long black cloak that disguised his form and transformed him into a shadowy puddle in the rear of the wattle and daub room. The fire was unlit, so his face was invisible within the cowl of his cloak. A heavy wrapper of coarse wool concealed his mouth and nose, while the fabric also disguised the man's voice.

'The route was difficult – and I dared not travel by daylight,' the smaller man replied, as he insinuated his body into the room through the derelict entrance.

The newcomer was even more heavily disguised than his master. Ragged travelling gloves disguised his hands and his beggar's robes turned him into a shapeless, verminous lump.

'Well, at least you're here now,' the third man stated roughly, causing the beggar to bridle within his coarse disguise. 'Have you found men who are suitable to our needs, men who'll keep their mouths shut?'

'Give me credit for some gumption,' the beggar responded irritably. 'The High King makes enemies easily, so I've encountered no difficulty in tracking down several men who have been thrown out of Cadbury for drunkenness or theft. They like their heads attached to their treasonous shoulders, so they'll obey me when the time comes.'

The third man snorted derisively and leaned against the far wall, cleaning his nails with a plain, wickedly sharp knife. Unlike his companions, he had chosen to bare his face, an unprepossessing network of puckered scars rendered more hideous by a sunken eye socket whose empty lid had been stitched shut. His plaited hair marked him as a warrior and a decorated eyepatch had been pushed up on to his broad brow for comfort. A heavy jerkin showed signs of hard use, although the leather was supple with oil, and bronze plates had been threaded on to the heavy ox hide to provide added protection. His kit was polished and in good condition, as befitted a mercenary.

'The time is right for us to strike,' the beggar hissed. 'And, with any luck, the High Bastard won't see any threat coming. He's grown soft on top of Cadbury Tor, bedding his serving women and avoiding his whore of a queen. He's old. And he's far too cosy with the Christian Church. It's the priests who'll own us all at this rate.'

The seated man in black made a sharp action with one shadowy hand.

'Artor is ready to fall.'

'I have no cause to love the man who killed my master,' the warrior began slowly. 'But it would be disastrous to underestimate Artor. He's survived this long because he's cunning and prepared. He manipulates our people and his bodyguard cannot be bribed.'

'The common people are stupid, because they love Artor.' The beggar sighed. 'Any number of them would inform on us in a moment if we don't take care.'

The black-clad figure laughed thinly, although neither of his companions imagined that he felt any mirth.

'The peasants have forgotten the old days before Pendragon, but there's much dissatisfaction in the northern towns,' the beggar continued, and smiled within the shadow of his cowl. 'We must capitalize on their discontent, and I've found a solution that might help our cause. I ask your permission to act on it.'

He aimed his request directly at the black-clad man, who was displeased at the tone of the demand. However, although his fists clenched reflexively, he visibly calmed his telltale hands.

'Continue.'

'We need a symbol to unify the common people and to lead them into a popular revolt against the rule of the bastard king.'

The beggar moved further into the bothie to reveal a

twisted, womanish mouth above and below the crude wrappings that disguised his features. Only the glint of his deep-set eyes, fanatical with madness, was visible below his cowl.

'I've found something that we can shape to suit our need. It's a gift from the gods, and it's so very old that it may have been held by the Old Ones themselves – a symbol that could promise a better life to even the lowliest of men.'

He could see that he had gained the attention of his two listeners.

'I speak of the Cup of Bishop Lucius of Glastonbury,' the beggar whispered reverently. 'I first heard of it when I gave shelter to an unfrocked priest who'd been evicted from the abbey. I swear that the goddess, Ceridwen, she who gave knowledge to men, sent this fool to me. I've searched out any talk of the Cup since the priest crossed my path. It seems that Lucius was a pagan Roman in his youth and the Cup came into his possession by some trick of fate. The priests count it as holy because Lucius owned it, but I swear I smell blood whenever I think of it. The priest had helped to bury Lucius, and he wept when he thought of his old master closed into the cold earth with only his cup for comfort.'

'Why not just use any old cup that we can find?' the black-clad man asked. 'Why disturb Lucius's bones for no reason? To attack Glastonbury will draw the attention of the Christians and Artor. Your argument is flawed, or perhaps it's motivated by your personal spite.'

The beggar's body bridled with affront.

'I have thought of the risks of my plan, but this cup has an inbuilt symbol with a potency that we can use to achieve our aims. The Christian faithful will honour Lucius's relic and will invest it with power. If we can transfer this reverence to Ceridwen and prove that Lucius stole her cup, we will add to the power of our imagery. I can make this powerful link, for I worship Ceridwen and can enact the old druidic ways. The gods are still under the surface of our skin, regardless of the whining of the priests. Many Celts are still pagan and have learned to distrust the growing power of the Christian priests. Strike at Glastonbury, and we strike at all Christian Celts. More importantly, we strike at Artor.'

'But he's not Christian,' the one-eyed warrior retorted. 'From all that I've seen and heard, he's not anything. He pays lip service to all faiths and tries to reinforce an aura of fairness and impartiality.'

The beggar smiled. 'Which is even more reason to attack holy Glastonbury, which lies at the heart of the Christian West. We can imply that the Church has stolen Ceridwen's gift to humankind for its own evil purposes. You may pick my ideas to pieces, but I know the people and they still fear the emerging power of the Christian religion.'

'Very well, then. Explain your plan.' The dark leader sat a little straighter on his rickety stool. His eyes gleamed with intelligence.

'If I can persuade those malcontents who have little cause to love the crucified god that this relic was truly made in antiquity, and that it was a gift to man from the time of the standing stones, then we would have a symbol that could be used for our own purposes. Then, if we incite the people with the old sacrifices, give them the hope of wealth taken from the Christian churches and promise them a return to the free, old ways, they will follow us.'

He paused and looked at his listeners in turn. 'If I have Ceridwen's Cup in my hands, the gods will surely show me how to outwit the Christian Church and return our lands to purity.'

The mercenary, who had little faith in anything, grimaced sourly. 'Ceridwen's Cup? The goddess is said to have owned a great cauldron from which all knowledge and disaster comes, but I've heard nothing of a cup. You're playing with circumstance!'

'The peasants are superstitious, and a cup will do as well as a cauldron if we can play on their hatreds and fears. The goddess Ceridwen is an oracle, and she is useful. She is enchantress, mother and hunter. She will nurture those who protect her sacred places, and wreak vengeance on those who turn away from her laws. She is old, she is young. Ceridwen is the sacred beloved and the crooked woman. She is a potent enemy to pit against Artor and his milky, cowardly Christian god.'

'Your eyes burn too brightly with belief, friend. I care nothing for your Ceridwen or her cauldron, whether you turn it into a cup or not,' the black-cowled man retorted. 'But if you can use your goddess to hurt Artor, I have no quarrel with your plan.'

The warrior nodded his agreement. 'At least a cup is more portable than an iron cauldron. I predict that whatever object we use will have to travel far before the people relinquish the years of peace they have enjoyed.'

'The peasants care only for full bellies and the freedom to squabble over women, wine and gold', the beggar said impatiently. 'If they think a cup will give them their hearts' desires, they'll follow where it leads.'

The warrior looked deeply into the eyes of the beggar. 'Do you know where the Cup is?'

'Of course, but I'll need to break some tonsured heads to get my hands on it.'

'What of the priest? Surely he'll expose you when you steal it.' The black shadow's tone expressed no particular concern. 'I've found that even failed priests can't quite relinquish their faith, rot them!'

'Dead men tell no tales and a drunkard rarely notices the taste of the wine he loves. The worms were after the priest not long before he left my door.'

'Very well.' The black shadow nodded. 'Get the Cup, and use it to gather the malcontents together into a cohesive weapon, especially in the north where Artor is vulnerable and starved of allies. And perhaps the Bishop of Glastonbury, Aethelthred the Pure, should be killed while you're at it. A different, less respected bishop will only aid our strategies. Can you do it? You must tell me now if you have any doubts, for too much depends on your dedication to our cause for half-hearted actions on your part.'

'Do you doubt me, sire?' The beggar's voice rose. 'Do you doubt my oath to the gods to cleanse the land of this Christian filth? If need be, I'll set fire to all the churches in the land to fulfil my vow to you and to my gods. There is nothing that I won't sacrifice in pursuit of our ultimate victory.'

The dark shadow acknowledged the beggar's words with a brief nod, although the tension in his shoulders and back suggested that he was not as nonchalant as he wished to appear.

'Our friend here will be your contact. He is able to travel

freely about the tribal borders and he will provide you with shelter and coin when you leave your base. He speaks for me and has my complete confidence, for his allegiance is to me alone. You will obey him in all things. If you wish to speak to me, you need only send a message to the Blue Hag Inn at Deva. My friend will always be able to find me.'

The beggar straightened his body and his shadow suddenly loomed larger across the wall as moonlight outlined his body. Something menacing seemed to rob the bothie of clean air.

'I will not fail, sire. Bishop Aethelthred is as good as dead. Glastonbury will be pillaged and the Cup will be mine. I've waited half my life to strike a blow against Cadbury.'

The beggar turned and slid into the night. His rag-wrapped feet were silent and all that remained was an odour of filthy flesh, corruption and a heavy, sullen perfume.

'That snake makes my palms itch, master.' The warrior's nostrils twitched with distaste. 'I hope you know what you're doing by entrusting our plans to a madman. Fanatics such as that one make me yearn for a good, clean knife.'

'What does he really know? Or matter? He's ignorant of our identities and he has no conception of the stakes we're playing for. All he cares about are his gods and some futile, fanatical search for revenge. He's a useful tool and if he makes an error and is caught, he'll be blamed for any insurrection. My plans run far deeper than his foolish diversions. Kingdoms do not fall over religious differences. Power, greed and envy are our real allies.'

'Good enough,' the warrior grunted. 'What do you want of me, sire?'

'Do you still have connections at the court of King Lot?'

The warrior nodded.

'Good. Then it's time for you to become a faithful hound to that fat fool. Dig in well at the Otadini court, for Lot has always wanted a network of informants to rival Artor's spies.'

The warrior nodded. Such an order was easy to follow, for he had sold his skills to every king in the north in the past.

'Keep your eyes sharp and your blade sharper. My plans depend on your ability to become a trusted vassal of King Lot. But remember where your allegiances truly lie.'

The warrior closed one fist over his heart in the Roman fashion. He bowed his dark head, then pulled his patch down to hide his ruined eye.

'I'm oath bound to you and yours forever, my lord. You need not fear that I'll weaken at the last. I remember my master's screams whenever I sleep and I've sworn that I will drag Artor and his allies to Hades with me when my time comes to leave this earth. Only then will Simnel rest in peace.'

The black shadow rose and adjusted its voluminous cloak.

'Simnel was executed by Artor when he foolishly tried to steal the Brigante throne. We will suffer his fate if we aren't careful, so keep your thirst for revenge under control.'

'I have waited patiently for twenty years,' the one-eyed warrior snapped. 'I can wait a little longer.'

'If I have need of you, I'll send to you to meet me at the inn where we first met. Once we have set the north ablaze, Artor will be forced to fight on our ground – and even that demon isn't immortal. He can't win without the tribal kings behind him and your task is to eliminate his alliances.'

The shadowy man departed, and the bothie became as cold, empty and ruined as the face of the warrior.

For a short moment, he stared at his strong, scar-webbed palms and wondered where his honour and his innocence had fled. And then he remembered the crows as they had feasted on his master's eyes, so he thrust away the last of his qualms.

'So it begins!' he told the gelid air as he crossed the threshold to find his tethered horse.

A solitary owl watched his departure with the unblinking patience of the predator.

The last conspirator rode away and, in a flash, the owl swooped and a small forest creature died. Only a tiny shriek from the underbrush indicated that something warm and furry had perished in indifferent claws.

CHAPTER I

A WIND FROM THE NORTH

> I was at the Cross
> With Mary Magdalene.
> I received the muse
> From Ceridwen's cauldron.
>
> *The Book of Taliesin*

Two tall men on powerful, clean-limbed horses came to Cadbury Tor as autumn turned the fruit trees to russet and gold. In the broad fields that surrounded the fortifications, the early winter wind ripped the fallen leaves into drifts of rust. With knowledgeable eyes, the young men noted the fruitful fields, the snug farms and the township that nestled at Cadbury's skirts, and they grew round-eyed at the beauty of this secure kingdom.

These outland warriors carried with them the scent of glamour and a faint shimmer of oddness that led superstitious folk to turn away in sudden alarm. Moreover, these men were twins, and many crossed themselves in dread, for even the smallest child knew that twins were both a curse and a blessing. The men were mirror images of each other, fair yet fearsome, and no common man could quite ignore the chill finger that stirred the hairs on the back of his neck.

At the first gate leading to the citadel, they sat proudly on their fine horses – one white and one black – and proclaimed their lineage clearly for all the men-at-arms to hear.

'We crave entrance,' the dark-haired twin demanded calmly. 'Our names are Balyn and Balan ap Cerdic, ap Llanwith of blessed memory, come to the High King at our mother's bidding to offer our swords to our liege lord.'

While the warriors who made up the guard were unfamiliar with the twins, every member of the garrison had heard tales of the legendary King Llanwith of the Ordovice clan who had assisted the young Artor to assume the throne of Britain. Rumour had long hinted that Anna, the matriarch of the tribe, was kin of Artor, a linkage that added a layer of mystery to an already distinguished family. The guards at the entrance to the fortifications straightened respectfully.

With low bows of homage, the watch permitted the twins to pass through the entrance to the citadel.

Upwards, towards the crest of the tor, the two men rode abreast of each other. One had hair of rich dark brown, bordering on black, and the other boasted hair of honey-red. One guided his horse with his right hand and one used his left, and the warriors on the walls remembered that their mother was rumoured to be the sister of the High King and the unacknowledged daughter of the previous ruler, Uther Pendragon. As they searched the faces of the twins, the warriors recognized that the shape and colour of the young men's grey irises belonged to only one other man in all these lands – Artor, the High King, who ruled the Cadbury fortress.

'The scions of legend are once again among us,' one old warrior said ruminatively when they had passed. He spat on his hands. 'We'll soon have some excitement.'

'They're fair young men, fresh fodder for the queen,' another responded wickedly.

'I'd keep my mouth shut if I were in your boots, Rhys, or the king will close it permanently. If Lord Artor chooses to ignore the behaviour of his wife, then who are we to notice?' a third veteran warned.

'May the gods send a fever to see that slut off,' Rhys said quietly. 'And then, perhaps, Cadbury can be hale and hearty again.'

Ignorant of the stir they were causing, Balyn and Balan rode higher up the defensive walls, noting with soldierly pleasure the cunning and strength in the earthwork construction that had been planned by Myrddion Merlinus so many years before. Then, abruptly, they realized they had reached the summit. Before them stood the wooden tower of a stone church with coloured glass set into the narrow windows of the building. Beside the Christian sanctuary, the palace of the High King towered over the land in tiers of dressed stone and timber.

At the carved doorway of the great hall, resplendent with its freshly painted dragons, the twins were halted by two tall warriors who eyed them from head to heels with cautious, unfriendly eyes. One warrior was close to fifty, with uncut hair of an extraordinary white-blond that was plaited to his hips and bound with silver. The other warrior was some years younger and open of face, with an upper body that was heavily muscled and hardened with exercise. Both warriors wore the king's dragon on their armbands and matching torcs could be glimpsed at their throats under the woollen tunics that covered their mail shirts.

'Stand aside, good men', Balyn ordered imperiously. 'We have ridden untended from Viroconium to offer our services to the High King.'

Balyn's arrogance made both guards bristle. No one entered Artor's hall without permission, however impeccable their lineage.

'Please?' Balan added, and his tanned face split in a wide grin.

Percivale and Gareth grinned instinctively in response to the darker twin whose hair had such shine and gloss, and whose grey eyes were like sunlight on a chill sea.

After a lifetime of service to the High King, Gareth knew the truth of Anna's birthright, and his chest contracted with an old pang of concern. He also knew that Artor's grandsons had come to offer allegiance to their grandsire in ignorance of the true ties of their bloodline.

'The High King is entitled to the protection of all loyal men who serve as his personal guard', Percivale explained gracefully. 'And we take our duties seriously.' His easy smile encompassed both young men. 'Please leave all your weapons at this threshold. Only the High King goes armed within the precincts of his Judgement Hall.'

Balan complied with easy good humour, but Balyn expressed his irritation with every muscle of his face. However, item by item, the brothers laid aside an impressive array of weapons and followed Percivale and Gareth into the presence of the king.

Artor's hall was resplendent with finely woven cloth that

acted as the perfect foil for the battle standards of Mori Saxonicus, the last great battle against the western Saxons under the command of the thane, Glamdring Ironfist. The eyes of the twins widened as they observed the symbols of one of the west's greatest triumphs. Around them, courtiers in brightly dyed linens and furs, and warriors richly caparisoned as befitted the servants of the king, rested on carved wooden benches or stood in corners, gossiping and drinking beer or wine offered by quiet-footed servants. It seemed to the dazzled eyes of Balyn and Balan that these vivid courtiers scarcely noticed the magnificence around them.

Peace had bred complacency and Balan read it in the plump, bland faces that gawped at them when they entered the King's hall. But he saw that farmers, shepherds and shop-keepers were also among the gilded throng. These ordinary men stood unabashed in the presence of the High King, firm in the knowledge that Artor would offer judgement in their various cases with impartial, unimpeachable justice. Balan felt a visceral thrill of pride that he could become a part of a world that was both beautiful and just.

His eyes were drawn to the man sitting on a simple chair at the far end of the hall. His tunic was snowy white, and he eschewed ornamentation except for his crown, a torc of red gold and a fine golden chain that disappeared into the neck of his robe. He was far less gorgeous than any of the aristocrats who lounged in the hall, but the force of his character was unmistakable. Here was the centre of this world; here was the source of song and story: Artor, High King of the Britons.

Artor himself longed for the open air. The aristocratic petitioners made his head ache with their constant demands for preferment over neighbours, for judgement over tribal borders and for relief from tribute. Their greed often made him feel nauseous.

On the other hand, his Judgement Hall also brought common men to the tor. Farmers, traders and town dwellers trudged up the spiral pathway, seeking arbitration from the one man whom they trusted to be fair. Untangling the complex familial or financial skeins of ordinary life gave Artor pleasure, for it reminded him of what it had been like to be a free man.

Although the hall was crowded with petitioners, the twins caused a stir as they strode through the crowd as if it did not exist. Within moments, they stood proudly on the decorated flagstones before the High King and his queen. Their booted feet rested at the claws of Artor's dragon mosaic, as if the twins were extensions of the great beast that reclined at the High King's feet. Smoothly, and with careful discipline, the brothers dropped to their knees and bowed to kiss the talons of the Dracos dragon.

'Rise, young princes, no child of Queen Anna need bow to me,' the king ordered, while Queen Wenhaver stared at the twins.

Artor listened to their salutations with a mixture of excitement and discomfort. Balan, who used the hand sinister, or the left, was tall and was similar in build to Artor himself. Not a hint of curl marred the sheen of his long, loosened hair, and his face under its dark, winged brows was calm and untroubled. Artor felt a painful stirring of affection for this clean-limbed young man.

Older by minutes, and as fair as his brother was dark, Balyn possessed hair that curled gently past his shoulders. The petitioners in the hall recognized the similarities between the two young men and the High King, and silence was replaced with a low hum of whispers. The other twin used his dexter, or right hand, which was believed to be more benign by the superstitious, although Artor wasn't sure that this grand-dam's tale was always true. His agile mind recognized an impulsive nature in Balyn, demonstrated through his swiftly moving hands and the ready words that spilled out his thoughts without the leavening grace of caution.

Both young men rose and waited quietly under the scrutiny of the High King.

For their part, the twins examined the face of their lord and noted the clipped, greying curls that gathered around his face. Artor was still handsome, strong and straight-limbed, but heaviness dragged at his mouth and clouded his wintry eyes with distrust. Lines of worry tugged the inner corners of his eyebrows close to his shapely nose, and the shadows under his eyes were deep, almost bruised.

'You will introduce me, Artor, won't you?' the queen interjected, tapping one foot on the dais.

Age had not dimmed Wenhaver's ostentatious display. She wore far too many fine gems for good taste. Her mouth was petulant and was marred by deep lines around her thinning lips. Although her hair was still extraordinary, her figure and face bore the signs of dissipation and encroaching old age, held at bay with the aid of rigid bindings and cosmetics that were better suited to a young girl than a mature woman. When Artor bothered to notice and remembered her former natural beauty, he felt stirrings of pity for her. Like a painting on wood, her looks were extraordinary until any movement broke the spell and revealed the hag waiting under the curls and the powder.

Both young men knelt before her and, characteristically, Balyn spoke first.

'I am Balyn ap Cerdic, my queen, second son of Cerdic ap Llanwith of the Ordovice, and this callow youth is my younger twin, Balan. Beware of his sweet words, my lady, for only I can offer the appropriate phrases that your beauty deserves.'

'How charming,' Wenhaver simpered.

Balyn's eyes were fervent and Artor sighed inwardly to see the boy so easily beguiled by Wenhaver's jewelled, practised and wholly superficial magnificence.

'My queen.' Balan spoke in turn with careful gravity. His gaze was direct and a shadow seemed to darken his eyes before he lowered them in homage.

Artor missed nothing.

'What news of your mother, Queen Anna, and your brother, Bran?'

'Bran enjoys the tribe's favour, and fortifies his lands with diligence,' Balyn responded in a slightly dismissive voice. 'He swears to you that Saxons shall never set foot on his soil while he lives.'

Artor nodded distantly. Gareth could have warned Balyn that any disrespect towards Anna's eldest son was dangerous ground, especially when duty was concerned. The High King had immolated himself on the fires of duty for decades, and fully understood the bitter price that Bran paid for his kingship.

'Mother sends her greetings and bade me remind you that

the High King remains her favourite warrior of all the lords of the west,' Balan added cautiously. 'I ask that you forgive her familiarity, my liege, but she swears that she has known you for as long as she has been alive.'

Balan's brief speech caused Artor to smile and some of the bleakness left his eyes.

'Is she well?' he asked the young man.

'Our mother is indefatigable.' Balan grinned widely. 'She's still beautiful, as you have no doubt heard, my lord, but she pays no attention to her physical appearance. She's the first to join the women in the apple harvest, and the last to bed during times of flood or pestilence. There are no children in all of Viroconium who don't sing her praises, while the little ones call her the Lady of Sunshine. They swear the sun glows brighter wherever she walks.'

'She was always a scamp.' Artor smiled fondly in memory of Anna's childhood in Aquae Sulis. 'Your mother was always scraping her knees and running off with the farm workers to explore the fields of the villa.'

'Why have I never met this Ordovice queen?' Wenhaver scowled at the compliments that had been heaped on another woman, especially on one whose lineage was rumoured to be so high. 'Why has she never journeyed to Cadbury, or even to Venta Belgarum?'

Artor's eyebrows drew together in controlled anger. Of the twins, only Balan was sufficiently alert to recognise Artor's displeasure at any implied criticism of his mother, and he smiled gratefully in response.

'Queen Anna prefers her adopted lands and she has told me often that she is reluctant to leave their borders,' Artor answered testily. 'I honour her preferences in this matter, for she cares nothing for courts or ceremony.'

'And her people would not readily permit her to leave,' Balan added. 'Even her Roman childhood is now seen as a virtue, for she insists on cleanliness and the old values of honour and respect for all souls who come in contact with her.'

Wenhaver frowned briefly, but then remembered that lines were beginning to deepen around her eyes. She forced her brow to smooth, although her blue eyes continued to glitter. Somewhere in her mean little heart, Wenhaver recognized that her husband loved Anna more than anyone. She smiled sweetly as she twisted the knife to show her displeasure.

'Does she really work in the fields like a servant?' she lisped in saccharine concern, as she examined her own hennaed and polished nails. 'Her complexion must be ruined!'

Balan whitened, and even Balyn flushed at the queen's insult.

'Desist, Wenhaver!' Artor raised his voice fractionally. 'Not all queens are amused by idle pleasures and personal vanities. Some, like the Lady of the Ordovice, are chatelaines in the Gallic sense, because they share those tasks that the common women must endure. In so doing, they understand their subjects much better. My sister Morgause is one such queen. She rules with King Lot and concerns herself with women's matters, where her orders are obeyed implicitly. I admit that we have had our differences in the past, but I have never doubted that my sister is a true queen.'

Wenhaver turned her fabulous eyes from one boy-man to the next, and then lowered her lashes to avoid seeing the anger on her husband's face. Her expression warned the king that tantrums were imminent but it left the twins totally confused.

Artor turned back to Balan, a partiality that was not lost on his twin brother, who stiffened a little and was imprudent enough to allow his cheeks to whiten with annoyance.

'So Anna has managed to civilize Llanwith's stiff-necked Cymru warriors? My foster-father, Ector of the Poppinidii, feared that she would never be accepted because of her Roman breeding, even though she was raised as a Celt.'

'Her personal qualities always triumph over any prejudices that might confront her, my lord. In fact, she still uses her Roman name within her household and the whole tribe knows it, but they accept her quirks and continue to love her.' Balan glowed with pride, although every word was chosen carefully. He imagined a chasm opening at his feet as the conversation threatened snares that he could not hope to avoid.

'Licia!' Artor murmured softly and, behind the throne, Odin stirred.

'Her name is magical and very, very old. She was named for the great matron of the Poppinidii, Livinia Major, who died before she was born.'

'Aye, we have been told the story of her birth by Lady Livinia Minor,' Balyn said, vying for the eye and favour of the king.

'You have been to Aquae Sulis?' Artor asked, his eyes flickering with sudden pleasure and his body leaning forward impulsively.

Wenhaver gaped at her husband's sudden animation. He obviously cared for these outlandish twins. He usually tired of visitors quickly.

'Many times, my lord. We have seen Gallia's Garden and the urn containing her ashes, and we have heard the legend of the wise healer, Frith. Local folk regularly visit the shrine, although few seem to know the history of Gallia. She died before Mother was born'. Balyn smiled as he realized he had Artor's full attention, even if his information was inaccurate.

'All the better,' Artor's inner voice whispered. 'What they don't know can't hurt them.'

'We've also said a prayer for Lord Targo, sword master of renown.' Balyn spoke quickly, as was his custom. 'And Grandfather Ector, of course.'

Artor wasn't disposed to like the boy, but he couldn't disguise the affection for Ector that infused his voice.

'Lord Ector was my foster-father and a man who was decent through to his bones. His dearest wish was to be buried in Gallia's Garden so that visitors could sit awhile over his resting place and ponder the natural beauty around them. He often expressed the desire to hear laughter and the soft music of the earth as he slept in death.'

'A pretty conceit,' Wenhaver murmured in a voice just loud enough for her husband to hear. Artor gritted his teeth and continued.

'Gallia was a Roman woman of little worldly account, lad, and she died long before her time. She was not yet twenty when she perished. I knew both Gallia and Frith well, so I can swear they were two of the finest women who ever drew breath in Aquae Sulis. They always had my undying respect, and their garden is maintained at my expense and by my direct orders.'

Wenhaver yawned delicately, but pointedly.

'But I fear we are boring the queen, who has little tolerance for tales of the past. She will be cross if we discuss paragons whom she has never met or understood.'

Like an indulgent uncle, Artor gazed down at the two young men who stood so upright and proud like two fine hounds bred for battle and the hunt.

'Gareth, my strong right arm, personally laid the garden during his youth. His brother and his nephews now tend it for me.'

Balyn frowned. He had no idea what lay behind this oblique conversation, but he was determined to discuss its issues with the king's 'strong right arm' in the near future.

Balan smiled easily, for he loved listening to tales of the past and was entirely wrapped up in Llanwith's scrolls, just as Artor had been when the Villa Poppinidii had been his home. But, unlike his brother, who always accepted circumstances at face value, Balan was wary of the waves of dislike that appeared to exist between the High King and his glittering queen. He promised himself he would think about the implications of the conundrum when he had more time.

The weak afternoon light warned the king that night would soon be upon them, so he accepted the twins' oaths of loyalty and offered them places in his militia where they could begin to prove their worth. Both young warriors greeted his decision with unconcealed happiness and Artor was reminded that they were still very young.

I shall avoid prejudgement, he told himself sternly, remembering a younger self, faced with the ill will of his own father.

As the twins bowed to take leave of their king, Balan stopped their hasty, excited retreat by gripping his brother's arm.

'Our thanks, my lord,' a confused Balyn muttered, but Balan nudged him.

'Tell them about the other visitors!' he hissed.

'Your pardon, Majesty, but the excitement of finally meeting you has driven all rational thought from my head,' Balyn explained. 'You are about to receive other noble visitors and kinsmen. We promised to serve as their envoys.'

Artor raised one mobile brow.

'Lord Gawayne is returning to Cadbury with his eldest son. We met upon the road, but Gawayne wished to view the resting place of the Lord Targo, so we parted at the crossroads leading to Aquae Sulis.'

Wenhaver smiled, and Artor cringed inwardly as he read her openly excited and lascivious thoughts.

The bitch is in heat, he thought savagely, but his face revealed nothing but polite interest.

'I remember Gawayne's boy well. He was a large and beautiful babe who almost killed Lady Enid during his birthing. The beauteous Nimue, the Maid of Wind and Water, managed to save both mother and son.'

With a brief flash of unholy amusement, Artor watched his wife's chagrin at his unwelcome compliments towards another woman. Myrddion's apprentice outdid the queen in beauty, intelligence, style and accomplishments. Regardless of the gulf of social position that yawned between them, Wenhaver knew that Nimue would always be her superior, and her hatred for Myrddion's woman hadn't wavered in the long decades since they had last met. In one detail only was the queen superior to Nimue – her enmity was eternal.

Wenhaver's dislike turned her doll-like face into a twisted and ugly reflection of itself. Yet sadness tinged his triumph, for he realized that he and Wenhaver had made a pointless, barren wasteland of their lives. He regretted the way they picked at each other, tearing off fragile scabs of mutual forbearance for the sake of a moment's satisfaction.

'What is the lad named?'

'His name is Galahad, my lord, and the Otadini claim he is the greatest warrior in the world.'

'Galahad,' Artor repeated, and somewhere beyond the mortal world, he felt a tremor in the void as the wheel of Fortuna shuddered and began slowly to turn.

'The boy will be welcome,' the king said softly, then the audience was over.

Far away in the cold north, Morgan swayed over her knuckle-bones and felt a fissure open in the fabric of the world. Her sister, Morgause, was in deadly peril. The bones presaged death, and the pattern warned Morgan that other deaths were promised. Her brother, Artor, was now threatened as never before, and she tried desperately to dredge up a feeling of triumph in his fall from eminence on Fortuna's wheel. She had hated him for so long that she should have felt something – even relief.

Her kinfolk were dying, but she looked in vain for a sign in the portents that revealed her own fate.

'Shite!' she exclaimed crudely. She brushed away a tear, for the Fey prayed for death every day of her pain-filled existence.

Then her eyes whitened and rolled backward in her head until all she saw was a battered tin cup that filled and overflowed with fresh, glistening blood.

'The Cup is come,' Morgan whispered through lips that were dried, cracked and oozing with the fragility of poisoned old age. 'The Cup is filling, filling, and we will all be washed away.'

Her vision cleared and she could focus on her withered, tattooed hands once again. Her ugly mouth smiled and her tongue flickered over her bleeding lips like a lizard kissing the sun.

'But Artor nears his end,' she whispered thinly. 'Praise be to all the gods! At last Gorlois will be avenged!'

But reason threatened her momentary triumph. Artor was close to sixty years, Morgause was older still and Morgan felt as ancient as the dead heart of the Otadini Mountains. They should all have died decades ago, and now the siblings existed as anachronisms of power and illusory vitality.

Her rational mind sighed.

What does it matter after all these years? Who remembers the ancient wrongs?

She answered her own question.

I do! And so does my pestilential brother. Fortuna's wheel turns ... at last.

CHAPTER II

BLOOD OATHS AND BATTLE BROTHERS

Artor paced up and down the length of his personal sleeping quarters. Bronze lamps had been lit and Percivale and Gareth moved around the spartan room, preparing for the king's rest and comfort, while Odin leaned impassively against the heavy, wooden door.

Their lord's frugal habits meant that Percivale and Gareth had little to do but put away the High King's scrolls in their fitted shelves and tidy Artor's collection of maps. Odin personally tasted the High King's water, stored in a beaten silver flask, and nibbled at the plates of nuts, cheese and flat bread that were prepared for him. Artor always remonstrated with Odin over his precautions and called him an old woman, but when Artor's safety was at stake, Odin simply ignored his master's wishes with a vague, agreeable smile.

Artor considered his three closest bodyguards and wondered why they had remained true to him for so long. Odin, the Jutlander, had to be well over sixty, but his tawny hair and greying beard suggested maturity rather than great age.

His muscles were still as hard as old oak, while his huge spine remained unbent. Odin had sworn a solemn oath to cleave to Artor until death took him and, regardless of the passage of time, Odin would never change his allegiance.

Gareth was almost a kinsman, for his grandmother, the slave woman Frith, had been Artor's mother in all but blood. Frith had died with Gallia, Artor's deeply loved Roman wife, whose memory had developed into the idealized beauty of a distant dream. Gareth had spent his youth caring for Artor's daughter, mother to those strong twins who had so shaken the High King's guarded heart. Gareth knew no other life than service to Artor and his family.

As for Percivale, chaste, Christian and a superb athlete, he was partly of Targo's making and partly a product of Gallwyn from the kitchens of Venonae. With his whole, passionate heart, Percivale had sworn to guard his king while breath remained in his body. Artor knew, to his cost, that Percivale would dare anything, risk anything and sacrifice himself beyond reason for him.

Suddenly, Artor was angry with both himself and his servants. Why must they love him? He could never care for them with that same, unreserved devotion. He wore their love around his neck like a chain of lead.

'I have waited so long for a sign that I'd almost given up hope of a solution,' Artor sighed, speaking to no one in particular.

'Lord?' Percivale looked up as he tidied the High King's desk. 'Is there anything I can do for you?'

'This matter goes beyond your understanding,' Artor growled. He continued to pace, but he felt ashamed of his outburst of temper.

Gareth set down the draught of clean water in its silver jug which was heavily decorated with a dragon swallowing its own tail. He placed one hand gently on his master's shoulder and stilled the king's frenetic movement.

'Yes, my lord, they are your grandsons. And, no, you cannot share the secret of their birth with them, for such knowledge could lead to their deaths.'

Percivale tensed at Gareth's effrontery, while the stolid Odin raised his white eyebrows.

Artor shook his leonine head and Gareth almost flinched, but his faith in his master held true.

'You are among the few men left alive who know the tale of Gallia and my childhood at the Villa Poppinidii,' the king hissed in warning.

Percivale's mouth gaped open.

As always, Artor saw everything. 'Keep your mouth tightly shut on this matter, Percivale. You'd be wise to remain silent about my secrets. I am an old man, and my temper is uncertain.'

Percivale wanted to protest that he knew no secrets but he heeded Artor's warning and closed his mouth.

Artor resumed his pacing. 'I know that neither of the twins can be told of their birthright. Rumours that Anna is my sister places them in an invidious position as it is. But in spite of the danger, I cannot help but wonder if one of them has the temperament and the ability to become the heir to my throne.'

'Perhaps,' Odin rumbled.

Gruffydd hobbled into the room, leaning on a cane and swearing as one swollen foot came in contact with the door-frame. The sword bearer was now decrepit, and his temper and health hadn't improved with the passage of time.

'Perhaps you can offer an old man a goblet of good wine.' He smiled. 'I know you favour water but, as far as I'm concerned, it's only good for pissing, making things grow or washing my beard. You're the king, so there must be something drinkable stashed away in here.'

Artor nodded, and Percivale opened a chest where flagons of wine awaited the king's pleasure. Pottery mugs were lifted on to the king's desk, for Percivale knew that the king would expect his guard to drink with the old sword bearer.

'You should have cast off that slut you married when you had the chance,' Gruffydd muttered darkly. 'And found yourself a real woman, one who could bear the son that would carry on your line.'

'Even you, old friend, should learn to keep your mouth closed over your teeth.' Artor's glacial stare promised dire consequences if Gruffydd continued to offer unsought advice. 'I'll speak to you first if I want the matter discussed.'

'Damn it all, Artor, you can glare at me all you like, but nothing changes because you're in a bad mood,' Gruffydd responded tactlessly. 'Targo was dead right about that bitch of yours. It's not too late to remove her, and you can't throw everyone out of Cadbury who speaks the all too obvious. She'll be the death of you and, with her luck, she'll survive to a disgusting old age, whining and carping as she fondles those young men she seduces.'

'Enough!'

'A winter or two at Tintagel would do wonders for the queen's temperament,' Guffydd persisted, ignoring Artor's stormy expression. 'It's far away and bleaker than a witch's tit in a snowstorm. Your mam never took to it overly, by all that I've heard, and Duke Gorlois managed to spend most of the year in his summer capitals. Even Morgan, who professes to love all things pertaining to her father, avoids Tintagel like the plague.'

Artor's expression was stony, and Odin read something dangerous in the shark's glare that had never quite deserted his lord's countenance. He concentrated on cleaning his nails.

'It's an excellent idea, my lord. Just send her away,' Percivale soothed. 'And no blood will have been spilt.'

'I'll think on it,' the king said curtly. Then he threw his arm over the thin shoulders of his agent in belated welcome. 'Now, spymaster, how go my lands?'

Gruffydd was very grey and had the disreputable look of a townsman down on his luck. During the period since Myrddion Merlinus had disappeared, only Gruffydd seemed able to resurrect and maintain the web of spies who provided Artor with intelligence.

The spymaster felt a familiar ache in his chest whenever he thought of Myrddion Merlinus. Cadbury had survived the scholar's departure but a light had been permanently extinguished in the eyes of the High King when his friend had deserted him. Without the fair Nimue, the Maid of Wind and Water, the glamour of life at court had vanished, along with magic and long peals of honest laughter that offered hope to the sternest and most adamantine heart. In the long years of loss, Artor had avoided mentioning the name of his friend. Even the memories of the common people relegated Nimue to the role of fair, inhuman enchantress who had stolen Myrddion away.

Gruffydd sighed and considered his own mortality as he sipped Artor's excellent wine. Events of the recent present were less clear to him now than were the deeds of yesteryear, and he knew that he would soon pass on the care of Caliburn to his eldest son. In private, Gruffydd admitted that the blade was almost too heavy for his thin arms to lift.

Gruffydd kept Myrddion's spy network ticking along, but he was a realist and knew that he added nothing of significance to a formula decided by that wise old courtier so many years earlier, when Artor's kingdom was still young and fresh. Since the departure of Myrddion, the free west went on, for Artor expended his blood and his soul to ensure the kingdom endured, but Cadbury was frozen in time – and hovered on the brink of decay.

'Stop dozing off over my excellent wine and tell me how my tribal kings are faring.'

Gruffydd started, grinned apologetically and put his scrambled thoughts in order.

'Well,' he began. 'I can say that Wynfael is no epicure like his father, the gods be praised, so Leodegran's kingdom fares better without him. When he dropped dead while trying to mount a slave girl, his whole tribe was mightily relieved. The man was so corpulent when he died that he could barely walk, unless it was to stuff his face with food. Wynfael is a Christian, so his oath to the Union of Tribal Kings will hold. Those maniacs seek martyrdom at any price, so I'm convinced that you could cast off your troublesome wife and her brother would confine himself to praying for her soul. He disapproves of his sister.'

Artor remembered Wenhaver's father as a man with expensive, exotic tastes. How strange that the son should deny his father's vices for the dubious attractions of religion.

'Bran and your Anna hold the Ordovice lands with strong

hands,' Gruffydd continued. 'In fact, the last of the Demetae who have managed to survive seem to welcome Bran as their master. And the Cornovii remain true to your cause. The faithful Bedwyr has emerged from Arden – with a wife, if you can believe it. I expect him soon, my lord.'

'Everyone seems to be coming to Cadbury of late but, of all my guests, Bedwyr is most welcome. Mori Saxonicus would have been harder won without him, and the gods alone know when we'd have cracked the lice in Caer Fyrddin if Bedwyr hadn't let us in through the old sewers.' Artor's brows drew together in a frown. 'What of the south? What of the Dumnonii, the Durotriges, the Belgae and the Atrebates? Have the remnants of the eastern tribes joined the Regni with whole hearts, or do they still long for the old days?'

Gruffydd blinked in surprise. Artor's parents both came from southern tribes who had always formed the core of the High King's power base.

'Aye lord. Perhaps they are a little complacent, for there has been no Saxon attack for three years and our borders appear to be accepted by the barbarians. But some displaced Celts from the east are disappointed that you haven't driven the Saxons into Oceanus Germanicus. However, they are not fools, for they understand how deeply rooted the Saxons and Angles have become. Some Iceni are even calling their old country by the name of Angleland. And the South remains faithful.'

'Any sensible man regrets the passing of good and righteous things,' Percivale murmured.

'Aye, but any sensible man recognizes when the time has come to relinquish foolish dreams of glory,' Gruffydd retorted.

'The Saxons, Angles and Jutes are entrenched in the lands of the east, and they can't be dislodged. Still, they haven't advanced a mile since Mori Saxonicus.'

'Nor will they while I remain alive to hold them back,' Artor vowed softly. No man present doubted his words. 'But the north is not so secure, is it, my friend?'

'I can hardly credit that any descendant of Luka could foment troubles within the northern tribes. There's bad blood in this new Brigante king, but he's a clever young bastard. Modred is a scheming, ambitious youth who seems to have inherited none of his grandfather's charm.'

'I don't like his name . . . it has an ominous sound,' Odin growled from his station near the doorway.

'You'll like the young man even less when you meet him, Odin. Rumour whispers that Morgause spent a night in Verterae on her way back to Segedunum after the battle of Mori Saxonicus. Luka's youngest son was very fair and Morgause was still attractive, if you ignored her total lack of charm. Apparently the young prince was smitten, and a child, Modred, resulted.'

Artor wondered at the depth of his spymaster's knowledge of his sister.

'Morgause was none too pleased to be pregnant late in life, and King Lot wasn't amused either, so Modred was sent back to his father as soon as she whelped him. The boy survived Simnel's rebellion and was raised by Luka's last living heir, in case he begot no sons. So now you have another unpleasant kinsman, one who intends to use his bloodlines to further his own ends.'

'All women are much the same in the darkness, whatever

their age,' Odin remarked, causing Percivale to blush scarlet, to the amusement of the older men.

'Still chaste?' Gruffydd stared at Percivale, amazed.

'Still!' The High King laughed with genuine mirth.

'You're being unfair, my lord,' Percivale pleaded. 'I've only ever loved one lady . . . and she's long gone. I'm determined to wait until I meet the right woman.'

Artor knew that his servant dreamed of Nimue, his childhood friend. Percivale had never moved beyond a young man's first infatuation and his lack of experience blinded him to his hopeless idealization of Nimue. The High King would have laughed at the childish delusions of men if he had not recognized that Gallia had become his own idealized, perfect woman.

'What has marriage to do with rutting?' Odin asked with bland interest. 'Celibacy is a very strange solution to an unsuccessful search for a true woman.'

'One I doubt you ever practised, my large friend,' Percivale retorted, his face still flaming in embarrassment.

Odin simply grinned through his grey beard in his snaggle-toothed way. Only his brown and broken teeth showed the weakness of old age.

'So,' Artor mused, 'Gawayne and this Galahad approach Cadbury, as do Bedwyr and his nameless wife, and Modred, who is Morgause's youngest son and the illegitimate king of the Brigante. We already have Anna's twins with us. The next generation is gathering to pick my bones clean while I'm still alive.'

Among the warriors in the room, only Gruffydd remembered Uther Pendragon as another High King who had clutched at immortality. Gruffydd shivered, fearing the sins he might have to commit in his master's service. Whenever he remembered the king's foster-brother, Caius, as he lay writhing on a bloody pallet, Gruffydd thanked the Tuatha de Danaan that he hadn't been required to carry out Artor's orders. Another hand had stopped Caius, so Gruffydd was clean of the assassin's taint Of course, he would obey his beloved lord for as long as his hands could hold a blade. Long years of proximity had taught the spymaster that Artor never acted maliciously unless he was pushed into a blind rage, a condition that rarely troubled the king in his old age. But would Artor order an assassination if such a cowardly act would save the west? Of course he would. And could Artor live with the consequences of such shame? For the sake of the Union of Kings, and for the preservation of the people, Artor would learn to endure.

'If he can do it, then I can,' Gruffydd whispered, and Artor's eyes swivelled towards his sword bearer as if he could read his old retainer's mind.

'This turmoil you feel is the way of old age,' Gareth said lightly. 'You are still hale and vigorous, but you approach sixty years, the same age as your father when he succumbed to death. The young wolves will always gather as the leader of the old pack greys with time, so you must beware of jealousy and rage. That foolishness was Uther's way.' He smiled at his king. 'My grandmother and your old friend, Frith, would have told you that what comes will come.'

Artor nodded and stared down at the pearl ring on his thumb. Many years had passed since his hand had been so slick with blood that the pearl had glowed from within encrusted gore. In Artor's jaded imagination, the pearl had resembled a blinded eye.

'Aye, our Frith was a wise woman, as was my friend, Myrddion. I wish they were still with us. But Frith's ashes lie in Gallia's Garden, and Myrddion must have succumbed to old age by now.' He smiled gratefully at Gareth. 'It's neither death nor the end of things that I fear.'

The warriors and the spymaster were not inclined to respond, but Odin sensed the danger in allowing Artor to fret, so he answered for them all.

'Those among us who care for you know that the kingdom will eventually be lost after you have gone beyond the shadows, master. We don't fear this fate, for we know it is inevitable. But we dread the pain of slow decay, and a return to the bad old ways of the past.'

'You're my second self, Odin,' Artor answered him. 'Sometimes I wonder why you've stayed with me for so long, why you've forsaken children, love and comfort for my cause. Why, my friend?'

'We each gave an oath, master. And I've never regretted my part of the bargain.'

The autumn wind that stirred the fruit trees of Cadbury wound sinuously through forest, mountains and grey, glacial valleys. In far-off Cymru, the breezes sought impudent entry to the stone villa built around the ruins of a venerable oak tree. Persistent as cold winds are, they managed to find entry through tightly sealed shutters that had worn a little at the hinges. One single tendril of frigid breeze stirred the hair of a woman who sat by a guttering fire.

Gradually, the wind died in the heat of a room that was awash with colour. The black, close-knit walls, the aged timbers and the smoke-blackened rafters were brought to life by great woven and embroidered hangings that coiled with strange creatures and the persistent image of a black-clad man. Hanks of vegetable-dyed wool, in every imaginable shade of green, gold, orange, red and woad blue, hung from the ceilings ready for the great loom that glowed with hand-polishing in the corner. Dried herbs, flowers, leaves and even seaweed hung in another corner, their heads hanging downwards and the fading colours adding to the rich ambience of the room and its occupant.

The floors were flagged, an unusual feature in these climes, and were softened with woven rugs and knotted whorls of brilliantly coloured rag. Soft, brain-tanned hide was stretched over cunningly shaped wooden benches to provide seating and, in a series of pegged shelves, racks of crude glass jars stood like miniature soldiers along the stone walls. Those jars had survived the long journey from Cadbury, and now the flames from the fireplace played over their surfaces, hiding their contents under the sheen of scarlet and gold.

The woman turned as she felt the cold air stir her knee-length, braided hair. She rose with unconscious grace and moved to the troublesome shutters with a hank of new wool in one hand. Her eyes sharpened in the chill draught and, with concentration, she rammed the wool into the narrow gap, checked with her hand that no more cold air could intrude into her sanctuary and then returned to her seat.

The grey-muzzled wolfhound at her feet didn't bother to rise from its comfortable rug.

Beauty and sorrow hung on Nimue like a rich, invisible cape.

Her face remained unlined, although she was almost thirty-nine years of age. Unlike Queen Wenhaver, the advance of middle age had only brought Nimue gravity and fine-boned elegance. Her hair was still silver, but it was now exceptionally long and was bound at several lengths by argent clasps. She wore grey, as was her habit, but the colour was pale and tinged with a memory of green, like still water under full moonlight.

Nimue's face was unchanged, but her eyes showed the passage of long, hard years. The deep blue of her irises no longer snapped with the curiosity and the fire of her youth, for the Maid of Wind and Water was now wholly dead. Her essence had fled on that doleful evening when Myrddion Merlinus went to his gods upon a huge pyre on the mountain peak. The Lady of the Lake now ruled her inner depths with patience, compassion and a never-ending, adamantine determination.

As she twisted her spindle and drew out the raw, cleansed wool into a fine thread, her mind ranged upon the night wind, far to the north, to the west, and to the south – seeking, asking and questing for the object of her search. Nimue had never cared for magic, nor truly believed in the secret world of spells and curses. Such primitive superstitions had been the subject of much mirth between herself and Myrddion in those happy days when her children were young, before his eyes clouded with blindness.

'I see better now that I'm sightless than ever before, sweet Nimue,' he had consoled her. 'My spirit leaves my body, and sees you as you are. It journeys far, beyond my fleshly strength, to watch my friend, Artorex, and the struggles he must fight in the south and in the east. Even Morgan, poor sad Morgan, feels the edges of my presence. How she jumps as she darts around her malodorous, old woman's room and searches for me.'

They had laughed without malice, but in her heart Nimue had not believed him. Myrddion had sensed her anxiety that his mind was failing and her blue eyes had welled with tears, even while she had laughed at his jokes. There were times, deep in the night, when he had woken and begun to speak in a voice she scarcely knew, describing strange wagons that needed no horses, spears that destroyed cities of glass and the great tapestry of human history that stretched out before his eyes to the ends of time. She wondered then if her husband was truly the wisest man alive, or only lost in the dreams of crazed old age.

She had recorded his visions, for he had no memory of them once he had spoken them aloud, and then husband and wife had puzzled over their meaning.

'Most of the future is closed to me, my dear,' he had told her, his craggy, still-handsome face turned towards the light. 'You should consign my dreams to the fire. Magic doesn't exist but, perhaps, some inner vision does. And if such insight is true, it can trick us into relying on it when our minds and hearts are what should guide us. So put my dreams aside, my beloved, for they are only the shadows of shadows.'

But Nimue had disobeyed him and had begun to weave and embroider her wool into a fitting record of the glory of his blindness. Nimue believed in her heart that her man was not a magician but a great poet and that towering images crowded his still-young brain. But then, after the funeral pyre, so filled was she with hot, scarfing grief that her three sons had had to carry her back to their mountain villa and her mind had descended into a pit of madness.

Wild-eyed, she had threshed and fought through unspeakable nightmares until her sons had been forced to bind her to her bed. Bleeding willow trees, scorched rosebuds, crucified women and blind dragons had assailed her in her horrors, until her sons had quailed to see the welts rise on her white flesh as she mutilated herself.

Then, as sudden as her violent descent into madness had come, her senses had returned. That night, she had dreamed of struggling through a wilderness of half-sentient trees that guided her towards bloody water and a willow tree that hid an unimaginable horror. Screaming, she had been impelled by unseen hands to part the weeping foliage of the tree while her eyes had willed themselves to close, for she knew she would find her own self beneath the blood-soaked branches.

But her strength was as nothing against the power of the dream.

'Nimue!' the demon had called. His strong, right hand had gripped hers, while his left hand had shielded her eyes. Then, just as she was fainting with terror, he had drawn her back into the hollow tree and the comforting nest of her bed. Her darkhaired lover had kissed away every burn, scald and tear that her hands had branded on to her flesh. His dark eyes had drunk her in until she feared her soul would be lost to this demonic creature of the shadows and the chaos between the worlds, and she had wept in her loneliness and her loss.

'It's only me, Nimue. I'm your old husband. Don't you know me?'

And then she knew that the dream still consumed her, for this creature was not Myrddion in withered age but in all the power of mature youth. How beautiful he was, and how his hair caught at hers in a net of darkness. She would have pulled away, but his eyes were the same as when she had first met him, lustrous, amused and full of pain.

'But you're dead, Myrddion! You must leave me to my sorrows, for your cooled ashes already lie in the burial urn. I would rather be crazed or lifeless than trapped in a hopeless search for you.'

He had kissed her thread-scarred fingers.

'You will live on, my beloved. You will live long, and when you call, I will come and we will talk and laugh as we did when I breathed in the fashion of men. You can send for me in your thoughts, and I will be here.'

So Nimue had been forced to acknowledge what Odin, the least learned of her old friends, had always instinctively known, although they had never spoken of it: the soul goes on, and some fortunate few can send their spirits out upon the wind and find the souls of those who call to them, beyond grief, beyond sorrow and beyond the small indignities of death.

'Mother?' a voice called from the kitchen.

Her reflection was broken.

As she entered the room, a servant girl from the hill people was in the act of clouting Nimue's youngest son with a crude ladle. He had stolen bread and was dipping the crusts into the mutton stew. Her eldest son, Taliesin, was attempting to wrestle the dripping morsel from his brother's hand.

Nimue simply raised her index finger. 'Enough!' The word fell like a single pebble into a still pond.

'Forgive me, Mother,' Taliesin apologized and dropped his brother's arm. 'I should know better than to disturb your peace.'

'You owe me no apologies, but Gerda shouldn't be made to look foolish by the behaviour of any of my sons.'

Like all of her kin who eked out a precarious living in the mountains, Gerda was short and very dark. Both of Nimue's sons towered over the irritated woman whose ancestry must have gone back to the little painted people who had lived peacefully in the isles for thousands of years. Nimue felt a flash of shame for her thoughtless children and pressed Gerda's hand lightly in apology.

Taliesin promised to present his second greatest song to Gerda if the servant would deign to forgive him. His eyes were so distressed that the maidservant put away her indignation.

'Have done with your glooming, boy. I knew you and your brother when you were both still soiling your loincloths, so neither of you had better touch Gerda's stew until I decide to give it to you.' The kitchen maid, who was little older than a girl herself, brought the wooden ladle down sharply, but without hurt, across the crowns of two repentant heads.

Nimue's sons were the wonders of the hill country. The boys were alien creatures to the simple folk because they were so unlike each other that, had the people not known of the lovers' devotion towards each other, they would have sworn cuckoos had been placed in the Stone House nest.

Taliesin was a reincarnation of his father, a symphony of black and white, but with eyes that were almost too blue to be human. He had fashioned a harp during his youth and had found the gift of music in his fingers as he learned to play the instrument. The grandams in the village spied the mark of white hair at his temples and nodded in archaic understanding of his qualities.

Glynn ap Myrddion was Nimue's middle son. He was barely seventeen years of age, and was as fair as Taliesin was dark, but his eyes were wholly inherited from his father. Glynn's black eyes were made doubly powerful by the fairness of his eyebrows and the golden hue of his skin. Taliesin's passion for music, poetry and song did not lure Glynn, but the healing trade called him, as it had his father, and he had trailed old Myrddion like a small shadow as the old man collected and prepared his herbs and medications. Seamlessly, Glynn had become his father's strong right hand and, even now, the lad was treating sick children with feverwort at a village over the hills. The hill people swore that his hands had some magic in them, but they also understood that Taliesin's fingers were likewise blessed.

As for Rhys, now sixteen and very full of his mathematical talents, the art of construction was his métier. Tinkering always, he had constructed his mother's favourite loom, he adored the menial tasks of thatching and he coaxed wood and stone to give up their ancient secrets.

All three were well versed in the small miracles of the soil and green and growing things, so Nimue had little cause to find fault in any of her tall and slender sons. Rhys was the most powerfully built of them all, recalling ancestors that Nimue had never known. And now that he had heard of a smith in a nearby village who needed an assistant, Nimue expected him to depart for several months before returning to construct a working forge of his own.

Yet she sighed.

The wind blew fiercely on their hilltop. Even as they shared their meal in the kitchens with Gerda and her mute, sheepherder husband, Col, she could hear the voices as they called on the night gales.

'Taliesin must leave the hill country to stand with King Artor in Cadbury and beyond', the voices told Nimue. 'Obey us, Woman of Water, for your son is needed. Artor's way is ending. Although your son is still young in years, you must allow him to finish what his father started, for the Bloody Cup is soon to come.'

Nimue had heard the voices for three successive nights, and even though she stuffed all the wool in Powys into the corners of her house to silence the intrusive wind, the messengers of her dreams would not be muffled.

Taliesin reached across the table and stroked her left hand gently, massaging her palm with his thumbs just as his father had once done.

'Why are you so unhappy, Mother?' he asked. 'Are there no songs that would lighten your load? Or must I write a new trifle to sing you back to happiness?'

'Whether I want it or not, it's important that you be at Cadbury by Samhein,' she told her son, and Taliesin watched her eyes mist with tears. 'I don't fully understand why you must go there and I don't desire you to leave my house in the dead of winter, but the voices tell me that you must record the passing of the king.'

Taliesin's mouth gaped, but Rhys laughed in the fashion of a simple countryman at the consternation that was written plainly on his older brother's face.

'Cadbury? What would I do at such a place?' Taliesin exclaimed irritably. 'How could I serve the High King? Father shamed us with his brilliance and my skills are few by comparison. Surely my place is here with you?'

Nimue smiled ruefully. 'I wish I could keep you by my side forever, but the wind would never let me rest if I ignored its message. You've been called, so you must sing for the High King. You will offer comfort to him with song and fable, and through lessons too, if the great King Artor will listen. He must be told that the Bloody Cup is coming.'

Rhys laughed. 'And what might that be? Did the wind bother to explain itself to you?' His laughter died as he realized that his words were wounding his mother. 'Please forgive me,' he apologized. 'But the wind, or whatever it is, asks a great deal of you. Father has only been dead one year.'

'Taliesin must go to Artor's court,' Nimue repeated. 'I cannot prevent it, for a mother sends a son down perilous roads if she stands in the path of her child's destiny.' A single tear snaked down her cheek.

Abruptly, Nimue wiped away her fears. Her spine straightened and she tossed back her marvellous hair.

'The family of Myrddion Merlinus has always served the High King of the Celtic tribes, and it was only for love of me that your father deserted his adored Artor. I'm sending Myrddion back to the High King in the guise of my firstborn son. You must do your duty, Taliesin, so your father can be proud of you from beyond the sea of death.'

I don't want to go, Taliesin thought mulishly. He was angry at the voices that spoke to his mother. He resented the needs of the High King that disturbed his life, but he was excited too, for young men love adventure. Above all else, he could deny his mother nothing, for the skeins of her love bound him more strongly than iron chains.

So Taliesin agreed to put aside his doubts and prepare for the journey, choosing to spend his idle hours, few as they were, with his mother and his brothers. If Glynn or Rhys resented his part in the history of the west, they never permitted him to see their envy.

But, late at night, when the wind blew from the east, he struggled with the warning implied by the Bloody Cup. He imagined a large golden goblet decorated with huge, raw-cut stones. It hovered in the deepest recesses of his mind, growing daily in size as his imagination fed on it. Ghastly and grisly, blood spilled down its sides and blurred the rich embossing and the fair gems. Within the rim, the blood swirled in a viscous spiral that dragged Taliesin down into impossible and fathomless depths.

He woke from such dreams drenched in sweat and trembling with terror but, in his waking hours, he mastered his face so that Nimue would miss the telltale pallor of his dread.

Both mother and son lied wordlessly to each other.

Winter had gripped the mountain country in its iron fists when Taliesin prepared to leave the only home he had ever known. On the morning of his departure, he rose early, expecting to find his mother in the kitchens or drying fleece before the fire, but the house had that curious, empty hollowness that only manifests itself when its soul is absent.

Two bare feet had tracked a path from the kitchen quarters, across the coarse stubble of field, and into the line of wild forest. The light footsteps had barely disturbed the dead grasses, but where a light dusting of frost had settled, Taliesin could trace the route taken by his mother.

As quiet as any wild young animal, he followed her footsteps into the trees and along the edge of an ice-bound rivulet that sank into a steeply sloping fold in the hills. At the bottom a black mere lay partially frozen over, glistening in the weak morning light like a slice of polished agate.

Taliesin halted and watched as his mother stepped on to the frozen lake. Her furs trailed from her shoulders, dark and slick as an otter's coat under the silver fall of her unbound hair. Words sang in Taliesin's head as Nimue cast off her furs and stood half-naked on the frozen lake, with her slender white arms raised upwards towards the rising sun. He could see the mark of the dragon as it coiled up her leg, and he could visualise the ice beneath her feet puddling slightly beneath the warmth of her feet.

Before she turned to retrace her steps to the Stone House, she bowed to the sky, the water and the willows that defined the far edges of the mere. Around her neck, Myrddion's electrum necklace gleamed like fish scales.

'She is, in truth, the Lady of the Lake.' Taliesin hugged the trunk of the oak tree that hid him in its shadow as his mother glided past him, her furs now returned to her shoulders and her flesh pearly-white in the half-light.

Later that day, when a weak sun had risen in a grey sky, the song was already growing in Taliesin's head as he rode away from his home with only his favourite hound for company and protection.

Nimue wept.

Three other women faced the same sunrise with similar stirrings of emotion, powerful and scouring.

Far to the north, in a bothie of thatch, willow lathes and mud, Morgan brooded over her shrunken flesh. The polished silver mirror that had been Uther Pendragon's cruellest gift to her revealed a face and eyes that were as sunken and desiccated as her stepfather's had been at the time of his death. Uther had hated her as much as he had needed her potions to keep him alive. The old king saw the betrayed Gorlois in his stepdaughter's face, and Uther understood how deeply she had damaged his last, painful days. Had the old monster known that she would live long enough to discover that her face was even more ugly than his had been? Had Uther known that his mirror would expose her bitter, cruel thoughts and acts in many decades of ugly, vicious living? She pondered on the boundless strength of malice that had burned away every trace of womanliness in her nature. Childless, friendless and empty, she had traded all her possibilities for a promise of revenge. Morgan would have wept, but her obsessions had sucked away even the temporary relief of tears.

How Uther Pendragon must be laughing, beyond the veils of death.

Petulant and mean-spirited, Queen Wenhaver writhed in her sumptuous bed. Her loins hungered for the salacious, thrilling touch of a man, any man, but her lust was secondary to a more primal need. She would renounce all pleasure for a means to make Artor bleed. She, too, no longer found solace in her mirror, for silver threads were visible through the gilt of her hair. With her old, careless arrogance, she consoled herself with the small number that she had removed from her scalp with delicate, golden pincers. She still had time to have her revenge for a lifetime of real and imagined insults.

Elayne woke to find herself covered by travelling furs in a nest of autumn leaves. Half asleep, she realized she lay in a small tent that blocked out the feeble rays of the winter sun. Sleepily, she wondered where she was and who snored beside her. Then she remembered, for Bedwyr's heavy arm was lying across her body.

I am a wife, she thought, with some surprise. And I go to Cadbury to meet the High King.

Then she smiled and loosened her nut-brown hair.

And woke her husband.

CHAPTER III

THE LADY OF THE LOOM

> What is woman that men forsake her
> to follow the old grey widow-maker.
> Old Norse Song

Gawayne emerged from a deep, satisfying sleep with the unnerving sensation that he had fallen from a great height. Gradually, memory returned, prompted by the warm and naked body that lay in the curve of his painfully numb left arm.

I've done it this time, he told himself, as memory slowly returned. Not only will Galahad be furious with my little slip, but I seem to remember that this lady really is a lady.

Gawayne had never been particularly sharp-witted.

The prince was now in his mid-fifties and ought to have been sliding gracefully into dignified old age. But nature had combined his limited intellect with reckless courage, superb athletic grace and the almost ageless, icy beauty of his mother, Queen Morgause. His jaw was a little thickened by time and the white lines around his eyes were a tribute to years spent in the saddle. His russet hair had faded a trifle, but male vanity forced him to retain the shaven cheeks of youth. Unfortunately, his reckless libido still governed his undisciplined body.

'I hate being hairy,' he had explained to Enid, his wife, as he ritually shaved with a special blade that had been honed to whisper sharpness. 'But I'm not a Roman with the bravery necessary to pluck out my hair, root by root.'

He had shuddered and Enid had kissed his smooth, still-unlined cheeks with passion.

Gawayne's son, Galahad, seemed set to eclipse his father, which made the prince feel uncomfortably irritable. It wasn't that he resented growing old, for so far the process had been quite pleasurable. Nor did he envy Galahad's brilliance at arms, for his uncle, King Artor, had always possessed greater martial skills than he himself had. The prince enjoyed his reputation as one of the finest Celtic swordsmen of his generation, while his son's extraordinary physical beauty and purity of face were constant sources of pride to him. What he really loathed about his son was the odour of sanctimony that Galahad wore visibly, like a hair shirt. The young man had turned virginity and celibacy into virtues, conditions that Gawayne considered downright foolish.

As the eldest son, Galahad had family responsibilities. But did the boy listen to his father? Whenever the topic of bedding women came up, Galahad simply smiled innocently and informed his father that he would leave such fleshly pursuits to other men – such as Gawayne. In Galahad's grandiose vision of his future, he was born to a destiny that surpassed any talent in the martial arts or his role as heir to the throne of a Celtic tribe.

Lying in this strange bed, carved quixotically to resemble a boat, Gawayne ground his teeth in impotent irritation.

He had hoped that the boy would be tempted to indulge himself in the exotic fleshpots of Aquae Sulis, but the charms of fair women, whether noble, common or professional, left Galahad unmoved. Nor did the charms of men, boys or even animals appeal to his son for, as far as Gawayne could judge, Galahad was as sexless as a rock. Galahad actually had the presumption to lecture his father on the duties and responsibilities of marriage, an experience that left Gawayne longing to clout the boy across the ear.

In fact, the only time Galahad showed the slightest interest in anything that Aquae Sulis had to offer was when he viewed the Garden of Gallia at the Villa Poppinidii. This shrine to the Roman way of life in Celtic Britain now included the urn of Targo of blessed memory, whom many soldiers begged to intercede for them with their gods when they were in the extremity of death. While Galahad disapproved of such superstitions, he extolled the virtues of Gallia who was said to exemplify Roman womanhood, even though she was rumoured to be a pagan. The garden itself had touched Galahad's glacial heart.

'It's humbling to hear that a slave and an aristocrat died together and that their ashes are now mingled,' Galahad told anyone who would listen. 'The Garden of Gallia has helped me to reflect on my fellowship with our Heavenly Father.'

'Please, Galahad!' Gawayne begged. 'I've been lectured all the way from the Wall.' He wished his son would show enthusiasm for something other than the Christian god.

Journeying south towards Lindinis, the closest settlement to Cadbury, they reached a river with wide meads along its banks and an island within its broad, slow swell. On the island, a villa with an odd, defensive tower spoke of ancient occupation and both men were charmed by the water gardens, where wild marsh flowers grew lustily and reeds formed a dense, almost impenetrable barrier to the river. The air was thick with dragonflies, butterflies and bees.

Both men attempted to ignore the biting gnats that feasted on their unprotected flesh.

As they lazed in the shade of a large tree, a wooden boat made its way to a shelf of silted mud close to where they were dozing in the shadows. Shortly thereafter, a sturdy man approached them. He was no taller than middle height and was decorated with whorls and spirals of woad-blue tattoos that covered all his exposed limbs. After stepping ashore, he brushed away the collected mud that was clinging to his woollen robe. This strange creature, almost deformed because of his abnormally broad shoulders and short, womanish legs, wore a silver band across his forehead that held back the remains of sparse grey hair that had never been cut.

'My lords,' he addressed them in a deep, guttural voice. 'My mistress, the Lady of Salinae Minor, bids you welcome and invites you to accept her hospitality in her villa. We are unused to visitors but she would welcome word of the world, for we are isolated in this remote spot.'

Gawayne brightened immediately; a soft bed under a snug roof would be more than welcome after the discomforts of life on the road – even better than a good vintage wine.

Galahad, however, was unimpressed. His eyes narrowed sharply as he scowled at the stranger. His delicate nostrils twitched as if he scented pagan blood. This creature actually wears perfumed oil, he thought with disgust and wrinkled his upper lip. He looks like a Pict.

'Thank you, friend,' Gawayne responded hastily, to counter his son's all too obvious contempt for this offer of hospitality. 'I am Prince Gawayne of the Otadini, journeying to Cadbury in the company of my eldest son, Galahad.' He smiled. 'I've always believed that Salinae lies in the lands of the Ordovice. Is your mistress some distant kin to Bran ap Cerdic?'

'Her father was distant kin to Llanwith, my lord, and he rebuilt the fortifications of Salinae. He settled here many years ago in company with my mistress, who was his only child. A blood dispute over his wife's infidelity caused him to be banished to this place after he had her executed under the laws of the Romans.'

Gawayne barely restrained an instinctive wince. Like the High King, he was contemptuous of any man who insisted upon exercising his full rights as paterfamilias.

'If you'll join me, good masters, I'll row you across to the isle,' the small man suggested gently. 'My mistress calls the island Salinae Minor in memory of her old home. My name is Gronw and I am the spiritual adviser to the Lady of Salinae. As you must have many questions, you may ask of me what you will.'

Galahad shot Gronw a suspicious, hostile stare. 'And what shall become of our horses and packs in our absence? I doubt they'll fit in your boat,' he retorted rudely.

Any natural resentment that Gronw might have felt was

55

suppressed under a polite smile. He responded with perfect, impassive courtesy. 'The village that provides us with our grain, meat and servants has been warned of your approach. They will care for your mounts, so you need have no fears for their safety.'

'I haven't seen a village and I can't imagine how you could have contacted any peasants so quickly,' Galahad declared pugnaciously. 'How do we know you're speaking the truth?'

'Galahad!' Gawayne admonished, but Gronw waved away Galahad's slur.

'We have known of your approach for many hours, so we contacted the village in advance. As soon as we embark for the isle, the villagers will collect your mounts.'

'How?' Galahad persisted.

'If you mean how do we contact the village, we do so with mirrors,' Gronw responded mildly, without a hint of impatience in his voice.

'You have your answer, Galahad, so don't harangue this poor man,' Gawayne ordered. 'Gronw, we're in your hands.'

The short journey across to the island was accomplished with minimal effort, for Gronw was an expert oarsman. As they approached a small wharf, Gawayne saw that the island was small, although the last few leafy trees of autumn gave an illusion of size. The villa sat upon its highest point and was surrounded by gardens and fruit trees that stretched down to the water's edge.

As they walked through the bare peach and apple trees and the fallow gardens, Gawayne admired the statuary carved in the Roman style that had been tastefully placed among the bare winter trees. He was struck by the peace and tranquillity of the place. The villa itself, in name as well as style, was Roman.

'Your tower has an odd appearance,' Gawayne commented to Gronw with some curiosity. 'It's not what one would expect in a villa of Roman design.'

'The tower serves to give us warning of the approach of strangers and my lady spends many hours at her loom in the upper room. She calls it her eye upon the world. The tower was already very old when the villa was built around the existing structure shortly after we settled at Salinae Minor.' Gronw smiled at Gawayne with a friendliness that smacked of familiarity. His eyes were amber with green flecks and, despite the man's apparent pleasure in their company, Gawayne suspected that something peculiar stirred in those quiet, intelligent depths.

Gronw handed the guests over to quiet-footed servants who ushered father and son into a spacious sleeping chamber that adjoined the Roman baths. Although smiling and polite, the servants were mute, except to inform the guests that the mistress expected them to dine with her in two hours.

Galahad strode around the tiled and painted room, clutching a crucifix that hung at his throat. He stopped to examine a dreamy fresco of nymphs and satyrs at play in a charming woodland setting, sniffed derisively and then uttered a short, barely audible prayer.

'No more of your piety, Galahad,' Gawayne snapped. 'I respect your right to practise your religion as you wish, although where your faith comes from is beyond me. Our family has never been interested in anything spiritual unless it's useful. But I'll not tolerate rudeness to our hostess because you disapprove of her faith. You'll keep your mouth shut, whatever your feelings might be.'

Galahad's cold, hazel eyes showed his intransigence and Gawayne groaned inwardly. Galahad's chilly contempt for anyone who failed to reach his exacting standards was insufferable.

'This place stinks of corruption, Father, and luxury and ostentation tempt you too easily. You should be thinking of your immortal soul, rather than pleasure.'

'I suppose you'd prefer that we slept on stone after we dined on dried meat and water?'

'Rather hardship than the temptations of pagan licentiousness,' Galahad retorted.

'How did I father such a supercilious prig? No, Galahad! Don't say another word! You'd do well to remember that neither I nor your grandfather ever failed in our tolerance of other faiths. You will be a king one day and you'll have to rule over men who follow all manner of gods. In such an event, you'd be unwise to prohibit other religions for, if you do, you'll find yourself vastly outnumbered in these isles. Even King Artor, whom I've never known to worship anything other than duty and loyalty, is more Roman than Christian. Perhaps you should use this night as an opportunity to practise some common courtesy.'

At least he's not taken to wearing a hair shirt and refusing to bathe, Gawayne grumbled to himself, remembering a disreputable Christian priest who had arrived at King Lot's hall in the summer. The putrid stink of his unwashed robes had caused the hardiest Otadini warrior to almost retch.

At the appointed hour, dressed in their best clothing and

shining with health and cleanliness, father and son were delivered to a triclinium furnished with dining couches in the old Roman style. Galahad perched awkwardly on a gilded and carved couch, and sat as close as possible to the archway as if his immortal soul was in imminent peril.

Gawayne remained standing. Familiar though he was with the Roman custom, he still found reclining to eat a very awkward proposition. As he glared a warning at Galahad's mutinous face, Gawayne wished that his son could learn to smile, if only occasionally.

Gawayne's irritation evaporated when the mistress of the house glided into the room.

She was exquisitely beautiful with long, uncut black hair that was elaborately dressed, as befitted a maiden. Her face was unnaturally pale, as if she rarely ventured out into the sunlight, and Gawayne noticed that her fingers were unusually long. But it was her eyes that charmed, and her wide, full-lipped smile. Her eyes were deep brown, warm, and feathered with long lashes. Her eyebrows were dark and turned up at the corners so that their expression appeared both knowing and surprised. However, within a few moments of conversation with the lady, Gawayne was convinced that her facial features protected a nature that was shy, unpretentious and childlike.

'Greetings, great lords, you honour my table with your presence.' She smiled becomingly at both visitors. 'I hope that we may provide good food, fine wine and peaceful rest so that you will remember Salinae Minor with affection.'

Even unsusceptible Galahad was momentarily robbed of speech by the mistress's aura of charm. Her dress was simply cut and styled, but the fabric chosen was dyed a changeable hue of blue and green, beautifully embroidered at the neck, sleeves and hem, so that she appeared to float in a pool of moving water.

Gawayne was the first to regain his voice. 'Your courtesy does us honour that I fear we have not earned, my lady. Salinae Minor is fair, but the isle lacks the charm and beauty of its mistress.'

Their hostess blushed and laughed. Her voice was warm and deep for a woman, and her laughter infectious.

Despite his best intentions, Gawayne felt a familiar stirring in his loins.

'You have a clever tongue, Prince Gawayne. Too clever for me. I'm a simple girl, and unused to flattery.'

Galahad twitched one eyebrow in ironic tribute to his father's skill with women. If Gawayne could have read his son's thoughts, he would have been shocked, for Galahad was certain that the lady's intention was to titillate and his father was rising to the occasion like a gaffed fish.

'Your servant neglected to tell us your name. I'm loath to refer to you as my lady throughout the evening,' Galahad stated baldly, without an iota of diplomacy or charm.

The lady embraced him with her brown eyes, but she found neither admiration nor liking reflected in his direct, frigid gaze. Gracefully, she returned her attention to Gawayne.

'I apologize, Prince Gawayne, for I've been remiss in courtesy. My father, Rufus, named me Miryll after the old ones of our family. Although we are of the Ordovice, Roman blood runs through our veins and he didn't follow the Christian god until late in life.' She smiled and Galahad chose to read a challenge in her moist, pink lips.

'Your son purses his mouth, I see, so he must believe in Jesus, the carpenter's son,' she continued pleasantly. 'I've found that Christian believers have no room in their hearts for those of us who follow the old ways.' She sighed prettily. 'But I'll say no more as I have no wish to offend my honourable guests. Let's eat and drink well and you shall give me the tidings from the west. I'm isolated here at Salinae Minor and visitors rarely entertain us.'

It was Galahad's turn to blush, for Miryll had neatly pointed out his prejudices. She had left him with little to say in his own defence, especially as Gawayne shot him a glance that promised trouble if his son's rudeness continued.

Miryll reclined elegantly on her couch, nodded to her guests to join her and then clapped her hands.

Food and wine jugs came quickly, carried by silent maidservants. The meal was epicurean, sophisticated and exotic. Galahad closely inspected each morsel with a doubtful eye. Throughout the meal, Mistress Miryll maintained a steady, light-hearted flow of conversation that she aimed primarily at the more polished attentions of Gawayne.

As soon as the meal drew to a close, Galahad stiffly excused himself, claiming fatigue. Gawayne recognized the signs: a period of sulking and awkward silences would greet the morrow.

'You'll not be long, Father, will you?' Galahad said pointedly. 'We must be on the road early tomorrow.' His demeanour was so stern and parental that Gawayne felt like a recalcitrant child. And, as such, the prince resolved to defy his eldest son and heir.

Perhaps Gawayne responded to Mistress Miryll because he was determined to put his son in his place. Perhaps habits of seduction were simply too deeply ingrained in his nature. Or perhaps Gawayne simply missed the company of women who flattered him. The oil lamps were guttering by the time he excused himself and made his weary, inebriated way to his sleeping quarters.

Even before he had refused the last cup of wine, Mistress Miryll had wrung a promise from him that he would stay at the Isle of Salinae for one more day. Predictably, Galahad was peeved by his father's decision but, for once, he wisely refrained from complaining.

Gawayne had learned from Mistress Miryll that the river passed close to Glastonbury and its tributaries provided the rich waters that made the religious centre one of the wonders of the west. When he suggested that they could take a trip to Glastonbury by boat, Miryll had laughed and explained that Glastonbury was landlocked, although it had once been surrounded by water, hence its name, the Isle of Apples.

Galahad concentrated on learning more about the mistress of Salinae Minor, Gronw and the history of her family. Why he distrusted Miryll, he was unable to explain exactly, except that he felt awkward in her company and suspicious of the circumstances that had led to their brief sojourn in this strange, timeless place.

Miryll smiled admiringly at Gawayne's most inane stories and Galahad wondered how such a young, intelligent and beautiful woman could be entranced by the attentions of an older man.

Gawayne felt none of his son's alarm. He was charmed by the garden, the pool with its hazel tree, the artfully wild roses and even the fields of dying marsh flowers and swaying bulrushes. When Miryll invited him into the tower, he was eager to explore the ancient fortification, which was so at odds with the luxurious villa it protected.

'The building is very old and its origins are lost in the sands of time,' Miryll said, her dark eyes misty with affection, fascination or some darker emotion. 'It was old even before the kings made peace with the Romans. We sealed the stone interior with a mortar of mud, dung and horsehair in the old way.'

Gawayne examined the stone used in the construction of the walls and the design of the winding stairs. He instantly recalled another tower at Glastonbury where he had made a prize ass of himself as he attempted to grasp the sword of Uther that had been embedded in the wall just beyond his reach.

He cleared his throat. 'It reminds me of the tower on Glastonbury Tor.'

'The Maid's Nipple. Aye, so it does.'

Gawayne felt some slight discomfort until Miryll slipped her warm hand into his. 'Do you fear legends from the old days, my lord?'

Gawayne shook his head.

'The villagers tell tales of an old man who journeyed from alien lands to Glastonbury,' she continued, 'where he built a church devoted to the Christian god. They believe he planted a thorn bush taken from a crown and then, for safety, built this tower to guard a treasure. Can you imagine such a crown?'

Gawayne displayed immediate interest.

'You needn't look so eager, Prince Gawayne. No treasure is hidden within these walls. If such a cache had ever existed, we would have found it when we rebuilt the tower. When Father came to the island, the structure was mostly in ruins, and many months of labour were needed to make it habitable.'

'Who was the old man who built the original church?'

Miryll permitted a flash of annoyance to cross her face. 'Who knows, Prince Gawayne? I've heard him called by many names. Some scholars have called him Josephus, but others have called him the Trader, or simply the Outlander. Five hundred years, at least, have passed since he came this way, and his true name has been forgotten in the river of time.'

Gawayne shrugged off a vague premonition of danger as he followed the lady up the winding stairs to a remarkable circular room.

Great stone apertures opened the tower to the elements. They were uneven, but attractive in their rustic simplicity, and light flooded every corner of the upper room. Gawayne could see that heavy panels of wool could be rolled across each window to keep out the winter chills, but the faint shimmer of cobwebs showed how rarely they were moved to counter the cold winds.

A large slab of undressed stone dominated the floor in the very centre of the tower, and Gawayne trailed his fingers over the heavy piece of limestone that had been raised with much labour to catch every shaft of light. A richly woven length of cloth softened its harsh, tomb-like appearance.

One corner of the room housed a frame on which the flowers, reeds and meads that grew beyond the window had been translated into woven thread. The half-completed work was oddly beautiful. He raised one eyebrow in inquiry at Miryll, who smiled back shyly.

'Yes, this is my work. I weave and embroider what I see through my windows. My next task will recall the scene of you and your son resting by the oak trees, with Gronw in his skiff coming to fetch you to the villa. My weavings reflect my life here on the island.'

For a moment, she seemed very sad, and Gawayne wondered what weight lay across her spirit like a malevolent spell. Then her eyes widened and her lips parted.

Gawayne's breath caught in his throat and his easy, seductive compliments were immediately forgotten.

The prince's day passed in a waking dream as Lady Miryll strolled with him through the gardens and whiled away the afternoon with stories designed to amuse her visitor. Before he was aware that the light was fading, evening came with a gentle reminder that they should return to the villa to bathe and dress for the evening meal.

Galahad was uncharacteristically silent when Gawayne joined him in their room, and the prince had to coax his son into speech. The young man had spent the day amongst the shelves of the scriptorium, looking through dusty rolls of fine vellum and Egyptian parchment.

'Father, there's a large collection of pottery jars stored here, all very ancient, to judge by the dirt and dust that covers them. I found documents that were rotten and still others that were brittle with age. I couldn't understand the language, but I found notes written by Lady Miryll's father that speak of an ancient relic that has been hidden here for safekeeping.'

Gawayne was surprised to see his son's excitement, for the young man rarely expressed enthusiasm for anything but his god.

'That may be so', Gawayne said slowly. 'Miryll spoke to me of some treasure that was supposed to have been hidden in the tower.'

Galahad was silenced for a moment, before rushing back into speech.

'I believe the scrolls may have been written in Aramaic. I'm only guessing, but the notes written by Rufus refer to the original builder of the tower as having spoken in that heathen tongue. The name, Josephus, also suggests that he was of that cursed race – a Jew.' He gazed piercingly at his father. 'Can you imagine the wealth of knowledge stored here?' he asked in awe. 'It must become the property of the Church.'

'The Church! The bleeding Church! Don't you think of anything else?'

'Not often, Father. Except, of course, of my duty to you.'

As Galahad paced about the room, Gawayne reflected that his son had at least found something on the island that captured his interest.

'Salinae Minor is neither a fair nor a healthy place, Father,' Galahad added stiffly. 'I can smell the decay that pervades this villa and lies under the scent of the perfumes.'

Gawayne dismissed his son's warning with frank incredulity. 'Really, Galahad! All I can smell here is good cooking and cleanliness. Surely, Salinae Minor and its tiled floors make an exquisite change from the rushes thrown over flagging stone, the odour of your grandfather's hounds and the odd old fish head that stinks up Lot's hall. Grow up, boy, so we can enjoy this brief sojourn while we can.'

Galahad couldn't deny that Lot's house was lice-ridden

and dirty, especially during winter, so he retreated into a sulk.

'I am certain there's a relic here in this villa, Father. I believe it's a holy object and I do not trust the hands that protect it.'

'Well, whatever it was, it's long gone!' Gawayne turned away. He was accustomed to Galahad's odd obsessions and was impatient with the prejudices that so easily blinded his son.

That evening, Gawayne drank freely. The wines were sweetened with honey and were liberally poured during the meal. Afterwards, he had little recollection of the stumbled journey to the top of the tower and even less of the intense sex that took place on a pile of furs in the very centre of that looming, circular space. As he grunted and moaned over Miryll's sweet young flesh, he imagined he heard the sounds of chanting in a strange tongue, but his mind was muddled by the needs of his body and the heady perfume of the moist loins below him. Puzzlingly, he found his erection remained painfully and stubbornly unsatisfied, no matter how often he spent himself inside the woman beneath him.

Eventually, he found himself being led from the tower on trembling legs and taken to the luxury of Miryll's soft bed. When his body permitted him to sink into an exhausted sleep, he dreamed of women who wound white arms around him and drove him painfully with the whips of their desire.

When he reluctantly left the embrace of sleep, he looked at Miryll lying beside him, tousled and still endearingly beautiful. He scowled at the awkwardness his lust had caused. The girl had been virginal! This much his sluggish brain remembered.

Well, I can't marry her! She knows I have a wife over the Wall, Gawayne thought gratefully. So there shouldn't be any tears. But she'll want something – women always do!

To punctuate his thoughts with some form of action, Gawayne planted a perfunctory kiss on the dishevelled black hair that fanned out over the pillow.

Miryll opened sleepy eyes and watched the naked Gawayne climb from her sleeping couch. She stared at the softened belly and the sagging neck of her ageing lover but, other than a small grimace of distaste, she said nothing. Her eyes were flat and enigmatic as she stretched like a sleek kitten.

'I imagine you'll be eager to depart for Cadbury, Prince Gawayne.' She smiled perfunctorily up at her guest. 'You must forgive me if I'm still abed when you're ready to depart. I've asked Gronw to oversee your passage back to the riverbank.'

Then Miryll stretched once more, folded her long, narrow hands under her pillow and went back to sleep with the ease of a small child.

Gawayne had expected tears, arguments and angry demands from a forsaken young lover. He had been braced to cajole and to flatter, so his abrupt dismissal was both surprising and deflating. The prince had little option but to tiptoe back to his room, leaving Miryll to her careless slumbers. Fortunately, Galahad was still asleep.

Gawayne felt manipulated and used. Ignoring the obvious truth that he had left a hundred women over the years with as little affection as Miryll was now displaying towards him, Gawayne indulged in a middle-aged sulk that lasted through a cursory meal, a silent journey from the island and the recovery of their mounts and provisions.

Galahad pursed his flawless, chiselled lips in annoyance when his father swore vilely after dropping a pannier on one foot.

'I trust you slept well last night, Father?'

Gawayne grunted in reply.

'You didn't take your rest in our quarters,' Galahad continued. 'I hope Lady Miryll was worth the effort.'

'What would you know, boy? And I don't wish to speak of Salinae Minor any further. I'd lief pretend the place doesn't exist.'

Galahad had the impudence to laugh at his father's discomfort. 'Was the lady unappreciative of your charms? Could the great Gawayne be growing old?'

Gawayne clouted his son as if he was still a fractious boy. Twin spots of colour mounted on Galahad's cheeks and his eyes took on a distinctly unchristian glint of anger.

'Shut your mouth, laddie, and treat your father with some respect. How I spend my nights are my business, not yours.'

Galahad refused to retaliate, but he skewered his father with one last observation that would trouble Gawayne for the rest of their journey.

'If she could have persuaded me to break my vows, Father, the woman would have taken me. Have you considered why she wanted one of us in her bed, and why we are so summarily dismissed when she has achieved her goal? The lady has a purpose other than your charms.'

Gawayne leapt carelessly on to his mount in an attempt to convey a nonchalance he did not feel. Something old and musty stirred below the splendour of Salinae Minor, and Galahad had recognized it in Miryll's eyes.

'You're an infernal irritant, Galahad, far worse than any black-robed priest,' Gawayne snapped. 'In fact, you're almost as infuriating as Morgan, your great-aunt.' His gaze met his son's amused, hazel eyes as their horses moved closer together. 'But in this case, I'm afraid you could be right.'

CHAPTER IV

KIN, LOVERS AND SUNDRY OTHER ENEMIES

A southerner with dark braids and shifty eyes slid into the least reputable alehouse in Deva, the Blue Hag, and approached a simple slab of sawn logs that served as a makeshift bar against the far wall. His eyes darted nervously around the room and he wiped sweaty palms down his stained woollen shirt.

Inside the shoddy room, which was thick with fire smoke, the smell of some kind of fish-head soup and men in various stages of drunkenness, the stranger stood out simply because he reeked of fear.

'I'm looking for Octa, the owner of this shit heap,' he demanded of a shepherd who was hunched over a wooden bowl of greasy soup. The man shook off the stranger's hand.

'Get your paws off me,' he snarled. 'Octa's over there by the pot.' He pointed a grime-stained finger at a man ladling out bowls of soup and pottery jugs of beer to his customers.

The stranger nodded, and then slithered his way through the press of men until he reached the innkeeper.

'A man called Pebr comes here from time to time,' the stranger began.

The innkeeper allowed his gaze to slide away from his ladle and focus on the newcomer.

'A one-eyed man,' the stranger added.

'Perhaps he does, and perhaps he doesn't. Who's asking?'

'It's none of your business,' the stranger rasped. 'Just tell him that I'm in Deva and I have his cup. The message is that it's begun. Have you got that? It's begun. I'll be here again in three days to see if there's an answer from Pebr.'

The innkeeper filled another bowl and slapped it on to the rough-sawn bench. Some of the oily grey sludge splashed on to the stranger's hand.

'Do you understand?' the stranger repeated, sucking the greasy mess off his fingers.

'Aye. You've got his sodding cup. As if I care! It's sodding begun – whatever it is you're talking about. It's in three days, if you say so.'

The stranger dropped a few worn coins into the smear of soup on the planks. 'That's for your trouble.'

Then he disappeared into the press of men packed into the Blue Hag.

'Sodding southerner!' the innkeeper cursed, but he picked up the coins and reflectively licked them clean.

Had the stranger chosen to check behind him, he would have seen a tall shadow leave a moment or two behind his retreating back. Had he been listening carefully, he would have heard deft feet slide into step behind him as the moon disappeared behind a bank of cloud.

An iron-strong arm suddenly encircled him from behind

and gripped his throat. A knife blade ended any sound he might have made, as it sliced through his larynx. Carefully avoiding the sudden jet of arterial blood, the one-eyed man let the stranger's jerking body drop into the spreading puddle of his lifeblood.

The last thing the stranger felt was Pebr's boot as it caved in his ribs in silent contempt. As the stranger's hearing and sight failed, the one-eyed man was already walking away.

'Men who use my name never speak another word,' Pebr One-Eye muttered softly.

Inside the alehouse, Octa wiped his sweating brow and reflected on the dangers of the world. But he said nothing. Silence ensured that wise men kept breathing.

Cadbury stirred like a hornets' nest as winter deepened and each day welcomed some new visitors of note for the population to gawk at. Balyn and Balan had initially been wonders but, now, within hours of each other, two more sets of visitors had ridden up the spiral fortification that led to Cadbury Tor, with an accompanying panoply of personal guards and packhorses.

Modred ap Cynwael had been the first to arrive. The citizens of Cadbury were cosmopolitan and accustomed to visits by envoys from the continent but, even in such exalted and exotic company as visitors from Gaul and Spain, Modred stood out.

Like all the scions of King Luka of the Brigante, Modred was lithe, dark and finely shaped. Yet, despite his natural comeliness, the man projected a sense of narrowness and crookedness. Perhaps such impressions were tricks of the light, for Modred's limbs were clean and robust, if a little too thin for military beauty. He rode his richly caparisoned horse without any need for the cruel mouth restraints favoured by so many lords. Like the fabled centaur, his body rose smoothly from the trunk of his mount, his legs hidden by a capacious woollen cloak clasped at the throat with a golden boar's head. White-haired grandfathers shivered at the sight of the golden emblem, as if the bad days of Gorlois and Uther Pendragon had returned.

Modred dropped his reins and slid from the back of his horse, ignoring the stable boy who ran to lift the dangling leathers from the mud.

He bounded up the steps leading to Artor's hall and pushed open the doors unceremoniously, brushing Percivale to one side as if the king's bodyguard was invisible. With Gareth and Percivale close behind him, Modred strode jauntily towards the twin thrones.

Artor rose from his seat.

'Who are you to break the peace of the High King's house?' Artor asked the question courteously, but those warriors present could have warned Modred that the king's eyes were as cold as the gales of winter.

Odin was the first to move. He drew his battleaxe and stepped forward. The remainder of Artor's personal guard loosened their weapons in their sheaths and Percivale drew his sword with a sinister little hiss.

'Why, uncle, such a welcome!' Modred's eyes gleamed with intelligence and laughter. 'If your servants want my weapons, they only have to ask.'

The young man, no older than the twins and, in his own

way, as comely as Balyn and Balan, ostentatiously held his arms away from his body while Gareth and Percivale thoroughly and roughly disarmed him. As Percivale removed a murderous, narrow blade from Modred's boot, the King of the Brigante laughed sardonically.

'Take care of my little plaything, boy. It was a personal gift from my mother.'

Percivale flushed to the roots of his russet hair in embarrassment, while Artor's brows knitted in irritation at the twin insults to his bodyguard's honour and to his own position as High King of the Britons. The emblem of Morgause on the blade, with its entwined serpents, was clear demonstration of where Modred's allegiances lay – with himself.

'Be careful, good Percivale.' Artor smiled with a sweet insincerity that was as polished as Modred's arrogance. 'My sister could quite readily have poisoned the blade.' Artor's chill smile remained fixed on his nephew. 'Royal, or not, Luka's grandson or not, you'll not carry arms within the precincts of the High King's hall. Nor have you earned the right to insult lords such as Percivale and Gareth who have far higher stature in this land than you do. You'll curb that sharp tongue that has been the birth gift of your mother, else men here may be tempted to call you to task as a deedless bastard who lacks honour.'

Modred stood very still and his face whitened under his blue-black hair. With visible self-control, the young man unclenched his fists and allowed the insults to pass over him.

'If I have given cause for offence, my liege, then I beg your pardon and the forgiveness of the noble Percivale and Gareth. It was not my intent to disrupt the order of this house. I was eager to meet and offer obeisance to the great Artor, as a friend and defender of my grandfather, and to swear allegiance to your house forever. I believe we are distant kin.'

The fair words stung Artor with their delicate taint of derision.

King Luka had been close to the High King's heart, so Artor had exacted bloody vengeance on those cowards who had murdered the Brigante king, Percivale thought nervously. Now Luka's grandson claims the High King's favour because of his blood ties and an old friendship. But kin or not, no one is permitted to insult the High King.

'Your apology is accepted, Modred. As the grandson of my old friend, Luka, you hold a special position in the hearts of my courtiers, for your grandfather was an admirable man who was my mentor when I was a young man. I still owe him the greatest of debts.'

Modred smiled at the king's omission and Odin stirred threateningly at Artor's shoulder.

'I believe the debt was cleared when you placed my cousin on the Brigante throne, my lord. Your justice was wise and swift.' Modred bowed deeply in mocking respect.

'We'll speak again later, King of the Brigante and grandson of my friend. I tell you now that I value your oath of fealty, especially after such an inauspicious beginning to our friendship.' Artor smiled thinly. 'You'd do well to consider what your grandfather would have done in my position. Luka would've separated your head from your body. But my friend was a hasty and a passionate man, while I am neither.' Artor's eyes were as devoid of emotion as a shark's.

Wisely, Modred remained silent and backed away, his head

lowered modestly between black wings of hair that hung about his narrow, handsome face.

As the Brigante king left Artor's hall, Odin made a covert sign against evil, while Wenhaver devoured the young man's retreating body with her blue, vacuous eyes.

More man-flesh for my lady, Artor's inner voice hissed. And this one is a dangerous, careful snake who'll inveigle her into carrying out his desires rather than the other way around. Perhaps sending Wenhaver to Tintagel may not be such a bad idea.

Artor continued meting out justice to petitioners, but one ear was keenly attuned to catch the ripples of laughter and conversation that rose around Modred's head like a murder of crows.

The High King was at table when, days later, Bedwyr and Lady Elayne craved an audience. Bedwyr would have retreated immediately and waited until his king had finished his meal, but Artor stood on no ceremony with his Arden Knife, the man who had delivered the Saxons to him at Caer Fyrddin.

Wenhaver pouted at the interruption, for Modred was an amusing companion, entertaining her with his wicked observations concerning Artor's personal guard, who all bore a striking resemblance to their king.

'Artor's personal guards are his bastard sons,' Wenhaver tittered. 'Can't you tell?'

How clever, thought Modred. Unacknowledged sons, especially those elevated to high positions in court, had powerful incentives to remain loyal. And a father's love and affection guard against assassination. Modred's thoughts swirled, as they alternated between admiration and bitter jealousy.

'I mean, my dear, just look at them,' Wenhaver whispered. 'They're pale imitations of their father, and they make me a laughing stock in the process.'

Amazing, Modred thought incredulously. The woman is not only barren, she's also stupid. Why does he bother to keep her?

When Lord Bedwyr and his wife ventured apologetically into the dining hall where space had been made to accommodate them, they became objects of curiosity for all eyes.

Bedwyr was grizzled, like a good mastiff just beginning to grey around the muzzle. The Master of Arden carried his battle scars and slave marks with distinction, and his brown eyes, so like the trees of his forest, were filled with genuine love and respect. He knelt in homage to Artor and would have kissed his master's feet had the High King not deftly diverted him.

'I'm told that my Arden Knife has chosen to wed,' Artor joked. 'It's about time, my old friend. You've enjoyed the benefits of youth almost into old age.'

'The years have passed gently over you, my king. I can believe that you will thrive until the end of time, just like ancient Myrddion.'

Artor's eyes reflected a dim shadow of remembered pain and Bedwyr reproached himself for causing his king any twinges of memory. In atonement, he lurched into speech with a plain man's pride and awkwardness.

'This lady is my wife, Elayne of Arden. She is the fairest flower of the Cornovii.'

Wenhaver snorted scornfully and Artor responded by kicking her shin below the table.

Elayne had waited patiently, with her eyes downcast and with her cloak's cowl covering her face. She was dressed in russet, the exact shade of autumn leaves, and even beneath the heavy robes, Artor could discern that her body was lissome and strong. Her sun-bronzed hands lifted back the hood on her cloak and she faced the High King for the first time.

Artor gazed at Elayne, the wife of an honoured friend, and his ageing heart fluttered in his chest.

Elayne was neither fair nor beautiful in the accepted fashion of Celtic or Roman Britain. Both Wenhaver and the legendary Nimue outshone her in form and feature, while the long-dead Gallia had possessed a face that held greater piquancy and prettiness. Elayne's skin was amber from the sun and her fingers were scarred from apple and berry picking. Her hair was very thick and sword-blade straight, but its russet-brown length glowed with health and sunlight. Artor imagined that he could smell the scent of sunny days in her travel-tumbled plaits. Where stray tendrils had escaped, they crackled with life in the charged air and fanned her uplifted face like a halo of flame.

Elayne's nose was narrow, but a little too long for orthodox beauty, while her nostrils flared slightly as if she could scent the moral malaise that festered around the feasting table. Her eyes were warm and amber, with flecks of green surrounding deep, black pupils. Such eyes never flinched, not even when the king stared deeply into them with his flat, grey stare.

'What need I fear?' her eyes seemed to say. 'I am Arden and the trees are forever.'

Elayne's brows were winged and mobile, rather than the thin crescents that Wenhaver had made the fashion at Cadbury. They were a pleasing foil for a mouth that was wide and full-lipped, topping a firm, determined chin.

And, for all her slender strength, she was as small as Gallia had been, and as unafraid in the presence of great men and women. She bowed low with the impudent grace of his long-dead Gallia, and Artor's heart was irrevocably lost.

'Lady Elayne is indeed the fairest flower to come from Arden,' Artor stated clearly so that the assembled guests could not help but hear. 'My congratulations on your choice, Bedwyr, and I welcome you both to Cadbury Tor. I'm fully aware of the many years of service you have given since you left your beloved forest to serve the people of the west, so I'm forever in your debt.'

Bedwyr flushed with pleasure at the High King's acknowledgement and guided his wife to a bench seat that Artor indicated with a negligent hand. Wenhaver was the only person present who noticed a slight trembling of Artor's fingers and his unwillingness to meet Elayne's eyes.

'What? Is the indestructible Artor afraid of a woman?' she exclaimed so softly that even her husband missed her words. 'I don't believe it!' She smiled slyly at Modred to see if he had noticed Artor's indiscretion. The bastard is lusting after another man's wife, she thought acidly. And the woman of a friend at that. Perhaps blood does flow through Artor's veins after all.

Modred tapped her hand with one long, white finger, as if to warn Wenhaver that her expression was making her thoughts transparent to any person who cared to notice.

Wenhaver lowered her eyes and wiped away the self-satisfaction on her face.

Artor was assiduous in his role of host to both Bedwyr and Elayne, taking care not to give particular preference to his friend's wife. Balan, who was seated beside Elayne, quickly engaged her in conversation and Artor watched her glow with pleasure as she described her husband's land holdings, the fecund fields and the villagers who had already taken her into their hearts. The High King imagined that her flesh would smell of newly baked bread, clean hay and the milky sweetness of young animals. His groin tightened with desire.

'The people are very kind but they're so poor,' Elayne told Balan with the simplicity of truth. 'I intend to do whatever I can to make their lives more comfortable. As chatelaine, it's my duty, and my pleasure, to give what I have to my husband's people.'

'Your devotion does you honour, my lady,' Balan replied earnestly. 'My mother, Anna of the Ordovice, always says that her day is only ended when the last of the children are fed.' He was mesmerized by the warmth of Elayne's eyes and, like the High King, he struggled to find the words that would cause her to gaze on him with pleasure.

Damned cub, Artor thought with mounting irritation as Elayne shyly smiled at the young warrior. Her unconscious charm had ground Wenhaver's florid beauty into dust.

My wife converses easily with these great ones, Bedwyr thought with pride. She's bringing me lasting credit in the king's court.

What an artful creature this Elayne person is, Wenhaver seethed. She's pushing herself forward, and is thriving on the attention of these stupid men.

Well versed in the foolishness of males, she recognized the admiration in Balan's eyes.

'I have just noticed your poor hands, Lady Elayne,' the queen spoke confidingly. 'You must allow me to send you some fine oils to soften and whiten them. I find that lamb's wool gloves at night are also helpful. The ladies at our court are noted for the fineness of their fingers and we must do our best to make your hands pretty.'

'Oh dear.' Elayne seemed genuinely upset. 'I never think of my hands when I'm working. You're very kind to offer me your help, Your Majesty.'

Artor gritted his teeth while Balan stared at Wenhaver with critical, clear eyes. Like a raw-boned hound, Bedwyr bristled at the queen's condescension.

'Since my Elayne was a young girl, she has always done the work of two full-grown women and our people call her Little Mother, for she won't order servants to do any simple tasks that she can complete for herself. Nor does any sick man, woman or child go untended, even if my dear Elayne must ride out at dawn and return to her home at dusk.'

Elayne smiled at her husband in modest embarrassment and gratitude at his defence of her worth. His obvious love for her warmed her heart.

'For the gods' sake, Wenhaver, let the girl eat,' Artor interrupted. 'Her hands do her credit and I have no doubt of Bedwyr's claim that her people worship her. In fact, she reminds me of my foster-mother, Livinia Major, who ruled the Villa Poppinidii with tender care. I wish all women were so virtuous.'

The king's retort was a crushing public rebuff for Wenhaver, for it was aimed squarely at her shortcomings. Wenhaver immediately retreated into a silent, fuming impotence. Artor's reprimand sealed Elayne's fate forever as an enemy of the queen.

A week before the first fires of Samhein, Gawayne and Galahad reached Cadbury. It was a time when a dizzy round of feasts, hunts and celebrations were beginning. Gawayne had always possessed a talent for fun and the close, heated air of Cadbury seemed cleaner for his boyish enthusiasm. The old year was dying and all the citizens of Cadbury set their eyes and hopes towards the new year, to mend the tiny tears that were appearing in the fabric of the land.

Gawayne threw himself enthusiastically into hunting. Like all aggressively healthy male animals, he adored the chase and Artor loaned him his mastiffs and great hounds so he could run down stags, wolves and the odd, unwary fox, even though the snow was deep and the hunted beasts wore their white winter camouflage. The prince rarely failed to return without a brace of coney, a handful of wood pigeons or, on occasion, a wild boar. Artor's court, including the High King himself, enjoyed the long nights of feasting.

On the eve of Samhein, heavy snow drove Gawayne, Balan, Balyn and Galahad back to Cadbury before noon. No hint of sun could be found in the lowering grey skies and the trees in the woods were coal-black against the whiteness of the snowdrifts.

'The silence out in the forests was eerie,' Balan informed the ladies as he warmed his numbed hands at the brazier. 'I know that midwinter is the stillest time, but even the trees weren't groaning under the weight of snow, as they usually do when the snowfall is heavy.'

'Aye,' Balyn interrupted. 'And the light in the forest was so fey that we swore we could see things that weren't there. I still shiver in awe when I think of them.'

'What manner of things, brave Balyn?' Modred drawled as he toasted his long legs before the huge central fire pit.

'The boys are speaking of a giant stag that we spotted when we were in the snowdrifts,' Gawayne began. 'A truly gigantic beast with a rack of horns that the animal could barely lift. What a noble deed it would be to sink an arrow into such a regal creature. I would have given my knife hand to hunt and kill that stag.'

'You're over-tired to make such a wish, Father, but I agree with you that this animal was amazingly large and elusive,' Galahad said. 'But what surprised me most was the reaction of the hounds. They were terrified and wouldn't pursue the beast. We rode after the stag and followed it into the thickets, but it kept out of bowshot with ease, almost as if it was protected by some magical charm.'

'A stag, even a huge old male, is hardly an object of fear,' Artor remarked with a slight smile. While he listened, he continued putting an edge on his dragon knife where it had become a little blunted on the previous day's hunt.

'It was a trick of the light, a shaft of sunshine, or something that fooled us into seeing these peculiar ... well ... fantasies,' Gawayne continued. 'I even thought I could see a crown caught in the horns of the stag. Then the animal foundered in a deep drift of snow and we thought we had managed to trap the creature at last.'

'But somehow it heaved itself out of the snowdrift and it was gone! Poof!' Balyn completed the tale with a dramatic flourish.

'You saw a crown?' Modred asked, and grew a little pale.

'And also a falcon,' Galahad added. 'Just after the stag vanished, we saw a large peregrine. It was snow-white and barred with gold. The bird appeared out of the same thicket as the stag and then spiralled upward until it, too, disappeared into the snow clouds.'

'I think your vision was a portent of evil,' Wenhaver breathed excitedly.

'Am I supposed to be the stag?' Artor asked, scarcely diverting his attention from his whetstone. 'And is the falcon some heir or pretender? I think not. And, with the greatest of respect to your keen eyes, sirs, you were probably affected by snow blindness.'

Without pause, Artor continued to stroke the whetstone over the edge of his knife with a hollow rasp that intensified the mood of drama in the warm room.

'It's possible, my lord,' Gawayne acknowledged thoughtfully, but his lips were twisted with doubt. 'But for those of us who were there, the stag and the falcon seemed perfectly real.'

'They probably were real,' Artor replied, dismissing all further discussion of portents and visions. 'But not supernatural.'

'You may expect a visiting traveller shortly, my king,' Galahad suddenly remembered. 'We could see a far-off man on horseback heading in our direction as we were climbing the tor. He's alone, apart from a staghound that accompanies him through the snow.'

'He's probably a beggar, come to throw himself on our mercy in the depths of winter.' Wenhaver scowled unpleasantly.

'The cold outside is dangerous, it's a miracle that any wayfarer can survive,' Elayne murmured, the softness of her heart evident in the sympathy in her eyes.

'My subjects are always welcome at Cadbury Tor or in the villages,' Artor stated with certainty. 'No traveller should be turned away on a night that is as cold as Morgan's teat, especially with the approach of Samhein. Besides, of all the beggars I have seen, Wenhaver, none was ever in possession of either a horse or a dog.'

The darkness came swiftly that afternoon, as if the unseasonably heavy snow had blinded both the sun and the moon. The lone rider continued to climb the spiral road leading up to the tor, avoiding the black ice reflected in the flare of torches that were placed at regular intervals on the wall. On Artor's orders, the traveller was unhindered during his journey, although several warriors looked sideways at the huge staghound that padded silently alongside its master.

'Well met, traveller, for Samhein is upon us,' Percivale greeted the man at the final gate of the fortification. 'The snow is wicked and deep, so I'm glad you've reached shelter on this vile night.'

'Have no care for me, good sir,' the heavily mantled man answered. His voice was muffled inside the layers of wool and fur that thickened his form. A heavy pack bowed his back and a smaller hide of wool disguised some implement that was strung from one shoulder. Even the staghound carried a small pack, but as the beast stood taller at the shoulder than a seventh year child, its load barely encumbered it.

'You're to be given shelter in the stables this evening on the orders of the High King, but I must ask for any weapons that you carry.'

The traveller wordlessly removed a worn but very sharp knife from his belt and handed it, hilt first, to Percivale.

'You bear no other arms in this harsh winter?' Percivale was mystified as to how anyone could survive, alone, in such inclement weather.

'I have my Rhiannon to bring down game and she's better than any sword if a thief is foolish enough to attack me. All else I need I pay for with my art.'

Percivale raised an inquisitive eyebrow.

'I am from Caer Gai in distant Powys, where winters are far harder than in these soft lands. I'm a harpist and I have come to sing for my supper at the table of the High King.'

'Then you're doubly welcome, traveller, for my lord always welcomes diversion. Please rest and wash, if such is your custom. I'll fetch you within the hour.'

The two men had reached the stables where a vacant, hay-filled stall beckoned the tired traveller. His horse and hound were quickly accommodated, while a boy prepared to rub down the wet hides of both animals. With natural courtesy, the traveller bowed low to Percivale and promised that he would be ready when the warrior returned.

As soon as Percivale closed the stable door behind him, the traveller eased off the heavy pack and dropped it on to the floor. The smaller pack was hung reverently from a hook on the wooden half-wall that separated the man from a large bay horse in the next stall. Several weary youths stirred from their task of oiling leather to stare with undisguised curiosity as the traveller shed his outer coverings, layer by layer.

The man who emerged from the cocoon of cloth and fur was nearly as tall as the great King Artor himself. As he stripped to his bare skin, the ostlers had ample opportunity to determine that the itinerant entertainer was broad of shoulder, narrow of hip and virtually hairless except for a mane of raven black hair that hung down his back. His feet and hands were very long and narrow, while some quality in him sent one youth, unasked, to collect two pottery jugs, one of warm water and the other of cold. When he offered the water jugs to the stranger, the man smiled with such sincerity that the lad felt warmed to his toes.

'My thanks, young sir. As you have heard, I must wash before I entertain the king.'

'It's nothing, lord,' the boy replied, tugging on his forelock with respect. 'The horses have plenty and we can heat more for our supper.'

'Then I will fashion a song for you. What is your name?'

'It's Gull, sir. My mother once lived near the sea and she says I was a squawking babe.'

The traveller laid his left hand upon the boy's forehead and immediately Gull felt warmth radiate through his flesh and bones.

'Like the bird after whom you've been named, Gull, you will sail far in this world. And I hope you remember that it was Taliesin who told you this, for I know it to be true.'

Gull backed away from the traveller, for this Samhein was proving to be a night of marvels and he was a little afraid. He rejoined his friends among the bales of hay and gently placed his grubby hand upon the spot where Taliesin's fingers had rested.

Taliesin grinned ruefully at the look of awe and expectation that brightened the boy's face. He was no mountebank, handing out prophecies like greasy, base coinage; Gull's inquisitive eyes had spoken to Taliesin more clearly than any foresight could have done. The harpist knew that the boy was a born traveller who would be gone from Cadbury long before he was a full-grown man.

When Percivale returned for his charge, the traveller was washed, scrubbed and dressed in a long robe hidden by a black cloak and hood.

'I am ready, my lord. Rhiannon has been ordered to await my return, so I'll collect my harp and we shall meet my new master.'

Percivale looked up at the long, shrouded form and noted the clean-shaven jaw and sensitive mouth exposed by the light of his torch.

'I hope you're in good voice, traveller. The king has had a trying day and needs amusement.'

'I'll do my best, for I'm duty bound by a familial oath to serve the High King.'

As Percivale led the way towards the feasting hall, he could feel the strong presence of the dark stranger close behind his heels.

All we need is more discord, Percivale thought to himself. Artor's court is already a hornets' nest that is stirred to fighting against itself, so I hope this man can charm away some of the evil that permeates our house.'

Percivale's ever-loyal heart knew that fate was rarely kind, even to the good and the pious, so he prayed silently to the Christ to protect his Artor from any malice that had entered the goodly house of Cadbury Tor. But in his heart, he could feel time running quickly towards an unknown and grim destiny.

CHAPTER V

THE SINGER AND THE SONG

In a room full of warriors, prominent citizens and genteel ladies, Artor stared around his feasting tables and glumly endured this Samhein feast. Braziers and wall sconces provided illumination and caught the soft glitter of gold, bronze, silver and a variety of gems. Their wearers posed and pouted, and spoke to each other with animation, while their eyes gauged the responses of their fellow guests. Warrior vied with warrior over the splendour of their harnesses, the rareness of their furs and the artistry of their torcs, arm rings and hair ornaments. Women in wool, dyed in every conceivable shade, shaped to reveal and conceal, preened and smiled under darkened eyelashes in pretence of maidenhood. Earrings tossed and caught the firelight, elaborate braids and curls gleamed with perfumed oils and bodies swayed towards and away from each other in the promise of forbidden delights.

Cynical, and disposed to doubt that any truth remained in Cadbury, Artor sat on his curule chair and saw no beauty in the glimmer of fine, lying eyes, nor courage in the exaggerated boastings of loud-mouthed men. His mouth twisted. Who was he to pass judgement on the warriors and courtiers who modelled themselves on their king? He, too, was a liar. His marriage was a sham, his child had been raised by others because he had discarded her, using her safety as a convenient excuse, and he had committed sins larger and more damning than anything these light-hearted, frail creatures could even imagine.

As Artor brooded and frowned, Odin watched his master with concern. Although he was ignorant of the reasons for Artor's misery, Odin could make an educated guess. The king's afternoon had not been restful.

Earlier, he had been re-reading the Caesar scrolls given to him by Llanwith pen Bryn so many years before. He had one leg hooked comfortably over the armrest of his campaign chair when the queen swept into his private quarters on a wave of heavy perfume and fury, shattering his pleasant solitude.

'What do you have to say for yourself?' Wenhaver had demanded in a shrill voice, her mouth tightening into an unattractive line, stitched across with ageing little wrinkles of disapproval. Egged on by Modred's whispered poisons, the queen was incensed and ready for a scene.

Artor sighed, put aside his scroll and rubbed his tired eyes. His sight was weakening; a concern that did little to improve his mood, for no man cares to confront old age or infirmity.

'What have I done to offend you on this occasion?' He steeled himself to repel his wife's angry and impatient attack. From experience, he knew that Wenhaver would nag him until her anger was assuaged.

'You know why I'm offended, you hypocrite. You've openly shown your partiality for another woman in my presence, so my reputation will be the subject of common speculation.'

Uncoiling his body, Artor laughed sourly. Wenhaver glowered at him with her face thrust forward on her neck like an indignant lapdog. As Artor considered her overly rouged face, he compared his shrewish wife with the lost Gallia, which led his thoughts to the gentle nature of Elayne and her sweetness of spirit.

His pent-up frustrations surfaced like hot, scarfing steam. Who was she to censure him?

'Your reputation? You're already well known to the common folk as a slut who would make the wife of Emperor Claudius seem virginal. You've cuckolded me for years and I've been forced to close my ears tightly to gossip, or else I'll hear those things that even the most ignorant of Cadbury servants whisper. I couldn't possibly compromise your reputation any more than you've done yourself with any number of men who have attended this court.'

Wenhaver stood tall and straight, quite unlike her usual pretentious posing, and Artor felt a fleeting admiration for her. Wenhaver seemed far more regal when she was defending her position rather than generating trouble or acting with arrogant, ostentatious display.

'I insist that you don't rub my nose into your indecent attraction towards that brown-skinned nobody,' she said haughtily. 'She's not a servant girl who can be tumbled to beget another bastard son for your personal guard.'

Regal or not, Wenhaver had gone too far.

Artor hit her with his open hand, but carefully, so her skin would bear no bruise. She grunted with shock like a kicked sow and would have struck back at him had he not thrown her on his bed and pinned her down by her arms.

'Don't speak to me of Elayne, Wenhaver, when you're not fit to even voice her name. I tell you now that if I weren't encumbered with a sterile old cow, and if Elayne wasn't wed to my friend, I would beg to enter her heart and her bed. But I'm old, while she's still very young – and you're so depressingly alive!' He paused, pressed down cruelly on his wife's wrists and then continued threateningly, 'Take care that you don't go the way of Caius, my late and unlamented foster-brother. He placed me in a position where he had to meet with an accident that wasn't of his choosing.'

Wenhaver gasped. She shook off her husband's weight and tumbled to the floor. Her husband's eyes were stark and emotionless, and she felt a cold finger of alarm slither down her spine.

'I've warned you in the past that you're expendable, but you've paid little heed to my warnings. Even your brother, Wynfael, has been embarrassed by your behaviour. Your beauty is fading daily and you're forced to paint yourself into a grotesque parody of a real woman.' Artor made an exclamation of disgust. 'You've one item of luck in your favour. I won't consider taking Elayne over your dead body, much as that option appeals to me. For I would then be forced to kill my friend, Bedwyr, and he is of much greater value to me than any woman, especially you, my very own drab.'

Against her will, Wenhaver shivered. The king's demeanour was so cold that her pretensions died instantly, to be replaced by an all-encompassing terror. She felt as if her bladder would empty if Artor continued to drill her with his unforgiving eyes.

'And so, Wenhaver, you're going to be very, very dutiful in

public from now on. You'll not compromise Gawayne further, nor will you seduce his son or any other guest who dwells under my roof. I'm sick to the death of you, Wenhaver! I'm tired of your pouting, of your rages and your endless, stupid vanity. I demand that you be silent, or I'll have your mouth stopped permanently. This isn't a threat, it's a promise!'

'You wouldn't dare to kill me', Wenhaver wailed, but her voice lacked conviction. She began to shiver in fear as thoughts of poison, accidental falls and even the assassin's knife began to crowd her suddenly imaginative brain.

'Wouldn't I?' Artor replied silkily. 'You give me no pleasure at all, either as a wife or as a woman. Most of Cadbury would rejoice if you vanished.'

Wenhaver gagged as her stomach threatened to empty itself on to Artor's wooden floor. She had been capricious and wilful for so long. She had flaunted her vices in his face to provoke some sort of reaction that would prove she still existed. Some part of her inner self, the part that still hoped for love and the comfort of family, began to cry softly with her loss, all to no purpose. When she was a foolish girl-child and unaware of the seriousness of her actions, she had caused her husband to reject her. Now, as she flinched away from a man beyond her control, she recalled the excesses and cruel reputations of his father and his sisters.

Wenhaver lapsed into a shocked silence and curled herself into as small a target as possible.

The terrified expression on Wenhaver's face caused the king to feel a genuine pang of shame. Yes, his wife was a disgrace. Yes, her lust had compromised his firm hand over his subjects since she was a girl. But had he ever given her a chance? Had the loss of Gallia been so all-consuming that no woman could have filled her place in his heart?

The answers rolled through his brain.

Yes! Yes!

Had he turned a blind eye to her excesses because he cared less for her than for his most useless hound? And had he demonstrated plainly to his wife just how little she really mattered?

Yes! Yes!

Then Artor realized that his threats to Wenhaver's life were as pointless and as wicked as any duplicity that she had inflicted on him. His father, Uther Pendragon, had responded with cruelty on those occasions when he was hurt, insulted or threatened, and Artor had struggled, lifelong, to avoid Uther's errors.

But his personal dignity hung in the balance. Artor looked down at his terrified wife. She may have been venal, and had earned every spiteful description that he had hurled at her, but Wenhaver could, so easily, have grown to be a true queen and a generous wife. She had been married to him for longer than she had lived under the idle, vain influence of her father. With patience, she might have been deflected from the worst aspects of her character, and cajoled and flattered into following more benign paths.

What could have been! Such a pathetic excuse for self-pity.

Artor could play that particular game no more, but neither could he inflict harm on his wife. She was incapable of change, and that was his fault. He must live with what he had made.

Artor reached out one hand to grasp her pale arm and help her to stand upright. For a second, he almost assisted her to straighten her robe, but this small consideration was more than he could offer, for the gesture would require him to touch her with some compassion.

He resisted the impulse, and hated himself at that moment – almost as much as he hated Wenhaver.

The queen hiccuped with the start of desperate tears.

'Who was Claudius?' she asked her husband unexpectedly, her fragmented thoughts grasping at a single idea that was, as always, vain and irrelevant.

Artor began to laugh, causing Wenhaver's face to colour with embarrassment, and she dropped her wounded, accusing eyes.

Artor's mirth died abruptly. Wenhaver couldn't understand because she'd been denied the education that he took for granted.

'He was a Roman emperor whose wife was more lascivious than the meanest whore. I wronged you with such a comparison, for your behaviour could never be such a blight on the sensitivity of your subjects. Nor have you imperiled the throne, and I don't believe that you would ever use your sexuality for treasonous purposes – at least not deliberately. I apologize for the comparison.'

'I hate you, Artor,' Wenhaver stated without any discernible emotion.

'I often hate myself,' Artor replied with a small grin.

Even now, after all these years, he could not fathom the nature of his relationship with his wife. But Artor was tired of mulling over problems and he longed for the saddle and action to once again give purpose to his life.

'Just remember, my dear, the real truth behind my threats,

even though I was cruel to speak to you in such a manner. You've no right to accuse me of infidelity, for I've never betrayed my marriage vows. Yes, I've used willing servants, but I haven't loved them or done more for their children than to give them a measure of regard, considering their birth. Such admissions do me no credit, but I'm a man and I haven't chosen to be celibate. But, Wenhaver, you've betrayed me with my own kin, which shames me to the heart. And you've been sufficiently indiscreet that I have been publicly humiliated, although no one has dared to speak openly about the matter.'

He gripped her chin and forced her to look at him.

'I won't do the same to you, I swear. I wouldn't compromise any married woman of high birth, and I won't harm my friends by abusing their trust. You and I have been caught in a continuing battle for years, but I'm bringing my requirements into the open now, along with the promises I am making to you. There will be no more unseemly affairs. No more dalliances with Gawayne. You frighten him, and he has no control over his sexual nature where you are concerned. I cannot censure your thoughts, nor prevent you from hating me, although I regret our bitter relationship. But don't undermine me. If I am assassinated or stripped of my throne, then so are you.'

She had left him then, with a swirl of skirts and a final, darting glance that was nearly as flat and as emotionless as his own. Wenhaver had rarely left him with as much dignity as she did on this dreary afternoon.

Now, in the overheated feasting hall, as he surveyed the brilliant throng of guests and watched his wife engaging Balyn in quiet conversation, he was sunk in gloom. Then Percivale slid into the airless room, followed by a tall figure in a long, black cloak. A diversion, the king thought gratefully. Blessed Percivale.

'Pray let me see your face, stranger, and give me your name.'

The younger generation attending the feast had never known Myrddion Merlinus, except through the many legends of sorcery, shape-changing and inhuman cleverness that had grown around his name, so they did not understand the gasp of surprise that swept the hall when the young man removed his cloak.

Artor whitened with shock. 'What is this trick?' His heart stuttered at the resemblance to Myrddion that was so vivid in the countenance of the young man.

Taliesin wore his best robe, woven and embroidered by his mother in intricate patterns of birds that edged the hem and the neckline. Silver thread glittered against the black wool and a single spike of electrum, inherited from his father and worn in one ear, was his only adornment – except for his long, flowing hair with its distinctive white streak.

'I am Taliesin ap Myrddion, son of Myrddion Merlinus. I have been sent by my mother, the Lady of the Lake, to bring music to my king on this auspicious night.'

The room seethed and swelled with whispers. Here was a true Samhein marvel.

'Is your father well?' Artor managed to ask, his hand clutching a locket secreted beneath his robe.

Taliesin bowed his head. 'My father has gone to the shadows, my king, but he loved you until the day of his death. My mother, Nimue, begs you to remember how deep were his feelings for you.'

'You play music, Taliesin, son of Myrddion?' Wenhaver asked courteously, her face as flushed as her husband's was pale.

'It is the only gift I possess that is fit to offer my king and his fair queen,' Taliesin responded without a trace of boasting. Then, reverently, he freed his harp from its fleecy nest.

As Taliesin slowly drew his fingers across the strings, the entranced audience saw that his harp was an object of singular beauty with a carved woman forming the main structure of the instrument. Under his exquisite fingers, its mellow sound was coaxed into life.

Positioning himself to face the guests, he began to sing the tale of the crowning of the king. Beyond the shadows of time, the youthful Artorex came to life in song as he faced the vicious spectre of his father, Uther Pendragon. The long dead Lucius played with riddles at Glastonbury, so the heir could find his sword and crown and become the High King, as was his destiny. Taliesin sang of glorious battles, dead heroes and old loves and, when the tale reached its crescendo in the coronation of Artor, the strings soared, exulted and then were silent.

The room shook with applause as men pounded the tables and shouted praise at the power of the ballad. Even Wenhaver was moved to tears as she remembered the hopes and promise in her younger self.

'Where came this song?' Artor demanded, as memories of the lives and deaths of old friends surged back to haunt him through the magic of Taliesin's harp.

'I wrote the tale exactly as my father related it to me, my lord,' Taliesin answered. 'If my small skill pleases you, then I am content.'

'You are a skilled song-master, Taliesin ap Myrddion, but I should have expected no less from the son of my oldest and wisest counsellor. Please continue to play.'

Under his inspired fingers, Taliesin sang songs that described the simple hill people and created flights of birds and hunting eagles. He filled the entire hall with joy and melody.

Towards the end of the recital, Taliesin sang of the Lady of the Lake and her aged lover, and the words caused Artor to weep unashamedly as he recalled the Myrddion of his youth. The young man then brought Nimue to life with such poetic inspiration that even those men who had never seen her great beauty loved her a little. Instinctively, the listeners knew that they were the poorer for her absence.

Then Taliesin's song changed and became lilting and delicate as he described Wenhaver's arrival at Cadbury. The golden tresses, cerulean eyes and full young mouth lived once again in hope, pride and passion.

It was now Wenhaver's turn to weep bitterly. Every word of the argument of the afternoon struck her anew, and she felt deep and honest regret for the many mistakes she had made so blithely and thoughtlessly.

Taliesin paused and drank a goblet of spiced wine to ease his throat. During this short break, Artor's quick eyes noted that the young man's fingers were raw. His right index finger was bleeding sluggishly.

'We have made you work hard for your supper, young man, and it's now time to rest.'

Taliesin nodded his appreciation to his king.

'Lord Artor, when my skill first came upon me, my father

bade me write a special song for you as a gift, and as a reminder of your friendship. I will finish my entertainment with one last tale of the Garden of Gallia.'

Deep, slow and sweet were the notes conjured from the strings as Gallia was brought back to warm flesh in words. Taliesin's tale recounted how she and Frith had died at the hands of Uther Pendragon's warriors, and how they were mourned and honoured with living flowers. Once more the water trickled over the woman stone, that ancient monolith from the Old Forest, and filled the crooked cup that fed the roses and the herb gardens. Targo lived and died once again, to rest at last in the garden where Gallia also slept, drowsy with the hum of bees and the seductive perfume of flowers. And, over this scene of harmony and natural beauty, Ector presided and protected, in death, as he had in life.

The guests in the rich feasting hall, many of whom had never even seen the garden, were transfixed by Taliesin's simple message of peace and beauty.

> The sword, the distaff and the plough
>   are blunted by the ruin of the years.
> Heroic deeds become as arid dust –
>   for enmity must always end in tears.
> Crowns are lost. The finest blade must rust
>   and all man's strength is measured by his fears.
> How soon the petty powers of kings grow weak –
>   how swift they wither and their hopes are dead,
> and women's beauty ages as they seek
>   to clutch at shallow youth that soon is fled.
> But flowers will bloom, an hour, a day, and more,

A thousand years in one eternal breath,
And Gallia's Garden proves the sacred law
that love, alone, redeems us at our death.

A well of silence followed the final chord.

'Mere sounds cannot hope to illustrate the god-given cleansing of love, my liege,' Taliesin said into the silence. 'My father told me often that the roots of the garden lie deep in the soil of this simple, all-encompassing truth. How can I hope to create words to do love justice?'

Artor stood and bowed low to Taliesin, as if their places in the world were reversed.

'Only my old friend was wise enough to remind me how to be a king. Only my old friend's son has the skill to remind me how to be a man.'

'Thank you, my lord,' Taliesin replied, his clear young eyes shadowed with confusion.

Then, with a boyish laugh, Artor tossed his wine cup over his shoulder and reminded his guests of the night's purpose.

'Come, my friends. We'll light the fires and cleanse our souls for the beginning of another new year – a year when we shall be forgiven for all our faults.'

'Rejoice! Rejoice!' the assembled personages called. 'For the new year has come.'

The pyre of wood was soaked in oil and pitch, so it caught fire quickly when the king and queen thrust torches into its base. Women threw holly berries and sweet garlands of hoarded, dried flowers into its blazing maw, while still more citizens fed its flaming energy with the sweetness of dried apples, fine cloth and cups of honeyed wine.

Men, women and children danced about the dozens of Samhein fires that turned the midnight darkness of Cadbury into a tapestry of russet, gold and scarlet. Fire etched faces into fine chiaroscuro masks set against a backdrop of light-reflecting snow. Voices sang and feet capered. Lovers kissed and old women spoke of grandchildren and asked for fecundity, good crops and a fine spring flood to provide feed for the newly born lambs and calves.

The world made merry as the king danced with his wife, for they were the servants of the renewal of all growing things.

'What a farce!' Modred whispered maliciously to one of his companions. 'An old man and a barren woman dance to bring rebirth to the land. But, look. Their hands barely touch each other.'

Modred's wicked words carried to the ears of the twins. Both men ceased to clap and laugh, and Balyn took a step towards Modred's languid shadow.

'I take offence at what you say, Modred. Your comments could be construed as treason when you voice such doom against the king and queen.'

'Horseshit, boy! Wenhaver's no better than she should be and Artor supports her fictions. Those details I remark on are common knowledge, both within and beyond the court. If they weren't so amusing, they'd make me ill.'

Modred's carefully ambiguous use of *they* was totally lost on Balyn.

'I advise you to take care, Brigante. By all reports, most of your kin were a murderous, cowardly gaggle of ambitious geese. I predict that a day will come when Artor separates your head from your neck, as he did for the other traitors within your tribe.'

Silently, Balan stood his ground on the frozen earth, leaving his brother to voice their shared disgust.

Galahad had heard the heated exchange and didn't hesitate to add his own warnings.

'Was your mother really a witch, Modred? Should you be sent to the fire to die, as was the custom of the pagans with their enemies in the days before Jesus saved these lands for the Holy Church?'

'You're nothing but a pious stripling, nephew,' Modred retorted. 'And you ought to know a witch when you see one, for our family has always practised the dark arts.'

'Silence!' Odin hissed. 'I don't fear the Beltane fires, so I'll gladly cut your throat if you say another word against my lord and master.'

Modred stepped back. He was justifiably nervous of this huge Jutlander, yet he was unwilling to relinquish his part in the game that these foolish young men were playing with him. He was forgetting that there was very little difference in their respective ages.

'Oh, isn't discord lovely? This court is a veritable treasure house of joy and happiness.'

Then Modred slipped away into the darkness, but his shadow lingered like a miasma of pestilence over the shoulders of the young warriors.

Artor strode towards them out of a fiery rain of falling embers and sparks.

'Dance, lads! Find girls to kiss and friendly arms to hold you, for Samhein comes but once a year.'

Shame-faced and uneasy, the young men moved away into the laughing throng.

'The Brigante king will have your head, Artor.' Odin spoke without rancour. 'Even now, he sets us all against each other. Let me kill him and have done.'

'I cannot kill the scion of Luka – I will not!' Artor smiled, and the reflection of the fire danced in his pupils. 'At least, not until he goes a step too far. So you may keep your axe blade sharp in anticipation of any change in circumstances.'

The night was full of laughter, wine and muffled figures. Within the king's house, even servants were as noble as lords on this night, and the corridors echoed with the raucous noise of revelry.

Eventually, Artor escaped to the peace of his apartments, where Taliesin waited patiently at the ironclad door, his harp cradled in its nest of sheep's wool.

'My lord, I bear a private message to you from my mother. I don't know what her greeting means and she told me that she doesn't understand it either. She sends warning of a deadly peril.' The young man was embarrassed by the vagueness of his message. 'She asked me to tell you that the Bloody Cup has come.'

'The Bloody Cup?' Artor repeated. 'Shite, boy, I've never heard of such a thing. Why should I fear any cup, bloody or otherwise?'

Taliesin shrugged expressively. 'She hears the whispers on the wind and dreams night after night of portents of evil. I sometimes wonder if her beliefs are simply the foolishness of an ageing woman, but I don't believe she's wrong, for I can smell carrion on the air.'

'In the words of old Targo, who was a true friend to your father, only a fool ignores any edge he's given, no matter how improbable it seems.'

Taliesin smiled gratefully. Across the small space, he saw the king's shadow loom monstrously like some hunched beast. He shivered.

'You may sleep here in the antechamber of my rooms, if you wish,' Artor added, thinking the boy might be feeling the chill of the winter night. 'You have my thanks, Taliesin.'

'The stables are good enough for me, my lord. The thaw will soon come and Rhiannon will weep for the open ground. I'll trouble you no more.'

Beyond his window, Artor watched impassively as the Samhein fires collapsed inward into dirty stains on the pristine snow.

CHAPTER VI

THE ENEMY AT THE DOOR

Spring came with a rush.

Myrddion Merlinus would have told his king, had he not been cold ash, that kingdoms are rarely lost in sudden, bloody, power struggles. The rot begins from within but is nurtured from without. The old tree cracks and warps with disease until a strong wind comes and blows it down. Even though the tree is riven, it still struggles to bear fruit in a last, poignant throw at immortality. The sweetest apples grow on the dying branches, but they are pitifully few and are attacked by the small pests that prey on new, bursting growth. Then, when the end eventually comes, the ripe apple proves to be only healthy, succulent skin that encloses bruised, corrupted and worm-eaten flesh.

And so Cadbury festered.

Whatever her fears for her safety, Wenhaver could not restrain a nature that had deepened and narrowed in its channel of vanity and self-aggrandizement over the decades. Mindful of Artor's demands, she avoided Gawayne but turned her still brilliant eyes upon that ardent youth whose impetuous nature made him easy meat.

Balyn. The twin who looked most like the young Artor.

She was never so foolish as to lower herself in his estima-tion by seducing him. Balyn's worship was a sweet anodyne to Artor's scorn and coldness. The young man's blood and allegiances burned hot, while Artor's passions were dormant, so she preened herself in the warmth of Balyn's regard and deluded herself that she was still young.

'You're making a goose of yourself, brother,' Balan told Balyn bluntly, after he had spent several hours dancing attendance on Wenhaver's whims. 'She's near as old as our mother.'

Balyn was horrified. With her working robes and tousled hair, Anna looked every day of her years, for she spared herself little time for anything but clean, warm water and the occasional use of precious oils on a holiday feast. Her wildly curling hair, now liberally sprinkled with white, was proud testimony to five living births and three stillborn children and, if her face bore telltale wrinkles around her eyes, in the long creases that ran to her mouth and in the sagging flesh of her neck, then Anna paid no mind to them.

By comparison, Wenhaver could never be old.

'Age has nothing to do with grace and youthfulness, dolt, and Queen Wenhaver is eternally gay and feminine. She knows how to make me laugh, and she's no sober-sides like you and Mother.'

Balan grunted in exasperation, for his brother's brows were glowering with the familiar, mutinous warnings of a prolonged temper tantrum.

'You don't understand how starved the queen is for amusing company and affection. She's younger than the king by many years and he has no interest in dancing, conversation or games of pleasure. She's lonely!'

'You can be such a birdbrain, Balyn. Did you never ask yourself why the king is too busy to dance attendance on the queen? He hasn't held the kingdom together for so many years because he plays at dice or amuses himself with idle gossip. He asks little of Queen Wenhaver but fealty, which many people say she has not been prepared to give. No, I won't make slurs against the queen's character, but you should watch and listen before you're seduced by superficial appearance. If our king seems harsh and dour, then perhaps he has good reason to be so.'

Balyn flushed hotly. Balan was always the more measured and serious of the twins, although Balyn possessed the edge in physical skills. To Balyn, it seemed that his whole life he had been told to 'think matters out like your brother', so rancour now rose in him like bile.

'You only have to look at the personal guard of the king,' Balyn complained. 'Don't you see the resemblances? Modred says that Artor gets bastards on lowly women and then recruits them into his guard to protect his back. If Modred is correct, the queen is much wronged.'

The brothers stood at the very edge of the citadel. A stiff breeze from the east blew their amber and dark brown hair into disarray as the measured grey eyes of Balan met the hot grey eyes of Balyn.

Balan felt his own slow anger begin to stir. 'Yet, brother, the queen has no child. And you must ask yourself why, if what Modred says is true, our king would turn to servant women in the first place? Then look in your silver mirror and observe your reflection and, afterwards, tell me what you see.'

Balan almost heard the two edges of the universe click together into a perfect, curved oval and the ground beneath his feet seemed to tremble and crack as if the foundations of Cadbury were breaking. He knew he had made a foolish and dangerous statement through his irritation, so he raised one hand to placate his brother. But Balyn cut him off.

'You impugn the honour of our mother with this talk. How dare you, Balan? How dare you suggest that we're the seeds of a despot? How *could* you? Your accusation strikes at yourself as much as at me.'

Balan threw his arms round his twin's stiff form, to avoid seeing the sudden wound that had appeared in his brother's eyes.

'No!' he whispered urgently in his brother's ear. 'No! You don't understand. Comac is surely our father! But I have heard rumours that Mother could be the High King's sister. Sometimes, matters are not as they appear, and only a fool would allow himself to be manipulated by gossip that could cause him harm. You aren't Artor's son, and nor am I. But look in the mirror, brother, and think carefully before you speak rashly. If we are Artor's kin, we are closer in blood to him than Modred is, so we should understand why Modred might want us to fall into conflict with the king. The Brigante king makes no secret of his blood claim to the throne. Who would have the people's approval as heir to Artor's throne? Modred, or you?'

In his distress, Balyn had scarcely heard a word of his brother's explanation. His agitated brain was comparing their features with the face of the High King. He pulled himself out of his brother's arms, violently thrusting Balan away.

'Careful, Balyn. Mother would be upset if we finally managed to kill each other,' Balan attempted to joke. But Balyn turned his stormy face away from his brother's pleading eyes and ran towards the stables.

'Hades should stopper your stupid mouth,' Balan admonished himself. 'And Hades should devour Modred, Wenhaver and all those rats that cluster at the feet of the High King if there is any justice in this world.'

Miles away from Cadbury, armed men were about to disturb the peace of holy Glastonbury. For centuries, no brigand or criminal had dared to seek easy pickings within the confines of its abbey or its surrounds, or to place impious feet on its flagstones.

Supposedly built by Josephus, the church was pitifully small and its walls lurched in different directions as its aged, wooden supports rotted in the earth. The tower, with its rough stone construction, was stronger and more impressive, but Glastonbury had never depended on the defensive strength of its walls for survival. Until now, holiness had kept its precincts safe.

Inside the church, narrow apertures allowed filtered light to enter the building, and the simple stone flagging, installed long after the church was raised, was spotless from scrubbing and sanctity. The altar was simple but the cross that stood upon it was made of purest gold. Woollen hangings warmed the little structure and covered the stained and darkened walls. Rough benches, laid out in neat rows, served to seat the brothers, and these could, if needed, be pushed against the wall to provide more space.

The priests and lay brothers slept in separate wooden dormitories with semi-attached kitchens. The order of this green enclave was restful, because the original builders had used a careful plan for the whole settlement. Of course, the passage of many centuries had welcomed growth and un-planned structures were added at need, so that Glastonbury's precinct had charm as well as order. Infirmaries, apothecaries, stables, forges, accommodation for travellers and even latrines surrounded the small, unpretentious church at its centre.

Murder was about to come to this ancient seat of power and religious piety.

The afternoon was cold but clear, so that sound carried as the attacking warriors fell upon the outbuildings like the sudden gale that presages a storm. The priests and brothers had no choice other than to flee, for they were forbidden by their faith to shed blood. Several lay brothers, however, attempted to slow the advance of the six determined invaders. But, as these courageous farmers were unarmed except for hoes and rakes, they were quickly dispatched by cold iron.

Fire bloomed like scarlet flowers from one of the barns where the winter supply of hay and grain was stored. A warning bell tolled forlornly over the enclave where figures in homespun robes scattered like disturbed ants in a nest. Like those same insects, a small group of brothers hastened to protect their church, the sum total of their lives.

Evening prayers had not long ended when the attack began, so Bishop Aethelthred ordered those priests with him to provide protection for the outbuildings.

'But master,' one brother protested, 'we can't leave you undefended! What would we do if you were killed? You are our master, and Glastonbury's heart.'

'I am an old man, Brother Marcus, and God is the heart of Glastonbury. My life isn't worth the destruction of a single building of God's city. Leave me and save our sanctuary. God will protect his church.'

But the brothers soon returned and begged Aethelthred to hide. A number of buildings were now ablaze, and close behind the brothers were the attacking warriors who were searching for the bishop. The smell of smoke and the reek of burning polluted the air.

Aethelthred rose from his knees, his body trembling with strain. He was very old, his skin had that transparency that comes with extreme age, and delicate blue veins were clearly visible under his skin at his wrists, temples and throat. He seemed as insubstantial as thistledown yet, when he spoke in his warm, firm baritone, the listener was left with a different impression, one of strength, wisdom and purpose.

'You are needed elsewhere, my sons. Please, save what you can without risking your lives. I'll be safe at the altar of our Lord.'

Argue as they did, the bishop refused to change his mind and, eventually, the brothers had no choice but to obey his orders. Under his gentle manner and ancient, withered appearance, Bishop Aethelthred was an inflexible autocrat.

The attackers spread out to achieve their respective goals. Five men armed with bright swords and axes moved through the buildings of the enclave like loping wolves, driving the churchmen before them.

But more terrible, like the Satan so hated by the priests, was a man dressed in black leather who stalked towards the church armed with a short, double-sided sword and a long, black staff of curiously carved ash and oak. So fixed was his purpose that the black warrior barely acknowledged the few terrified priests who scuttled out of his path like disturbed chickens.

The five brown-clad warriors made for the outside of the church, spoke together hurriedly, made some calculations and then began to dig with their axes at a grave site near the church wall. They worked with economy and precision, as if this disinterment was the purpose of their violent intrusion into Glastonbury.

Meanwhile, their leader was about a more terrible task, one that he had chosen with relish.

Inside the church, the intruder found the bishop alone at the altar. At prayer and on his knees, Aethelthred was at the mercy of the implacable intruder.

The bishop rose, genuflected and turned to face the impersonal eyes of the intruder. The malice he saw there told him that he would soon meet his God.

'If you must kill me, my son, then strike hard and fast,' the old man stated bravely. Years ago, he had been a sturdy peasant who had gone to the priesthood to learn the secrets of the Latin language and to quench a strange hunger in his belly. He had never forgotten the plain speaking of ordinary folk and he had long relinquished any fear of death.

'You will die slowly, priest,' the black-clad warrior hissed and struck the bishop on the chin with the butt of his staff, breaking the old man's jaw. 'But you'll die silently.'

As Aethelthred tried to pray through shattered teeth, the

warrior struck him again and again, each blow more ferocious than the last until, barely conscious, the priest lay at the feet of his assailant.

'I . . . forgive you . . . my son,' the bishop gurgled through the blood that seeped from his mouth.

'But I don't forgive you,' the warrior snarled and swung the staff down in a wide arc, striking the old man on the side of the head. Blood sprayed and splattered over the white cloth on the altar. Then, with eerie deliberation, the warrior drew aside his robes and urinated over the Cross and the precious scrolls that were laid on the altar before him.

As the warrior brought one heel down to stamp on the old man's head, a cry like the sharp keening of a girl caused the murderer to almost lose his footing. He spun quickly and searched the hangings and dark corners of the church with malignant, startled eyes.

A scuttling like the sound of disturbed rats on the flagging made the black warrior's hair rise. But no one was there. Nothing moved, so he turned back to Aethelthred.

One final, looping blow caught the bishop's skull with a dull, wet thud. But the tip of the staff was caught on the edge of the altar and the heavy weapon skittered out of the warrior's hands and slid away into the shadows.

Voices were rising outside the church – shouts, screams and the distant sound of horses.

The black warrior swung away from the corpse. Quickly, and without wasting time to regain his staff, the intruder drew his short sword and ran from the church towards the graves that edged its walls.

Time was short and his task was only half completed.

Behind one long hanging, a young priest sagged against the wall and vomited, careless of the mess he left on his sandalled feet. As he edged out of his hiding place, a trickle of blood from the body of the bishop ran towards him like an accusing finger.

Balyn brooded as the afternoon lengthened.

Although he was obsessive, hot-headed and stubborn, Balyn was not completely foolish. He had heeded the words of Balan throughout his whole life, for he valued his brother's ability to see clearly to the heart of any problem. Now, thoroughly confused by the deceit that lay under ready smiles at Cadbury, he blundered through the passages of the palace like a blind man.

While Artor's palace was not overly large, it was complex, having grown haphazardly to accommodate growing demands as the High King's court became more sophisticated. Modelled loosely on the form of a villa, with a hugely enlarged entry which had become Artor's Hall of Judgement, the structure had once had an atrium which had now been divided into further rooms, leaving long, narrow corridors that led to still more corridors, off which small rooms opened, most of which were dark and lacked adequate ventilation. At the rear of the structure, a second storey rose with wooden stairs linking the floors. In some ways, Artor's palace was primitive and lacked the opulence of southern climes, yet the raw-sawn wooden floors above and the stone flagged rooms below were clean, sweet smelling and free of the straw used in so many Celtic homes to disguise the stench and dirt, especially during the winter months.

Exploration and constant usage were the only methods by which the inhabitants mastered the maze of corridors, so Balyn became quickly lost. His blind temper was a further impediment, for Balyn lost all reason when his moods overcame him. He was apt to stride away from whatever had upset him without any sense of where he was going.

By sheer accident, he met the High King in one of the passages.

Artor was in an expansive mood. He had been watching his guard as they exercised and paired off for weapons practice, and he had been entertained by the skills of two of the warriors. One was a very tall man in his early forties called Gwydion after one of the old Celtic gods. Artor remembered Gwydion's mother well, a laughing farmer's daughter called Olwen. Gwydion's hair was blond like Olwen's and held Artor's wild curls. The boy had grown into a cheerful, open man who was as sunny-tempered as his mother had been. Gwydion had wed when he was still young, and had since sired a son who had also been inducted into the guard.

Gwydion's partner in weapons practice was a much younger bastard son called Vran, who was only eighteen years of age. The lad was dark and intense, slender and steely of muscle, but he lacked the height of his sire, being short and neat like his mother, Fearn, who was reputed to be a descendant of an enslaved Pict. Unlike that dour race, Fearn had been a graceful, vivacious and fiercely intelligent young woman, and she and Artor had remained friends. From time to time, the High King would visit her snug cottage in Cadbury Town and she would welcome him in the old way, with laughter, earnest talk and comfortable passion.

Artor felt a warm surge of pride as the two warriors, both so dissimilar, fought each other to a standstill. Although Gwydion had superior reach, he couldn't find a chink in Vran's defence which was fast, acrobatic and intelligent. When the bout was over, Artor congratulated both men, who bowed in homage and flushed with pleasure. He clapped Gwydion on the back and ruffled Vran's hair as he marvelled at the devotion that was so nakedly obvious in the eyes of both men.

How very strange, Artor thought. I never openly acknowledge my bastard sons, and yet they are still fiercely loyal. I believe the guard would die to protect me.

'We thank you, lord, for your faith in us,' Gwydion murmured, clenching his right fist and holding it over his heart in the manner of the Roman legions.

'You have given an old man pleasure, boys. Remember me to your mothers, and remind them of my respect and affection.'

Both men stood a little taller in gratitude for Artor's words. The king accepted their mothers and themselves as his, although they would never be legitimate and had no expectations of formal largesse from the High King.

So, when Artor ran headlong into a heedless Balyn running at full tilt, he felt a moment's irritation, but his good mood was too warm and mellow to be easily cast aside.

Drawing back from the youth, Artor eyed Balyn with concern. The young man had virtually no ability to hide his emotions behind a smiling façade. That he was deeply troubled boded no good for Artor's peace of mind and the king felt, rather than heard, his protective Jutlander as Odin moved carefully into a striking position behind him.

So deeply was Balyn enmeshed in his own chaotic thoughts that he would have blundered on carelessly through the palace, but Artor gripped his arm and swung the lad round to face him.

'Hold up, young Balyn. I swear you're as skittish as a frightened horse. Where are you heading in such a mad rush, and who's put that frown on your face?'

Balyn paused, blushed and stammered out his apologies.

'I'm angry and confused, my lord. I didn't see you. I crave your pardon for my haste and discourtesy.'

'That's not good enough, young man. I'm on my way to see the queen, but she can wait a few moments more. How may I help you?'

The boy's eyebrows knitted together, just as Gallia's had done when she was worrying away at a particularly troublesome problem. The king's chest contracted painfully with this small trick of memory. Artor wondered how he could remember such fine details about his beloved's mannerisms and yet couldn't recall the details of her face. For Gallia's sake, he chose to ignore the mutinous flash of anger that passed through the expressive eyes of this grandson who scowled and stared mulishly at his feet.

'I argued with my brother, my lord,' Balyn replied. 'It was only a passing squabble, not worth keeping you from your duties to the queen.' Balyn shuffled his feet like a small child caught out in a lie. His telltale eyes dropped to stare fixedly at his hands.

'Come, Balyn. Wenhaver can wait, but I fear that you cannot do so.'

Firmly and patiently, Artor began to draw the young man

towards his private apartments, acutely aware of Odin's disapproving scowl.

Balyn protested half-heartedly, but he permitted Artor to lead him into his spartan quarters where he was firmly pressed to accept a cushioned bench. As the boy's eyes roamed this inner sanctum, Odin gave him a goblet of light Spanish wine. The golden alcohol was the same colour as the tiny yellow flecks that lay in Balyn's grey eyes.

'I'm an old man, lad, but I've seen too many summers come and go to confuse a brotherly squabble with a serious disagreement. Tell me the nature of your argument.' Artor used the full force of a voice that had always had authority. Balyn blushed, even though the king's tone was kindly.

'You'll be angry with me,' the youth began, then stopped abruptly.

'I'm often angry, but tell me anyway.'

'We argued over you, sire . . . and the queen.'

Artor ran one hand through his close-cropped curls. Balyn was almost childish in his lack of tact. The blurted-out words washed away any impatience that the king still felt. He raised the boy's mutinous chin with one hand. For a moment, he wished that this beautiful youth had half the poise of Vran or Gwydion.

'As you are so confused and upset, I'll permit you to ask whatever questions you choose of me. I'll answer them as honestly as I can, as long as I don't besmirch my honour in the process. I've nothing to hide from you, young man.'

'Modred says that your personal guards are all bastard children that you've sired,' Balyn stated baldly. 'I felt sorry for the queen and Balan told me I was being hasty.'

Artor became a little pale around the eyes and one booted foot jerked unconsciously.

'And?' Artor raised one quizzical eyebrow. 'I know that small piece of gossip wasn't enough to send you rampaging through my halls like a blind young bull.'

Dismayed, Balyn tried to retreat from the king's all-seeing eyes but, like many better men and women before him, he could not. Artor missed nothing.

'Balan told me to look in a mirror,' he said quietly. Torment stared out of eyes that had the same quick passions of the long-lost Gallia.

Instead of words of comfort, or the truth, Artor drained his wine cup in one swallow.

Odin immediately refilled it.

'Do you really think that I made a bastard out of *you*? And a whore out of your *mother*?'

Artor's tone was regretful, but not angry, and Balyn's heart ceased to hammer ferociously against his ribs.

'Not exactly,' he stammered. 'Balan said I was crazy to think such treasonous thoughts. But what am I to do when every time I shave my face, I see your image in the mirror? Kings have been known to beget sons on aristocratic women before now. Modred has told me of the failings of my family.'

'Modred is an adder who'll soon find my heel on his neck,' Artor murmured and rose to his feet. He looked down at the handsome young man whose shining plaits and glossy, golden skin was so much like his own had been. 'Still, you've a right to know your mother's history, so you'll hear it from me and not from rumour-mongering or innuendo. Your confusion is understandable, Balyn, so I'm not offended. Yes, my personal guard is composed, in part, of my acknowledged but illegitimate sons whom I've chosen not to abandon. The queen has borne me no heir and, although we work together for the good of the realm, I'm long past the age of love and romance. Our marriage was arranged for us, Balyn, and we have suffered some of the consequences of such affairs of state. I'll not lie to you. Neither of us has been particularly happy in the match, but we do our duty as best we can.'

A little mollified, Balyn gulped a mouthful of wine. The king's explanation seemed so reasonable that his anger began to waver.

'Would you begrudge your king the odd entanglement with a willing servant girl if I do my duty by any child born out of a moment's lust?'

Balyn raised his eyes and shook his head.

'As for your likeness to me, what can I say to calm your fears and to kill Modred's seeds of suspicion? Your mother, Anna, and I are kin. We are close kin. Your elder brother, Bran, is probably my direct heir, although I'll never lay such a heavy burden upon him. Many years ago, I privately acknowledged that your mother was my sister, the child of Uther Pendragon, who was sired on his deathbed. This blood link is not common knowledge, for Anna would be shamed by any suggestion that she was illegitimate.'

Balyn gaped. He was now thoroughly disarmed.

'Both my older sisters deny the link between Anna and Uther Pendragon for personal and ambitious reasons. I have also been deliberately vague with Anna, so she has never been sure who was her birth father. Fortunately, she accepted Lord Ector as her foster-father. I was pleased, partly for political reasons but, more importantly, to protect her from the lying rumours of curs such as Modred. I have publicly been silent on the matter to spare her feelings and to protect her from men who would have much to gain had they got a child on her when she was young. Your father, Comac, on the other hand, was the son of one of my dearest friends. I ensured that Anna and her children were safe.' Artor smiled into the gawking eyes of Balyn. 'Was I wrong to protect her from the ambitions and slurs of the unscrupulous?'

Artor's words were direct and seemingly free from guile. Balyn felt his confusion weaken under the High King's steady gaze and something melted within his chest. Had Artor known how totally his words were believed and how passionately Balyn accepted his king as the head of his family, he would have been ashamed at the half-truths that fell so glibly from his practised tongue.

'I'm humiliated by my wicked thoughts, my king. I've allowed myself to be used and enraged by rumour, when all I had to do was ask and the truth would have been made clear to me. I've been foolish.'

'No, lad, you're simply young and you're new to the jockeying for power that is a large part of life at court. But you must beware of Modred, for he's happy to foster the belief that Morgause is his mother, that she betrayed her husband with Luka's youngest son. It suits him to become known and accepted as my kin. Perhaps that's why he's so slow to return to his lands, although I've hinted several times that his subjects must miss him in his absence. Modred plays his own games. I don't know if Modred speaks the truth or not, but he has the look of my sister, Morgan the Fey. Modred believes he is a claimant to the throne, along with Gawayne and his brothers. Modred, therefore, cannot be trusted.'

'Balan tried to explain Modred's motives to me, but I wouldn't listen.' Chagrin was written plainly on Balyn's face.

The two men finished their wine. Balyn rose to his feet and bowed deeply to his king.

'I know so little of the world, but I promise to listen to cooler heads in future. I'll maintain my silence about what you've told me, lord, and I swear I'll never betray you.'

'I don't want your blood on my hands, lad, because your mother would never forgive me. But, I want you to think before you act. When I was young, I was fortunate to have Targo who taught me to exercise patience, rather than make a snap decision I would come to regret. Your twin brother serves this same purpose for you.'

With profuse thanks and with the glow of ardent hero worship shining out of his eyes, Balyn left the king's presence with the endearing clumsiness of a puppy.

Artor remained seated in his favourite chair and hooked one leg over its raised end piece for comfort, his intended visit to the queen apparently forgotten. His brows were drawn down in irritation and he felt a momentary self-disgust for the lies and half-truths he had told to perpetuate a necessary fiction.

'You spoke too frankly with that young man, Artor,' Odin chastised him. 'The boy feels too much and thinks too little. He lives on the edge of a knife and he'll never forgive you if your small lie is revealed to him.'

Artor shrugged off Odin's words. Balyn was only a high-spirited, passionate young man. Roughly, he told the Jutlander to be silent. Odin obeyed, but he clutched a small leather bag that hung on a cord around his neck. Inside the soft leather, Odin felt the smooth outline of small stones marked with northern runes. There was little that he feared in the whole green earth, but Balyn's eyes were windows to his thoughts, and what Odin saw there filled him with foreboding. The boy teetered between the extremes of exultation and despair, and Artor was ignoring Balyn's flaws, terrible weaknesses that could bring him to ruin.

For a time, Artor sat, nibbled on a dried apple from the winter storehouse, and considered the vexing nature of Modred, his nephew.

As befitted Modred's position as a tribal king, Artor had invited the young man to a private audience not long after he had arrived at Cadbury. Neither man enjoyed the occasion.

Modred had dressed exquisitely in black and red, a flamboyance that suited his colouring and slenderness. When he entered the High King's private apartment, his eyes had scanned the room efficiently, filing away all those small details that revealed aspects of Artor's character. With every movement of the young man, Artor was reminded of Morgan the Fey, his dangerous half-sister.

'Why have you come here, Modred? You are welcome, of course, to stay for as long as you wish, but I'm curious about the motives that have driven you to travel so many weary miles.' Artor offered his nephew the same easy, lying smile that Modred gave to him.

'Why, uncle, we have never met till now, and the death of my king and my unexpected crowning seemed to necessitate some communication between us. Luka was my grandfather, as you know, and I was raised as a Brigante.' Modred grinned. 'A shortage of heirs to the throne resulted in my elevation.

'When my cousin died childless from a lung disease, I was fortunate to be on the spot, so to speak, the motherless and fatherless outsider who was the last heir of Luka. My cousin was ill for some time, so the council of old men are quite used to ruling in the name of the king. While you might frown at my casual disregard for my throne and my people, I can assure you that those squabbling old lords can't agree on anything but the simplest actions of rule. The young warriors follow me, so I don't fear that I'll be deposed. But I'm curious about my grandfather, and even more eager to learn the history of my mother's kin. I'm sure that you can understand my position, having been raised in a similar fashion yourself.'

In fact, their childhoods had been very different. Modred's mother had rejected the boy as an error of judgement, and his father had been assassinated before the babe could ever know him, leaving the infant to be raised by retainers and treated as an inconvenient bastard, albeit one who was well-born. He was scorned by other boys of his age as a landless orphan.

Artor could imagine how despair, loneliness and bullying had blighted Modred's life and embittered him beyond his years. Modred was unloved, he had been ignored and rejected; he had lacked a Frith or a Targo to humanize him. Those aspects of his nature that had ensured his survival during his barren youth had also cemented his position as king of a troublesome and passionate tribe, but they were not comfortable skills, for Modred was ambitious and coldly efficient. With a spasm of recognition, Artor acknowledged that the young Modred had inherited his chill, rational nature from the same source as he himself had. In this, Modred was the one kinsman who most closely resembled the High King.

Yet Artor couldn't bring himself to like Modred, and would never be able to trust him. The High King had never known the whips of ambition that drove some men to commit terrible crimes to achieve their heart's desires. Yet he had known many men and women who were afflicted by an excess of desire. Ambition had driven Glamdring Ironfist and Caius, although both men had been very different in nature and motive. Ambition had driven Simnel's rebellion and caused the death of Luka. Ironically, Simnel's ambition had ensured that Modred was elevated to the position of King of the Brigante.

Could Modred wish for more? Would he raise his eyes as high as Artor's throne?

Artor had resolved to watch Modred closely.

Now, his spirits lifted as his thoughts returned to the twins. They might prove to be a blessing. If one of them became his heir, Modred's expectations would be denied; both Balyn and Balan were skilled warriors and, more importantly, they were still young.

Two days later, as rains threatened from out of a darkening morning sky, riders were seen approaching at speed from the north. They had already reached the orchards beyond Cadbury Town when the guard called the alarm.

Warning bells pealed over the tor.

Accompanied by his bodyguard, Artor rode out to the first rampart to greet the tired horsemen as they climbed the hill on their foundering horses. The five men had set out from Glastonbury at a fast pace that they had maintained all the way to Cadbury. The least experienced rider of the group was a tonsured priest in a bloodstained habit that was only partially covered by a ragged cloak. This exhausted man, almost unconscious with weariness, was lying along the neck of his shaking horse as it shuddered to a stop. Its chest and withers were covered with bloody foam.

'Who disturbs the peace of the High King?' Percivale demanded, already kitted out in hastily donned battledress.

The four warriors dismounted and bowed low while the priest continued to hang over the neck of his mount. Percivale helped the man to dismount and to stand on trembling legs.

The leader of the warriors addressed Artor directly.

'I am Ked, my lord. I'm a vassal of Glyndwr of Lloegyr come to report Saxon and Jute activities to the east. Two nights ago, we observed a number of fires in the distance. We rode to Glastonbury the next morning and found it had been attacked and several buildings gutted by fire.'

Artor curled one hand into a fist. Glastonbury lay under his personal protection, and any attack on it was an attack on the crown.

'What else?' He looked at the exhausted priest. 'This matter is clearly both serious and urgent. The priest has ridden hard for a man unused to the reins.'

'The Bishop of Glastonbury has been murdered,' Ked replied evenly. 'He was killed at his own altar.'

One of Ked's men handed over a tall rod of office, similar to those used by Druids. The crude carving at both ends was matted with hair, blood and brain matter, all long dried.

Artor gave an exclamation of dismay, but Gruffydd took the staff from Ked and examined it closely.

'Five other priests also died in the attack, but they were struck down by knives and swords as they attempted to put out the flames,' Ked went on. 'The altar was desecrated with piss, as were the sacred scrolls of the church. Worse still, the grave of Lucius, the previous bishop, was desecrated and an attempt was made to steal Lucius's skull from his grave.' Ked shuddered with remembered disgust.

'How large was the force that attacked holy Glastonbury, Ked? You're a woodsman and a warrior, so I imagine you could read the signs.'

'Aye, my lord, I could follow their spoor clearly. There were six men in the party that attacked the holy place, but only one man was riding a warhorse. The other carrion were afoot when they attacked, although they stole two horses when they made good their escape.'

'So they live close to the community of the priests. The foot soldiers wouldn't have run far, not if they wanted to fight at the end of their journey.'

Ked nodded in agreement. 'The sign was clear. They headed north, so we chose to bring the attack to your attention rather than follow them.'

'You have our thanks, and your master will have our support if he feels imperilled. Rest now, for tomorrow we ride to Glastonbury to discover what we can of this cowardly action.'

As the men of Glyndwr were led away to comfortable stables and sleeping quarters, Artor rode back to his citadel. The showy roan under his strong legs was impatient to stretch its stride and he was forced to curb its enthusiasm by brute strength. Artor regretted the loss of Coal and his offspring years earlier, but there was no avoiding the relentless passage of the years.

He was sunk in gloom when he handed his roan to the ostlers and strode into his quarters.

'Lord Artor, will you spare an hour for an old servant?' Gruffydd asked, wheezing in his efforts to match the king's longer strides.

'Of course, Gruffydd. And you'll bring Gawayne, Galahad, Bedwyr and the twins to our discussion as well. I need fresh minds rather than the counsel of cautious old men.'

'Such as myself, my lord?' Gruffydd asked quickly, his grin not quite hiding something vulnerable that lay behind his eyes.

'I've never considered you to be an old dodderer, Gruffydd,' Artor answered the spymaster with a grin. 'You're far too nimble-witted. This situation provides an opportunity to test the young ones. Balyn and Balan are strong, I know, but are they quick-witted and flexible in their thinking? Is Galahad the paragon that he is reputed to be, or the sulky hypocrite that Gawayne's enemies describe? Either way, my knowledge of these young warriors is increased.' He smiled at Gruffydd. 'You might also invite Nimue's boy to join us. I know he's not a warrior, but perhaps Myrddion passed on more to his son than quick fingers and an eloquent tongue.'

'I live to obey, sire,' Gruffydd replied with an impertinent grin that briefly lit his craggy face.

'You're an old flatterer,' Artor said with affection.

We're all getting older, Artor thought pensively as he watched Gruffydd hobble away on swollen feet. And what of those who follow? Where will they stand, and what will they be prepared to die for?

An hour later, Artor gazed around his spartan room where Llanwith had once put his muddy boots on the table and laughed until the room seemed too small for his mirth. Myrddion had stood in that far corner, guarding his thoughts, as his nimble mind sought answers to the troubles that beset his king. The mercurial Luka had banged this table with his knife hilt in frustration, and the wood still retained the impressions of his blows. And Targo – honest Targo – had sat at his right hand and reminded him that having an edge was the most essential part of combat.

Perhaps, thought Artor, it might be better if he, too, was at rest with his beloved ghosts.

Llanwith's face swam, grinning, through Artor's thoughts. He could still hear that redoubtable man's demand of him, so long ago, when he was barely twelve years old.

'Are you fast, boy?'

'Fast enough!'

Artor grinned reflectively. How had he dared to answer Llanwith with such impudence?

Aye, the years had proved that he was fast enough, and strong enough, to overcome almost any hurdle – other than his loneliness. Llanwith had died twenty years ago of a burst vein in his head that sent a rush of blood pouring out of his ears, nose and eyes. He was replaced first by one son and then another, but his great strength hadn't been passed on to his tall, virile sons. Only Comac, the youngest, had lived long enough to marry Licia, to father children and to hold the Ordovice tribe together. But he, too, had died tragically before he reached old age. His eldest son, Bran, now ruled in his stead and the line of the Ordovice kings seemed set to rule for generations. Artor smiled nostalgically. What would his old friend have said if he had known that Artor's grandson would eventually rule the Ordovice in his place?

'He'd have laughed, loud and long!' Artor spoke aloud to the empty room, and hoped that his dead friend still watched over him.

Ignorant of their king's black mood, the next generation of warriors trooped into the chamber, rather over-awed to have reached the inner sanctum, and surprised by its lack of luxury and decoration.

'My tastes are simple, young men,' Artor offered in explanation, while Odin filled plain campaign cups with mead, ale and wine. 'I have little patience with golden plates or fine fabrics, for possessions would only slow me down and deflect me from our cause. Ultimately, we must all be ready to surrender everything we own if we want to win the battles that are coming.' He turned to his spymaster. 'You've brought the staff used in the attack on Aethelthred, and you're the expert on Druids. What can it tell us?'

Gruffydd shook his head. 'The Druids had no part in making this staff, my lord. I've served the old ones for all of my life, so I know and understand their symbols. I can swear without hesitation that this false object has no part in their ceremonies.'

'How so?' Balan asked carefully. 'It looks authentic.'

'Only to an untrained eye. The carving is very crude and I can't recognize any discernible link with the old faith. For instance, this leering face where the hand sits against the wood is a satyricon, and that's a Roman symbol. Besides, the decoration was carved long after the staff was made. See? The wood is cleaner and it has a different texture – in fact, it's a different wood altogether.'

'The Druids are in decline,' Galahad interrupted. 'There are few of them left since the Romans exterminated them on Mona Island. Could this attack mask an uprising against Christianity by disaffected Druids for the sins of the past?'

Galahad's prejudices were obvious and Gawayne shifted awkwardly on his stool, more sensitive than his son to the feelings of those who followed the old ways.

'The Druids were teachers, lawmakers, healers and intellectuals.' Bedwyr's voice was flat but Artor could trace the faint shadow of disapproval under his words. 'They've not fallen so far or become so stupid that they'd kill the Bishop of Glastonbury, a man who lives under the protection of the High King of the Britons. It's well known that our king tolerates many religions.'

Bedwyr had embraced the Christian faith in his youth, and had then become a pagan. But what religion did he follow now? Few men would dare to ask the Arden Knife what allegiances he held, other than loyalty to the High King.

'Many of my people still cleave to the old ways, although the Christian religion has begun to make some inroads in Arden,' he added. 'But, like all sensible people, we pay lip service to both faiths.'

Galahad snorted in derision.

'Why would anybody try to take the skull of Bishop Lucius?' Balan asked, stabbing to the heart of the conundrum. 'He can't be very important, for I've never heard of him.'

'The desecration was aimed at me,' Artor stated with conviction. 'Lucius assisted at my coronation, and he saved my life when I was a babe by sending me to the Villa Poppinidii to be fostered by Lord Ector. Lucius was a man who displayed both Roman reason and Christian faith, which is a rare and valuable combination. Perhaps the skull was required for some symbolic ritual that was designed to draw me out of Cadbury.'

'Why would you leave the safety of your fortress?' Balyn asked.

'Because he must, my lord,' Taliesin answered. 'The murderer considers Lucius to be responsible for pains, real or imagined, that he feels have been exacerbated during Artor's reign. If Artor ignores this insult, he will demonstrate to his enemies that he and his warriors are prepared to sit behind safe borders until the Saxons destroy all the kingdoms of the west.'

'Thank you, Taliesin,' Artor responded. 'Like your father, you speak clearly and with brutal honesty. I'd rather stay at home and find peace at the fireside, but such a fate is not for me. My witch of a sister, Morgan, foretold my destiny many years ago.' He smiled wryly at Gawayne and Galahad. 'I apologize to you both for speaking of your aunt in such a manner.'

'No offence taken, Artor,' Gawayne responded. 'She's always been a thoroughly poisonous woman.'

'Aye,' Galahad agreed primly. 'She's heathen and her spells are works of the devil.'

'So who are our enemies?' Artor asked the assembled group. 'And where are they?'

'The priest may know something,' Balyn suggested. 'He must have had a good reason to come here on such a wild ride. Has anyone asked him yet?'

Artor laughed and, slowly, the other men joined him.

Balyn flushed to the roots of his amber hair.

'Well done, Balyn. It seems that Queen Anna has true sons in her twins. You've asked the obvious question while we've wasted time in speculation.'

Balyn blushed even more hotly.

Artor turned to his bodyguard. 'Find the priest, Odin. And try not to frighten him witless.'

'You joke, lord,' Odin said reproachfully as he left the room.

'He frightens *me* witless,' Bedwyr quipped, 'and I've known him for years.'

Before the priest eventually stumbled through the doorway, he had found time to clean his face, dust his habit free of the dirt of the road and to bolt down a little food, so his boyish face had regained a little colour, while his slender body stood a little straighter and more at ease. His thin hands were pale and free of calluses, except for swollen and cut palms caused by the reins. From the damage to his tender hands, Artor judged that this priest had never ploughed the fields or worked in the orchards of Glastonbury.

'What is your name, priest?' Artor demanded.

The willowy young man shifted nervously from foot to foot and a tic jerked along his weak jaw.

'My birth name is Eldric, sire,' was the whispered reply. 'But I'm known within the church as Brother Petrus.'

'Come, Brother Petrus, you don't need to fear blade or cudgel here,' Artor told him. 'What are your duties at Glastonbury?'

'I'm a scribe, my lord, and I'm copying and repairing the old scrolls for the glory of Mother Church. Glastonbury has become a place of learning as well as piety.'

Artor rubbed the stubble on his chin and promised himself the luxury of a long bath and a close shave with his special blade when time permitted. This clean-faced stripling was making him feel withered and dishevelled.

'Were you present when your bishop was killed? If you were, I order you to tell me all you saw or heard. Speak boldly.'

Brother Petrus wrung his swollen hands together nervously without any apparent thought for the cuts and bruising that must have been causing him pain. Dreadful memory or fear seemed to distort his young face and he was obviously distressed. Taliesin was certain that this shy, pallid man was reluctant to relate his experiences in the church at Glastonbury because the recitation would do him no credit.

'It was near to dusk when they came to the monastery, just after we rose from evening prayers. We smelled the smoke first. Had they not paused to set the hay barn alight, they would have had us trapped within the abbey.'

'Why were these attackers so stupid?' Taliesin murmured to no one in particular from his corner of the room. 'Everyone knows at what time evening prayers are said in Christian churches. Besides, what would the attackers achieve by setting fire to valueless outbuildings?'

Brother Petrus wondered briefly whether he was expected to answer these questions.

'The bishop ordered the brothers to hasten outside to quench the fires,' he said. 'I stayed behind with Aethelthred, who was very old and frail.'

'How many priests stayed with Aethelthred?' Taliesin asked.

'None of the brothers remained with the bishop. Why do you ask?'

'I'm simply trying to imagine exactly what happened during the attack', Taliesin replied innocently. For Taliesin, Petrus was either a coward who avoided the fires or a dutiful young priest who wanted to protect his bishop.

'Several brothers returned and told the bishop that the Glastonbury enclave was under attack. Again, they begged him to go with them and seek safety, but the bishop refused. Aethelthred ordered the brothers to put out the fires without risking their own lives, and assured them that God would protect him.' The young priest almost spat out these words, and his mouth twisted unattractively. When the eyes of the warriors registered their surprise at his manner, Petrus coloured and looked away in embarrassment.

Irritably, Artor cleared his throat and Petrus resumed his narrative.

'I heard the sounds of violence outside, so I tried to convince the bishop to leave the altar and flee to a place of safety. No matter how I begged, he wouldn't see sense and remained with his sacraments. When the black warrior entered the body of the church, I tried to stand between my bishop and the ruffian, but he was armed and I couldn't defend myself. Aethelthred simply continued with his prayers.'

Artor wondered why Petrus hadn't simply carried the ancient bishop to safety against his wishes. Petrus was young enough to perform such a simple task. Artor felt his lips curl, for he suspected that the sour-faced young priest had left his frail master to die.

'The attackers must have desired the death of Aethelthred alone', Artor stated drily, 'for you're unharmed. What became of the brothers who left the church?'

'They dispersed to fight the fires, or tried to defend the church against the ruffians,' Brother Petrus whispered nervously. 'I thought they'd be murdered, but other brothers came in from the fields when they saw the flames. The villains eventually took to their heels and left.'

'Did you flee the church?' Artor asked impatiently. 'What did you actually see with your own eyes? You must be precise! I don't care about your part in this incident, or if you were hiding in the church to save your own skin. Far better men than you have found it prudent to run when they were outnumbered. So tell me, without embellishment, exactly what you saw.'

Brother Petrus stared beseechingly at Artor and his mouth quivered. Like many ineffectual men, he could not face the knowledge of his own inadequacies. What he saw in Artor's stern countenance gave him no help and he lowered his eyes.

'I watched my bishop die while I hid in shame behind the altar hangings.'

'Describe what you saw, Petrus,' Taliesin said gently. 'No one will blame you for protecting yourself because we're fortunate to have a witness to the murder of the bishop. All we ask is that you help us to identify the murderous animal who committed this atrocity.'

The kindness in Taliesin's voice brought a fuller response.

'There were six men. Five of them were servants of the man who was their leader, who was dressed in black. The men wore leather jerkins with plates of iron set into them and simple helmets without any emblems or symbols on them. They looked more like village ruffians than warriors, even though they carried knives and cudgels. The leader ordered them to leave the church, and I heard them digging outside. He paused for a moment, as if to gather his resolve.

'The man in black was different from his minions. He wasn't tall, but his body was thick and powerful and he was heavily armed. I saw him clearly as he moved past me. He wore a black robe that was cinched at the hip with a silver belt of small skulls. His body armour was made of black leather with iron plates set into it, and he wore a helmet topped with black horsehair. The visor was down, so I couldn't see his face.'

'And?' Gawayne urged impatiently.

Artor glared at his nephew when Petrus flinched away from the Otadini prince.

'He beat the bishop to death with his staff, that one there.' Petrus pointed at the staff in Gruffydd's hand. 'The leader beat the bishop until Aethelthred's head was cracked like an egg. Then the staff became caught under the altar and the killer was forced to leave it behind. I had to jam my fist in my mouth so that I wouldn't make a sound.'

'Did you see anything else?' Artor's voice was hoarse, for the tale was sickening.

'The man's hands and neck were tattooed, for I saw them when his robe fell open. There were more on his arms in the gap between his sleeves and his gauntlets. There were tattoos of serpents and strange monsters over his lower arms where the flesh was visible. The man was perverted and he cursed the altar in the old tongue, although I couldn't understand the words. But I recognized the language. Then he urinated on the altar.'

The young man gagged and would have vomited, but Taliesin pushed a cup of strong red wine into his unresponsive hands and forced him to drink. When a little colour had returned to the priest's face, he continued.

'When the black warrior left the church, I tried to see what he was doing through one of the window slits. His servants had opened the grave of Bishop Lucius and the black warrior reached through the exposed bones to remove something that I couldn't quite see. Then our brothers arrived and the attackers fled. Their leader rode away on a black horse.'

The young priest crossed himself to ward off evil. Palpably, the room's heat seemed to dissipate in a chill of superstition. Petrus began to weep, his face twisted as if he was a child.

'I don't want to return to Glastonbury! Please! I beg you not to send me back to the monastery, my lord, for the devil came to Glastonbury – and I don't believe he has departed. I'll hear the sound of that staff breaking my bishop's skull for as long as I live.'

Artor looked at the quivering priest. His bottom lip was twisted in terror, and Artor felt a mixture of pity and scorn for the effeminate youth.

'You may journey south to the monastery at Venta Belgarum, if you so wish. It's for you and your church to decide what must be done with the life that your god has allowed you.'

Decisively, Artor turned back to his warriors and put all thought of Petrus out of his mind. Odin nodded his head towards the door and the young priest scuttled from the room.

'Our investigation of these atrocities shouldn't be complicated by superstition,' Artor stated bluntly. 'These abominations were enacted by a man. A murderous human killed the Bishop of Glastonbury and Gruffydd has expressed his doubts that this creature was a Druid. This murderer acts like no Druid I ever met, but whatever he is, he must answer directly to me for his crimes. On a clear day, the tower on Glastonbury Tor is just visible from our fortress, so this black warrior has struck very close to me – too close. I depart for Glastonbury at dawn.'

'I wish to go with you, sire,' each of his courtiers requested in turn.

Even Taliesin nodded his head in agreement.

Artor acknowledged their resolve and was content. A new generation was eager to be tested in a crucible of vindictiveness, cruelty and murder. Who knew what he would discover about these flushed and eager faces that watched him with such excitement!

Gawayne felt a strange prickling along his spine. Did his sexual adventure on the journey to Cadbury have any link with the black warrior? Not possible! Yet he recalled that he had seen a number of tattoos on the arms of Gronw, Miryll's servant, but he had been an oily, subservient creature and hardly capable of the bold, brutal slaughter carried out by the black warrior. Surely he couldn't be the murderer. Gawayne determined to put that uncomfortable idea out of his mind.

For his part, Galahad enjoyed a surge of righteous wrath. He believed that his purpose in life was to smite those pagans who lifted impious hands against the Church. And, as the knowledge of his destiny hardened in his mind, he remembered the tattoos that he had seen at Salinae Minor on the body of Gronw. The young man tried to catch his father's eyes, but Gawayne pointedly ignored his son, going so far as to turn his back.

Every man at Artor's council viewed the coming journey to

Glastonbury through the mirror of his own nature, his fears and his ambitions, except for one.

Taliesin bit his lip and stared fixedly at his feet. Talk of the Bloody Cup was only rumour, or his mother's nightmare, so why did he fear that the Glastonbury killing was the first sign of its malign presence?

When he finally drifted off to sleep in the stables, a bloodstained goblet continued to mock him in harrowing dreams.

CHAPTER VII

THE BLACK WARRIOR

The ride to Glastonbury was short and gruelling, but un-eventful. When the warriors left at first light, Artor set a fierce pace and even the twins were stiff and aching by the time the quiet green vale came into sight in the late afternoon.

The ride had been made more difficult because Artor insisted on full battle kit which meant that the horsemen were encumbered by their breastplates, shoulder guards, gauntlets and leg guards which, because the young men were nobles, were either solid, embellished iron or were made of ox hides covered with iron plates. Either way, the riders and horses were heavy with unaccustomed weight.

Packhorses carried the equipment and arms needed for a sustained campaign on horseback. Each warrior required at least one spear, a fighting knife, a sword and an axe as a basic weapons kit. Although the weather was still cool, the inexperienced warriors were soon sweating and uncomfortable within their shells of protection. Their supply escort, well used to Artor's lightning fast cavalry strikes on those occasions when the Saxons ventured out of their compounds, saw to the baggage train and followed at the rear of Artor's cavalry force.

Artor, Gawayne and Odin, all seasoned cavalrymen, viewed the younger men in their midst with amusement. Sore backsides, chaffed underarms and aching muscles would cause most of these youngsters to suffer that night. Although well trained and fit, none of the younger men had experienced Artor's version of a fast journey. They would soon learn.

Only Taliesin still sat easily in his saddle. Uninterested in combat, he had rejected body armour in favour of a heavy jerkin of boiled ox hide and crude but comfortable leather leggings. His head was protected by his father's helmet, a skullcap of some blued, shining iron that had supposedly fallen from the heavens. The metal was abnormally strong, although it was much lighter than the usual iron. As his hands were precious to him, Taliesin's gloves were soft and flexible, as were his simple boots, and his hair was plaited to form a cushioning protection under his helmet. With his hair no longer framing his face, his northern eyes were even more striking, and his clean-boned face reminded Artor strongly of the features of Myrddion Merlinus.

'This valley is part of Glastonbury,' Artor proclaimed as his arm encompassed the rich land that opened up before the tired eyes of his warriors. Dykes, streamlets and marshy ground caught the waning light in silvery sheets of water. Considering the violence that had taken place here just a few days earlier, Glastonbury drowsed in the beauty of an early spring afternoon, lulled by the sleepy hum of early bees, the heady scent of new growth and the rich aroma of newly turned loam.

'Cadbury might be fair, but Glastonbury is a small slice of paradise,' Balan said with youthful exuberance. 'Here, all green

145

things grow huge and even kine and cattle are more fertile than in any other place in the west that I've seen.'

'To desecrate such peace strikes at the heart of the Christian faith,' Galahad fumed. His hazel eyes were muddy with anger.

'Ah, Glastonbury,' Gawayne reminisced. 'I made a fool of myself here once, didn't I, Artor? It was only my lack of height that saved me from disaster that day. I must have appeared very silly, leaping upwards and trying to grasp Uther's sword, when it was obviously far beyond my reach.'

'You wrong yourself, nephew,' Artor responded cheerfully. 'The fates saved you from the burden of sword and crown, so you should be grateful for that blessing.'

'Believe me, Artor, I am,' Gawayne agreed with honest good humour. 'Being caught between the ambitions of my mother, my father and my aunt is a fate too gruesome to contemplate.'

As the warriors rode between the green spear points of newly planted crops that had already begun to send out shoots, the priests who toiled in the fields stood upright and waved them on.

'To work with the soil is truly God's way at Glastonbury,' Galahad murmured.

'All men give what is their portion in this place, son,' Gawayne said. He was nervous that his wayward son might cast off his weapons and pick up a hoe.

Several burned-out buildings came into view. Their desecrated walls rested on scorched stone foundations that left obscene scars in this gentle place.

Then a group of priests and lay brothers came forward to meet the king's retinue. Under their fresh, ruddy cheeks and downcast eyes, their mouths were glum and unsmiling. Few eyes rose to meet the gazes of their visitors and caution stiffened their bowed shoulders. Surprised by the absence of an open welcome, Artor searched among the closed ranks for a familiar face.

'Brother Simon. Simeon who was. Do you still defy time?'

A knotted, arthritic old man in a simple homespun robe stepped forth from the group and bowed low. His ancient eyes warmed as he looked up myopically at the king.

Time had not been kind to the old Jew. His black hair and beard were wholly white and he was left with a sparse fringe round his shaved tonsure. He had once been of middle height and had been whipcord thin, but now his spine was bent with the bone disease and Artor could tell that his hips pained him. His hands, those clever, artistic tools that had wrought the beauty of Caliburn and the dragon crown, were concealed within his robe.

'Do your sword and knife still serve you well, sire?' the old man asked in a hoarse baritone.

'Aye, Brother Simon.' Artor smiled back at the priest. 'My weapons are still as young and as strong as we once were.'

The twins looked at the ascetic face of the churchman and then at the hilts of Artor's weapons. Was this husk of a Jew the metal-smith who had wrought Caliburn, the legendary sword wielded by King Artor in the great battles against the Saxon hordes?

'I'm flattered to hear you say so, lord. Those blades were the last really fine work I completed. I can do nothing now.' He held up two twisted, arthritic hands and Artor felt pity wash over him at the thought of such a prodigious talent betrayed by the weaknesses of the body.

'Don't mourn for my lost dexterity, lord, for I have two fine apprentices who struggle to learn my skills. A man must serve as best he can and, on most days, I am content.'

'Where is your bishop?' Artor asked. 'Have you appointed someone to step into Aethelthred's shoes?' Artor's eyes swept the group of churchmen, all of whom were dressed alike with their hands hidden in their capacious sleeves.

A sturdy, black-haired man stepped out from the throng. Artor noted that he wore the Aryan tonsure, rather than the Roman version, and this priest had the confidence of a Celtic warrior. His origins were not written on his quick, clever face, but his length of limb indicated an eastern heritage.

'I shall stand for my bishop until a new appointment is made in Venta Belgarum. My name is Mark.'

'Has your bishop been buried yet, Mark?'

'We waited for your arrival, my lord. Brother Simon was certain that you would come to Glastonbury because your ties to this place are so strong. Our bishop has been laid out in his vestments on the altar where he died. He'll be interred beside Lucius after you've viewed his body, near the church wall that he perished to defend.'

This priest is a dour, direct man who possesses neither humour nor charm, Artor thought as he dismounted and handed the reins of his horse to one of the retinue. Still, he's honest, and he meets my eyes without fear.

'I wish to pay my respects to your dead bishop,' Artor requested gently. 'I must see with my own eyes what has been described to me.'

Mark bowed and guided the warriors through a simple stone entryway that led into the church. The younger men couldn't resist satisfying their curiosity by examining the site of such a blasphemous murder. Of the noble warriors, Gruffydd and Gawayne remained behind in company with Odin and Gareth. Percivale followed his master, falling to his knees as he entered the church and moving his lips in silent prayer.

The body of the bishop had been washed, oiled and dressed in ceremonial robes, but the gaping wounds that crisscrossed the bishop's head were plain to see. And neither nard nor precious oils could disguise the sweet scent of corruption. A thin strip of gauze covered the dead man's face and Artor drew it back exposing more wounds. A clear imprint, as cruel as any torture that Artor had ever seen, showed that a booted heel had crushed the bishop's nose into shapeless pulp.

Galahad crossed himself. Even Balyn, who had no fear of death, stepped back from the sight of such desecration.

'This poor man has been butchered,' Artor said evenly, although Percivale felt the undertow of anger that surged from beneath his master's veneer of self-control. 'You can see that he held his hands up to protect himself against repeated blows.'

The bishop's hands had been broken in many places from the force of the attack, even though gentle ministrations had straightened the fractured bones and folded the gnarled fingers into the position of prayer over the bishop's thin chest.

Taliesin moved forward and carefully parted the robe covering Aethelthred's torso. Another heel imprint was visible across the old man's throat; his killer had used his boot to shatter the larynx and the spine below it. A strip of linen ran under the corpse's chin and around the crown of the head.

'It's only this cloth that keeps the skull together, my lord. As

149

the bruises show, he must have lived for a short time during this beating.' Taliesin pointed out swollen, blackened marks that stood out hideously in the waxen pallor of the old man's ruined face. 'A single, well-placed blow would have given the bishop a quick death, but the murderer took pleasure in inflicting pain. His heart was filled with hate.'

Sickened and shaken, Artor replaced the gauze over the bishop's face.

'Rest well,' Artor muttered. '*Ave*, brave heart!'

After a moment's silence, Artor turned to face Mark.

'Take me to the grave of Lucius,' he ordered.

'May your god save this black warrior from the anger of the king,' Bedwyr whispered to Balan. 'For Artor will have his revenge. The black warrior will suffer before the king lets him die.'

'Is the king so brutal?' Balan asked.

'When wicked men practise evil, they must be forced to fear for their lives.' Bedwyr spoke softly. 'He practises the old ways of justice that he learned from the Romans who raised him. For men such as Artor, punishment is meted out to the exact measure of the crime committed, and it is carried out with complete impartiality. His justice is harsh, but it's effective against the sort of barbarity that was inflicted on the good bishop.'

'Can this form of cold-blooded justice create a peaceful civilization?' Balan was sceptical.

'Perhaps you should consider Cadbury and the peace that has been created there. A generation ago, it didn't exist. Harmony and plenty reign in the west, and you rode here from the north in perfect safety. The only reason that such security exists is because Artor has meted out retribution to thieves and plunderers and he's not afraid to get his hands dirty in the process.'

'But what of his soul?' Balan murmured.

'Ask him yourself,' Bedwyr replied and hurried after his king.

In the lee of the church wall, a grave had been partially excavated. The stained and rotted shroud had been ripped away so that the skull bones and the clasped fingers of the long-dead Roman bishop were partially exposed. Out of respect for Lucius, a piece of embroidered cloth had been placed over the pathetic skeletal remains.

'To bone and dust we all go eventually, friend Lucius,' Artor whispered as he stroked the worn thumb ring gifted to him by the long-dead bishop at his coronation.

Artor knelt so he could remove the fragment of embroidery and carefully examine the partially exposed bones.

'Is this grave exactly as it was left after the attackers were driven off?'

'Aye, my lord. We knew you'd want to see this desecration for yourself, so we only covered the bones with planks to protect them from the elements.'

'Why would these animals expend so much effort and place themselves at such risk to open an old grave?' Artor looked up at Taliesin, who was also puzzled. 'The black warrior had few men and little time, while Glastonbury has many potential defenders. The villains stole nothing. The attack appears to have been carried out with the intention of killing Aethelthred and opening Lucius's grave. These actions are bizarre, because the black warrior must have known that these churchmen would fight to protect the bones of their dead bishop. A diversion, perhaps?'

'The skull doesn't seem to have been disturbed, my lord,' Taliesin replied quietly. 'See? The earth is still tightly packed around the bones. Perhaps there was something else in the grave that the black warrior wanted. Petrus seemed certain that something was taken.'

Artor turned to question Brother Mark. 'Was anything of value placed in the grave of Bishop Lucius when he was interred?'

'I don't know, my lord. I wasn't here when Lucius ruled Glastonbury. God hadn't called me at that time in my life.'

Artor smiled thinly at the priest. 'Fetch Brother Simon. He was outside the sanctuary earlier. And bring any other greybeard who served the church when Lucius was Bishop of Glastonbury.'

Men didn't dawdle when Artor issued orders, especially when the king was visibly upset. Brother Simon soon arrived. Breathless, he leaned heavily on a sturdy staff and winced as he gazed down into the gaping grave. The empty eye sockets of the skeleton flickered with a counterfeit of life.

Four other ancient priests joined the group standing in the burial ground. Their eyes slid over the open grave as if they, too, couldn't control the primal curiosity that living creatures feel for the dead. Age-mottled hands clutched at crucifixes and made the sign of the cross.

Artor addressed the elders of the monastery.

'Was anything placed in the grave of Lucius at the time of his death and burial? Is something missing? It's important that we are properly informed if we are to capture the men who killed your bishop. Today isn't the time to preserve old secrets. Look closely, keen-eyed Simon, and try to remember if there were any objects in the grave that have been removed.'

The old priests came forward and stared down into the grave. Confusion and regret dulled their eyes.

Then one lurched into hurried speech. 'I recall seeing something placed in Lucius's hands as his body was laid out on the altar.'

'What was the object?' Artor demanded.

The old monk was frightened into a panic of incoherent mumbles.

'It was his drinking cup, Lord Artor,' another priest said earnestly. 'Lucius was interred with his old campaign cup. He used it at every meal.'

'I know the object, my lord.' Simon sighed and lowered his eyes. 'I remember that its dull metal had been scratched and dented by time. Before he died, I even offered to make Lucius another cup more befitting his station, but he refused my suggestion. He told me his cup had travelled over half the world and had, at times, been drenched in blood. He didn't elaborate on how it came into his possession, but he did say that it was fitting that it should now contain clean water to quench the thirst of a simple priest.' Simon hesitated. 'I'd quite forgotten his battered old mug.'

'The failure is not yours, Brother Simon,' Artor replied distantly, as if he could sense some evasiveness in Simon. 'I, too, recall seeing him drink from that same vessel all those years ago. I remember that it was round at the base with a simple flange of metal to serve as a handle. Was that the cup you recall?'

'Aye. He treated it as if it was a commonplace thing, but it was a memory of his past and he used it daily.'

'But why would these brigands take a simple cup?' Taliesin whispered to Artor, his mind haunted by images of the bloody goblet he had seen in his dreams. 'Unless the object is some relic with a history of its own, it would have no value to anyone, apart from Lucius.'

'I don't really understand either, but the cup must mean something to the black warrior.' Artor switched his attention back to Simon. 'What did the cup mean to Lucius, my friend?' he asked softly. 'Come, Simon, you'll not harm your old master by telling me what you remember about this object.'

Simon's eyes appeared clear and honest as he considered the king's request. He was obviously thinking carefully and only Taliesin and Percivale saw a fleeting shadow appear, and then disappear, in their guileless depths.

What is Simon hiding from the king? Percivale wondered warily. He's very cautious, even for a man of God.

Percivale turned towards Taliesin, who raised one eyebrow in mute agreement.

Is this cup the source of Mother's dreams? Taliesin wondered to himself. His hand itched to make the sign that wards off evil. The cup must be something of far greater significance than an old campaign mug.

'Lucius once told me that it had come into his possession when he was a soldier.' Simon's brow knitted with the effort of remembering, or hiding, the memories passing through his mind. 'He was ashamed of the violence in his early life and rarely mentioned his youth, but I remember that he referred to it once in a way that I didn't really understand.'

'I also remember speaking to Lucius about the cup,' one of his fellow priests added. 'I, too, asked him why he had kept it for such a long time. He told me that its design appealed to him. I took his meaning to be that the cup had been made in the land of his birth.'

Another old man joined the conversation. 'I remember I once spilled some water by overfilling it, and Lucius brushed aside my apologies by saying that water stains were cleaner by far than the bloody hands that had befouled it in the past. The bishop smiled in that sad way he had when he spoke of his younger days. I remember that we were very curious about it at the time, for the bishop was such a romantic figure to us when we were young men.'

'But it's only made from base metal,' Balyn protested. 'Why would anyone want to steal it?'

The king and his retinue stared into the grave, but it gave no answer to the enigma they faced. After a moment, Artor turned back to Mark and broke the uncomfortable silence.

'Did you see the direction in which the black warrior and his men fled?'

'Those men who were afoot headed across those small hills towards the river,' Mark replied, grateful to change the topic. 'The black warrior separated from them and circled round to the north on his horse.'

'Then we'll begin our search by following their trail towards the river. Guard Glastonbury well during my absence, Brother Mark, and keep a sharp watch at night. I'd be surprised if any other marauders return to shatter your peace, but continued vigilance will ensure your safety. Perhaps you can remember us in the prayers you make to your god and, if he's willing, we'll find the dogs who murdered your bishop.'

Despite Mark's invitation to remain for the night, Artor knew that any sudden shower of rain could destroy the spoor of the fugitives and leave them with a very cold trail. They prepared for an immediate departure and rode off into the softening evening light.

Bedwyr led the way, accompanied by Taliesin on foot. As fleet as any woodsman, Nimue's son was well versed in hunting and could easily keep up with Bedwyr's horse as the two men sought their quarry through the telltale signs of broken leaves, dislodged stones and scraped bark.

Shortly after leaving the last of Glastonbury's fields, the party came to the river that was flowing slowly between gently sloping banks.

'There are signs that coracles have been drawn up here,' Bedwyr called back to Artor.

'Aye,' Taliesin agreed. 'Rain has blunted their traces, but they've left many footprints behind to show their presence. The tracks of two horses have also stirred up the mud.'

'These traces would be of the two horses they stole,' Bedwyr murmured.

He stared intently at the earth and leaned forward, snatching up a single bedraggled feather that had been trampled into the soft mud. 'One of these men wore a raven's feather on his cap. A fitting reward for scavengers.'

'Keep it safe,' Artor ordered economically. 'Which way did they go? Did they make a fast escape downstream? Or did they travel against the current?'

'It would be easier to continue travelling towards the east if they were on foot,' Gawayne offered. 'Why would they run so far and then paddle back over ground already covered?'

'I agree,' Artor answered brusquely. 'We'll follow the river downstream.'

The waning light slowed their progress. At some fords, Taliesin and the twins crossed to the far bank to look for signs of a landing by the coracles, but they found nothing.

When full night came and the horses were imperilled by rabbit holes and poor ground, Artor drew his troops to a halt and they ate a frugal meal under the willows. On the far side of the river, Taliesin sang softly of his home and the twins were entranced by the magic of his voice. Slowly, to the soft whickering of the horses as they cropped grass in their hobbles, the force settled down to sleep.

At noon the next day, when Gawayne rode past the Isle of Salinae Minor, he felt only a momentary pang of guilt, but Galahad's brows furrowed suspiciously as he considered the isle and its inhabitants. The thought of Gronw's deceiving eyes made his nerves twitch, although the young zealot kept his thoughts to himself.

Later that afternoon, Artor's men came to the grey sea. The pebbled beach and the mournful cries of seagulls chilled the hearts of the warriors. No matter how carefully they scoured the banks of the estuary, there was no sign of the coracles.

Angry and defeated, Artor stared at the leaden sea with its treacherous currents.

'No small craft could survive in that mess.'

'A man can easily carry a coracle on his back, but we've seen no spoor to indicate they came this far, Artor,' Bedwyr said. 'It's likely they left the river at some point upstream, perhaps along one of those small tributaries we passed on the way.'

'There's been no sign at all,' Taliesin added, 'although both the men and the horses could have walked through the shallows to hide their presence.'

'They haven't flown away,' Artor retorted.

'They're more familiar with the terrain than we are,' Taliesin offered evenly, refusing to take offence. 'Perhaps we should investigate those tributaries upstream. Although . . .' His voice trailed away.

'What?' Artor snapped.

'Look!' Taliesin pointed towards a flock of gulls that rose from a partially concealed streamlet. 'Over there! Those birds must be feeding on something.'

The harpist would never have noticed the birds if a falcon hadn't hovered on the wind above the flock, disturbing the gulls and sending them into the air in panic.

'Bedwyr, check it out!' Artor ordered.

Bedwyr wheeled his horse and Taliesin swung up behind him. Together, they rode back up the pebbled beach to the sluggish, wide river mouth and urged their horses to enter the water. After crossing the flooded inlet, they disappeared into the marshy, reed-choked watercourse on the far side of the stream. Within minutes, Taliesin reappeared on a small knoll and waved to the waiting horsemen.

'I've found something, Artor,' he said as the king and his retinue joined him at a spot where the stream flowed around a series of natural stone steps. 'The gulls have been feeding on a corpse.'

A bloated, water-sodden body was caught in a cleft between

two wet boulders. Even now, gulls were returning and beginning to tear at the exposed flesh with their long, hooked beaks.

'I never liked those birds overmuch,' Gawayne muttered. 'How did we miss this body?'

'We were looking at the ground for signs of men and horses, not in the air where the birds fly,' Taliesin replied. 'Nobody notices the cries of gulls when they're near the sea.'

Balan dragged the battered corpse on to dry land.

Artor recognized a worn leather jerkin set with iron plates, which fitted the description given by Brother Petrus. The king grunted in disgust.

'So, where are the others?'

As if he had heard the words of his master, Bedwyr reappeared. He rode out of a small copse of stunted trees that had been partly hidden from the riverbank by rising ground. To gain the attention of Artor and his warriors, Bedwyr whistled piercingly and then returned to the shadows of the copse.

Artor's retinue remounted and hastened to join the scout.

The copse of trees was twisted and gnarled by the force of the offshore winds that prevailed in these climes. Scudding over low cliffs that hunkered above the gravelled beaches, the wind swirled back to eddy over the lower river flats. A heavy grass cover grew around tortured trees that provided shade and shelter and there, beside a long-dead campfire, lay four corpses in contorted, unnatural positions. They had died violent deaths in hideous spasms of agony, yet none of the bodies bore a single wound.

'Be careful, Taliesin!' Artor warned from the back of his horse, but the harpist was already kneeling beside the nearest bloated body, his nose close to the convulsed, purple mouth. The other members of the hunting party looked away in revulsion.

Taliesin rose to his feet and dusted off his knees. 'They've been poisoned, Artor. The black warrior obviously believes that dead men can't tell tales.'

Taliesin picked up an iron cap from which two bedraggled raven feathers still dangled. After a few moments of searching, he discovered a coarse pottery bottle, sealed by a leather plug.

Artor shook his head slowly. He could imagine the proffered bottle, the unsuspecting servants drinking deeply, then the first burning pangs in the gut.

'Shite!' Gawayne swore. 'The poor sods must have trusted whoever killed them.' He looked away in revulsion. 'Animals have been feeding on their bodies.'

'All God's creatures must feed, Father,' Galahad responded piously, although Gawayne noticed that the young man's complexion was very pale. Galahad leapt from his horse and approached the bodies. A couple of the victims had vomited and their twisted mouths were encrusted with a vile, yellow residue.

'Forget them, Galahad,' Artor ordered shortly. 'They'll rot where they lie. I'll accord them the same respect that they gave to Bishop Aethelthred.'

The twins and Galahad looked shocked at Artor's callousness, but Taliesin merely nodded in understanding.

'We'll ride on for a few miles and try to find some trace of the black warrior.' Artor's body was rigid with controlled fury. 'He's managed to elude us so far, and he's made sure that there are no live witnesses to betray him, but I intend to find him.'

Eventually, the hard ground revealed some telltale traces of passage. Both Taliesin and Bedwyr dismounted to examine a series of horse tracks that they found on patches of softer earth. Two horses had galloped off in one direction, heading back towards Glastonbury, while another set of tracks showed that one horse had cantered away on a path running parallel to the river.

'Ignore the trail of the two horses,' Bedwyr grunted. 'You can see how much shallower the indentations are than the single hoof prints. Those two horses have no riders, and they've been set loose to lead any searchers astray. There's a keen intelligence at work that devises diversionary tactics without knowing whether we are in pursuit.'

'So we'll follow the single track,' Artor stated grimly.

The king's retinue remained prudently silent.

Gawayne was uncharacteristically introspective as the troop returned along the riverbank.

Finally, when they were once more close to Salinae Minor, he approached the king and begged his pardon. Then, hesitantly, and with eyes that couldn't meet those of his master, he explained his experiences at the strange island in the centre of the river.

Taliesin noticed that Gawayne took care to remain beyond the reach of Artor's sword arm.

When Gawayne had finally run out of words, Artor pulled on the reins of his horse until he faced his nephew. He pushed his horse as close as possible to Gawayne's beast, grimaced, and then struck Gawayne across the face with his gloved fist. Dumbstruck but little hurt, Gawayne was tumbled from his horse by the force of the blow and landed squarely on his plump backside.

'Are you a complete cloth-head, Gawayne? No! Don't bother to answer! We've wasted a day in the saddle while the black warrior has probably run to ground on this damned island of yours. Shite!'

Gawayne scrambled to his feet, his dignity in tatters. With a horseman's ease, he leapt on to the back of his horse, taking care to remain beyond Artor's reach. Artor turned his back on his nephew, leaving Gawayne looking unhappy and ashamed.

'I was deceived, uncle. But when have I ever been able to resist the ladies?'

'You have a grown son, Gawayne! You're no longer a boy who smiles charmingly and expects to be forgiven for the most heinous of crimes. In this case, we rode right past a place that could harbour a murderer and what did you do? Nothing!'

'I was embarrassed . . .'

'Is that sufficient reason to send your king on a wild-goose chase?'

'No, but we did find the black warrior's accomplices.'

Uncharacteristically, Artor spat on the stony ground in disgust and stared down along the banks of the river.

'I disliked the place,' Galahad interjected piously. 'But Father found the lady to be particularly pleasant company.'

Both Gawayne and Artor stared at the young man's complacent face with amazement, reproach and disgust.

'Galahad!' Gawayne warned.

'And you failed to tell your king that she has a squat servant whose body is covered with woad tattoos,' Galahad finished with a triumphant flourish. 'I never trusted those pagans.'

Artor furiously kicked at his mount's ribs, causing it to rear and whinny shrilly, while Gawayne stared at his horse's mane as if the earth was about to swallow him.

'You always think with what hangs between your legs, nephew,' Artor admonished the prince. 'You're lucky I don't knock you on your arse again.'

Galahad smirked at his father's discomfiture, but he'd reckoned without Artor's sense of fairness.

'As for you, young Galahad,' the king began, one lip curling derisively. 'A son who tells tales on his father with such obvious pleasure has neither honour nor respect. I may chastise your father, for I am his liege lord. You are not! You, too, neglected to tell me of your visit to Salinae Minor, so take care that I don't punish you for your failure towards me *and* towards your father.'

Galahad's cheeks reddened, whether with shame or anger it was impossible to tell, but to Gawayne's relief the boy chose to remain silent.

The king forced his lips to remain regal and firm, disguising his contempt; Artor had little time for sanctimony and hypocrisy, least of all in one who lacked respect towards his elders.

'The lady's servant is called Gronw,' Gawayne said, as much to break the uncomfortable silence as to provide more detail. 'He is an unpleasant creature but I doubt he'd risk returning to the island if he is the black warrior. But he does have tattoos . . . he's pagan . . . and he's very short and quite squat.'

Gawayne quailed under the king's jaundiced expression.

'It's time I met this lady who's been banished from her own home to set up house on my doorstep,' Artor said decisively. 'I'll also enjoy meeting this Gronw person.' He smiled as a more pleasant thought occurred to him. 'Besides, if the villa has been built in the Roman fashion, it may have a bath. I'd kill for a chance to remove the grime from my body.'

Galahad sniffed. Like all good men beyond the Wall, he wasn't entirely sure that daily bathing was either healthy or manly. However, he could hardly accuse the High King of being a sybarite.

Artor knew exactly what the young man was thinking, and he was quietly amused. He booted his horse into a gallop and his warriors were forced to hasten to catch up with him.

That's torn it, Gawayne cursed mentally. Galahad will be the death of me, especially if Miryll tries her tricks with Artor.

Alerted by the message mirrors, a small flotilla of coracles and skiffs soon left the island of Salinae Minor and were rowed to the banks of the river where Artor and his party waited. To Gawayne's heartfelt relief, Gronw was nowhere in sight. Against his inclination and his nature, the Otadini prince felt pangs of responsibility, an unfamiliar and unpleasant sensation that he had avoided for most of his adult life.

As the villa and its gardens came into view, Artor's spirits lifted. If he ignored the looming tower, Salinae Minor could have been a pocket version of the Villa Poppinidii where he had grown to manhood. The High King realized that he was homesick.

'I'm getting old, Odin,' he remarked quietly to his bodyguard.

'Yes,' Odin replied in his calm, economical fashion.

'Am I finished, Odin?' Artor put one foot on the prow of the simple fishing craft and stared at his boot. His relaxed posture gave no hint of the sad nostalgia that coloured his thoughts.

'Not yet, Artor. There's still red work for us to do, and golden days like this one to enjoy.'

Artor laughed without mirth. 'That's your weird Jutlander instinct speaking, I suppose.' He sighed. 'Death never stops and the goddess of war is only taking a moment's rest. I suppose I shall die like Caesar did, killed by friends for the good of the realm.'

'This island has a bad smell, my lord,' Odin warned.

The High King paid attention, for Odin's instincts, Jute or otherwise, were rarely wrong.

Artor hadn't ridden to war for twenty years, but skirmishes occurred somewhere along his borders every year after the weather began to warm – when the 'Saxon summers' returned. It was inevitable when two civilizations rubbed against each other in such close proximity. Small sores were bound to form at points on the landscape where the two cultures were in direct conflict. Still, Artor pondered Odin's promise of future battles. Out and out warfare was ugly and destructive, but then so was the toadying, deceitful game of words and jockeying that took place in politics.

At the small wooden dock, Lady Miryll waited with her servants, bearing trays of wine and sweetmeats. A house servant approached the king and his courtiers.

'No one is permitted to carry arms on Salinae Minor, my lord,' the slave said nervously.

Artor recognized the man's status as a slave by the iron collar that was bolted round his throat, and the king was forced to smother a sharp exclamation of disgust. Artor had always detested slavery, partly for long-dead Frith's sake, but mostly because it destroyed the soul of both master and servant. As if reading his master's mind, Odin gently eased the servant out of Artor's path.

'The High King of the Britons and his guard always remain armed,' Gareth replied gravely. 'We are his bodyguard and we do not disarm for any person, friend or foe.'

'And I do not relinquish the sword of the High King to any hand other than my sword bearer, Gruffydd, who remains at your village,' Artor stated clearly so that the mistress could easily hear him. 'I would consider any such demand an insult and a slur upon my honour.'

The servant scuttled back to the lady where he whispered Artor's response.

Miryll's face didn't change, but remained as smooth and featureless as an egg. Then she smiled and Artor felt her glamour for the first time. His eyes became flat and wary.

He responded to Miryll's deep obeisance with a courtly bow, and they exchanged words of welcome that were gracious, empty and elegant.

At Artor's back, Odin's expression was frozen.

As Miryll led the way to the villa through the terraced gardens, Artor drew pleasure from the Roman order that she had imposed on the British flora. Her gently swaying hips invited his attention, but the sense of geometry and peace that he found in the typical Roman garden brought him far greater satisfaction.

He said as much to Lady Miryll and she bowed her thanks.

As the villa came into view, Artor's experienced eyes perceived subtle differences from Livinia Major's style. The sculptures were sophisticated and depicted such violent, antique subjects as the rape of the Sabine women and imaginary scenes of Jupiter and his inamorata. Violent sexual activity was subtly celebrated, but overall there was a clutter of ostentation, too many fountains and too much colour in a display that wasn't quite pleasing to the eye.

But Artor was inclined to be generous on this bright day, so he forgave Salinae Minor its slightly jarring imperfections and determined to enjoy the good will and luxury that it offered.

The simple elegance of the villa's atrium gave Artor great pleasure. The lady's father must have enjoyed enormous wealth, for even the Villa Poppinidii with its vast resources had only a simple bronze fish to decorate its fountain. Miryll's father had commissioned a large statue of an erotic half-fish, half-woman, with a tail and spiked fins along her spine. The figure was set amidst a profusion of fanciful shells that filled a large marble bowl.

'Do you like our fountain, great lord?' Miryll asked. 'My father took pride in his Roman ancestry, so perhaps you'll find our ways a little strange.'

Miryll was a practised flirt. Her full attention was aimed directly at the High King and her smile was as brilliant as the light reflecting from her enormous, doe-brown eyes. But Artor had been pursued by many of the most beautiful women in western Britain for decades, so he was more than equal to the arts of seduction. In fact, her shy glances and fluttering hands were a little too feminine and artless; Artor felt a need to count his fingers and toes to reassure himself they were still firmly attached to his body.

'Not strange at all, Lady Miryll. I was raised by a Roman family and have always been thankful for the advantages I gained from my childhood. My home was a rural Roman estate outside Aquae Sulis. In fact, I have longed for a Roman bath for some time and I hoped you'd have your own hypocaust.'

A momentary shadow passed fleetingly over Lady Miryll's features. She hadn't expected Artor to be more Roman than herself.

Artor had been watchful all his life, and he noticed the widening of the pupils that revealed her discomfort.

'Of course, Your Majesty. The baths are at your disposal. But surely your visit is for some more pressing reason than the luxuries of my villa?' Then she coloured and covered her mouth with one hand, her eyes wide with embarrassment. 'I beg your pardon, my lord. It's not for a mere woman to question the intentions of the High King. You reign over the west, so you're entitled to come and go as you please.'

Methinks you are trying to be clever with me, Lady Miryll, or whoever you are, Artor thought, while his lips framed the graceful, empty words that brushed away her feigned, or accidental, discourtesy. You're not truly Roman, for all your protestations. I make you nervous, because you think I might see through that lovely façade you present to your guests.

The baths were not extensive, but the sides and bottom were lined with fine marble and were beautifully appointed. Artor thoroughly enjoyed the use of perfumed oils and a strigil, the calidarium, the frigidarium, a tepidarium and the pleasure of a very close shave by his servant, Odin. Artor trusted no one else to place a naked blade against his throat.

Dressed in a spare tunic that was neither regal nor ostentatious, Artor's quality still shone through his careless appearance. Apart from Taliesin and Odin, the king was far taller than any other man in his retinue and he dwarfed the lady's servants, while his measured tread and calm, imposing face impressed. Even his faded hair retained a memory of its tawny beauty and the curls hadn't thinned with age. The twins and Galahad seemed mere children in his presence and, by comparison, Gawayne became a cheeky, middle-aged libertine.

Lady Miryll's eyes widened slightly as she stared at him from her dining couch. Artor knew that particular pretence of guilelessness and sexual attraction only too well, just as he recognized the raw invitation that lay under it. Inwardly, the king chuckled. Gawayne must have been like warm, malleable clay in Miryll's hands.

Unlike his companions, Artor reclined on the Roman divan as naturally as if he had done so every day of his life. Percivale prepared to act as cup bearer and taster and, if Miryll was insulted by the king's lack of trust, her smooth face hid her feelings. The rest of the company of lords managed to drape themselves awkwardly over the dining couches of the triclinium.

Taliesin waited unobtrusively against one of the walls, cradling his great harp in its woollen cocoon.

The meal of exotic delicacies began. Balan and Gawayne ate freely but Balyn and Galahad eyed the small stuffed birds with horror and waved the dishes away. For different reasons, each man was iconoclastic in his tastes, and Galahad chose to embrace simple meals in the belief that he followed in the footsteps of his carpenter lord, Jesus.

Balyn's mercurial nature gave him a vivid imagination, and he could see the process of plucking thrushes, stuffing them with wild mushrooms and then inserting them into the breasts of pigeons with more minced offal, herbs and water chestnuts inside a larger peacock. He was repulsed by the whole process, but excited by it as well.

Had Artor been capable of seeing the rapid images that coursed through Balyn's mind, he would have been concerned. The young man was frequently tortured by graphic mind-pictures, and he acted precipitously in response. Simplicity drew him because simplicity offered quiet and peace.

Percivale tasted each complex dish and drank the clean water that Artor chose, while Balan declared that the wine was exceptionally good and asked the lady where she had found it.

Miryll laughed graciously. The mellow beauty of her voice was both a promise and a caress, but Artor was pleased to see that Balan was unmoved.

'Our island is small and we are remote, Lord Balan, but we aren't barbarians. Personally, I have never enjoyed the heavy red wines that my father loved, so my servants purchase the sweet white wines of southern Gaul. I am glad you enjoy my choices.'

Artor ate sparingly, using a narrow blade. His fingers rarely touched his food and Galahad was surprised by the High King's easy assumption of Roman manners throughout the meal. As he struggled with a joint of waterfowl that Artor had neatly spitted and divided for him, Galahad wondered if, perhaps, he had been too hasty in his snap judgement that Artor was just another version of his grandfather, King Lot.

As young men often do, Galahad had relegated all persons over forty to the scrapheap of old age. His grandfather was simply a fond, fat man who lived like most Celts, and was neither particularly clean nor learned. In truth, Galahad found it difficult to imagine that either King Lot or his queen had ever been powerful people. They were his grandparents, and so very old.

These same prejudices were transferred to Galahad's view of his great-uncle. No doubt Artor had once been a mighty warrior and a clever king, but those years were long gone. In his youthful arrogance and Celtic scorn for all other races, Galahad had scarcely seen the real man below the grey curls. Because Artor permitted pagans to practise their faith, Galahad had further damned the High King as barbaric and amoral.

Now, he was forced to recognize that Artor was genuinely sophisticated and, what was more impressive, completely immune to the charms of Lady Miryll. As far as Galahad could see, Artor was neither pagan nor Christian, and expected a high moral code from all faiths. With a pang, Galahad began to face his own inadequacies. He was ignorant of other religions and civilizations, even the people of his lord, Jesus. So, carefully, he began to emulate Artor's economical, graceful movements.

'Who is the young servant in the corner, my lord?' Lady Miryll asked, one white hand languidly indicating Taliesin and the other placed familiarly on Artor's forearm. As she leaned towards him, Artor glimpsed her full, white breasts.

'He's no servant, Lady Miryll,' Artor answered calmly, as Taliesin stepped forward into the light to be introduced to her. 'This young man is the son of Myrddion Merlinus, who was the wisest seer in all of Britain. His mother is Nimue, the Lady of the Lake, who is a woman of extraordinary beauty and brilliance. As befits any child of Myrddion, Taliesin comes and goes as he pleases.'

'I've heard of the great Myrddion.' She smiled at Taliesin. 'Was your father truly a shape-shifter, as men say he was?'

Taliesin frowned briefly and raised his head. His hair was neatly combed and was nearly as long as the unbound locks of his hostess. It was certainly thicker and darker than hers.

'Lady, my father had no need to change his human form. However, he could foresee what might happen in the future. He read souls from the faces of their owners, he healed the sick and he helped to change the west. So why would he have any need for paltry tricks of magic?'

Taliesin's expression was courteous and was designed to take the sting from his message, but his words exposed Miryll's lack of genuine respect for her guests. Miryll blushed becomingly and lowered her long eyelashes, so the men in the room, with three notable exceptions, forgave her for everything.

Taliesin turned back to Artor, breaking the spell.

'Would you have me sing for the lady's pleasure, Lord Artor?'

Artor nodded, so Taliesin drew the harp out of its woollen nest with exaggerated ceremony. From the first stir of the strings, the diners were captivated.

The first song spoke of Nimue's loom and the wonders she wrought on it. Without a trace of her earlier artifice, Miryll became lost in the music and Gawayne remembered her description of her 'own window on the world'.

The harp seemed to mimic the thud of the shuttle and the hum of warp and weft as Taliesin coaxed the instrument to show the brilliance of his father's vision as it emerged on the loom. Again and again, the harp thrummed and vibrated, until the rapt audience could almost see Nimue's woollen hanging, pregnant with symbols and unknown images.

Then as this song finished, Taliesin made the harp weep and wail, like a woman who has lost her heart's desire forever. He sang of his father's blind, white eyes staring skyward on his high bier, of the storms that raged around the mountains when he perished and of Nimue's demented wanderings and madness. So much love was poured into strings and vocal cords that the lady wept, in spite of her attempts at self-control. As he watched her out of the corner of his eye, Artor began to like her the better for her empathy.

Finally, Taliesin sang of the coming of the king in such picturesque language that Gawayne was forced to slap his thigh and laugh as he relived that mad ride of his youth when he had raced the young Artorex to Glastonbury. Once again, his futile attempts to reach the sword that had been buried in the stone of the tower were celebrated with laughter. In glorious pomp and ceremony, the song came to its conclusion, and all present felt the golden shadows of those long-gone times.

The silence, when it came, continued to vibrate with images of the past.

'Your mother must have truly loved Myrddion Merlinus,' Miryll said seriously, her rich voice still raw with emotion.

'And she loves him still,' Taliesin replied. 'I believe that their love has transcended death.'

The lady leaned forward, her eyes unnaturally bright. 'What do you mean?'

'My mother swears that Myrddion comes to her at night, or when she calls him at times of need.'

'But how can such a thing be? No one can thwart death.'

Taliesin smiled distantly. 'I'm certain in my own mind that

purity of heart and love transcends everything for those few who are hand-fasted forever. My parents overcame age, the expectations of the world and the power of mighty men to swear their wedding vows to each other. For them, death was simply one more obstacle to overcome through the strength of their love.'

'I've never known such an intensity of love,' the lady replied sadly. 'And I suppose I never shall.'

The men around the table examined their hands, unsure how to act or what to say. They themselves did not fully understand Taliesin's words.

'I did, but once, and then fleetingly,' Artor remembered slowly. 'Once experienced, such a love is never forgotten.'

Miryll turned towards the High King, her eyes full of questions. Artor saw no artifice in them and wondered at how much her beauty grew when she was herself.

'Has Lady Wenhaver always been your great love, my lord?'

Odin stirred angrily behind his king, and Artor felt the pressure of his huge knee in the small of his back.

'Be careful,' Odin seemed to be saying with that gentle pressure.

Artor was, as always, diplomatic.

'No, mistress, Queen Wenhaver has never been my great love, for arranged marriages rarely induce that madness in the blood that is called passion,' he replied softly, with regret in his voice. 'However, I enjoyed a young man's romance many years ago, and it was no less powerful or pure for all my relative youth. Young men often enjoy a brief, first love. As it happened, that beloved girl returned to the earth that formed her before she became a grown woman, but I never forgot her.'

He sighed. 'Her memory still haunts my dreams, but I am grateful that I knew such an early passion, even though it was only for the briefest time.'

'Did you marry her, lord, and know the completeness of desire?' Miryll asked. Several of Artor's men looked shocked at the lady's presumption and Gawayne was inclined to be insulted on his king's behalf.

Odin's knee pressed harder into Artor's back.

'I was a landless man, and young men in my situation are rarely permitted to marry their beloved,' Artor replied, and few noticed the ambiguity in his answer.

The pressure from Odin's knee relaxed.

Miryll sighed. 'How sad to love so deeply but never know the felicity of marriage with that person.'

As her eyes dropped in contemplation, the dangerous moment almost passed. To break the mood of melancholy that was threatening to dampen the spirit of the dinner, and to divert any close examination of his words, Artor raised his wine cup.

'Let us drink to love, whether we are old or young. Fortuna judges what we deserve by the measure of our hearts. I wish love to you all.'

The men, with the exceptions of Artor's bodyguard and Taliesin, rose and lifted their cups to their lips.

Miryll also raised her silver goblet.

'To love!' they roared, and laughter soon replaced the mood of a feast that had been in danger of maudlin sentimentality. Wine flowed, and love soon became the chief topic of conversation for the men, while Miryll blushed, giggled and entranced the warriors with ease.

Shortly afterwards, she excused herself gracefully and left the men to their drinking.

Artor also left the dining chamber early, for there was much for his suspicious brain to mull over. The island's mistress had provided much more than good food and drink to occupy his thoughts. He also knew that his bodyguards needed relief, so they could eat their own meals in the kitchens and take turns to rest from their duties.

Escaping from the revelry, Taliesin decided to stroll through the quiet gardens where the sound of Artor's retinue, still drinking and gorging, could no longer be heard. The young Cymru poet looked up at the strange tower and was surprised to see an oil lamp sending out shafts of light through the open window slits. Periodically, the lamp was shuttered in the delivery of some kind of message. From his vantage point, Taliesin couldn't see the mainland and any answer to the insistent light.

Does the lady watch through the night? Taliesin wondered. Or does she speak to an enemy under cover of darkness?

After a few minutes, the light signals between the villa and the unknown ceased. Taliesin waited for some time, but the moon was beginning its downward slide towards morning, so the young man decided to retire to his bed. The corridors of the villa were maze-like and he felt disorientated by weariness and the moon's madness.

Suddenly, a thin, high cry echoed through the halls, and then was abruptly cut short.

Taliesin cursed under his breath and hurried in the direction of Artor's room. In his haste he tripped and fell over the shod feet of Gareth who was lying, unconscious, in the doorway.

'Help me, Mother,' Taliesin whispered as he struggled to pull the prone, unresponsive form of Gareth out of the way. He's been drugged, he thought wildly. But what of the king?

Taliesin pushed on the partly open door, expecting some resistance to his entry. He almost sprawled full length as the door gave inward easily and a shaft of light from the setting moon showed that the king's bed was empty.

Taliesin's heart rose in his throat. He heard his own frenzied breathing.

But the night was utterly still. Except for himself, the whole villa appeared to be asleep.

Taliesin ran across the inner court, dragging doors open and searching rooms as he went. In one room, a bleary-eyed Odin struggled to rise, while in another, Galahad cursed and searched for his weapon. Taliesin continued with his frantic quest, his thin sandals almost silent on the tiled floors as he retraced his steps.

At the end of a long corridor, a thin sliver of light beckoned from under a closed door.

Taliesin hit the door running and was immediately enclosed damply in a thick white mist.

The baths. I'm in the baths, he thought as he edged his way along the wall.

Behind him, the door closed of its own accord.

A flicker of white skin loomed out of the mist for a brief moment and then vanished with a low gurgle of laughter. Taliesin tasted danger like the rust of iron on his tongue. Such was his confusion that he almost fell blindly over Artor's feebly threshing legs. He could vaguely see a dark figure looming over the long body of the High King, holding Artor's head under the water.

Taliesin had no time to think. He lashed out with stiffened fingers strengthened by years of practice on harp strings and struck the enemy somewhere below the black cowl. The figure grunted, loosened its iron grip on Artor's shoulders and sprang back with one hand clawing at its throat.

Impelled by need, Taliesin turned his back on the dark figure. Every instinct told him to drag Artor from the hot water. So, with a strength he barely knew he possessed, Taliesin pulled his king by the ankles until the unconscious man lay prone and dripping on the wet tiles.

As he bent over Artor's body, Taliesin felt a stinging sensation along his upper arm and he fell backwards, with one hand searching automatically for the site of the pain.

The black figure came at him and Taliesin scrambled out of the way. As he struggled to his feet, his mind was beginning to compose his own death song, for he realized that he was unarmed and vulnerable. Then, like a dream slowed down to impossible, exquisite clarity, the door to the baths slammed open and a half-naked warrior charged into the room with a wild Otadini scream.

The black figure seemed to hunch in upon itself and then kicked once more at Artor's prone body, before leaping away into the densest part of the mist. The sound of footsteps skidding on wet tiles drifted back as Taliesin threw himself towards the king's prone body.

He turned him on to his back. Artor's upturned face seemed unnaturally white and still. A great bruise marred the side of his brow, oozing a thin line of blood where the skin had broken. The king did not appear to be breathing.

Taliesin began to beat on Artor's chest with the whole force of his body. The ribs of a lesser man could easily have broken, but a few gulps of air began to surge in and out of Artor's lungs within a few moments. The ragged breaths were accompanied by a thin trickle of water.

The king's breathing stopped.

'Do something!' Galahad screamed in panic, quite oblivious to his half-naked state. His drawn sword was pointed directly at Taliesin's throat.

'My father often breathed into the mouths of newly-born infants who weren't able to breathe for themselves.'

'In God's name, do it then!'

With silent apologies to his king, Taliesin took a deep breath and, fixing his mouth to Artor's lips, blew air deep into the lungs of the king.

Galahad dropped his sword, and expelled the air from Artor's body by pushing down on his ribs in a duplication of Taliesin's original actions.

With another mental apology to his king, Taliesin slapped Artor across the cheek with his open hand. Artor drew a short, involuntary breath and began to cough hoarsely and uncontrollably. Gouts of water gushed from his open mouth and nostrils.

Over several minutes, Artor began to breathe raggedly by himself, but he was still barely conscious. Taliesin sighed gratefully, and then was surprised as the room began to tilt violently.

'You're bleeding like a slaughtered hog,' Galahad pointed out. 'You'd best tie your wound off. The tiles are already slippery enough without your blood making them worse.'

'Am I bleeding?' Taliesin asked dully. Galahad began to tear a strip off the harpist's robe to fashion a rough bandage.

'I will need some help to return the king to his room,' Galahad said, as he attempted to lift Artor's bulk with a painful grunt.

'I'll join you shortly, Galahad,' Taliesin replied. 'The villa isn't secured yet.' His knees felt like jelly.

'If you must go, take Artor's knife with you. It's over there, beside the brazier.' Galahad's keen eyes had sought out the dragon knife, kicked into a corner during the earlier struggle between Artor and his assailant.

Breathing deeply, and with his head slowly clearing, Taliesin ventured into the mist that he now realized came from the brazier and whatever rubbish was smouldering on it. Only the constant drip of water remained to intrude into the wet silence once Galahad had staggered away, half-dragging and half-carrying the king's sodden body.

I'm hunting blind, Taliesin thought irrelevantly as he moved out of the mist and into a room where the bath was filled with cold water.

The spoor of several pairs of wet footprints skirted the pool and disappeared through a door beyond the bath. One set of prints was booted and one was bare.

Cautiously, Taliesin began to follow the footprints.

When he passed through the next doorway, he found a dressing room where a number of wet towels lay in puddles on the floor or had been tossed over rough wooden benches. The footprints continued onwards, although they were already beginning to dry.

Beyond this chamber, a door led to a narrow vestibule and

an exit from the villa. A set of man-sized footprints led out on to the dewy grass. But the vestibule also contained a flight of stairs that coiled upwards. On the third step, a small puddle glinted like a blind eye.

At the threshold of the door to the gardens, a single black glove lay like the discarded skin of some diseased reptile.

Taliesin picked it up gingerly, conscious that a slow trickle of blood was still dripping from the fingers of his left hand. What to do? He cautiously mounted the stairs until he reached a round room at the top of the tower.

Lady Miryll lay beneath a fur coverlet on a bed-shaped block of stone. Her head turned as he entered and she looked directly at him with unfathomable eyes. He presented a strange sight with matted hair, wet and blood-soaked clothing, and his normally pale skin as white as the waning moon. But she remained composed and seemed unsurprised by his condition.

Wordlessly, she lifted the corner of the covers as if offering herself to him. Under the furs, the lady's naked body was alabaster-pale and very beautiful but Taliesin was repulsed, as if he had been shown so much sacrificial meat. He rubbed his hand over his tired eyes and, when he looked at her again, Miryll had pulled the furs up to her pointed chin.

'Has anyone come this way, my lady?' Taliesin croaked.

'No. I've seen nobody.' She smiled endearingly at him. 'May I help you? You seem unwell.'

'Were you in the baths just now? I thought I saw you leaving.'

She lifted one black tress of hair to her lips as if to taste its wetness. 'I was there about an hour ago. Why do you ask?'

'Forgive me, my lady,' he stared suspiciously at her, 'but

there's been an attempt on the life of the king from inside your house.'

Miryll's eyes flared, but Taliesin felt that she was surprised by his choice of words.

'Does the king still live?' Miryll asked softly as she reached for a small silver bell. 'Surely no one here would wish to harm the High King of the Britons.'

'The king lives,' Taliesin responded carefully.

'Then Fortuna may yet save us. You must excuse me, my lord, for I must dress.'

Once again, Miryll rang her small bell to summon her handmaidens, an action that surprised Taliesin for he hadn't seen anyone as he was mounting the tower stairs.

Taliesin left the room and staggered down to ground level, pressing his body to the wall as a wide-eyed and terrified serving woman suddenly materialized and ran past him in the direction of the tower room. He made his way through the baths and along the corridors that were already boiling with servants and armed warriors until he reached the doorway that led to Artor's room.

'So there you are, Taliesin.' Galahad pushed a disorientated Gareth out of the way and stripped off Artor's sodden clothes. 'I was about to send out a search party to find you.' Although the tone of his voice was gruff, his relief at Taliesin's safety was clear. 'Can you help me with Artor? He's not the lightest person to manhandle.'

As Taliesin moved forward to assist Galahad, Odin surged through the door, shaking his ursine head in confusion and rage. The huge Jutlander had bared his axe and his eyes glittered with the deep-red glow of madness.

'Don't touch the king!' Odin roared.

Taliesin put one bloody hand on Odin's chest.

'You can put down your axe, Odin. Artor lives, largely because of Galahad's efforts. Your master must be stripped, warmed and put to bed so that I can examine his head wound.'

'And who'll minister to you, harpist?' Odin growled, but his eyes were returning to their usual faded shade of blue.

'I will survive. I've managed to stop most of the bleeding.' He turned to the still confused Gareth, slumped on a bench in a corner of the room. He looked deathly ill.

'I suggest you go outside and put your fingers down your throat, Gareth,' Taliesin ordered him. 'It'll serve to remove most of the poison from your blood.'

'I failed our master, Odin,' Gareth mumbled and rubbed his wounded face as if to rob it of the drug that continued to call him back towards sleep. 'I left him in a position where he was vulnerable to attack.'

'Get outside, Gareth,' Taliesin repeated. 'Throwing up can't hurt you, and it'll make you feel better.'

'Who did this treason?' Odin asked in a quiet voice so deadly that Taliesin felt a surge of pity for any unfortunate creature the Jutlander suspected of causing harm to his master.

'One of the culprits managed to leave this glove behind him as he fled,' Taliesin responded. He threw the black leather glove on to a chair where it lay deflated, like a severed hand. 'Galahad was correct. This villa was the lair of the black warrior.'

Then, for the first time in his life, Taliesin fainted clean away.

CHAPTER VIII

OLD SINS AND WASTED LIVES

The song-master wasn't unconscious for long. Someone had shoved a piece of soft, folded cloth under his head and another had stripped off his torn robe and exposed his smooth chest and shoulder. They were now hurting him a great deal by probing his wound.

'Let me up,' Taliesin hissed through his clenched teeth. 'I'll stitch myself together, thank you.'

'You sound just like your father, Taliesin.' The hoarse voice was Artor's. 'You must forgive Percivale, because I ordered him to discover the extent of your injuries. Shite, boy! If you die on me, I'll never know exactly what happened tonight. Fact is, I don't remember a thing after I entered the baths.'

Percivale flushed with embarrassment and handed Taliesin the damp cloth that he had been using to clean a deep slice across the muscle of Taliesin's upper arm.

'May I have my pack from my room, Percivale? And a spare robe. The wound seems clean, but it's very deep and the edges need to be sewn together. My assailant retaliated with his blade after I hit him in the throat.'

'Who was he?' Artor's voice seemed sharper and more focused than before.

Taliesin struggled to his feet, discarded the rags of his robe and saw a still-shaky Artor seated on the side of his sleeping couch.

'I don't know, but I saw the vague shape of a naked person running through the baths.'

Artor looked totally mystified. His brow was furrowed and he winced as a lance of pain ran through his head. 'Some noise surely woke me, but it sounded like knocking at the door. I took my knife and almost fell over Gareth in the corridor. When he didn't wake up, I knew that something was dangerously wrong. Fool that I am, I managed to set myself up like a tethered goat, rather than calling for the guard. I recall hearing a strange, gurgling laugh around the corner of the corridor, so I followed the sounds. And I seem to remember seeing a light,' Artor murmured, as he stared off into the distance and struggled to recall the events of the early morning.

'The light was in the baths,' Taliesin told him. 'That was how I found you. Do you recall hearing a scream?'

'I remember a thick, foul-smelling mist as if something green had been thrown on the brazier. Gods, I couldn't even see my own hands in front of me. But I heard something, so I struck out at it and then the roof seemed to fall in on my head.'

'Then you must have managed to strike your attacker,' Taliesin said. 'Did you use your knife? Or your open hand?'

'I used my fist.'

Galahad interrupted the conversation. 'You heard the scream, Taliesin. Was it a man? Or a woman?'

'I *think* it was a woman.'

'So where, then, is Lady Miryll?' All of Galahad's prejudices were evident in his distrustful eyes.

'She was dressing when I left her in the tower to return to your room, my lord,' Taliesin answered. 'She should have joined us by now.'

'Damn and shite!' Artor cursed. 'This is her villa. Who else would know best what is going on within these walls? I've waited long enough. Any innocent host would have been knocking at my door as soon as they heard of the attack.' Artor seemed re-energized now that he had an enemy to pursue. 'Odin! Galahad! Find this woman and bring her to the atrium. Search wherever you wish, and use whatever force is necessary. This villa is a snake pit.'

'When I left her in her tower, I noticed that her hair was damp,' Taliesin added slowly and with a degree of regret. Miryll was too young and too beautiful to die for the sin of treason.

'I think we can accept that she's involved in some way in this attempt on my life.' Artor's voice was silky and implacable.

'But she wasn't the person who tried to drown you, sire, and I doubt she struck you either. Those sins may be laid at the door of the man dressed in black.'

'Galahad told me I was unconscious and you saved my life by dragging me from the bath. He insists that I would be dead were it not for your intervention. I thank you for your courage.'

Percivale re-entered the chamber with Taliesin's light pack in his hands. Taliesin fished out a leather bag and withdrew items of medical equipment.

'We each serve as best we can, my lord,' he replied awkwardly. He found a needle and a length of thin gut inside his pack. Oblivious to the shocked stares of Artor and Gawayne, who had just entered the room, Taliesin began to stitch together the gaping wound in his arm.

'Do you have to do your needlework right now, Taliesin?' Gawayne complained testily. 'My stomach and my head are quite queasy enough without such a sight this early in the day. Why are we all awake anyway? And why are the guards in from the stables? What's going on?'

'I don't know how you've managed to sleep through all the fuss and noise, Gawayne,' Artor said ruefully. 'There has been an attempt to assassinate me. Galahad was right when he said that this place was poisonous.'

'Don't be ridiculous!' Gawayne retorted, only half awake. 'Lady Miryll can hardly be the black warrior.'

Galahad returned in time to hear his father's last comments. He gave an expressive shrug.

'What?' Gawayne asked. 'What's the matter?'

Gareth entered the room considerably paler than when he had left it, but now he was almost alert.

'You look like a sickening cat! What's wrong with you?' Gawayne aimed his frustration squarely at Gareth, who simply managed to look miserable.

'Gareth and Odin have both been drugged, Gawayne, and an attempt has been made to drown me,' Artor explained. 'Lady Miryll appears to be implicated, but it's equally possible that she was simply the tasty bait in a honey trap set by conspirators.'

Gawayne gaped.

Odin stepped silently into the room.

'So, Odin, what have you discovered?' Artor asked.

'We found Lady Miryll as she was about to board a skiff to leave the island. A few more moments and both she and her maid would have been gone. They would have escaped easily, but she delayed herself by pausing to collect jewels and clothing that she'd packed beforehand. Greed and vanity have caught more men and women than hatred', Odin intoned. 'And you'll be interested to know that the lady has a fresh bruise on her breastbone.'

Artor's lips set like stone. So he must have struck the lady in the bathing room during the assassination attempt. Miryll wasn't simply a honey trap, she was an assassin.

'Where are they now?'

'As you instructed, the captives are under guard in the atrium', Odin replied with a satisfied grin. Within the tangle of his reddish beard, his brown and crooked canines seemed even more predatory than usual. 'The mistress of Salinae Minor has a foul tongue, my lord', he added conversationally.

'Your information does not surprise me, Odin. The lady is not a lady'. Artor turned his attention back to Taliesin. 'Are you finished your sewing yet, song-master? If I'm to think clearly and pursue some reasonable explanation from Lady Miryll, I'll need to have my head wound examined and have my wits about me.'

Taliesin snipped off the last piece of gut with his sharp knife and climbed to his feet.

'Aye, my lord, I've finished treating my wound.'

He found a tunic in his pack and pulled it over his head.

'Now, my lord'. He grinned at Artor. 'How many fingers do you see when I hold my hand before your eyes?'

✝ ✝ ✝

Artor allowed the nervous imaginations of Miryll and her servants to stretch out painfully while they were held in the atrium. For Artor, an hour or two meant a light doze and physical renewal. For the captives, it was a period of increasing tension as they contemplated their separate fates.

The king finally entered the atrium, sipping a cup of hot water with a little honey spooned in for warmth. Even with salve smeared on his forehead, the king still looked rested and physically strong. Behind him, his bodyguard and the lords of his retinue seemed far more worn and queasy.

Artor seated himself negligently on a conveniently placed marble bench where he could watch both the fountain and Lady Miryll. He noticed immediately that the neckline of her gown was sagging open, revealing the edges of a growing bruise. Her eyes were furtive and frightened, although she attempted to appear calm and regal.

'I bid you a fair morning, Lady Miryll,' he greeted her conversationally. 'How old do you think I am?'

The lady's brown eyes became muddy with dislike, and her hands pressed together with such force that her knuckles shone whitely.

'You're far too *old*,' she retorted unpleasantly. 'Ugly, disgusting, arrogant and *old*!'

Artor smiled with such convincing sincerity that Taliesin's blood ran cold. He remembered his father, Myrddion Merlinus, speaking of Uther Pendragon's last, bitter days; Artor showed no signs of degenerating into the violent monster his father had been, but perhaps he was becoming something worse.

189 ✝

'I congratulate you on your self-control, woman.' Artor's tone hardened. 'You seemed perfectly at ease in my presence last night when you were parading your body for my appreciation, yet I've come to realize that you must hate me and all I stand for. Am I correct, Lady Miryll? If such is truly your name.'

'I am Ceridwen!' she hissed. 'I am the maid, the mother and the hag! You are nothing, and you have no legitimacy! Your reign is a sham!'

Indrawn breaths were the only response from the ring of men. Such arrogance and blasphemy were shocking.

Taliesin took an involuntary step forward. 'You're not my great-grandam!'

The charged tension was released by Artor's booming laughter. He explained to the gathered warriors that a legend persisted in the west that Myrddion Merlinus was a direct descendant of the goddess, which, if true, would make Taliesin her great-grandchild.

Artor looked at Miryll. 'You may pretend to be whatever, or whoever, gives you comfort. I really don't care, but Taliesin might object to your choice if you're claiming him as your kin.'

Lady Miryll spat inaccurately towards Artor. Her face was twisted with hatred.

'I'm disappointed.' Artor spoke conversationally. 'I've been searching for grand plots and conspiracies among my enemies, and what have I found? A foolish woman who thinks she's a goddess. A stupid, ignorant woman who has been the tool of ruthless men who care so little for her that they have abandoned her to my justice.'

Lady Miryll spat again, her eyes wild.

'You have a lovely face, my lady, but terrible manners. Didn't your mother school you better?'

Miryll whitened at the mention of her dead mother.

'If your plan was to kill me, then it has failed, but only through the keen reactions of Taliesin, son of Myrddion of blessed memory, and because of the ineptitude of your accomplices. Still, failure is the greatest and the most damaging of faults, don't you agree?'

The lady's face contorted into such ugly lines of loathing that Gawayne was amazed that he'd ever considered her to be beautiful.

'Come, answer me, woman, for it's only my curiosity that's keeping you alive.'

'You are the fraud!' Miryll screamed out at last. 'There's no Roman blood flowing through *your* veins, but I'm descended from Augustus and, through him, back to the Caesar himself.'

'Not that old, tired refrain again.' Artor shook his head. 'I'm very disappointed in you, Lady Miryll. Are you just another moon-mad claimant to the throne of the west, or do you have some deluded desire to restore the Roman Empire? Or, crazier still, do you truly think you're a goddess?

'My father, the Pendragon, was the son of Constantine II and the grandson of the great Maximus. No Roman blood, Miryll? But, I am proud of my mixed heritage, for I am Briton first and last.'

Artor gazed sorrowfully into Miryll's eyes as if she were a child, caught stealing by a concerned parent. The mock affection on his face was more shocking than a stinging slap.

'Gawayne, my nephew, has a far more worthy heritage than you, Miryll. And Galahad has a legitimate claim. In addition, he is a Christian, which would serve him well in any dispute in the south about his succession to the throne. I assume your father convinced you that your bloodline comes from some bastard son of Augustus. If so, he was misguided or deranged, for such a bloodline would be worth nothing in the west after all this time, even if it were true. The Rome of the Caesars is dead. In these isles, succession is always followed from the present king to the next person in line. I can't imagine the Celts accepting Julius Caesar himself, even if he could manage to escape from Hades.'

'The Bloody Cup will see you dead, Artor.' Miryll spat the words out. 'And that same Bloody Cup will christen my son and will drive all your followers into the sea. I follow the old ways and our cause will prevail.'

Miryll's speech had wiped the merriment out of Artor's eyes, a change that none of the warriors present considered propitious for the lady's health.

'So. Now we finally have your version of the truth. Of which old ways do you speak, Lady Miryll? Do you believe in the Tuatha de Danaan? Do you submit yourself to the laws of the Druids and the justice of the wicker man? Are you dedicated to the Roman gods? Or is it something older still?' The High King paused and gazed reflectively at the mermaid fountain. For a long moment, he seemed almost mesmerized by the steady, rhythmic flow of water. Then his grey, chill eyes turned back to Miryll, and Taliesin could read no pity in them.

'Or are you following blindly behind the aspirations of another?' Artor asked. 'I admit to wondering about the manner of man who pulls the strings that control a beautiful woman such as yourself.'

'You'll not know the truth until it's far too late to do anything about it.' She huddled triumphantly in her black cloak, all her voluptuousness leached from her face and her muffled body.

'So where is Gronw, Miryll? Where is your little priest?'

She started in surprise, but quickly recovered her self-control.

'He's not here,' she replied defiantly. 'He returned to his people.'

'The blue Picts from beyond the Wall?' Galahad interrupted, his voice laced with contempt. 'I thought the Celtic tribes had cleared those vermin out of civilized country, but it doesn't surprise me that Gronw is a heathen, slimy Pict. He's surely got the tattoos and the objectionable personality of the Picts. That lot are nothing but pagan scum for the Otadini to hunt down like mad dogs.'

Miryll's face whipped towards Galahad like the head of a striking snake. 'Even though you treat them like animals, you've failed to make them bend their knees to you. My mother was Gronw's mistress, and she was a Pictish queen! You didn't know *that*, did you? Her ancestors ruled these isles long before the Celts and the Romans came here. She led my vain father around like a bull with a ring through his nose.'

'Then you have my sympathy,' Galahad retorted. 'It's no wonder your father ultimately removed her head.'

Gawayne felt a moment's pleasure in the cruel words of his son.

'Enough!' barked Artor. 'Galahad, instead of exercising your prejudices on Miryll, who seems to have been spun a concoction of lies for most of her life, you will send a rider at speed towards Aquae Sulis with instructions that our warriors are to scour the wildest routes between here and the Wall for Gronw. You know what he looks like, so make sure that he is forced to run like a rabbit. Or the rat that he more closely resembles!'

'That would be my pleasure, sire.' Galahad left the atrium with much dignity and self-importance.

The High King turned back to Miryll. 'Now that my impetuous young kinsman has gone, you might wish to tell me about your son. I'd like to know more about this infant who will take my place on the throne.'

'He's in a place where even you can't touch him,' she whispered and then placed her hands protectively over her belly. 'He's in here.'

'Of course he is,' Artor responded. 'The babe was fathered by Gawayne, I presume.' He did not wait for a response. 'Did he provide his seed willingly? I thought he had children enough.'

The lady's lips curled. 'His body was eager, for all that it's old. I had a preference for Galahad to sire my son, but that fool is drunk with his god. The father was much easier to manage and was very diligent in his task. I'm happy, for my child will be the end product of many royal bloodlines.'

'Artor, I swear I didn't intend to . . .'. Gawayne's voice trailed off, his stomach churning with bile. 'I know I was drugged, but I'll admit that I was willing enough. I beg your forgiveness, my lord.' Gawayne abased himself before his king. His eyes were filled with tears.

'If I was angry on every occasion that you bedded a slut, Gawayne, I would have burst into flames years ago. This woman was just a tasty morsel for you to dine on. I attach no blame to you, so stand up and stare her down. She's only a woman, and not a very clever one at that.'

Artor delivered his cruel taunt with such timing that his entire guard burst into raucous laughter. Every man present knew that Lord Gawayne chased anything that even pretended to be female. Taliesin winced at the contempt for women expressed in the men's mirth.

'My lord', he said loudly, 'does Gronw have the talent for such a complex plot? We have a dead bishop, a stolen campaign cup from the grave of another sanctified man, a servant who considers himself to be a Druid, the daughter of a Celt and a Pictish queen, who has been raised to believe that she is a reincarnation of Ceridwen, and these strands are so entangled, Lord Artor, that only a subtle brain could create any pattern in them. As fair and clever as Lady Miryll might be, she lacks the experience to put together such a conspiracy. Listen to her, my lord. She mouths what she has been taught like the child she is.'

'Be silent, Taliesin!' Artor ordered angrily. 'I need no lessons in understanding from you.'

Artor's expression brooked no argument and Taliesin backed down. 'My apologies, my king.'

Scarlet spots tinged Miryll's pale cheeks and she leapt angrily to her feet. Odin freed the axe that hung from his belt.

'It's very easy to pile scorn on a mere woman, Pretender,' she snarled. 'I am far better born than you are. My revenge is the knowledge that the Cup will have you in the end, for Gronw will be certain to spread the tale of what happens here. If you kill me, you'll be known as a monster. Your Lucius left a small, poisoned dart in wait for you that will bury you in your own dung heap.

I'll enjoy watching you smother in it. You may call me an ignorant fool if you want, but I'll glory in your punishment.'

'But, my lady, I thought you understood your position. You will perish. Your pitiful beliefs, your spite and, regrettably, any child that you carry in your womb will go into the shadows with you.'

Miryll finally understood that she would die when this inquisition came to an end. Her servants shuffled and glanced about with darting, wild-eyed stares. They saw their own executions looming and their thoughts began to scramble for some means of self-preservation. Miryll lowered her eyes. Her unborn child would never draw its first breath and she wondered, perhaps for the first time, whether ruthless men and their plans for glory had simply used her up as bait to further their own ambitions.

Her thoughts were visible in her pale countenance. Artor watched her, and his expression softened fleetingly.

'The west would never embrace the bastard son of Gawayne if I should be murdered,' he told her. 'I have so many presumptive heirs that I could start my own village with them, and I have nephews and great-nephews all over the north. You and your unborn child are a cruel diversion that has been devised to trick attention away from the real point of attack. Gronw's real plan was centred on achieving his purpose at Glastonbury. Perhaps, in time, your infant could have caused me problems, but I doubt it.'

'Gronw wouldn't use me,' Miryll whispered brokenly. 'He raised me and cared for me as part of a great and noble plan.'

'And he's filled your head with lies. Why, Miryll? The black warrior has succeeded in drawing me out of Cadbury but, had

I not come to Salinae Minor, you would have borne your child and suffered an arranged death in childbirth. Don't shake your head in disbelief, Miryll, for where is your protector now that you have need of him? Sooner or later, you were doomed to die. But Gronw understood me, for he knew I couldn't allow dissent within my kingdom. He left you behind so that I would be delayed in my pursuit of him.'

The king smiled regretfully at Miryll, much as a disappointed father would have done.

'The kingdom would have collapsed if Gronw had been successful and if I had died in last night's assassination attempt. Such an outcome would have freed Gronw to build a secure base at Salinae Minor where he would be ready to pick up the pieces after the inevitable civil war had run its course. You were always expendable, my dear, regardless of what direction his path followed. You're female. Had you been born a male, Gronw's plans would have been quite different.'

Taliesin could see the flaw in Artor's argument, but the rest of his troop stood gape-mouthed as the king unravelled the plot. What part did the Cup play in all this? Taliesin was certain that Gronw could not be the main conspirator in the plot. He did not possess the necessary knowledge of court life or of Artor himself. A more influential personage was moving the human pieces around the board game.

'You lie!' Miryll screamed, but her words lacked conviction.

'I'm truly sorry for you, Miryll,' Artor replied with sincerity. 'You're an accomplished and beautiful woman who was born to marry and to be loved. Gronw has taken your future and poisoned it without a thought for the woman he used as a weapon to suit his own purposes.'

Taliesin watched as the truth of Artor's words was reflected in her eyes and in her agonized face. His heart ached for her youth and naivety, and he feared for her as well.

Artor took a single step towards her and extended an open hand. 'I could excuse your betrayal if you chose to reveal what you know of the Bloody Cup. For that information, I'd happily extend mercy to you and to your servants. I'd also allow your child to be born, for I'm not a monster who makes war against innocents. I'm particularly intrigued by the history of the relic, for I know that Bishop Lucius wasn't always a priest, but was a Roman who served throughout their world.'

Perhaps Artor would have kept his word and taken back his earlier threats. Maybe he would have spared Miryll even if she knew nothing that was of importance to him. After all, Gallia had been pregnant when Uther had ordered her death; Artor had no wish to follow in his father's footsteps – the very thought haunted him.

But all this would remain conjecture, for Miryll believed that the king truly desired her death. Backed into a corner, and with the fabric of her life in tatters, she chose the Roman way. Had she possessed a sword, she would have fallen on it. Instead, she tore a long golden pin from her hair and leapt towards Artor, intent on stabbing him through the eye.

'No, Odin! No!' Artor roared, but too late.

Faster than the flicker of a serpent's tongue, Odin struck her head off at the throat with his axe.

The lady's body stood quivering for one poignant moment, spurting blood from the stump of her neck. Then her knees began to buckle and she fell, some distance from her staring head which had landed several feet away.

The servants wailed and covered their heads with their robes.

Artor sighed wearily as he fastidiously stepped away from the growing pool of blood.

Taliesin was the only person present who wept for the lady. He would remember that twisted face, turned ancient by betrayal, for the rest of his unnatural life. He alone saw that in the course of a single winter, Lady Miryll had been a maiden, then a newly impregnated mother, and then had died wearing the face most feared by any woman, the mask of the hag.

Carefully and reverently, Taliesin stepped forward and closed Miryll's eyes, then reunited head and body. Immediately, her face became smooth and young again, as pale as moonlight and as silent as shadows. The spurting blood had darkened her hair further, so she appeared to be a creature of light and shadow, a carved effigy of a fair young woman who had never truly lived.

Her blood didn't touch Artor's sandalled feet, but he was aware that it stained his hands.

'What could she have been had you never ridden on to her lands, Gawayne?' Artor mused. 'And how would she have fared with a different father and another adviser? They are to blame, as are you and I, for no guilt can be apportioned to any of my servants for her death.'

Artor surveyed the carnage in the atrium from behind the careful façade of his royal responsibilities. But what he felt beneath its mask, even Taliesin couldn't fathom.

'Her servants will be set free after they've been questioned,' Artor instructed Gawayne. 'They'll be permitted to leave the villa, but they may take nothing with them, for this house is now part of Galahad's wealth. Her possessions are forfeited to your son, for he understood Lady Miryll's intent when he first met her. We'll let her people wander until they find a tribe who'll give them shelter, for I'll permit no more bloodshed in this place.'

'What of that one there?' Gawayne asked, pointing to a servant with a broken arm. 'He shouldn't be permitted to walk away. How did he break his arm?'

'You can question him if you wish,' Artor said, 'but he will remain unharmed. I'll not waste more lives when my real quarry has escaped and is miles away from this place.'

Galahad entered shortly after Artor had given his orders and the king's bodyguards had commenced to shuffle the servants away for questioning. He was momentarily taken aback by Miryll's corpse, but Artor searched in vain for any compassion in his fiercely beautiful face.

'Excellent,' Galahad pronounced pompously. 'The slut has gone to meet her maker. It saddens me not at all, for she was an abomination.'

Artor was shocked; Galahad's callousness was so at odds with the Christian code he embraced so enthusiastically. The young man looked so smug that Gawayne stepped forward and slapped his son's cheek as hard as he could.

'What was that for?' Galahad was genuinely unaware of his heartlessness.

'Lady Miryll is as she was made, my son,' Gawayne said. 'And, to my shame, so are you. I wish that you had some pity in you, as your Jesus demands.'

For once, Galahad found he had no glib, easy reply.

Gawayne turned back to Artor and bowed very low to his

kinsman. 'I ask that you allow me to place her in a skiff, my lord. If no one wants to wash Miryll's poor body clean, then I'll do it myself. Let me send her to the sea so her soul may be cleansed in the great ocean, and so my unborn child might sleep on the bosom of the waves.'

'As you wish, Gawayne,' Artor replied. Then he turned to Galahad, but no liking softened the king's features.

'I grant you ownership of this isle as of today, Galahad. You will hold it secure for me.' And with that, he left the atrium.

Evening came softly and the spring flowers had begun to close their petals with the approach of darkness as Gawayne, Odin, Percivale and Galahad bore the body of Lady Miryll to the small dock at the end of the island. The twilight air was sweet and, to Gawayne's tired senses, it seemed to skirl its way through the gardens back towards the villa. By morning, it would have scoured the stucco and wood of the building clean of Gronw's stink. Perhaps the smell of blood in the atrium would also be leached away.

In the end, Taliesin had aided Gawayne in the women's ritual of cleaning the mutilated corpse. The harpist had watched his mother serve this same, final office to his father's desiccated remains and he understood the dignity involved in performing these last rites.

Stripped, cleansed and perfumed, Miryll lay upon a simple bed frame with her hair fanning out around her face. Gawayne had plundered her jewel box and found a golden necklace that now covered the severed neck and acted as a bond that joined throat and face together in a semblance of sleep. Her body was decked in fine cloth, while her arms were decorated with bangles.

After their ministrations, Lady Miryll was, once again, the mistress of Salinae Minor.

Before Odin and Percivale raised her bier on to the skiff, Gawayne placed his left palm upon her gently swelling belly. He allowed himself to wonder, for one brief moment, what their child might have been like ... but then he reminded himself that he had many sons.

Galahad accompanied the bier because he had searched his heart and found it wanting in Christian charity. He realized he had been jealous of the lady, not of her body, but of the easy manner in which she had cast a spell over his father, a man he could never truly understand or love.

Odin bore her frail corpse because he knew that he owed her spirit a debt for shedding her blood. He had no regrets, for his duty lay squarely with ensuring the safety of the king, but blood guilt is a hard burden to bear for those warriors who were born in cold northern climes. By offering Lady Miryll this last dignity, Odin hoped that her shade would not await him at Udgard when death finally embraced him.

Percivale attended the ceremony for Artor's sake. The king couldn't attend, for to do so would be to imply guilt over his actions. Only Percivale knew how Artor had pounded the wall of his apartment with both fists when he left the atrium. Only Percivale knew that the High King had fallen on to his knees and prayed to the Christian god for forgiveness. For Artor didn't know if he had truly intended to execute Miryll out of hand.

A king's way was to sweep all threats aside. The man's way was to protect the innocent and the frail. Artor could not be faithful to one duty without failing in the other. And now the High King would never be sure what his final choice would have been. The memory of his beloved Gallia lay across his heart like an ingot of lead for the first time in his long life. Had he been Uther Pendragon, he would have killed the woman and her unborn child without any qualms of conscience but, being Artor, he suffered.

Percivale carried Artor's end of the lady's bier, his lips moving soundlessly in the prayers of atonement.

Taliesin waited patiently at the end of the dock, his harp uncovered in the crook of his arm. The skiff was still tied securely, but its sail was set and it was ready for its final voyage.

Once the corpse was in place, Gawayne loosened the rope at the tiller and the skiff leapt away into the current, bearing its effigy of ruined beauty.

Taliesin sang the lady's death song.

The sweet male voice travelled far on the evening breeze, disturbing the birds as they nestled in the reeds and causing hunters to shiver with superstitious dread as they worked at their trap lines. Those few fishermen who heard the distant thread of song or saw the skiff skim past them on the waves felt as if they had been dealt a sudden blow, and they mourned a loss they could not name.

For beauty itself was riding on those waves and in the notes of the song, haunting and unearthly.

Gawayne watched the skiff and its pale burden until the flood bore them away into the growing darkness. Against his will, he wept silently now that no one could see the sheen of tears on his smooth cheeks. Concealed by the shroud of darkness, Gawayne could not tell if he wept for Miryll or himself.

CHAPTER IX

Aпother Saxoп Summer

'She's dead, mistress! She's dead! Your child! *Our* child! And the High Bastard lives because I failed in my task.'

Gronw slumped over the neck of his failing horse and tried desperately to recall the face of his long-dead mistress. She had died when Miryll was an infant and Gronw had to struggle to recall the details of his lover's face.

'Our Miryll is dead,' he sobbed in contrition, lest the gods send her shade winging after him on the night air. 'She *must* be dead by now!'

Gronw was largely indifferent to Miryll's fate, for she had willingly played her part in the execution of the hurried plot to kill Artor. It was she who had placed the drugs in the food given to the guards. And it was she who had knocked at Artor's door and then lured the king along the corridor to the baths. Naked and laughing, she had plunged into the fug of the calidarium and had played her part in Gronw's attack on the king. Even when Artor had knocked the breath out of her body with his fist, she had giggled while Gronw attempted to drown the king.

The glorious task that filled his brain with promise was far more important than the life of a girl child, he told himself. She *knew* the implications of what they plotted.

Gronw felt a sudden rush of hot tears stream unchecked down his face.

Miryll had been a sweet child when they had settled at Salinae Minor, and he had almost come to love her as she played in her favourite places in the villa. But when he saw the reflection of her dead mother's face in Miryll's eyes, and smelled the perfume of her mother in the child's newly washed hair, a storm of loss rolled over him and any affection he might have felt for the young girl was washed away in a tide of bile and bitterness.

After leaving Salinae Minor, Gronw had ridden for days, pausing only to rest his horse and steal a little food before taking to the back roads again. Several times, mounted men had swept past his hiding places beside the old Roman road and he knew that Artor's warriors were in hot pursuit.

But when fear and weariness were so heavy that he felt crushed by his burdens, he had only to feel the Cup inside the warmth of his leather jerkin to have his spirit restored. The smooth metal edges eased the feelings of guilt that niggled at the edges of his reason. He had Ceridwen's Cup, the Cup of Lucius, and he would fill it to the brim with fresh blood, again and again, to give renewal to his mistress and her daughter.

'I can sleep when I reach Deva,' he whispered wearily into the night. 'I've only to reach Deva, and all will be well.'

He chanted this mantra over and over as his horse moved painfully into the north.

✢ ✢ ✢

In Cadbury, the High King stalked through his halls like a caged beast. He found no comfort in conversation, in the hunt or in his fruitful fields. His lands closed around him like a stifling shroud so that he felt like a living man prematurely buried in his grave.

Nothing had changed since he had led his troop out of Cadbury for the journey to Glastonbury. Superficially, Artor could see no changes in the faces of his court, in the security of his treaties with the Celtic tribes and in the continuing lack of coordinated resistance from the Saxons.

But Artor knew that everything had shifted out of focus since he had returned from Salinae Minor. The shades of Miryll and her son troubled him little, for they were small voices in a great tide of dead who waited at the edges of sleep to trouble his dreams. But the implications of the attack on Glastonbury disturbed his rest every night.

Beyond doubt, someone had plotted his downfall, and that conspirator was clever and well-organized. Gronw had vanished as if he had never existed; only a very efficient cadre of sympathizers could hide the Pict from Artor's warriors and agents. The formation of such a web of co-conspirators required careful planning, great patience and fierce determination. Gronw, an unknown Pict from the north, could not set up such an organization; he did not have the power or reach to find, enlist and organize malcontents.

Gronw was an opportunist. He had managed to capitalize on the visit of Gawayne and Galahad to Salinae Minor with dashing effrontery. Likewise, when Artor had arrived at the isle with his troops, Gronw had immediately devised an assassination attempt that could have achieved his aims as effectively as his original plan might have. Chance had saved Artor, rather than any flaws in Gronw's hasty changes of plan.

'Whoever my enemy is, he is far more dangerous than my Saxon adversaries, because I am being attacked from within and the aggressor has remained invisible,' Artor muttered to himself. 'I cannot defend myself against an enemy within my walls who is so very well-entrenched.'

Artor's angry path had taken him back to his apartments. For a moment, he stood at the door, trying to gather his wits. Then he recalled that, in his concentration on plot and counterplot, he had forgotten the petitioners for his judgement. With a show of unnecessary force, Artor hit the door with his palm and strode into the quiet room.

'Lord?' Odin raised his head from the sleeping couch that he was straightening.

'I'm an ageing fox caught in a trap by one foot. Dare I gnaw off my own limb to be free?'

Odin stared at his master with concern.

Artor was dressed for his Judgement Hall, and now he threw his golden torc across the room with as much force as his arm could muster.

'Artor!' Odin protested. 'How can I help?'

'You can't, unless you know some way to spirit me out of here.'

The king's brow furrowed and Odin thought for a moment that Artor might weep.

'But where would I go, anyway, if I deserted my duty and ran? There's nowhere open to me but here!'

Odin retrieved the king's torc and straightened his master's robes.

'I'm afraid, Odin. I see no way out of this mess!'

The last words were shouted, and Percivale ran into the room.

'More of you to witness my shame?' Artor threw himself into his chair and lowered his grizzled head into his hands.

Artor had studied the teachings of the philosophers and he fully understood that his kingdom was in decline. He smelled decay in his land like the rot that appeared in the folds of old parchments. Unerringly, he recognized its corruption in the squabbling carelessness of his warriors and the malice in men like Modred.

The nobles and the warrior class had forgotten the horrors of life caught between the twin evils of a despotic ruler and ruthless invaders. Artor had banished war and enforced peace and the rule of law, so very few of the denizens of Cadbury Tor remembered the distant past when the fortress was in ruins and its great defensive walls were unkempt and blurred with young trees and rubbish. They had either forgotten the rule of Uther Pendragon or had not been born when that ancient madman held the land in the grip of his terrible lunacy.

Human beings quickly forget the taste, the smell and the agony of pain. After several decades of stability, some Celtic aristocrats had forgotten how exceptional Artor had been during his youth and, even in the embers of his life, he still kept Celtic borders secure from invasion. Some arrogant nobles, who had never learned the lessons of history, had come to believe that they could rule in the High King's place.

'Even if my kingdom was hale and strong, I would still be under attack from the growing weakness in myself,' Artor told Odin with a catch in his voice.

If truth be told, Artor recognized the smell of decay in his own growing rage at everything and everyone around him.

Neither Odin nor Percivale found any comforting words that could ease Artor's distress. Dumb and miserable, they could only show their love and faith, twin burdens that bowed the High King's shoulders even further.

Later that day, after his judgements were complete, Artor took his misgivings to the one person who listened impartially to his distress.

'You've ridden too far these last few weeks,' Lady Elayne told him, her fingers pressed against his forehead as if he was a sick child. 'And you must be very tired.'

By all the rules of Church and man, Artor should have avoided the company of Bedwyr's wife. The court would be quick to judge her as a faithless wife if they were discovered together. Of course, he would be judged guilty as well, although no one would dare to raise a hand against him. In the rough justice of public opinion, Lady Elayne would be damned as a whore if she was compromised in the company of the king. But Artor needed a confidante, and one who had a cooler, less biased brain than his loyal bodyguards. Selfishly, he often sought private conversations with Lady Elayne. If he felt any obligation to Bedwyr, he silenced his conscience with the reminder that neither he nor Lady Elayne had committed any impropriety.

Artor sighed. 'The Saxons don't care if the king is tired. Nor do those elements of Celtic society who plot against me. They wish to turn back the sand glass to those lawless days before Ambrosius brought the tribes out of barbarism. Yes, I'm tired, but I can sleep later. Today, tomorrow and for many days to come, I must be prepared to ride at need.'

With his whole heart, Artor wished that he could rest his aching head against Elayne's cool hand and take courage from her concern.

'My lady, I'm old and my body betrays me after every hour I spend in the saddle. Were I young again, this Saxon summer wouldn't stretch my strength so far. Sadly, the west has grown complacent after many years of peace.'

It was now Elayne's turn to sigh. Her new role as the king's confidante was inherently difficult, and she had been forced to struggle with her conscience over the last three months since Artor had returned from Salinae Minor.

She loved Bedwyr dearly, as a man and as her husband, and she had no intentions of betraying her marriage vows with King Artor. She blushed at the thought, for the king had never importuned her sexually. However, Elayne was aware that Queen Wenhaver and gossips within the court would make a world of sin out of her innocent role. By being alone with Artor, she exposed Bedwyr to ridicule. But some visceral kinship linked her with the High King, and encouraged her to accept Artor's confidences. She understood his vulnerability and his growing need, for no man who possessed blood in his veins could survive without someone to share his innermost thoughts. Those few who ignored the necessity for intellectual intimacy with others ultimately descended into madness.

Also, because Elayne was an honest young woman, she acknowledged that a part of her took pleasure in her growing importance to the High King of the Britons. She couldn't deny how very flattering it was to be sought out by a powerful man, not for her sexuality, but for her intellect. For perhaps the first time in her life, Lady Elayne was truly needed, and such heady knowledge was difficult to relinquish.

'Are the barbarians truly stirring, my lord? I've heard tales of their savagery, but we've not felt their menace in my lifetime.'

'They stir, Lady Elayne. And this time, they'll come on horses. They've learned from us, so this time I'll need more than dumb beasts to hold them back behind the mountain spine. Ratae, Venonae, Lavatrae and even Portus Adurni have sent messengers seeking reinforcements to repel the wolves who are now baying at their gates. Fortunately, no leader has risen to unite the Saxon enclaves, so we can pick them off piecemeal, thanks be to Mithras and the other gods of war and soldiery.'

'But aren't such widespread engagements difficult for our troops to manage? Surely they'll have to ride many miles to confront the enemy at places such as Ratae and Anderida?'

Artor bowed over her hand and kissed it. She blushed, and conscious that Artor had crossed the bounds of propriety in their relationship, she pulled her hand away and hid it in her skirts.

'Dear lady, I have strengthened the fortresses to repel invaders in these situations. Pelles, Gawayne and your strong husband have trained with our warriors over many years so that they can deal with any number of separate Saxon forces. It's only when the Saxons unite under a single leader that they will cause us trouble.'

'And you're confident you can repel the force that comes out from Anderida?'

'Aye. Anderida has been my sole responsibility since my

twenty-second year. I'm looking forward to riding out against the Saxons from that pestilential place.'

Elayne gazed earnestly into Artor's eyes. She saw irritation and fear in his grey irises, but excitement as well. Artor lived for challenges and, in his advanced age, the Saxon menace had ceased to be his primary fear.

'Do you have reinforcements to send to the fortresses, lord?'

'Not yet, my lady. But your Cornovii kin will ride to fortify Ratae and Venonae, where Gawayne is already stiffening the spines of the defenders. At this stage, I hold no fears that the Saxons will slip through the forest.'

'Yet your brow is furrowed,' Elayne murmured. 'If the tribes remain true, the Saxons will be forced to face the power of our border garrisons as they always have.'

'But what if they don't hold true? I've wondered at the motives of the Brigante tribe recently, because they've been slow to move troops to Lavatrae. Modred mouths all the right platitudes, but his troops stay within his borders. They continue to keep themselves isolated, and I've been forced to rely on the courage of Galahad's warriors to defend the north, bolstered by Morgause's hatred of all things Saxon. Fortunately, the Ordovice tribe will advance under the rule of Bran and the wishes of his mother, Anna.'

Elayne flinched instinctively as Artor shared these details of his family in such casual language. Although she was flattered by the trust that the king placed in her, she was also appalled by the interplay of hatred, politics and distrust that powered the Union of Kings. The High King's confidences revealed a world that was usually closed to women, and the insights she gained from his openness were almost oppressive.

'Don't you fear that the walls might have ears, lord? The Union of Kings does not encourage friendship or trust, so there must be spies in your household. No doubt you have spies in theirs.'

'Of course. Gruffydd is skilled in finding talented servants who keep him well supplied with information.'

'Don't you fear that someone could be listening to what we are saying right now?'

Artor shrugged without expression.

Elayne moved to the far side of Artor's hall and twisted back the long, woven hangings that softened wood and stone. Satisfied that no ears but Artor's bodyguard could hear their conversation, she turned back to the king.

'Lord Modred makes much of his kinship with you,' she said quietly, approaching the king more closely than was her custom. 'He claims his mother is your elder sister, although we have only his word that Queen Morgause seduced his father. Modred whispers that he's your true heir and that you're too old to control our lands. He preaches revolution, but furtively.'

Artor slammed his fist down upon the carved arms of his royal chair. Then his eyes narrowed suspiciously. For a short moment, Elayne knew that he doubted her.

'How did Modred permit you to learn all this? Modred is far too clever to openly reveal his plans.'

'Modred never says anything that is directly critical of you. His listeners draw obvious conclusions from his hints and lies and he leaves them to cast any slurs. He can deny that he has ever encouraged treason while creating a climate where it is bound to flourish. Beware, my lord. I sit quietly in the queen's arbor and I listen to them when they talk.'

'Modred's not my true heir. He doesn't have the breeding and he carries all his mother's bitterness without possessing an iota of her justification. I'd sooner die without an heir and risk the safety of the west than expose the kingdom to a vain pretender like Modred. Nor need I worry that he'll find support for his claim after my death. His illegitimacy will always be a handicap for him with the tribes.'

The High King lapsed into silence, but Lady Elayne couldn't relinquish the conversation so readily.

'The Brigante tribe controls a huge territory,' she said, her voice low. 'And they have a large population – dangerously large. I'm fearful of Modred, my king. Something in him repulses me, although he can be very charming when he chooses. There's something womanish in the way he delights in cruel gossip.' Elayne flushed, and Artor could clearly see a dusting of golden freckles across her cheeks and nose. She seemed to realize that her insights insulted her own sex, so she lurched back into explanation.

'If Modred was a man who finds his pleasure in the love of men, well, that would be no impediment to his succession. Many warriors have put aside the love of women for men, so few Celts would be critical of Lord Modred on that account. But something in the way he looks at me makes me feel soiled and poisoned, as if he takes pleasure in any predicament that causes pain. Servants who are clumsy, fools who are caught in some crime – Modred enjoys their fears and punishments. Such sadism isn't healthy in anyone, and in a king it is terrifying.'

Now Lady Elayne blushed scarlet, for it occurred to her that her conversation with the king was quite improper. Artor saw her embarrassment, and laughed.

'I'm sorry, my lord,' she apologized. 'I really didn't consider what I was saying. Forgive me if I have been overly frank.'

'I don't mind, Lady Elayne. I agree with everything that you say, but such talk might not be appropriate in the queen's bower.'

It was now Elayne's turn to laugh. 'Lord, if you believe that, then you haven't been privy to many of the conversations of well-reared maidens.'

'Anyway, I've never considered Modred as a viable heir – never! I know far too much about that gilded young man to countenance his flaws as a ruler, or even as a member of my family.'

The king's strong hands twisted in a way that Elayne had come to associate with shame. Artor seemed to be screwing up his courage to share a secret with her that he found deeply distasteful.

'Modred isn't even a true man!'

Elayne looked puzzled and Artor wished he'd remained silent. Some secrets were better left unsaid, and some nasty habits were bearable only when they were kept from the light of day.

'I don't understand, sire.' Elayne's open face glowed with concern and curiosity in the semi-darkness of the hall.

'Forget everything I've said about him, Lady Elayne,' Artor murmured. 'I was rambling like an old grandam, and I should learn to keep my opinions of my kin to myself.'

Artor had been nurtured in the Roman world and had absorbed their sexual tolerance with the milk of his wet nurse. Where a man chose to find his sexual gratification was a matter between his conscience and his gods – and no concern of the High King. But Modred had gone beyond what Artor could condone, and had raised an ancient spectre that troubled the king's already burdened spirit.

The High King had discovered Modred's secret life by pure chance, for the Brigante understood Cadbury too well to hunt for prey within the confines of the tor. A crofter had approached the king when he was riding with his guard and had spoken the unspeakable to his lord and master.

The farmer had leapt out into the roadway, almost under Artor's horse.

'By the gods!' the king shouted and wrenched back on the reins so that his horse almost fell backwards on its haunches.

Odin drew his fighting axe and for a moment the roadway was a mêlée of wheeling horses, drawn weapons and angry men.

'My lord! Save me! Save my son!' the crofter cried out, his face streaked with dust and tears. As the man pawed at his leg, Artor caught the reek of fear and filth.

'Leave him be, Odin,' the king ordered. 'He's unarmed and can't harm me.'

Artor dismounted and helped the man to his feet from where he was kneeling in the dust of the roadway.

'Why have you stopped me at such risk to yourself? My bodyguard could have killed you for your foolishness. Come, man! Speak up if you want something of me. I cannot guess.'

'I can't speak in front of them,' the farmer whispered, and pointed in the direction of Artor's bodyguard. 'Please, my lord, I'm fearful and ashamed.'

The farmer couldn't have been above thirty years of age, but his back was twisted as if he was twice those years. From his unkempt hair to his mended clothing, he stank of poverty.

Pitying the man, the High King drew him a short distance away from his bodyguard so they were just beyond earshot. Odin expressed his displeasure in every muscle.

'We are a poor family, my lord, for our land is not as rich as it could be, and I owe part of my crops to my landlord. Otherwise, I'd never have sent my Finbarr off with the young master.'

Artor nodded in understanding.

'Finbarr is my oldest boy, but he's small, and not much use on the farm. The young lord rode past our croft one day, saw my boy and offered to take him into service. I couldn't see any harm in it. I swear, my lord, I'd not have taken his coin if I'd known there'd be any hurt done to the boy.'

Awkwardly, Artor patted the man's shoulder in a gesture of sympathy, although he wondered if the farmer was too full of excuses to be completely innocent.

'Finbarr went to Cadbury and we heard nothing of the boy for some weeks until he arrived home three days ago. He was bleeding, and he told me he'd been raped and beaten. His spirit is crushed, and he lies beside the fire and won't eat. What can I do, my lord? I've already spent the coin that the young lord gave me.'

Even then, Artor felt little concern. The man had sold off his eldest son and now, in the aftermath of his greed, the crofter wanted some kind of justice for the boy. Contempt creased the High King's features.

'How old is Finbarr?' Artor asked.

'He's eight, my lord, but he's small for his age.'

217

'Faugh!' Artor made an involuntary sound of disgust. The boy's youth made the father's crime even worse, for what innocent reason could a noble want with a small child? In his heart of hearts, the crofter must have suspected that his son was in danger.

The abuse of children was the taint of every society and frowned on by all. A memory returned to Artor of a hellish crypt that he had entered during his youth, a place where young boys had been taken by perverted men, now mercifully dead, who had indulged their sick fantasies on the children's tender flesh. With the memory came the smell of decomposing flesh and the keening of bereaved women. It haunted Artor still.

'Who was the young lordling who purchased your son?' Artor's voice was wintry and hard, and his words didn't spare the sensibilities of the cringing father.

'He didn't give his name to me, but Finbarr called him Lord Modred.'

Appalled, Artor wheeled away. He ordered Odin to give the farmer a gold coin to care for his son and, later, sent a trusted healer to visit the croft.

Artor attempted to assuage his conscience as best he could, for he chose to avoid raising the subject with Modred. What was there to say? The Brigante alliance was far more important than a tow-headed boy, but Artor carried the guilt of his inaction.

As Artor explained to Taliesin that evening, the Union of Kings had cost him dearly, for he had been forced to tolerate behaviour that he found repugnant. When Lady Elayne was unavailable, Taliesin had become an excellent sounding board for, unlike the lady, Artor could tell the young harper anything he desired.

'You didn't consider the tribes when you punished Luka's murderers,' Gareth murmured as he offered his king a flask of clean water and a bowl of apples. 'You rode roughshod over your own rules.'

'That was different!' Artor snapped.

Odin raised one eyebrow and Artor had the grace to colour.

'Very well. I lost my temper when Luka was killed and I didn't wait for the tribal kings to pass judgement on his murderers.'

Odin handed his king a small paring knife to cut his fruit.

'My bad temper doesn't change the present situation. The Brigante tribe is important to our cause, because they control the central west and are essential to our campaign against the barbarians. Can you imagine what would happen if the Saxons made a concerted attack on the Brigante lands and defeated them? They could fight their way through Modred's lands to the Oceanus Hibernicus. The whole north would be cut off and defenceless. How, then, could we hold our enemies at bay? We couldn't! Eventually, we would lose the entire west!'

Or so Artor tried to tell himself. But, when he watched Modred sit among the women with his mobile brows raised sardonically and his well-shaped mouth spouting ugly nothings, the High King felt genuine disgust with himself.

Careful checking by Gruffydd soon revealed the full extent of Modred's sins. Girls, slaves, boys and vulnerable women were all food for the Brigante king's table, and anyone could become his victim if they fell under his power. Modred wasn't fussy, because what he enjoyed was the infliction of pain and humiliation, not the drive of sexuality. The sex of the partner didn't seem to matter, and Artor became certain that all his prey were stand-ins for that one person who had rejected Modred before he was even aware of what humiliation meant – his mother, Queen Morgause.

Modred might appear to be sophisticated and self-contained, but Artor was sure that he was seeking revenge on all the Brigante people, particularly those men, women and children who had bullied and brutalized him during his lonely childhood. A volcano of rage must boil under Modred's quiet face. With a vague sense of regret, Artor felt some empathy for Modred's motivation, for he could easily have travelled that same bleak landscape of pain if the three travellers had not come to the Villa Poppinidii forty-eight years earlier and if Frith had not given him her unconditional love.

'Modred will never be whole – never!' Artor muttered to himself. 'Caius was the same. He demonstrated that people cannot escape the damage done by the traumas and hurts of their youth. They can only hide their true selves for a time, for the poison festers and must find an outlet sooner or later.'

So he let Modred be, and knew that he was merely delaying the inevitable. But he continued to watch the Brigante carefully because he understood that the circle of his life was beginning to close.

Later that week, Elayne and Artor once again strolled round the king's hall in private. Artor was explaining the pleas for help from Portus Adurni and its fear of Anderida, the now-impregnable Saxon fortress on the southern coast, when he heard a small noise from outside the door. Still speaking naturally, he walked quietly to it and abruptly pulled it open.

Modred stood in the doorway with his body slightly crouched as if he had been caught rising from his knees. The King of the Brigante appeared unembarrassed by his exposure and continued to straighten slowly before falling into a low, ironic bow.

'Have you heard all you wanted to know, Modred?' Artor asked pleasantly. Elayne had noticed that the High King always controlled his temper around Modred.

'The population of Portus Adurni always jumps at shadows,' Modred drawled. 'Of course, you could repeat history by taking the Anderida fortress once again, but I'd be reluctant to crawl through mud if I were your age, my liege.'

'I wouldn't dream of asking you to do so, Modred. By all reports, the mud you favour is moral and beyond my understanding.' Full of false bonhomie, Artor clapped the smaller man on the back a little too enthusiastically. 'Besides, all the real heroes of Anderida, except for Odin and myself, are dead. Perhaps you'd not last long anyway, stripped of your little . . . comforts.'

Modred frowned, showing his discomfiture. The Brigante rarely revealed his feelings on his disciplined face, so Artor savoured his small victory.

'I don't know what you mean, sire?'

'Yes, you do!' Artor grinned. 'I don't suppose you ever dreamed I'd discover your secret. I've been riding out of Cadbury recently to meet my poorest vassals. It's amazing what they'll do for a few coins.'

Modred whitened.

'As for dealing with the Saxons of Anderida, that is soldiers' work,' Artor continued urbanely, 'and I've noticed you prefer the company of women – and children.'

'That failing seems to run through our family, my lord.' Modred smiled down the hall at Lady Elayne. 'I bid you good morning, my lady. Does the noble Bedwyr find life at Ratae congenial when he is so far from your arms? I'm sure he must miss the felicity of your presence.' Modred stared at the shadows beyond Lady Elayne.

'Aye, Lord Modred,' she replied pleasantly. 'He writes quite often to tell me so.' Her cool eyes met Modred's with a contempt that was palpable. She moved forward into the light that spread inward from the open doorway, and behind her came Odin and her maid. 'He bids me to take good care of our king, as all loyal subjects should. I notice you listen at doors carefully, my lord. Is it, perhaps, to learn whether our king has need of you?'

'Of course,' Modred answered, and inclined his head sardonically. He enjoyed these cat-and-mouse games, especially when he was on safe ground. It was unfortunate that Artor had discovered his secret and now had a potent weapon to hold over his head, but there was always some saving grace in any disappointing situation. Artor had said nothing openly. And he won't, Modred thought smugly, not when he needs my warriors more than ever, now that we have a Saxon summer upon us.

When Artor rode away to conduct his campaign against the Saxons, it was with a feeling of release, for he had put Modred on notice and was, finally, free of the stink of the court. That the Brigante king had seen him with Lady Elayne was unfortunate, but she had demonstrated that she was well-chaperoned at all times. Artor smiled reflectively as he remembered Elayne's ripostes to Modred's sly threats.

After the months of uncertainty, after the plots and counter-plots and all the talk of Bloody Cups and even bloodier rebellion, the business of sanctioned killing, with its clear boundaries, was a welcome change. In warfare, roles were defined and the sides were fixed. Of course, there was always the possibility of a trusted friend changing allegiance but, compared with the convolutions of politics, the position of friend or foe was straightforward.

The Governor of Portus Adurni had dispatched a courier to Cadbury with an urgent message for the High King. Lying at the end of Magnis Portus, some eighty miles away from Cadbury, the harbour town's populace was quick to respond whenever the Saxons of Anderida began to stir. Clausentum and Portus Adurni guarded the roads that led to Venta Belgarum and the coast, so when their spies told them that the Saxons had left their coastal citadel by both land and sea, they called for help.

The battle of Anderida had been fought when Artor was very young and too inexperienced to realize how heavily the odds weighed against the success of his attack on the well-defended fortress. Now, the king was returning to the beginning, except that the Saxons of Anderida were coming to him. In this respect, the world had changed; the Saxons were no longer content to dig into their fortresses and defy Artor to drive them out. They, too, felt the movement of Fortuna's wheel and knew instinctively that their time would soon be at hand.

This Saxon summer could be his last, Artor knew, but it still called to him with the old excitement, in spite of the ache in his old bones as he rode. While he lived, Anderida and all the other strongholds of his eastern enemies would not attack his borders with impunity.

The Saxons were pouring out of Anderida, out of Durobrivae and out of Lindum. In response, Artor moved his Cadbury forces to Venta Belgarum. The defenders of Ratae, Lavatrae, Venonae and Verterae were also on the move and had been placed on full alert. The force led by Artor consisted of cavalry and archers only, for the Saxons from Anderida had always been reluctant horsemen.

As Artor watched his campaign tent rise at his bivouac, Wenhaver enjoyed the summer months lazing in her bower, embroidering and gossiping. Her ladies were obliged to join her, as were any young lordlings left at the tor who took her fancy. Modred was a special favourite, for he was adept at framing elaborate and wicked jokes at the king's expense, to the chagrin of the twins, Elayne and the silent servants who proffered wine and sweet, oaten cakes drenched in honey.

Fortunately for Modred's safe existence, Artor decided that the twins should be blooded and sent a message ordering them to join him. Their energy would be useful and they would have the opportunity to prove their courage and strategic skills. The Saxons had ventured into the lowlands and forests of Anderida Silva, where they would be difficult to dislodge without significant loss of life. Wild courage and cool heads were necessary, an excellent description of Anna's sons.

Modred felt certain that Wenhaver cared little whether her husband survived this providential campaign. But Modred underestimated Wenhaver's self-interest.

The queen's mirror spoke the unvarnished truth, and Wenhaver was finally forced to listen. She realized she was irrevocably middle-aged and barren, and her sole great achievement during her life had occurred when she became High Queen of the west. Should Artor perish, no new suitor would claim her as the spoils of war, and she would be forced to dwindle, a legendary beauty fallen into ugly decline. Should such a disaster occur, Wenhaver would soon be forgotten in the poverty that lay in wait for unwanted, sterile old women.

No, Artor must live, and heaven help those Celtic nobles who attempted to come between her and the throne of the High King. She marshalled her not inconsiderable influence as queen to stand behind Artor as the just and legitimate ruler of the west. In her solitary bed, she vowed silently to endure celibacy, if it would keep her beleaguered husband upon his throne. She rode through Cadbury and comforted the wives of Artor's warriors, and would have ridden further if the land had been safe. In addition, she sent messages to the Union of Kings, reminding them of ancient debts, and ensured that recalcitrant rulers provided their share of the levy in men and money that would fund Artor's campaign. To his surprise, even Modred was shamed into capitulation.

Languid and idle, Wenhaver was considered by most of the court to be as useless as a lapdog. Her yellow hair was curled and perfumed, her exquisitely clean hands were rouged on the palms and her feet were as soft as those of a small child. But those who thought she was negligible were wrong. As queen of the west, she played her part.

Artor had sent Balan to patrol the lowlands of Anderida

Silva and the forests to the north of Noviomagus and Anderida, where Artor played a Saxon game by digging in along a low ridge line with his cavalry hidden in the rear. With fresh enthusiasm, he set up his bowmen behind the defensive lines with their wicked log spikes, so perfect for impaling horses that were charging uphill. While the use of cavalry had been adopted by the Saxons, it was still a rather alien concept to them and Artor was trusting that the barbarians would not realize the crushing disadvantages of the battleground that he had chosen for them.

In his campaign tent, Artor revealed his battle plan to his captains. Daring and simple, Artor intended to engineer a ruse that gave the Saxons a tempting target, one that would trap and destroy them.

Balan had looked at Artor with rapt admiration as he assessed the gamble that the High King was about to take with such nonchalance.

'Saxons are new to the kind of discipline that is needed for effective cavalry charges', he explained to Balan. 'Unfortunately for them, raw courage isn't enough for success. As the warriors of Anderida have never used cavalry as their main strategic thrust, they'll be at a disadvantage. I'm sure they'll charge straight at us and will expect to overrun us – much as we tended to dominate them in the past.'

'But what if they don't charge?' Balan asked. 'A strategic stand-off could be disastrous for our forces.'

'In that event, my archers will decimate them where they stand. If they decide to resume the attack, the bowmen will fall back, regroup and let our cavalry mop up those Saxons who manage to reach the top of the hill.'

In the morning, Balan's troop was sent out to locate the bulk of the Saxon forces and then ride back to the Celtic positions at full gallop, as if in alarm. Artor was gambling that the Saxons would pursue Balan's horsemen and blunder into the High King's trap. But, to ensure that they would actually charge his defensive position, Artor would take to the field himself, dressed in full battle armour and carrying his shield and helmet. His panoply would proclaim to the Saxons that the High King had come to Anderida Silva to teach his enemies a lesson in person. Artor hoped that the Saxons would rise to the bait.

Back in Cadbury, the court knew that the king was involved in a risky endeavour. Wenhaver was surprised to discover that she was actually on edge. When she learned from her couriers that Balan was returning to Cadbury in haste, she paled a little under her cosmetics, for it indicated that the battle for Anderida Silva must already be over. After a few tears, Wenhaver soon rallied and gathered her women around her for support.

Balan, or Silence, as Wenhaver's cronies had dubbed him, came to the queen's shady rose garden in a hasty response to her urgent summons. His stern face shone with boyish enthusiasm and, although he carried a light wound on one brown thigh, he was bubbling with excitement.

'If I read your face correctly, you come with good news, Lord Balan.' She smiled at the young man. 'Give us your tidings from the field. Tell us everything, and don't spare our female sensibilities.' Wenhaver waved a rosebud under her nose to cover the scent of strong, masculine sweat.

'Forgive me for coming into your presence without first

making myself presentable, my lady. It is my duty to ensure that you are the very first to know that the High King has smashed the Saxons in the forests and has sent them scurrying back towards Anderida. You would hardly credit how brilliant was the strategy used by our lord to secure victory. He had the courage to draw the Saxons into his trap by fighting afoot – yes, afoot – while carrying a shield that was clearly marked with his dragon symbol.'

To an audience that was hushed and awestruck, Balan began the tale of the rout of the Saxons at Anderida Silva.

The young man had led his small troop into the still forest of oak, hazel, alder and beech trees. Uncannily, the woods were silent and no birds sang in the deep indigo shadows of the foliage. In open glades, the summer sun barred the horsemen with stripes of gold and bronze, while the hock-high grasses muffled the passage of the troop.

Balan forced himself to remain calm in the face of his rising excitement and nervousness. Irrelevantly, he wondered how his brother was coping with his duties as he rode with Pelles Minor and Bedwyr and the forces patrolling the mountains around Ratae. Balan felt a moment's envy for the experiences that his brother was enjoying with two of the great commanders of the west. Balan's modesty was such that he hadn't realized the importance of the task given to him by the High King, for he was the necessary decoy who would bring the Saxons to Artor's maw.

An experienced cavalryman riding on the point raised one hand to catch Balan's attention, so the younger man ordered the troop to a halt with a hissed command. Something stirred several hundred yards through the trees. Balan could hear the telltale sound of metal plates grinding against each other, the slap of leather on flesh and the jingle of bits and reins.

Horsemen were approaching fast without any attempt at concealment.

Balan's troop waited deep in the shadowy thickets, as still as centaurs, their senses probing towards the sound of incoming riders. Then, with much cursing and crashing in the underbrush, a group of Saxons burst into a small clearing ahead and pulled their horses to a shuddering halt.

'Ready?' Balan hissed to his men. 'Then let's go!'

The Celts were away at a brisk gallop. Fortunately, their mounts were skilled in this brutal, dangerous world of rabbit holes, fallen trees and low branches. The Saxons milled in confusion for a panicky moment and then set off in pursuit, with several warriors whooping in excitement until a shouted command ordered them into silence. Deftly, the Celts avoided the raw enthusiasm of the slightly larger Saxon troop and led their pursuers towards a large clearing.

There, concealed in the trees, a small detachment of archers waited in ambush. As soon as the enemy riders appeared, a hail of arrows rained down on them. Balan's men mopped up the wounded and dragged their slack bodies into a narrow, malodorous ditch that ran down to a streamlet, while the archers retrieved their arrows and the captured horses. Over the next week, the pile of bodies grew steadily as Balan played a rather nasty game of cat and mouse in ambushes where the mice died, every time.

Just when Balan began to believe that his own small troop would destroy the entire Saxon army, one contingent at a time, the Celts rode through a lighter area of woodland

and discovered the main body of the Saxon invaders in bivouac.

The Saxon force consisted of some two hundred cavalry, plus foot soldiers and supporting troops. The cavalry was well supplied with horses, at least two per rider, and Balan was impressed at the organization displayed by the Saxon campaign, and the meticulous, surreptitious planning that had ensured that horses were purchased in large numbers, without alerting the Celtic spies. At long last, the Saxons were learning how to do battle against the Celts.

Balan paused for breath, leaving his listeners to lean forward intently. Wenhaver clapped her perfumed hands in excitement, before handing him her rose as a sign of favour.

'I can hardly believe Artor's boundless luck when he conducts his campaigns,' Modred murmured. 'So you found the Saxon cavalry by accident, did you?'

Balan was still for a moment while he absorbed the implications of Modred's mockery. Then he looked at Modred with such icy contempt that Modred's eyes dropped. For a moment, the young man's likeness to Artor, his kinsman, was written clear in his stony face. Even Wenhaver shivered.

'You are safely domiciled here, lord, not because of luck but because of the military prowess of the High King. You are hardly in a position to speak so dismissively of a week-long campaign in which you played no part whatsoever.'

'I meant no offence, noble Balan,' Modred apologized easily.

Balan ignored a needle of irritation.

'Tell us what happened next, Balan,' Wenhaver said eagerly. 'I'm agog to discover what you did when you found all those Saxon warriors.'

'Well, my lady,' Balan responded, 'like any sensible Celt who's outnumbered by at least twenty to one – we ran!'

The Saxons saw Balan's troop almost immediately so pursuit was swift. Balan ordered one of his warriors to ride like the wind to Artor's trap in order to warn the king of their imminent arrival. Meanwhile, the rest of his troop would delay the arrival of the Saxon force until Artor's men were in position.

'We'll keep the Saxons off your back, Euen, but don't spare your horse,' Balan ordered.

For over an hour, the Celts led the forward detachment of the Saxons through the oak thickets, careless of the branches that tore at leather jerkins or slashed across unprotected faces. Then, when they were almost trapped by the wings of the Saxon advance, Balan led his men, shrieking and yelling tribal challenges, through a narrow gap in the Saxon front and off towards a wooded hill. The horses were almost done as Balan's men began the climb. In the distance, the main body of the enemy trotted through the tree cover in a more cautious pursuit. Balan hoped they would follow their advance party into the attack area but, if they held back, Balan was sure that Artor would have devised a solution. With complete faith in his king, the young man rode like a crazy savage, screaming defiance as the troop attempted to remain ahead of the pursuing Saxons.

The chasers sensed an advantage and drove their equally weary horses after the Celts. One warrior charged at Balan's mount and, drawing level, slashed wildly at Balan's back with his sword. Without checking his mount, Balan bent low over its neck and avoided the deadly sword thrust while drawing his own blade. Then, with daring worthy of Artor himself, he checked his horse for a moment so that the Saxon warrior began to draw past him. With deadly precision, Balan buried his sword in the Saxon's back.

So great was the forward momentum of the galloping horses, that Balan's sword was ripped out of his hands. The Saxon swept past him on his wild-eyed horse, pinned upright by Balan's weapon. With a whoop of triumph, Balan swept on, driving his exhausted horse up the steep slope.

Suddenly a concealed pit, one of Artor's traps, yawned at his horse's feet and Balan only just managed to swerve his beast in time. The rest of his troop continued up towards the crown of the hill without mishap. Behind them, Saxon cavalry disappeared into collapsing screens of sapling, leaves and dry grasses – and the screaming began. Balan wanted to block his ears to shut out the dreadful sounds of impaled horses and dying men. Then Artor appeared, on foot, in full armour of a striking, blood-red colour. Around the High King was a line of warriors and bowmen, their eyes set and grim.

'Even before I had dismounted and begged a blade from a Celtic bowman, the Saxons were upon us,' Balan stated matter-of-factly, 'and our arrows were mowing down the forward cavalry.'

'How very fortuitous,' Modred said blandly, his smile just a little too wide.

'Your sneering does you no credit!' Balan snapped.

'Really, Modred,' Wenhaver reproved him, 'you should show some respect towards our warriors. Balan is correct when he says that we sit safely in Cadbury because of the wars fought by my husband.' Her rosebud smile was as warm as ever as she tapped him lightly with the silver stick of her fan, but the disdain that coated her words took Modred by surprise.

'Please continue, Balan,' Wenhaver ordered and pointedly turned her back on Modred. 'I shudder with fears for the safety of my husband.'

Now both men looked puzzled. Neither was accustomed to hearing the queen voice words of concern for the High King's welfare. Both men wondered fleetingly what new game Wenhaver was playing.

'King Artor annihilated the main Saxon force when he enticed a direct frontal attack. By keeping our cavalry concealed at the rear, they were convinced we were vulnerable. I suppose they believed that they were using our own tactics against us, and that we were at their mercy. But the pits and traps set by Artor surprised the first wave of attackers, while Artor's foot soldiers held the line. Once the Saxons were committed to making their attack, our cavalry was unleashed from their hiding places to chop the Saxons into bloody strips of meat.'

Wenhaver's courtiers clapped joyously and a wine cup was pressed into Balan's hands.

'Let us drink to Artor. Long may he reign as King of the Britons,' Balan shouted. He raised his wine cup into the air and the assembled company repeated the toast. Even Modred exhibited patriotic zeal.

'What were our losses, Lord Balan?' Lady Elayne asked quietly, and the faces of Wenhaver's women fell. Women understand that even victories are costly.

'The Saxons all perished, Lady Elayne, and there will be

much weeping in Anderida in the weeks to come. We burned their bodies so their widows would see the smoke above the forest and know the Celtic answer to their attack on us. Those few Saxons who fled were hunted down.'

Balan squared his shoulders and broke the little bubble of silence that had opened up around his words.

'As for our own losses, Artor won the victory, but good men went to the shades before their time. Ulf of Caerleon, who was a survivor of Mori Saxonicus, perished with some thirty of our archers, while twenty of our cavalrymen will come home to their families in funeral urns. But I know that our dead would count their sacrifice worth such a stunning victory. After the battle, King Artor spoke to the living and to the wounded in praise of our dead, and he told them that every sacrifice contributes to our survival. As is his custom, coin will be sent to the families of those who were killed or wounded in the battle, for the king will never allow wives and children to starve. Nor will he allow old mothers to wander the roads, starving and homeless. Such is the wisdom and the love that our king gives to us.'

'The loss of any young man is very sad,' Wenhaver murmured. 'But why did the Saxons venture out of Anderida after so many years? They must have realized what the outcome could be. Have they so many men to lose?'

'We can only guess, my lady. A number of freed slaves have told the High King that the Saxons were convinced that their cavalry would place great pressure on our borders. They believed our warriors would be forced to retreat, and allow them to gain control of more of our land. By all reports, their settlements need more farmland to provide for their growing populations. I don't wish to frighten the ladies, but the Saxons will come again, because they have no choice.'

Even Modred looked subdued and all the good humour in Wenhaver's bower fled away.

Battles were subsequently won at Ratae, where Balyn distinguished himself with reckless courage, while Artor's forces continued to skirmish with the Saxons for all of that unseasonably mild summer. The king's golden touch hadn't deserted him. In those combats where he raised Caliburn, the sword of kingship, and where the Red Dragon banner snapped in the summer breezes, Saxons died and the Celts carried the field.

From Ratae to Anderida, the crows and ravens gorged. As always, where Artor rode, death followed, for the king used an arsenal of strategies to bring the Saxons to ruin. In one battle, cavalry and archers harried the Saxons like a swarm of bees, until the enemy was driven to a river and the Celtic foot soldiers pressed forward to leave the Saxons with no place to run.

Later, at a ruined Roman fortress near Ratae, Artor winkled the Saxons out of an impregnable position by poisoning the wells with rotting corpses. While neither Balyn nor Balan approved of such methods, there was no doubt that sick Saxons were easier to defeat and Celtic casualties remained minimal.

As Artor increased pressure on the Saxon invaders, they were forced to beat a strategic retreat back towards the east and the south, and to their respective sanctuaries. The Jutlanders, in contrast, nibbled surreptitiously at the lowlands near the Wall, sinking in roots that would last for a thousand years.

Artor called his captains to Venonae fortress to discuss strategy. The motley group sprawled around his rooms and talked desultorily.

'The Saxons are like ants,' Bedwyr growled, his dirty campaign boots resting on a scarred table in Artor's war room in Venonae. 'They build a nest and dig in to strengthen it. Then, when they're ready, they scatter and extend their network, further and further into Celtic lands.'

'In some ways, it's even worse than that,' Gruffydd said, 'because the Saxons are starting to apply military strategy rather than relying on brute force. Bugger me, but the bastards are even starting to look like us, except that they're so damned big.'

Artor nodded in agreement. 'You know we're just putting off the inevitable. We'll never dislodge them from our island now that they have such a foothold.'

Galahad looked disgusted, as if sickened by a rancid smell. Gawayne dozed on a hard seat after the long ride to Venonae, while Taliesin examined his hands from his position in the corner of the room.

'True Celtic hearts can drive the invaders back into the sea, my king,' Balyn protested naively. 'All we need are a few more troops and a united faith in the justice of our cause.'

Artor sighed irritably. 'You're wrong, Balyn. The Saxons, Angles and Jutlanders are here to stay, so we must be realistic. They've lived in Britain for a hundred years or more, so they are Britons now, not invaders. A united enemy attack by them would finish us. Once all our young warriors were slaughtered, they'd annihilate the people. Saxon kin from across the waters constantly reinforce our enemy while we must grow our own warriors. It takes time to turn a babe into a man.'

'But the barbarians intend to sweep away our gods, our towns ... our whole way of life,' Balan whispered with a genuine shadow of fear in his grey eyes. 'We're fighting for our survival.'

'Just so, Balan,' Artor agreed. 'And they'll probably succeed in the end. We've been protecting our Celtic way for as long as I can remember. And my greatest wish, as it was for Myrddion, Luka and Llanwith pen Bryn, is that our enemies become more civilized before the days of the final conflict. Perhaps we should cultivate the Picts. We would both be stronger if they joined with us, but the Picts will never forgive us for stealing their lands in the distant past. Perhaps, like them, we will be forced to retreat to the wild places where we will taste the bitter bread of poverty and drink the sour water of defeat. But even then, the Celts need not wither and disappear. On days like this, when my shoulder aches from the old arrow wound taken at Mori Saxonicus, my mind can imagine no future for my people. But tomorrow, if I have no pain, my spirits will rise and I will remember that such sacrifices cannot be in vain. Celtic hearts will live. The question is, where?'

'How can you continue to fight the Saxons when you doubt our ability to win the war?' Balyn asked, his face shadowed with unhappiness. He was shaken to the bottom of his soul by Artor's brutally honest assessment of their future. He had always believed in the invincibility of his father's people, and he had never considered that the infrequent forays against the Saxons were anything but an exciting opportunity to initiate young Celtic warriors in their first blooding. Never, not even during his blackest moods, had Balyn considered that the will and cleverness of an old warrior, backed by loyal troops who were ready to die to the last man, were all that stood between the Celtic people and slavery.

'What's the alternative?' Artor smiled wearily. 'I would do almost anything to end the Saxon menace, once and for all, but I don't believe it is possible. Where would the Saxons go if we drove them out of these isles?'

Balan looked puzzled and held his tongue, but Balyn hazarded a response.

'Couldn't they return to their own lands? The Saxons must have come from somewhere.'

'Aye, they did. But if you travelled across the narrow Saxon Sea, you would understand that other tribes from the north and west are moving inexorably southwards. The Saxon homelands have been overrun by another people who won't permit the original inhabitants to return, just as the Picts, who once stood where we do, were overrun by invading Celts. We drove them out of their lands into the cold wastes that lie beyond the Wall.'

Balan nodded his head in understanding, but Balyn pursed his lips in denial and his grey eyes were angry and hurt.

'Balyn, you cannot close your mind to what is real. This is now the Saxons' homeland. We can either share it with them, or one of us must leave.'

'Not us!' Balyn swore. 'Never the Celts!'

'I hope you're right, Balyn.'

At this point, Gawayne roused himself. Any other vassal would have been embarrassed to have dozed off in the king's presence, but Gawayne simply laughed at himself. Artor did not begrudge him his rest after weeks of physical exertion and vigilance. Gawayne had always been able to shed his cares like a discarded snakeskin.

The Otadini prince had used his father's warriors to teach the Jutes a stinging lesson at Eburacum, where so much Celtic and Jute blood had been spilt in the past fifty years. The swamps had run red, instead of green, when the battle lines were drawn. Where once rushes had grown, the bodies of many dead men now lay. The Otadini singers were already composing songs of this vicious battle, where neither side had been prepared to cede victory to the other.

As Gawayne reported to his king, both sides had fought to a weary standstill, for their armies were almost evenly matched. Both sides were desperate, and both were fighting for survival, so the conflict was a dour, bitter affair.

'Eventually, the Jutes withdrew and granted us the field,' Gawayne told Artor grimly. 'They've retreated back inside their borders and won't be able to advance again for several years. Their losses were particularly heavy, for you know these huge, hairy barbarians hate to surrender.'

'I'd be careful what you say about Jutes within Odin's hearing,' Artor warned with a wide grin. His temper had frayed easily at the beginning of the campaign but although his eyes were hollow with weariness, his smile now came easily and his mood seemed lighter and more optimistic, for all that he preached disaster to the twins.

Perhaps he's just happy to be away from the court, Gawayne thought, and no one can blame him for that!

'The Jutes brought me bars of red gold in carts drawn by

milk-white oxen to purchase the bodies of their dead. They were noble adversaries, so I accepted their payment, just as we've done in the past. I've travelled with their gold for many miles to pay it to your steward. I've also taken a one-tenth share for the kin of our dead, which has been sent back to my father and the Otadini tribe. I trust this arrangement is acceptable to you?'

'Aye, Gawayne. You act with commendable common sense and dispatch in matters of warfare.'

Gawayne grinned and accepted a mug of ale from Odin.

Artor no longer saw Gawayne often, for his nephew had avoided Cadbury for years, having discovered, to his cost, that the queen was a ruthless hunter and he was easy prey. He was never able to resist her charms, even as she aged, and his answer to this weakness was to hide from the seductive siren call of his paramour.

'We'll let the Saxons retreat in good order and without undue harassment,' Artor ordered. 'Meanwhile, all the tribes must contribute to the fund needed to refurbish our defensive positions, except for the Otadini, as Gawayne has brought the Jute tribute with him. This instruction is especially binding on the Brigante tribe and they lie under threat of being cast out of the Union of Kings if they refuse to comply.'

Artor glanced at each of his leaders in turn, holding their eyes until they nodded in agreement.

'Modred's warriors will be responsible for the defences of Verterae and Lavatrae. I'll explain his duties to him in simple language that even he should understand. However, because I have little trust in my kinsman, his forces shall be merged with warriors from your tribe, Gawayne. You are in overall command of the north, so you must make those difficult bastards serve their king. You may use your fabled charm.'

'My charm only ever worked on women, Artor, but this task will give me a great deal of satisfaction. Shite, I'll enjoy extracting cooperation from those Brigante bastards!'

'You'll need to appoint a damn good second-in-command to assist you to fulfil all of your extra responsibilities. Numerous unannounced visits and inspections of your forces will be needed to ensure that all is well in the region.'

'I'll install my brother, Geraint, as my deputy. He's competent and overdue for promotion. I can trust him to carry out your orders.'

'I don't remember your brother, although the name seems familiar. Have I met Geraint?'

'Yes, my lord. But he was a spotty youngster when you last saw him. He's thirty-nine now, and was born only a year before Gaheris. He's very quiet, but he's a talented leader of men, even if I say so myself. His sons are almost fully grown, so he can devote his time exclusively to your interests.'

The reminder of Gawayne's youngest brother, Gaheris, was a wrench. Artor had always felt responsible for his nephew's death, twenty years earlier, at the hands of Glamdring Ironfist. Gaheris had taken Artor's place at an arranged meeting with the Saxon leader to offer an honourable truce. The murder of the envoys and their personal guard had resulted in Artor's last major confrontation with the Saxons at the battles of Mori Saxonicus and Caer Fyrddin.

'If he's half the man that Gaheris was, Geraint will be a welcome addition to the ranks of my captains,' Artor said.

'Aye, lord. He's an able fighter and his men love him. I trust him with my life.'

'As for Ratae and Venonae, the Ordovice and the Cornovii are already committed to defending their own lands.' Artor turned to Bedwyr. 'You, Bedwyr, will assume command of this united force.'

'Me?' Bedwyr yelped. 'I'm not a king to be given command of an army. A promotion like this would insult my neighbours and my own liege lord.'

Bedwyr's shock said much about the self-effacement of the Cornovii warrior. Now in his middle years, Bedwyr's reddish hair and flushed complexion had faded, but the marks of the slave collar that had once encircled his throat were still vivid. Scars across his face and evidence of a broken nose spoke of years of danger and pain.

'I've spoken to the kings of the Cornovii and the Silures and I have written to my kinsman, King Bran of the Ordovice,' Artor said. 'They've agreed to abide by my decision. Who else knows the mountains and the forests as well as you do? And, more importantly, I have absolute trust in your judgement.'

Bedwyr bowed his head.

'I shall bestow on you the title of King of Arden. You'll have no tribe to follow you, except for those men who come to you voluntarily. I cannot risk the alliance by gifting more men to you than you already have.'

'I'll obey you to the death, my lord. The title means nothing to me, but my family will be proud, and for that I thank you. The only boon I ask is that you permit my wife to remain at Cadbury under your protection, for she's dear to me.'

'You may be assured that Lady Elayne will always be safe in Cadbury.' Artor turned to Balyn and Balan. 'As for command of the south, this will be divided between you two. You will be charged with the defence of Venta Belgarum and the ports. It will be your task to prevent Anderida from spreading its poisonous influences any further. Although you'll be far from your home and you've no love for the south, I trust you both to act as I would. Balyn, you have natural authority and consider-able fighting skills, so you'll assume tactical command. Balan, you are a born strategist with your cool brain, and will assume strategic command.'

Balan dropped to his knees and bowed so low that Artor was embarrassed. Balyn was a little slower to respond, for his mind was fixed on the compliments that had been given to his brother, rather than to himself. He felt a twinge of jealousy stab through his vitals.

'What are my duties, my lord?' Galahad asked. He had acquitted himself well on the battlefield and wondered why he was having to wait for Artor to give him a role that was commensurate with his ability and his birth.

Gawayne winced as he saw Artor's eyebrows twitch. At this rate, his son's lack of manners would have him banished from the king's presence.

'You'll base yourself at Salinae Minor and will control all those lands that surround it. Gronw hasn't finished trying to destroy me, so you are charged with finding the Cup. I've heard word from Gruffydd that the black warrior still has influence in the district around the island, and that trouble will soon be developing from the hamlets near Salinae Minor. The villagers believe a rumour that there is a sacred relic in Gronw's care that can save the west. Unfortunately, the rumours also infer that I'm not worthy to hold Lucius's Cup.'

'Why did you choose me for this task, my lord?' Galahad asked, proving to his father yet again that the boy saw the world entirely through his own feelings and self-image.

'You have a nose for wickedness, Galahad, and you possess Christian righteousness that is coupled with a strong right arm. I trust you not to give up until you complete the task I have set you.'

Galahad still managed to look offended but before he could voice a complaint, Gawayne punched him hard on the arm.

Artor began to pace the room, needing to match actions with the orders he had issued. So much rested on these men, all of whom were flawed in some way. Then the High King shrugged for, as Targo had often said, he must do the best he could with what he had.

'I'll be riding to most of the major settlements in the west to spread a message of hope and reconciliation. This Saxon summer has cost us very little, but if we are to prevail, we must remain alert.'

'I understand, my king', Galahad replied. 'You fear the blows that can come from inside our borders. For my part, I'll carry out my duties with diligence.'

Then Artor addressed the whole group once again.

'You may go, my friends, for we have planned our work for the coming autumn and winter. Go with grace and the favour of the gods.'

Once his captains had departed, Artor allowed his squared shoulders to slump and he sank into his chair like the old man he had become.

Taliesin moved out of his corner.

'You're tired, my lord.'

Artor sighed. 'I wonder when I became such a manipulative creature, one who plays on men's faiths as easily as you pluck on your harp strings, Taliesin. Necessity, it seems, makes monsters of all men.'

'I understand how the love of your subjects burdens you, for you fear that you'll be forced to betray them for the sake of the kingdom. But if you asked every warrior in Venonae how they felt about dying for your cause, they'd answer that such a death would be the will of the gods – and not your fault.'

'I am glad your mother sent you to me. And I'm grateful that you're content to follow me across the country so that I have someone to complain at when I feel sorry for myself, which is far too often. Tired men make mistakes.'

'There's no need for pretence or apology with me, my king. I'm only Taliesin, your harpist, and no man counts me important enough to court my loyalties.'

'More fool them!'

Taliesin felt the force of the old king's character. Like a guttering candle, Artor's spirit still burned bright and clear. His grey eyes might be nestled within networks of old man's wrinkles, but the intelligence and reason that had governed the king's life shone through with purity. Although Taliesin had seen those same eyes freeze with pitiless calculation, he had also watched the deep and concealed compassion that swam in their cool depth, and enlivened Artor's rugged face with a special kind of love.

Artor had submerged much of his own humanity into the task of saving the west from invasion. Family, love, fidelity, gentleness, consideration and humility had been ruthlessly buried because circumstances had transformed these virtues into weaknesses. But Taliesin knew that Artor still possessed these characteristics in abundance, and he was sad to see Artor's constant struggle to keep his softer side alive.

'I'm proud to stand behind you, my lord, and I'm grateful that I've taken my father's place. I'm also privileged to see the last of your strength and, if the gods should permit it, to record the Passing of the King and the kingdom before I die.'

'Will you play for me, friend? Give me a folk song, one to remind me of our people and what they expect of me.'

'Of course, my lord. I'll tell you a tale that the villagers sing in the mountains at the time of the autumn threshing.'

His voice lulled Artor to sleep for a short time and, when the king awoke, they talked as friends do, late into the night. Artor could almost pretend that Myrddion and Targo were still alive and were speaking through the mouth of the young harpist.

Elderly men take what comfort they can from their memories of the happy past.

As the first autumn winds soughed around the ramparts of his fortress, Artor felt the inexorable advance towards physical death. A sudden gust shook the shutters and the king was reminded that the kingdom was under attack. Like the wind that battered at his walls, his enemy was also invisible, but if he reached out his hand, he could feel its presence.

With a chill, he admitted that nothing, and nobody, could stop the wind.

CHAPTER X

A WEB OF DECEIT

Gronw sat in a mean little hut built of wattle, daub and reeds, and stared sullenly at his tattooed hands. The hut leaked when it rained and the wind found its way through a myriad cracks and holes that made every damp winter night a misery.

The black warrior's refuge stood in a cleft between two windswept hills to the west of Deva, a large provincial town that lay at the end of Seteia Aest. Deva was situated on the main Roman road from Venta Silurum into the north, and any intrepid traveller knew that Deva was the gateway to the Brigante lands. In obedience to the instructions that had been hurriedly whispered to him at an inn in the town, Gronw had ventured on to the smaller, rutted road heading towards Mamucium and, from there, he had followed an almost invisible track that branched away into the hills. Few travellers ventured into these windy, barren slopes, so the murderous priest was relatively safe from discovery.

Only the hardy or the desperate braved the desolate track that served as a pathway for shepherds and farmers from the lowlands. While Gronw's quarters in the wild were ugly and uncomfortable, the families who provided the shelter were true believers who had long adhered to the old ways of worship, so Gronw was secure. They gave this shepherd's hut freely as a base for Gronw's work.

Malcontents, the curious and a number of ragged hill people had come to listen to the rantings of the black warrior, who was popularly believed to be a Druid of the highest order. In fact, Gronw bore no resemblance to the masters of the old lore and didn't possess the high status that he assumed so glibly. He clung to ancient, Prydyn woman's magic rather than Druid maunderings over mistletoe or oak.

The Prydyn, the ancient name for the Picts, recognized the Tuatha de Danaan, although the Celts could never get their mouths around the Pictish names. Gronw smiled unpleasantly. Ceridwen was fundamental to his faith, for Prydyn queens often decided who ruled the land in the name of the goddess. Many a Prydyn king governed only because his mother held the true reins of power in the name of Ceridwen.

'These Celtic pigs accept their Ceridwen in Her place. Her name is too holy for their tongues.'

The emptiness of the ramshackle shepherd's bothie echoed his words oddly, so that a second voice seemed to speak aloud with him. Gronw shivered within his cocoon of furs and rags. The goddess came rarely, but when She did notice the affairs of fragile, feeble men, every message was charged with meaning. Celts had killed Gronw's mistress Gernyr, Ceridwen's priestess, and Celts had killed Miryll, the daughter of Gernyr, so She was thirsty to drink their blood and feast on their raw and quivering flesh. Many years earlier, the Roman legions had castrated the Celtic Druids at Mona, and only the shivering remnants of those priests still worshipped in the sacred groves of oak. But She went on and on, wearing different names, and bearing different faces. The goddess was forever, and She would dance on the graves of the Celts.

'Men are fools when religion is used as an excuse for their failures,' Gronw muttered to himself as he stripped off his threadbare ceremonial robe and busied himself with heating a simple rabbit stew that had been sent by a member of his flock. 'Celts are easily convinced that the gods have turned their faces away from them – as if the gods would care if some petty chieftain loses a son or two in battle, or a disease kills all his cows. Rather than accept that they themselves might be inadequate, these Celts choose to blame Artor for their ills. He has angered the gods so they must suffer!' Gronw spoke aloud to relish the taste and sound of his words.

'Their selfish stupidity is an easy weapon to use against them, Mistress Gernyr,' he whispered. 'Yes. We'll use it, won't we? How these Celt pigs love it when I blame Artor for their poverty, the Saxon attacks and even the weather. They salivate to heap their sins on to the shoulders of the High King. Miryll has served her purpose, although I had not planned to use her in quite this way.'

The Lady of Salinae Minor had assumed a mythic martyrdom since Gronw had been forced to flee from his southern base of operations. A helpless, pregnant woman was an ideal symbol to illustrate that the High King was a depraved and murderous barbarian. Even an unborn child could not be permitted to survive if it threatened Artor's hold on the throne. Many men who had ancient quarrels with the Romans, or who possessed Saxon heritage that had its genesis during the reign of Vortigern, embraced any myth that fed their resentments.

Gronw giggled again, but louder, and the sound was manic and teetering on hysteria as it filled the bare, wooden room.

'Vortigern fell prey to Ceridwen. His wife, Rowena, was an adherent of the goddess, for all that she was Saxon. Those barbarians accept Her influence as well, although they prefer their gods of thunder and discord. Poor foolish Vortigern was old and frightened of his sons, so he invited Rowena's kin to enter his kingdom.'

Gronw snorted mirthlessly.

'Imagine, mistress, an old grey rat who is frightened of the sleek sons he had spawned. He welcomed in the cats to protect him – and the kin of Vortigern, High King of nothing, have been trying to get rid of them ever since. Vortigern was a Celtic fool, so Uther and his son have wasted Celtic lives to root out the Saxons the old man invited into the land. Good! Fewer for me to kill! But Vortigern left a legacy of hatred which we can use, mistress, as Ceridwen used Miryll in our holy cause. Miryll's death has served a great purpose. The people, great and small, will listen to the story of her death and weep for her lost love for Gawayne. It doesn't matter that there was no love on either side. The story is pretty, and they can weep over her innocence and her loveliness.'

Gronw was right. Legends achieve a life of their own. Miryll's tower, her weavings and her liaison with Gawayne had developed a distinctly sentimental tone. Even the tale of her watery burial had been adapted so that the lady sang her own burial song.

'Men are such fools, mistress. You'd smile to see how easily the Celts can be manipulated.'

Gronw never spoke to Miryll's shade. Her spirit did not

choose to visit him, although he had been present at her birth and had acted as her foster-father for most of her short life. Gronw still served the raven-haired Gernyr, Miryll's mother, who had been his secret lover before her husband, Rufus Miletus, exercised his rights as pater-familias. Even the passage of nineteen years had not dulled Gronw's deep hatred for all things Romano-Celtic, or for those people who preserved that hateful regime.

Gernyr and her servant, Gronw, had been the spoils of a skirmish beyond the Wall when she was little more than a child. They were captured on a rutted horse trail overlooking the soft landscape above Ituna Aest by Rufus Miletus, a prominent man in Salinae who had been visiting King Lot with his father, Miletus Magnus. At that time, hunting barbarians was a popular Celtic sport and ten-year-old Gernyr had been a valuable catch, had any of her rapists chosen to discover that her father was a Prydyn king. Ignorant of her status, Miletus Magnus had made the little girl a slave in his household.

Gernyr had hated secretly and with utter concentration for her whole youth. She did not soften even after Rufus Miletus had become so captivated by her beauty and spirit that he had taken her as his wife, and she had used her woman's knowledge, and Gronw's aid, to ensure that she never fell pregnant to the man she loathed. Miletus had not been cruel, and he had endured harsh censure from his dying father when he entered into marriage with a freed slave, so her coldness, promiscuity and visible dislike was an unbearable insult.

Over time, she had eagerly taken Gronw, or any other man of influence, into her bed so she could revenge herself on her husband for stealing her away from her homeland. That her daughter, Miryll, was born at all was a small miracle, and Gernyr was unsure who had fathered the babe that she had initially attempted to abort. Ultimately, the child had become just another tool of revenge that Gernyr used against the hapless Miletus, who could never be sure if he cherished another man's child. To his shame, the Celts of Salinae enjoyed gossiping about his disgraceful wife until he had no choice but to take action against her.

Gronw remembered the last, terrible battle of words that had resulted in Rufus Miletus striking off Gernyr's head. Since that dreadful, blood-soaked moment, Gronw's life had ceased to have meaning, and only his taste for revenge gave his life a semblance of reality. Rufus Miletus had been banished and had died peacefully at Salinae Minor. Who was left to hate but all Celts, and the High King in particular, whose laws perpetuated the enslavement of the Picts, the proud Prydyn?

Although the assassination attempt at Salinae Minor had failed, Gronw had discovered that Artor was assailable. The High King's true and utterly faithful followers were growing old, while the king's safety seemed rarely a matter of concern for the younger lords. Artor's fighting skills were legendary and his aura of invincibility was so strong that few of the High King's loyal servants could imagine that old age could dim his prowess. Complacency blinded Artor's court, and even the High King had become careless of his own safety through many years of peace and prosperity. So great was Artor's reputation that, in a few months, the vigilance born out of a narrow escape from death would begin to fade and he would once again become easy prey. Artor did not value his own life, although he would do nothing to end it. Gronw had no under-standing of why the High King might welcome death, but he was happy to oblige if he had the opportunity.

In the meantime, the Cup was in his possession.

Although Gronw was a natural conspirator, he had few leadership skills. After Gernyr died, Gronw had been alone, raising Miryll in bitterness and lies – until his new master discovered him in the sterile solitude of Salinae Minor and his life regained its purpose and direction. His new role was to spread sedition and distrust against Artor, and if religion could help serve this avowed purpose, then it would be used.

Gronw extracted the Cup from its hiding place beneath a loose stone in the floor of the hut. It was such a plain, unassuming object, considering it wielded so much power over human imagination.

When Miryll had first seen it, newly recovered from the grave at Glastonbury, she had looked at it in wide-eyed amazement.

'Why is the Cup so precious, Father Gronw? It's only a metal drinking vessel.'

'It's not what it is that accounts for its worth, Miryll, but who owned it. This battered mug once hung at the girdle of Mother Ceridwen. And she used it to ladle out drops from the Cauldron of all Knowledge. If you drink from the vessel, and your lips touch the rim once handled by Ceridwen, your heart will gain all her knowledge.'

The poor little fool had believed both his promises and his lies about her kinship with Ceridwen. A small lump stuck in his throat, for he had valued her worth to him, but his habits of obedience ran too deeply to be swayed, even by love. His new master had told him to kill the bishop when he took the Cup, and he had enjoyed murdering the Christian prelate at his own altar, but Gronw had been mystified by the need to kill him. Aethelthred was too humble to be powerful, and his death was of no appreciable worth to their cause.

Gronw carried out his master's wishes but master and servant had their own, separate goals. Gronw sought the destruction of every Christian Celt in the land, for nothing less than a river of impious blood would appease him. Let his master dream of power, but Gronw was at war, ultimately, with all things Celt – including his master.

Gronw's lips twisted in fleeting pleasure. He knew he was a pawn, and at times like these, when he was cold and hungry, he railed against his fate. But next week, he would leave these uncomfortable lodgings and find a new refuge where he could spread his poison to a wider audience. He wouldn't sleep soundly until all the Celts in the west were washed away and the shade of his mistress could finally rest. And then, perhaps, Gronw would no longer dream.

Galahad strode through the gardens of Salinae Minor, finally alone now that his father had taken up his duties in the north. Within the villa, Percivale slept in unguarded peace.

Before leaving Venonae, Galahad had sought out his king in a private audience.

'Forgive my rudeness, my king, but I need your assistance. It's imperative that I have someone I can trust to act as my second self at Salinae Minor during the search for Gronw. If we are to find the Cup, as you have ordered me to do, I'll need someone who shares my beliefs and thinks as I do. Moreover, we cannot afford to alienate the priests of Glastonbury, so I'll need a good Christian warrior as a companion.'

The High King chose to judge Galahad's brusque manner as a personality trait caused by a fixed and obsessive nature, rather than intentional discourtesy. Galahad's request made sense, although Artor doubted the prince's clarity of purpose. Faced with a choice between his god and the Celtic cause, Galahad could well falter.

Gruffydd had informed Artor that rumours of Ceridwen's Cup were circulating widely in the north. His spies could speak of little else, and solving the origins and location of the Cup was an urgent matter.

'Would my bodyguard, Percivale, suit your needs?' Artor asked. 'I'll be sorry to lose him, even for a short time. Percivale is more my friend than my servant, and I made a promise to Targo on his deathbed that I would keep Percivale by my side. However, this puzzle of the Cup is more important than my own needs, so I'll temporarily relinquish him to you.'

Impressed by the speed of the king's decision-making, Galahad nodded in agreement and Percivale was soon summoned into the king's private presence.

Percivale was now forty-five and a seasoned warrior. His face was boyish, but his scarred body was muscular and fit.

'I must ask you to leave the court and undertake a mission of great importance to the west,' Artor told his aide. 'If I had any choice in the matter, I wouldn't ask this of you, but Galahad needs you in his quest to find the Bloody Cup, a religious relic that is being used to rally forces against me. This Cup must be found, and Glastonbury is the key to its origins. Someone there must know where Lucius first obtained it. After all, the Cup was in Glastonbury for at least seventy years. Your god dwells there among the priests, so you will fare better than I, or even Galahad, for that matter, for he comes from the pagan realms to the north. The priests are more likely to speak freely to you than to either of us.'

Percivale sighed, and a world of sadness dwelt in the sound.

'I live to serve you, my lord', he responded. 'If this task is the best way to do it, then I am prepared to take my leave from you and perform my duty.'

Artor clapped Percivale on the shoulder.

'Good man. It's unfortunate, but I can't trust Galahad's judgement. He's mad with love for his god, so the interests of Christianity might not always be best for his king. I know that you'll always be loyal and true to your conscience.' Artor smiled at Percivale. 'You have one further task. As well as finding the Cup of Lucius, I want you to discover who is behind its use in what I suspect is a conspiracy against me. I believe that Salinae Minor may still have secrets that might be of use to me. And while you're in the area, visit Glastonbury and introduce yourself to the new bishop.'

Percivale nodded in agreement. He recalled Brother Simon's cautious reticence when the king had questioned him about Lucius's Cup; a courtesy call to the new bishop would provide an excellent opportunity to seek out the old Jew and question him further.

Percivale left for Salinae Minor in company with Galahad, but not before Odin had voiced his fears.

'The trine is broken, Perce. How shall Gareth and Odin serve King Artor without you? Two is unlucky and a dangerous number.'

Odin looked so disconsolate that Percivale almost changed his mind. But Taliesin stepped forward and volunteered his services as the third bodyguard.

'I know I'm a poor substitute for Percivale, Odin, but I have slain wolves and, on one occasion, I speared a cave bear. I'm not a weak-kneed youth, else my mother wouldn't have sent me to serve the king, so you can be sure that I'll guard Artor's back during Percivale's absence.'

Odin rapidly revised his fears and found them resolved.

'Myrddion's son lowers himself to labour like a servant,' Percivale answered slowly.

'But Nimue's son would never count the cost if there was any risk to the king,' Taliesin responded earnestly. 'If it was in my power, I would save him anyway. So what does livery matter? No badge of service harms my station if it raises my honour.'

Odin embraced Taliesin, and Percivale marvelled at the courage of the Jutlander, for some atavistic, superstitious part of Percivale's soul still feared the intensity that lay behind the eyes of the harpist.

He gripped Taliesin's sword hand and felt love and friendship replace the doubt in his heart.

'Take care during my absence, friends, for I can sense that our world is changing. I catch odd looks and whispers behind corners. Danger is close to the High King, so you must sleep with one eye open and drink only water, if you value the High King's safety.'

Both men laughed ruefully and embraced Percivale, who had only enough time to collect his few possessions and run to the stables. Characteristically, now that he had a purpose,

Galahad was eager to brush the dust of Venonae from his boots.

The days were shortening and the grey skies of winter threatened sleet when Percivale turned his horse towards Glastonbury. He had visited the religious centre many times in the past, but on this occasion he had the leisure to notice that, even with the onset of winter, Glastonbury's waters sprang cleanly out of the cold, aching earth and her sweeping, pale green slopes were still scattered with the last amber leaves of autumn. The soft, grey mists turned the skeletons of trees into dim and jewelled landscapes, and Percivale felt Glastonbury's attraction anew. He was struck dumb by the beauty of God's sanctified earth.

On arrival at the ancient enclave after the short journey from Salinae Minor, he quickly discovered that the priests had little liking for their new bishop. Otha pen Gawr, already nicknamed Rufus for the well-tended beard that spread over his chest in a fiery plume, was one of the younger Celtic clerics, although Percivale immediately noted that the man had a vague Saxon appearance and a greedy, arrogant eye.

When Percivale was ushered into the bishop's presence, he saw that Otha was a fleshy man under ornate robes that his predecessors at Glastonbury would have scorned to wear. His lips were full and very red, while his eyes were a guileless blue under his Celtic tonsure. As Percivale knelt and kissed the bishop's ring of office, he made every endeavour to keep his eyes veiled. Common sense warned him that Bishop Otha was the kind of man who set great store by superficial values of ostentatious wealth and luxury. He wondered who had secured Otha's meteoric rise – and why such an apparent sybarite had been gifted with the fruitful fields of Glastonbury.

For his part, Otha was unhappy with both the presence of Percivale and his quest. They were an irritation that the bishop didn't trouble to hide.

'Glastonbury is a religious order and, as such, it owes no allegiance to the High King,' Otha stated baldly, his lips pursed as if he tasted something foul. 'Although we are grateful that the High King has sent the staff that murdered holy Aethelthred back to us. We have prayed over this relic to cleanse it of the blood that it shed so intemperately.'

'You should be grateful. Your order thrives under the protection of the High King,' Percivale said bluntly but politely. 'Would you wish Lord Artor to withdraw his succour? I can assure you that there are brigands and Saxons beyond count who wouldn't quibble at cutting priestly throats, if the spoils were good.' Percivale stared pointedly at the golden rings that adorned Otha's chubby hands.

'Hhmf!' Otha snorted, pig-like, with disdain, and Percivale was forced to fight down a natural desire to slap the bishop across his fat, hairy chops.

The bishop had yet to offer his guest a seat, or even a cup of water, and Percivale compared this Otha creature with Lucius and his successor, Aethelthred, who were, first and foremost, men of poverty who never flagged in courtesy.

'I need only speak to the older members of your community to complete the task I have been given by King Artor. I've been instructed by the High King to locate and trace the origins of a cup that was used by one of your predecessors, Bishop Lucius. King Artor is curious as to why such a mundane object should have been stolen during the attack on your church.'

'I've heard of this heathen vessel. Fortunately, it has been stolen from Glastonbury, so it no longer taints this haven of peace.'

'I couldn't accept that anything possessed by the sainted Lucius could be wicked or ungodly, Bishop Otha, for Lucius was a true follower of Jesus Christ.'

'Hhmf!'

Percivale wondered if Otha always grunted like a pig when he was out of sorts. But, as the petitioner, Percivale kept his face pleasant and biddable, knowing that he looked like a farm boy and was therefore beneath the notice of a pretentious hypocrite like Otha.

'Are you Christian, lad?' Otha demanded.

Percivale managed to school his face, for he was a middle-aged man, a warrior and was almost certainly older than the bishop himself.

'Aye, my lord. I've followed the Christian way for all of my adult life.'

'I suppose that's one small mercy,' the bishop snorted insultingly.

'I've been to Glastonbury on many occasions, usually when the High King makes his annual pilgrimage. One of my tasks has been to cut a sprig of the white thorn on Wearyall Hill for Artor to wear on his bonnet at the midwinter festival. I trust in the Lord Jesus and I believe he walked on the soil of Holy Glastonbury, just as the old stories tell us. I also believe that Josephus of Arimathea built the church and planted the roots of the Christian faith in these lands.'

'Very well,' Otha grumbled, unable to find any flaw in Percivale's religious credentials. 'But you must not keep my brothers from their duties or their worship.'

Percivale bowed and removed himself from the bishop's presence with a sigh of relief.

A silent priest accompanied him to a long dormitory where spare rooms were kept readied for visiting penitents and other travellers. The small cell possessed the usual tiny bowl of holy oil, a crucifix and a narrow sleeping pallet. It lacked a window and seemed tiny and claustrophobic. Yet, spartan as his new accommodation was, Percivale felt immediately at home, for he had been raised in the kitchens of Venonae and had learned the value of warm, closed rooms during the freezing winters.

After he had stowed his travelling bag, he sought out the Jew, Simon, who was the overseer of a small workshop and forge in the outbuildings of the Glastonbury enclave.

Brother Simon's workshop was open at the front to allow the forge to be cooled by fresh air. A sod wall separated the workshop from the open fires used by the blacksmith, although an open doorway linked the two rooms. Wide shelves lined one wall and a heavy table of wooden slabs, nearly a foot thick, served as a workbench. The warm windowless structure bustled with activity as several lay brothers escaped the cold weather to sharpen every scythe, ploughshare, spade and hoe used on the farm.

Brother Simon looked glum, and seemed sunk in a suspicious, unresponsive mood as he sat at his workbench.

'King Artor sends his best wishes,' Percivale began, while Simon supervised the melting of a number of golden arm rings in a crucible his apprentice had placed in the fires of the forge.

'Feast your eyes on this nonsense – an altar plate of sheet gold!' Simon growled. 'Bishop Otha orders me to melt down Glastonbury's treasures to add to his vain trappings of wealth.'

Percivale winced at Simon's unwise rantings, and the priest's young apprentice made a small exclamation of surprise that was just audible over the scrapings of iron on whetstones. The lay brothers continued to work diligently, obviously inured to Brother Simon's unpredictable moods.

'Keep your ears closed and your eyes sharp, boy,' Simon snapped at the nervous, tonsured youth who clutched a red-hot crucible with long blacksmith's tongs.

'Then you've no love for the new bishop?'

'He's well enough in his way, I suppose, but he isn't a suitable bishop to head the Glastonbury order. The man is far too worldly and grasping.'

'You're harsh in your judgement, Brother Simon.' Percivale grinned at the priest to show his sympathy. 'Where does your bishop call home?'

'I couldn't say – and I wouldn't care to speculate.'

This curt response only added to Percivale's caution.

'Please understand my motives, Simon,' Percivale began. 'I've been sent by King Artor to discover the whereabouts of a drinking vessel used by sainted Lucius, a relic that seems far too ordinary to be causing the storm that is gathering around it.'

Abruptly, Simon fumbled a shallow mould of clay that he had been oiling, causing it to fall on to the hardened sod floor. The green-clay mould smashed to pieces and the young apprentice almost dropped the crucible in surprise and alarm.

'Good God of Abraham!' Simon blasphemed in exaspera-tion. 'Look what you've made me do!' His gaze fastened on the young apprentice who was trying to shrink into the floor. 'Don't drop that crucible, Ethelbert, or I'll skin you alive. Put the crucible back on the fire and let it re-heat. Then fetch me another mould from the shelf.' The cords of Simon's neck were straining with suppressed emotion.

Percivale waited patiently while another mould was found and laid carefully on the seasoned oak bench. Gradually, Simon controlled his breathing, visibly calmed himself and then knelt painfully on the bare floor. He began to pray in a whispered monotone, while the warrior and the apprentice looked at each other silently.

They waited.

Eventually, Simon had mastered his emotions sufficiently to struggle to his feet, dust himself off and sit on a stool beside the bench. His head rested glumly on one twisted hand.

'Could you please leave us, Ethelbert? An early lunch perhaps? Or even a walk? I must gather my thoughts, and I'm weary.'

'Of course, master. I'm sorry to have caused offence.'

'You didn't cause any offence, boy. Please ask the brothers to allow us some privacy as well. Give them my apologies for disturbing their labours.'

The brothers hurried out into the weak, winter sunshine.

'But Otha *does* cause me offence! May heaven damn the man! The younger men will be all atwitter now because the Jew has thrown a tantrum, and Otha will hear of it and use my intemperance against me. At least Lucius understood that a man might say anything and everything when the anger comes upon him. Never mind. Perhaps the lads will hold their tongues, for our bishop is not universally loved.' Simon looked at Percivale with a lopsided grin. 'I beg your pardon, young man, for you've offered me nothing but courtesy, and I've repaid you with rudeness and irritation.'

'I have nothing to forgive, Brother Simon. Just please tell me frankly what you know about this wonderful drinking vessel.'

Simon avoided Percivale's eyes. 'I don't know much. Lucius never shared his past life with anyone.'

Frowning with impatience, Percivale wondered how he could extract the truth out of this obstinate old man who was reluctant to discuss the subject. Why would such a dedicated priest flinch at the mention of a common drinking vessel?

'If you truly know nothing of the Cup, why do you act like a guilty maiden caught with her lover whenever it's mentioned? An innocent man would merely shrug his shoulders and proclaim his ignorance.'

'Otha would rejoice if he could cast me out of Glastonbury, regardless of my tonsure or my age. And he will eventually succeed, for Otha is a patient man. He hates my race because he believes we murdered Jesus, as I suppose we did.'

Percivale groaned audibly. Once again, Simon was attempting to change the subject.

'But Jesus was a Jew!'

'Otha ignores that particular inconvenient truth.'

'What does the Jewish race have to do with the Cup? I don't understand your fears or your reluctance to speak openly with me.'

Simon replied, 'You were there when Artor questioned the old priests. What none of them knew was that the Cup is of

Jewish manufacture. It's not Celtic, or Pict, or Saxon. It's Jewish. Any man of my race would recognize it.'

Percivale looked quite blank. 'I still don't understand.'

'I'll admit that I avoided telling the whole truth when King Artor questioned me. I asked my bishop how he came to own a Jewish peasant's cup. Lucius smiled at me, in that sleepy way he adopted when he didn't wish to discuss a particular subject. I knew he'd been a decurion in the Roman army of Gaul, for a man can't hide his origins entirely. I knew, too, that the ring that Lucius gifted to King Artor had once been thick with congealed blood, but the tears of remorse shed by the bishop over many years had washed it clean. From what my master let slip, I knew that Lucius had killed many men in ferocious battles across the Roman world. I, too, once wielded a sword, and I could see that Lucius carried his history in his eyes, in his stance and in the way he used his hands.'

Percivale nodded. He resisted the temptation to ask Simon why he had become a priest because he knew that Simon would have welcomed the diversion.

'Go on.'

'Simply put, Lucius told me that he had received the vessel from another warrior, who had taken it from yet another, who had been given it by another. He told me that the Cup had travelled many leagues, as if these tired old eyes couldn't see that fact for themselves.'

'There's still more to explain, Simon,' Percivale persisted. 'I know there is.'

The silence between the two men stretched out achingly, until Simon spoke at last.

'I asked the bishop about the Cup on many occasions,' he

admitted tetchily. 'I nagged at him and, eventually, he became a little angry at my persistence.' Simon's shoulders slumped as if he was ashamed of the recollection. 'In my stiff-necked pride, I hungered for something tangible that would link me with the sainted Lucius. Damn me, I think I've been vain and intrusive all my life. In the end, Lucius gave me an answer of sorts just to shut me up, although I never solved the riddle.'

'The riddle?'

'Lucius was a man who enjoyed devising complex puzzles – not the least being the one solved by King Artor when he became ruler of the Britons.'

'Aye. That story is well known to all who live in the kingdom.'

'Lucius said that I might understand what he knew if I could solve his riddle. I puzzled over it for many years but I never solved his word game. Perhaps you'll do better. For a saintly man, my master could be infuriatingly obtuse, although I've often wondered if he was struggling to protect me from the consequences of my vanity.' Simon smiled. 'Lucius managed to shut my mouth and silence my questions, so I suppose he achieved his purpose. I never asked him about the Cup again.'

'Recite the riddle for me, Simon. We no longer have Myrddion Merlinus to show us the answer, more's the pity, but I'll try the best minds in the kingdom to ferret out its meaning.'

'You may have the puzzle, for I could never forget the damned thing!' Simon sighed as if a weight had been lifted from his soul. 'Let others bear the responsibilities of knowledge. In return, I ask that you free me of any blame for whatever direction this rhyme takes you. I'm too close to the great hand of my god to carry any more sins on my soul, especially for errors made by others.'

Percivale nodded in assent, and waited.

Simon fiddled with the broken mould, pursed his lips, scraped his sandalled feet over an imagined imperfection in the sod floor and then launched into rapid speech.

> I travelled far in bloody hands,
> In army camps from arid lands.
> My worth is naught in gems and gold.
> No blood, nor sacrifice of old
> Can touch the centre of my pain.
> The hands that hold are changed again.
> Lest men still covet my dull shine,
> I carry water now, not wine.

'You may extract whatever meaning you can from this riddle,' Simon said. 'However, I'm certain of one fact. The Cup never belonged to the blue hag, Ceridwen, so the black warrior is a liar as well as a blasphemer and a murderer.'

Percivale had never learned to read so, through repetition, he committed the entire rhyme to memory.

'I swear by my hope of heavenly redemption that I know nothing else,' Simon told him.

Percivale bowed his head in gratitude and respect. 'I won't trouble you further, Brother Simon. You've aided me in every way that you can. I would only request that you don't tell Otha, or anyone else, of the riddle.'

Simon chuckled, a sound that resembled nothing so much as the friction of rusty armour. 'That's one promise I'll keep.

The Cup of Lucius should have lain with its owner in his grave until Judgement Day. It has already been the cause of murder, distrust and cruelty. It's my belief that only the hands of a saint are sufficiently sanctified to hold such a symbol.'

Percivale turned to go.

'One more thing, before you go, young man,' Simon said. 'Lucius asked me to ensure that the Cup was placed in his grave after his death. He swore to me that the Cup was perilous and to take every precaution, on pain of my mortal soul, to ensure that the vessel went into the earth with him. I did exactly what he asked of me but, within days, my hands began to grow steadily worse until they became as crippled as you now see them. I've searched through the words of Jesus for a message about a vessel such as the Cup, but my prayers have never been answered. In God's name, Percivale, I beg you to take care, for I'm sure that the Cup is dangerous.' He paused to add weight to his warning.

'I've forsaken my race and the faith of my fathers to follow the teachings of Jesus. No child of mine will cover my eyes when I die, and no Jewish kin will sing the last song for me. So understand that when I beg you to forget the Cup and let it be, I have no ulterior motives. I do not wish to see Lucius's curse again in this life. I've no doubt that it will kill any murderer who holds it, and it will madden even good men if they should lust after its insidious promises. If there is any fault in your heart, the Cup will discover it, as it found the blood that was still on my hands and ruined them forever.'

He smiled wistfully at Percivale.

'I speak harshly because you are clean and good, Percivale, and I want no part of any ill that comes to you. Look into your heart before you reach out your hand to clutch this vessel to your breast. And pray that such an object never finds its way into King Artor's court. It would destroy the king more certainly than any blade could. He is a good man, your Artor, for I saw the character in his face long before you were born. But a king must make compromises to rule as long as he has, and the Cup will find his weaknesses. As to his court, I haven't been to Cadbury and I cannot imagine those men who surround him, but the Cup would discover every vile detail and every ambition in their natures.' Brother Simon stared at his useless hands. 'I would regret my assistance to you if it should bring harm to the High King or to any of his loyal subjects. Better I should be dead than be a traitor to the man who labours to preserve God's church.'

Percivale could offer no comfort, other than to bow respectfully and then leave the old man to his regrets.

As Percivale left the room, Brother Simon turned back to the new mould and began to oil it with shaking hands that were mere clubs. Tears rolled down his leathery cheeks, not only in sorrow, but also in joy. Glastonbury would be the last home he would ever know; although the Cup may have taken his hands, God had given him Glastonbury. Simon's faith was as strong as the metals he had once mastered. For good or for ill, the Cup was loose on the land, but Simon believed that God would prevail.

That night, Percivale dictated a written message to a priestly scribe, addressing it to Bishop Otha. Then, before first light and in secrecy, he took his leave from the religious enclave. Otha couldn't be trusted so, as a precaution, Percivale had questioned all the older priests during the course of the one afternoon in order to divert suspicion away from Brother Simon.

In the letter delivered personally to Otha, Percivale pronounced himself defeated by the passage of time in his search to find the origins of the Cup.

Then, like the smoke from the kitchens he had once tended, Percivale disappeared into the welcoming darkness.

Four days away as the crow flies, Gronw tossed fitfully as he slept on a pile of filthy straw in a stone hut in Ordovice country. His dreams were filled with the many faces of Gernyr Raven-Hair, her lower lip gripped between her white teeth as she thought up devilry. Her dark eyes were agleam as she stroked his thighs, his groin and his lust-blinded eyes. The black warrior groaned as he remembered the texture of her white throat as it pulsed with fierce life under his kisses. Then he saw her beloved, fearsome face as it jetted blood from the severed arteries that fed the stuttering beat of her heart.

Her brilliant eyes still possessed him, body and soul.

He writhed in his sleep and wished that he could gaze on her remembered beauty for just one more moment. Even the unconscious release of orgasm couldn't soothe him, as her eyes burned themselves into his brain as they had for a thousand nights before this one.

Eventually, exhausted and numbed, Gronw slept on dreamlessly in his malodorous hut.

Nimue woke from a dream of blood and murder, and felt the shade of Myrddion stretched comfortingly beside her.

'Taliesin does well', she told her beloved. 'My heart tells me he eases the king's pain.'

In Nimue's imagination, Myrddion's voice gently answered her as he stroked her hair.

'He'll need to be stronger still. As will you, my beloved. The unseasonable winds from the south blow cold when they should be warm. Dire portents are coming and you must be ready to do your part. Those who live by the taint, smell and taste of spilled blood are growing stronger by the hour. You are one of the chosen few who can do what must be done.'

'But do I have the strength to play my part in what must be?' she asked, her eyes like deep pools of blue water as she looked out into the empty darkness.

'You always have the strength to do what must be done, my lady.'

Her arms embraced the nothingness that lay beside her and she dreamed of Myrddion's touch, uncaring of the wind from the south or the portents of evil that wailed on the dark air.

CHAPTER XI

DOGGEREL AND
DREARY DAYS

Salinae Minor dreamed in the night wind, her breast pressed against the cold, dark waters of the river and her trees and roofs shrouded in a thin blanket of snow. Her statues were pale blurs in a landscape of charcoal trees and glistening, diamond-white gardens, and the villa seemed to hover over the silver drifts.

Inside, a roaring hypocaust heated the floors and every window was shuttered and the doors barred. The furniture and servants had scarcely changed, although Galahad's personal guard had taken up residence with much noisy joking and young male sweat. Even the slow-falling snow that entered the atrium couldn't chill the glowing braziers and warm tiles that resisted nature's extremes. More long shutters sealed the atrium from the body of the house, dimming the light and containing a feeling of cosy contentment and safety.

Galahad had efficiently organized the good order and comfort of the villa, but even his energy could not hide the fact that the heart had been plucked out of Salinae Minor and had not yet been replaced with another. Already, in the cobwebs forming in corners and through the thin line of dust that was filtering down on to wooden surfaces, the absence of women spoke wordlessly of Miryll's fate.

In the scriptorium, Galahad and Percivale stared glumly at a line of puzzling words that Galahad had written on the tabletop with a piece of charcoal.

'I'm damned if I can understand the meaning of this sodding rhyme,' Galahad muttered irritably. 'Artor will skin me alive if we don't decipher Lucius's puzzle, so I'm doomed to become a pair of slippers for the High King's feet.'

Percivale was about to grin in rueful companionship at Galahad's little joke, but he realized that Galahad was serious. The young man's abundant hair was tousled and untied, and even his normally perfect eyebrows seemed to be tangled. Under weary lids, his fine hazel eyes were bloodshot from lack of sleep.

'Can we explore this rhyme from another direction?' Percivale suggested tentatively. 'Perhaps we should determine exactly what we do know – and work outward from there.'

'We know that Lucius brought the Cup to Glastonbury,' Galahad stated. 'He admitted that fact to anyone who asked.'

'If that's correct, the Cup has no history in this land,' Percivale responded. 'So it can't be the Celtic relic that you thought was hidden at Salinae Minor.'

Galahad looked thoughtful.

'I suppose not,' he said. 'So what was secreted away in the tower? It must have been something important for Miryll's father to write of it, so we now have two mysteries to puzzle over. Shite, but I'd prefer to be doing something rather

273

than sitting around trying to puzzle out silly rhymes and mysteries.'

Percivale was as humble as Galahad was arrogant, but Percivale saw no reason to ram his beliefs down the throats of his friends, unlike Galahad who saw conversion to the Church of Rome as his duty. However, their shared faith was proving to be an asset in their developing friendship, although Percivale had never spent so many hours on his knees, a practice that Galahad deemed necessary to support his spiritual health. Arrogant and difficult in character, as straight as a sword blade and as brutally direct, Galahad was the stereotype of a Christian warrior in the imaginations of those unfortunate men and women with whom he came into contact. Only close proximity and empathy revealed the uncertain, troubled man who was struggling to break the influence of an exotic and repellant family. Percivale understood that Galahad dreamed of lasting glory to wash away all memories of his famous libertine father, his grasping grandfather, his sorceress great-aunt and his hate-motivated grandmother.

'Has anyone mentioned anything to you about the Salinae Minor relic except for what you discovered in the scrolls?' Percivale asked.

'During my visit to this place with my father, both Gronw and Lady Miryll avoided me as if I carried the plague.' Galahad toyed with a reed pen. His fingers picked at the stem, splintering and ripping the delicate point until it was pulpy and useless.

'Do you think that Lady Miryll might have revealed something to your father, even inadvertently? Both Miryll and Gronw seem to have treated Lord Gawayne like a pet hound, and she spent a whole day in his company. They must have talked about something.'

'After we left Salinae Minor, Father complained incessantly all the way to Cadbury. The main topic of conversation was Salinae Minor and its past. He objected strenuously to my dislike of the place and, while I'm no longer sure what he said because I hardly listened, he mentioned the execution of Miryll's mother by her husband, Miletus, without giving me her name. Father was adamant that Salinae Minor was a venerable place, and that I was being unreasonable in loathing the whole menagerie.'

'Did your father give any reasons for his judgement? I'm certain you would have argued with him about it.'

Galahad laughed thinly. 'He takes no notice of anything I say. He's Gawayne, one of Artor's immortals!'

Percivale waited, much as he had with Brother Simon at Glastonbury. He understood that even the cleverest and most manipulative of men hate silences and so they hasten to fill the void.

'Have you heard the legend of an old man from another land who is reputed to have built the original church at Glastonbury?' Galahad asked.

'I vaguely recall the tale.' Percivale shrugged, careful to hide his knowledge of Josephus until he knew the direction of Galahad's thinking.

'Father told me that the man who built the church was the same person who built the tower on this island. He'd already found Rufus's notes on the old scrolls but Father was uninterested in the references to an old man.'

'Perhaps the legend of the old man might be the link we're

searching for,' Percivale said cautiously. He resisted the link between the tower on Salinae Minor and Glastonbury church. In his mind, Salinae Minor would always be pagan and drenched in blood.

'Damnation! I can't remember what Father was maundering on about. But if you give me a moment, I might remember.' Galahad paced the room, and Percivale wondered how difficult it was to be sired by a legend such as Gawayne.

Visibly, Galahad wracked his brains. 'Father just shrugged, and he agreed that he'd never heard of the trader of the scrolls . . . or another outlandish name like that.'

Percivale stared at Galahad in disbelief. For such a dedicated young man, and one who was a zealous Christian, the Otadini prince was occasionally remarkably obtuse.

'Could the name he mentioned have been Arimathea?'

'Possibly. I don't remember.'

'Do you recall the holy stories of the Church?'

Galahad looked blank, but then realization slowly animated his face.

'Is it possible? Could Joseph of Arimathea be the Trader? The same Joseph who brought Jesus to this land? Who buried the Lamb of God in his tomb?'

Both warriors stared at the words on the tabletop with eyes that were round with excitement.

'The legends insist that Joseph came to Britain, but I always assumed that the tale was a fiction,' Galahad said, his face shining.

'Perhaps the legend was a memory from times long gone and the tale has changed with the passage of time. Have you ever seen the likes of the Glastonbury thorn elsewhere in

Britain? Myrddion Merlinus believed the thorn tree came from a sprig of Christ's crown of thorns. But who can say after all these years?'

Galahad shook his head. His eyes constantly returned to the charcoal words scrawled on the tabletop.

'First things first,' Percivale insisted, noting his master's preoccupation. 'What was the relic that came from this place? And where is it now? Listen to me, Galahad, and stop leaping to conclusions about the origins of the Cup.'

'It must be in the tower. Where else could it be?'

Decisively, Percivale rose to his feet. 'Then it's time we searched the tower.'

'Aye.' Galahad smiled at his friend. 'Searching is far better than staring at that damned rhyme.'

Several fruitless hours followed.

The tower had been stripped of all trace of Miryll's existence and only the bare stone room with its many narrow apertures remained. A few leaves from the last winds of autumn had banked up in the corners, for the servants were unwilling to enter this ghost-ridden space where the air was almost frozen from the winter chill. The two warriors tapped the stones with knife hilts, checked the stairs and lay on their bellies and burrowed into the crude foundations.

But they found nothing.

'I wonder what this room contained before Miryll's occupation?' Percivale stared around the small space.

Galahad shrugged. He was seated cross-legged on the central stone that raised him some two feet above the tower floor.

'If you lived here, would you sleep on a cold stone bed?' Percivale asked him.

'I don't even like sitting on this thing. It clearly wasn't intended to be a bed and, if it's an altar, its presence in a tower room makes no sense. Who would put an altar here? Think of the effort and ingenuity needed to raise the stone into place.'

Percivale gingerly kicked at the slab of stone. 'Why is it here?'

Galahad ran his hands over the rough surface. There was no carving, and no pagan symbols. In fact, it was just a rectangular rough-cut stone in the middle of a tower, in the middle of an island.

Both men dropped to their knees and started to inspect it in earnest.

Percivale was a practical man, as is anyone who has once hewed firewood and cleaned dirty pots for his daily bread.

'The floor should collapse under the weight of this stone,' he muttered to himself. He strode to the nearest aperture. If he craned his neck, he could see huge oak slabs protruding some two feet out of the walls. They were little more than six inches apart in two rows all round the tower, and made it look as if it wore a crown of spikes.

Galahad watched Percivale as he crawled around the room and examined the iron-hard floor so closely that the tip of his nose was almost touching the timber.

'There are heavy beams, then thinner slabs of wood set on cross-pieces. And here is a groove in the flooring.'

'Are you sure?' As usual, Galahad spoke first and thought afterwards.

Percivale was dirty, tired and exasperated. 'See for yourself!'

he retorted irritably. 'A competent craftsman would have spotted this seam sooner. Unfortunately, I'm not a carpenter and I'm not remotely familiar with stonework.' Percivale was now talking to himself as a rush of ideas tripped off his tongue. 'I'm sure that this floor was built for a specific purpose.'

He looked at the bemused Galahad. 'Think, Galahad! Why would anyone go to all this effort ... years of back-breaking work by a team of skilled workers? I know that oak is difficult to shape at any time, even with iron implements. A small grove of old trees has been sacrificed for ... what?'

Percivale hurried on, ignoring Galahad's puzzled face.

'Now, do we try to move the stone? There's a seam there, but it's black with age. No. There's not a hope of moving it, even if we had the strongest warriors in Britain to carry out the task. There has to be another way.'

Percivale darted out of the tower room and down the stairs. Galahad followed.

'Yes!' Percivale stated excitedly. 'There it is, in the centre of the wheel.'

Galahad craned his neck upwards from the twelve steps that led up to the tower chamber. 'What am I looking at, Percivale? I swear I'll clout you if you keep mumbling nonsense at me.'

Percivale pointed upwards.

The great double spokes of a wheel made of ancient oak were clearly obvious. The wood was hardened through years of seasoning to the rigidity and colour of old iron.

'Look at the centre of the structure. It's six feet in diameter and inlaid with dressed timber.'

'So?' Galahad was curt. His expression remained blank, and

279

Percivale was reminded that the kin of Morgause weren't noted for their intelligence.

'If you wanted to hide something, where better to put it than under a slab of stone that can only be accessed by opening another slab of wood under the floor of the tower room. Does anyone ever look upward when they're in a place like this?'

Light was beginning to dawn inside Galahad's inflexible thought processes. If Percivale's calculations were correct, there had to be a circular cavity below the floor that supported the stone.

'We'll need ropes to check that cavity,' Galahad said eagerly. 'You'll need to find a pulley and some sharp chisels.'

Percivale laughed at the younger man's enthusiasm – although he was less impressed at being ordered about like a slave.

'I'd prefer to do this chore in the daylight when we can see what we're about. If you wish, you can try to find entry at night but I plan to eat, then sleep soundly through the hours of darkness. This hiding place has been here for hundreds of years, so it can wait until tomorrow.'

Unwillingly, Galahad agreed, but neither warrior really slept well through the long, cold night, although their reasons for sleeplessness were quite different. Galahad was in hot pursuit of a Christian relic and the reputation he would win with such a discovery. Percivale was searching for God's purpose, for he was sure that Joseph of Arimathea would never bother to hide a relic unless it was important to the Christian faithful.

And so the discoveries made during the next day were an anticlimax. Percivale was winched into position under the floor and risked life and limb by hanging over the empty, central well of the tower. Below him, the stone flagging threatened to break every bone in his body if he fell.

As he sought footholds on the stone that made up the wall, Percivale realized that relatively fresh iron hooks had been placed in position and painted black to disguise them from all but the closest scrutiny. With the assistance of the hooks, he reached the centre of the wheel in minutes.

'Someone's been here before us, Galahad,' he called down.

After peering at the solid wooden wheel for several minutes, he pulled on one of the slabs of oak that was part of the construction and the thin plank moved slightly, leaving a narrow, dark aperture. Percivale pulled more forcefully until the board slid a little too far and fell into the depths below.

A long length of woollen cloth tumbled out of the gap, unfurling as it fell.

Percivale felt inside the diagonal space that was left, but if a relic had ever been there, it was now long gone.

'Damn, shite and Hades!' Galahad swore from below. 'All that effort for nothing!'

Breathing raggedly, Percivale hauled himself back on to the tower steps.

'It wasn't for nothing, Galahad. We now know for certain that there is a relic, and that it was once hidden in this tower.'

'But we knew it existed before we looked.'

Percivale shook his head. 'We only *thought* it did. Now we know for certain.'

Over ale in the scriptorium, the men examined the length of cloth that had been left in the wheel.

The wool was ancient, unbleached and it had discoloured

to the hue of old honey. Oil stains marked the folds in the fabric, and they could tell that the wrapped object had been long, thin and almost six feet in length.

'The relic must have been a staff,' Percivale guessed.

'So what made this hole in the fabric?' Galahad countered, wiggling a finger through a small tear caused by friction wear at one end.

'Perhaps it had a sharp edge . . . or something.'

'Possibly,' Galahad said glumly. 'But it's long gone now.'

Percivale remembered the length of old, dark wood that had bludgeoned the Bishop of Glastonbury to death. It had been carved with a Roman satyr at one end, which had been covered in blood.

'Gronw must have found the relic,' Percivale murmured. 'Perhaps he thought it was a Druid staff, or an object of magic. It's even possible that Gronw didn't know what it was. Questions. There are always more questions.'

The two men folded the woollen wrappings and stared fixedly at them. Once again, they considered the words of the rhyme and the legend of Joseph.

'We have a staff, a Cup, a thorn tree and mention of the Trader of Arimathea,' Percivale muttered. 'But the tower was hiding a staff, when it should have been a spear . . . *the* Spear!'

The silence lengthened as Galahad considered the Roman spear that was said to have pierced the side of Jesus as he suffered on the Cross. His blood roared in his ears.

Abruptly, Percivale rose to his feet. 'We may have some of the answers to the questions in our puzzle, but we could easily be wrong.'

Galahad pointed to the words of the rhyme. 'The reference to arid lands fits the description of the land of Israel, and a Roman soldier speared the side of Jesus while He was dying on the Cross. The soldiers were said to have gambled for His possessions, which could have included His drinking vessel.' He smiled across at Percivale. 'Lucius said his Cup had once held wine.'

'Slow down, Galahad. We know of the staff that killed the bishop, but we know nothing for certain of a spear. A small hole in woollen wrappings is not proof of its existence. And to guess that the Cup of the Last Supper travelled all the way to Glastonbury is ... well ... *very* hard to believe.'

Percivale's cautionary words were just so much background noise to the feverish thoughts that circulated within Galahad's brain. 'All the facts fit,' he insisted. 'And the rhyme makes sense if the Cup of Lucius belonged to Jesus.'

'But why would Bishop Lucius keep the Cup of the Last Supper for his personal use?' Percivale cautioned. 'Why didn't he send such a sacred object to Mother Church for safekeeping? We are probably imagining a solution to the puzzle that suits our purpose, rather than following logic.' He closed his eyes in concentration. 'Lucius knew the danger of his Cup. He'd been a Roman officer, he'd seen the worst excesses of warfare. If he suspected its origins, he'd have known that such an object could become a powerful tool for any unscrupulous kinglet who desired to further his power and influence. Lucius must have wondered at the connection when he heard the legend of Joseph at Glastonbury and saw the white thorn growing in an alien land.'

'So why did he keep it?' Galahad demanded. 'At the very

least, he should have hidden it, even if his suspicions were unfounded.'

Percivale grinned. He had heard from Gruffydd the tale of how Lucius led Artor in the search to find the sword and crown of Uther Pendragon.

'Lucius was a subtle man, so he probably wanted to hide the Cup in plain view, just as he did with Uther's crown and sword. Who'd suspect that a battered old mug might have such a history? Besides, Lucius may have had doubts about the origins of the Cup. Nothing else fits the facts as we know them.'

'I agree. Lucius must have had some doubts.' Galahad's sluggish brain had been stimulated and was now working with greater speed. 'And his natural caution would have impelled him to have the Cup interred with his body after his death.'

Although common sense warned Percivale not to leap to conclusions, he was a Christian and he yearned for an affirmation of his faith. Heady thoughts sent his mind spinning with promises of God's love made concrete through Lucius's Cup.

'There are no other answers that make any sense,' he said slowly, his eyes shining. 'The Spear that pierced the side of Jesus, the Cup, and the fragment from the Crown of Thorns might have found a home in Britain. The thorn tree grows freely at Glastonbury, but the other two are in unknown hands.'

Percivale wanted the relics to be Christian to validate his life choices but, gradually, his eyes cleared and he became his normal, controlled self again.

'Perhaps these relics really are what we would like them to be . . . and perhaps they aren't,' he said. 'Either way, they could easily be manipulated by some ambitious and greedy person who was fortunate enough to gain possession of them. A man as pious as Lucius would never have made personal use of the Cup of the Last Supper if he'd truly believed that was what it was. But he knew how dangerous the Cup could be if it fell into the wrong hands. Lucius took great care to keep the Cup out of men's imaginations, for the very reason that he *didn't* believe it held religious power.'

'He could have been wrong,' Galahad stated flatly.

'Aye, but perhaps we yearn for proof that our faith is paramount. Perhaps we ascribe too much meaning to the Cup's purpose. Whatever the truth might be, we can never truly know – never. The Cup is dangerous because it could be made into Ceridwen's Cup, or the Cup of the Last Supper, or anything else we care to imagine.'

'So Gronw holds the most powerful relic in all of Christendom in his profane hands,' Galahad murmured. 'Artor must be told of this danger.'

Percivale nodded. 'The hunt for the crown and the sword of Britain was as nothing compared with this quest. No throne is directly at stake here, but this search leads to the very roots of Christendom. The Cup must be found.'

'We can't afford to waste a moment, can we, Percivale?' Galahad said impetuously, having absorbed little of what Percivale had said. 'God intended that you should come to Salinae Minor with me and that you would place the Cup of Christ into my hands.'

Percivale saw the light of zealotry and madness dancing in Galahad's eyes. Lucius's worst fears about the power of the symbol were evident in the young prince and Percivale saw his path clearly at last. The cold, ambivalent and largely godless

Artor would have the strength of character to see the Cup for what it really was. And, the High King must ensure that the staff used to kill Bishop Aethelthred must never fall into the hands of the same unscrupulous persons who now held the Cup. Percivale recalled that as he had stood at the last gate of the tor and listened to the news of Aethelthred's murder, Gruffydd had been given the staff. Artor must be warned of its potential for evil.

'We must ride to Cadbury,' he agreed, and Galahad needed no further urging.

If the gods of the Romans were watching, Percivale was certain that they would be laughing at the frailty of mere humans.

Galahad permitted their beasts to take no rest on the journey to Cadbury. The horses were near to exhaustion when the two warriors reached the southern road leading to the tor. Galahad demanded fresh animals from a group of pilgrims en route to Glastonbury. They saw the red fever in Galahad's eyes and handed over two of their horses without hesitation. As Galahad spurred his new mount into a gallop, the pilgrims crossed themselves.

Every fibre of Percivale's being screamed the need for caution, but Galahad's fervour permitted no argument. In vain, Percivale pointed out that Artor was likely to be absent from Cadbury and could be waiting in Venta Belgarum for more clement weather, in case the damaged Saxon forces of Anderida made another abortive attack on the Celtic forces in the south.

'All the more cause to hurry in case Artor hasn't left for the south,' Galahad insisted.

'But if he's gone, we'll have to follow him!' Percivale called after the prince's back. 'The horses will die if we keep up this speed.'

'Then they'll die, and we'll just take others,' Galahad shouted back.

Eventually, in an exhausted daze, Percivale glimpsed Cadbury Tor pointing skywards like the index finger of some buried giant, and he thanked God for His mercy. At the wall that ringed the tor, the sentries told unsettling news. The king was absent from Cadbury. Galahad ordered the king's steward to send a courier to Artor with a simple message.

'What you seek is found. Return to Cadbury.'

Privately, Percivale was furious. Galahad's eagerness had told the entire west, and its many enemies, that they had discovered information of great importance.

The court boiled with curiosity after the return of Percivale and Galahad. Within a few hours, Balyn and Balan also arrived to report to the king on other security matters, so the court was set abuzz with rumours before a single night had elapsed. Percivale thanked God that the arrival of the twins had diverted some attention away from Galahad's crazed intensity.

Modred appeared unconcerned by the frenzied activity in Cadbury but he listened in corners more than usual. Wenhaver was sullen with resentment; when she summoned Galahad to her bower, the young man refused point blank to tell her why he had returned to the court in such haste.

'But I'm your queen,' she demanded, her chin lifted arrogantly. 'I insist that you impart to me the reason for your return to Cadbury. I speak for the king!'

'No, Your Majesty. I am on pain of death from King Artor

not to discuss my mission with any person other than my liege lord, the High King himself,' Galahad replied evenly, and all her threats and tantrums had no effect.

When Wenhaver remembered that Percivale was also present at the court, she demanded his presence in her bower. Artor's warrior choked at the summons.

What could he say?

Artor might have affection for him as a friend and body servant, but Wenhaver had no reason to care a jot for him. In fact, Wenhaver resented Artor's friends and was inclined to believe that they conspired with Artor against her. She could have him put to death before Artor returned if he refused to accede to her demands. As the king's servant, Percivale had no rights during the absence of his master and, being peasant-born, no aristocratic family would give him protection.

Percivale dressed carefully to visit the queen, even though her messenger became angry at the delay. As he entered the sweet-smelling bower, he felt himself skewered by a circle of hostile eyes.

'Bodyguard, I expect the truth from you as you hold to your god,' Wenhaver began before Percivale even had time to bow. 'Why does Galahad demand to see the High King?'

Percivale succeeded in looking like the innocent kitchen boy he had once been, dressed up in borrowed finery.

'I don't know, my queen,' he answered as calmly as he could. 'I've been given no indication of what Galahad intends. I swear by the blood of the Christ that I've never been able to fathom the workings of Galahad's mind. He nearly killed us in his haste to reach Cadbury and I was terrified that the High King's peace would be broken when he took horses from pilgrims without any explanation or payment. He's mad, my queen, and I'd lief not ride with him again.'

Percivale had listened to Artor's strategies often enough to know that a man may tell the truth and yet lie through his teeth. With an internal prayer for forgiveness, he sidestepped Wenhaver's insistent questioning with much eye-rolling and waving of his hands, and the burred syllables of the countryman he was.

The queen's bower was a sweet-smelling, warm cocoon attached to the lower level of the High King's palace. Solid wooden shutters sealed out the cold winds and hid the garden from view, but bowls of petals, flower heads and dried herbs provided a memory of warmer summer days. The stone floors were softened with woven banks of brightly dyed wool and the walls were warmed with more woollen hangings in rich colours that reminded Percivale of roses.

The queen was dressed warmly in a robe of a soft pink-red that was mostly covered with a rich lap rug of thick, pale fur that was lined with more rose-coloured wool. Around her, Wenhaver's maids dressed in other flower shades such as pale yellow, soft yellow-green, ivory and even a pale woad blue. A few men added a splash of popinjay brilliance to the scene, except for Modred who wore his customary black enlivened by a cloak lined with a deep yellow-gold material. If Wenhaver had intended to create a human flower garden, she had been successful, but the queen's court was a hive of sharp gossip and Percivale struggled to maintain his equanimity amongst the brilliant, stinging insects.

Modred examined Percivale through black, acute eyes that threatened to unleash uncomfortable questions and accusations.

Modred was rarely fooled, and Percivale began to sweat in earnest. *He realizes that I'm playing with words,* he thought to himself uneasily.

But all servants learn to school their faces early in their careers, and Percivale kept his face open and puzzled, and his eyes guileless.

Wenhaver eventually accepted Percivale's explanation with much petulance and a threat to take the skin off his back if he had lied to her. In her view, anyone who had spent his childhood in the kitchens of Venonae was bound to be stupid, venal and lacking in subtlety. She had never bothered to examine Percivale closely before, because she considered that he was too far beneath her station to rate her attention.

But Modred wasn't so blinded by prejudice.

'I don't understand the need for such haste,' he commented with feigned confusion. 'Warriors such as Prince Galahad never risk men and horses for something trivial.' He raised his mild glance to impale Percivale. The bodyguard felt cold sweat trickle down his back.

Hell's master! He furiously tried to keep his mind clear, while his frightened glance darted from face to face. His panic was only partially feigned, for Modred's eyes unnerved him.

'I don't know, my lord, and that's the honest truth! Lord Galahad ordered me to ride, so we rode. Lord Galahad was obeying King Artor's instructions and told me nothing. I don't understand any of this, your lordship.'

Percivale's careful language and accent had slipped badly under questioning.

'Very well.' Modred pursed his lips. 'Leave us.'

Percivale fled from the rose bower and the accusing,

observant eyes of the queen and her friends as if he was escaping from the demons of chaos. So this is how good men learn to tell lies, he thought as he hurried back to the safety of the servants' quarters. Perhaps the Cup has already begun to poison my mind and stretch the limits of my scruples – and I haven't even seen it yet.

Percivale was beginning to understand that when honest men learn to parlay with scoundrels, no matter how just or holy their cause might be, the contagion of lies and trickery leaves them weakened. Percivale crossed himself and prayed to his god for strength.

CHAPTER XII

Those whom the gods would destroy, they first make mad

'You speak in jest!' the High King snarled, his logic affronted by the superstitious mish-mash of legend and fable that Galahad was thrusting at him with such crazed enthusiasm.

The hour was very advanced, the cold of late winter was absolute and King Artor was in a nasty temper. A week after Galahad's summons, Artor had returned to Cadbury at the head of a small troop of tired warriors. When he spurred his horse through the gates of the citadel, he was in a towering, black mood. Only Odin dared to order his master to sit and eat when they finally reached the shelter and privacy of Artor's rooms – and now Galahad was insulting Artor's intelligence with his wild ramblings.

In order to return to Cadbury, the royal troop had been forced to heave their way through deep snowdrifts, for the weather had worsened, as if the gods intended to keep the cursing and sweating king away from his own fortress.

Consequently, Artor was exhausted, irritated by his physical weakness and irrationally angry with Galahad who had caused him to leave the comforts of Venta Belgarum in such inclement weather.

Nor did the High King have the satisfaction of even a small victory behind him to buoy his spirits. Stubbornly, the Saxons had stayed put in Anderida, sulking over their losses the previous summer and using the depths of winter to shore up their fortress. A month in Venta Belgarum, a town that had always set Artor's nerves on edge with its tangible memories of Uther Pendragon, was more than enough to cause the High King to brood on a future that increasingly seemed inevitable and bleak.

Now, as Artor listened to Galahad's disjointed report, only Taliesin and Percivale from his inner circle were permitted to be present.

Galahad's head reared back like the head of a disturbed snake at Artor's exclamation of doubt, but Odin put his hand ominously on the haft of his axe as a warning. With an effort, the Otadini prince calmed himself.

'What you're saying doesn't make much sense to me, lad,' Artor said more reasonably. 'A staff that's really a spear, which was spirited out of Israel and was later stolen from Salinae Minor? Please, Galahad, your tale sounds very far-fetched. Percivale, you explain it to me,' the king requested, for Galahad appeared ready to storm out of the royal apartments.

Percivale took one weary hour to explain their discoveries at Salinae Minor and Glastonbury, and the reasoning behind their belief in the existence of the Spear. Tempers in the quiet room were strained to breaking point by the time he finished answering questions.

From his position in the corner of the room, Taliesin stirred.

'We're all friends here,' he commented softly, 'yet the Bloody Cup already sunders us and weakens our unity. It makes no difference if the Cup is Galahad's Christian relic or Gronw's Druid symbol. Faith is a powerful tool, especially when it's manipulated by the wrong minds and held in unscrupulous hands.'

Percivale nodded in agreement. This so closely reflected his own thinking, he felt a new respect for the harpist.

'You shouldn't rely too much on the skewed perception of a devout adherent of Christianity, lord,' Gareth interjected. 'The Cup and the Spear could be anything. I've always believed that if something looks like a dog and barks like a dog, then it usually is a dog. In all probability, these objects are part of a complex hoax using an old, tin drinking mug and a wooden staff.'

In response to this slur on his religion and his integrity, Galahad leapt to his feet. His fists were tightly clenched and the red haze of anger blurred his sight and made his sword hand twitch.

'Don't flaunt my laws, Galahad!' Artor barked. 'I don't care who you are or how high your birth is. No one raises his hand, or his sword, against any other man in this room.'

With ill grace, Galahad resumed his seat.

Percivale felt feverish and dislocated. The king's eyes darted rapidly from one face to another, although his head didn't move, and Percivale's distressed imagination toyed with the suspicion that they were the only living parts of the king's rigid body. He shuddered.

The king broke the spell of the moment and turned his attention to Gareth.

'Find my nephew, Gawayne, and bring him to me,' he told the big man. 'He's somewhere in Cadbury at the moment, en route from the north to a council of war I called in Venta Belgarum. I have no idea why he broke his journey at Cadbury, but at least he shouldn't be too hard to find. Don't let him prevaricate, or even dress, unless he's stark naked. Drag him out of whatever bed he's in and bring him to me – now.'

Taliesin noted the strain that revealed itself in Artor's suspicious, down-turned lips. He's afraid that Gawayne is in Wenhaver's bed, he thought with a frisson of anxiety. He'll never trust either his wife or his nephew, no matter how many years pass innocently.

'Have you sought out your father, Galahad? Have you discovered everything he knows? Or does your foolish feud with your sire continue unabated?'

Galahad bridled, but Percivale stood on his booted foot, and the Otadini prince lurched into speech.

'We've exchanged pleasantries, my king, but nothing more. I was surprised to find him here when I arrived.'

Percivale coughed tactfully. 'Lord Gawayne explained that he sought a day of comfort before he made the final push to your summer capital, lord. When he learned you were coming here, he decided to await your arrival in the citadel.'

Unconvinced, the High King snorted irritably. Gawayne's excuses were always so infuriatingly simple, and believable! Why did his woolly-brained nephew decide to deviate from his journey south and visit Cadbury? For that matter, why did Gawayne do anything? On impulse, of course.

'So, Percivale. Is it true that you've been visiting my dear wife?'

The rapid change of topic left Percivale stranded in confusion.

'Er . . . yes, master,' he mumbled. 'She ordered me to explain why we had come to Cadbury in such haste, and what was so urgent that Lord Galahad sent a courier to you, sire.'

Artor winced at the mention of Galahad's peremptory message, and Percivale suspected the prince would regret the careless wording of that demand before he was much older.

'She threatened you, I suppose. Yet you've managed to survive with a whole skin. How did you deal with my wife's questioning?'

'I led the queen and her friends to believe that Lord Galahad acted impulsively and didn't discuss his motives with me. The queen eventually accepted my explanation but Lord Modred seemed suspicious and interrogated me very closely. I stuck to my answers and he finally tired of questioning such a stupid servant.'

Artor nodded his approval. He was surprised that Percivale had lied successfully; his faithful servant had always been an honest man and blushed a hot shade of pink whenever he tried to lie.

'I'll deal with Modred if he is so imprudent as to openly interfere in my affairs.'

'While we're awaiting the arrival of Lord Gawayne,' Taliesin began hesitantly, 'perhaps we should consider how much information your noble nephew should be told. Lord Gawayne isn't always discreet, especially in the presence of beautiful women.'

'True, but I'm forced to trust those lords who are close to me in blood. Who else can I depend upon for loyalty?'

Galahad had the grace to look shamefaced.

Gawayne entered the room a few minutes later, looking decidedly put out.

'How may I be of service, Artor? After Salinae Minor, you instructed me to go to the north, so I went to the north. Then I'm ordered to Venta Belgarum for no reason that you'll explain to me. Does everyone conspire to deprive me of sleep? Or are you angry that I broke my journey to enjoy a soft bed for a few days? As soon as I discovered that you had already left for the south, I packed up to leave, but then *he* turned up.' Gawayne pointed irritably at his son. 'I decided you'd return like the wind in response to Galahad's message, so I kept to my soft warm bed to await your arrival.'

'Did you say you were sleeping, nephew?' Artor's voice was silky.

'Well, I fully intended to sleep ... eventually,' Gawayne replied with a smug smile.

'Well, I'll endeavour not to keep you from your bed – and whoever you're currently sharing it with – too long. Then, after we have had a brief meeting in lieu of the Venta Belgarum conference, you can ride back to your northern fortresses. Now, what have you heard of Arimathea?'

Gawayne gaped. 'What?'

'You're not a fish to go gawping about in a pool, Gawayne, so shut your mouth and start thinking. What do you know about Arimathea?'

Completely at sea with the direction the discussion was

taking, Gawayne muttered a garbled reply that included references to traders, old towers and legends.

'If this question has anything to do with Miryll, then she was a deluded liar,' he finished triumphantly. 'Nothing she told me is dependable.'

'Some matters have come to my attention that require elaboration. I don't think you have the answers I need, so you have my permission to return to your bed.'

Gawayne rose to his feet. He was confused, but that feeling was nothing new.

'One further matter, Gawayne,' Artor added. 'You are forbidden to discuss this conversation with anyone, especially the queen and Modred.'

'I couldn't repeat this conversation if I wanted to, Artor, because I haven't understood a word of it. What a Jew who's been dead for at least five hundred years has to do with your court, I have no idea. As for Wenhaver or Modred, I don't speak to either of them if I can help it. Just let me know when you want me to leave.' With that, Gawayne stalked off.

Artor steepled his fingers in thought. 'As Taliesin said, perception, especially by the common folk, is everything. Therefore, whether or not the Cup and the Spear are real, I must either possess these items or nullify them completely.'

'You would destroy the relics?' Galahad's eyes were shocked and disbelieving.

'Yes. I'll destroy them if I am forced to, but only as a last resort.'

'But the Spear and the Cup belong to Mother Church!' Galahad's face reflected his anger and, with a sick certainty, Percivale realized that Galahad would kill Artor before he would allow any object of Christian reverence to be destroyed.

'In these lands, the Church owns nothing unless I permit it,' Artor stated brutally.

'The Spear is already in our hands,' Galahad bleated. 'We have only to find the Cup.'

'You're assuming that Gronw's staff is this hypothetical spear. I've no proof that your assumptions are correct.'

Galahad's eyes roamed around the room as he sought for allies. Finally, his gaze came to rest pleadingly on Percivale.

Percivale was silent.

'Only the Roman Church has the sanctity to care for these relics,' Galahad said desperately. 'The esteemed Lucius drank his mealtime water out of the very cup that Christ used at the Last Supper. That in itself was blasphemy.'

'Why?' Artor asked. 'Even if the Cup is as you say, Lucius was both a bishop and a Roman. The Cup was perfectly safe in his care, wasn't it? You would have us send it on a voyage of thousands of miles to the Romans, of all people – the very same Romans who now quiver in Constantinople.'

Galahad should have been warned by the tone of Artor's voice, but the young warrior was a zealot.

'The Cup will bring thousands – millions – of new souls to Christ. What do we poor mortals matter in the scheme of God's intentions?'

'I would hope your god is fond of the Celts as well. They need saving too, Galahad, and from enemies who are far more pressing than your devil. I have already charged you with finding Gronw, and the Cup. When you do, you'll bring it to me.'

Galahad abased himself. 'I won't fail you, my king.'

'Percivale will go with you, and you will both be equal in standing in the completion of this task. Percivale's mind is quick and he has the practical common sense of the ordinary man.'

Galahad flashed Percivale a grin. 'A wise decision, my king, for it was Percivale who solved the riddle of the Cup.'

Here comes the difficult part, Taliesin thought to himself. Artor has another surprise for Galahad, one that he won't enjoy.

'And Bedwyr, who is neither pagan nor Christian, will also go with you. I shall send for him – Ratae can survive without him for the present. And he will go under the same terms as you. You need his scepticism, his woodcraft and his knowledge of languages. Neither of you could walk safely among those worshippers who follow the old ways. Neither of you can dissemble.'

'No!' Galahad exclaimed. 'Bedwyr is not fit to undertake a task such as this.'

'Not fit?' Artor asked quietly, with an unreadable gleam in his gaze. 'I am your king, Galahad! If I say that Bedwyr is to be part of this endeavour, then Bedwyr goes. Either you accept my terms or your father will assume your role in finding the Cup. Gawayne will obey my orders completely and without question.

'Send a courier immediately to Bedwyr informing him that I require his presence at Cadbury. Ratae can survive without him for the present.'

'The Spear!' Galahad interrupted wildly. 'The Spear is still at Glastonbury.'

'We know that Gronw's *staff* is certainly at Glastonbury, but I don't intend to leave it there for much longer. Balyn needs to be tested, so I shall send him to the monastery to inveigle the spear away from Bishop Otha. I'm uneasy that any man who is jointly distrusted by both Percivale and Simon the Jew should hold sway over such a dangerous object. Once the staff is in my possession, we'll soon discover if it's a spear, as you believe! Meanwhile, Gruffydd will use his wiles to discover whose influence was instrumental in appointing Otha to the post of bishop at Glastonbury. Now leave us, for there's much for you and Percivale to do before you can depart on your quest. Gruffydd will have the latest intelligence concerning Gronw's movements. You must arrange provisions for your group carefully for the time that you'll be in dangerous territory. Your face stands out in a crowd, young man, so we need Percivale and Bedwyr to provide a screen for you.'

As the two men rose to leave the king's rooms, Artor laid one last injunction upon them.

'You'll depart as soon as possible after Bedwyr has arrived at Cadbury. Under pain of my punishment, you will not speak of your quest within the confines of this citadel. Even the walls have ears in this place, and there are enemies among our people who wait only for a chance to harm us. If you value the Cup and wish to ensure its safety, you will remain silent.'

After the two warriors had left the chamber, Artor's strength deserted him like ice melts in a fire. His shoulders slumped forward and he rested his head on his hands.

Inwardly, he thanked all the gods, Christian or otherwise, that he had returned to Cadbury before the snowdrifts had become too deep for travel. Galahad was as dangerous to Artor's reign as the Cup and the Spear combined. They were objects that were fixed and unchanging, whereas Galahad was an explosive mix of fanaticism, unpredictability, violence and bigotry. No ruler could depend on this young lord, for he had no inner compass, except his own interpretation of the will of his God.

'May the gods spare me from the extremities of all religious men,' Artor muttered, his doubts and formless concerns evident in the quaver in his voice. Odin looked up from the tray on which he was assembling a simple meal of bread, cheese and red wine. 'They'll destroy everyone and everything for the sake of their faith, even in the Christian Church where their Jesus preaches peace and piety. The gods make us crazy, and old Targo was right to be suspicious of them. Yet, when it came time for my friend to cross over to the shadows, Targo depended upon me to pay the Ferryman his due. We humans are strange, inconsistent creatures.'

A sudden gust of wind shook the shutters and the oil lamp flames dipped and danced.

'But what if the Cup isn't found by my searchers? God help the west! Any rebellion, no matter how small, draws my eyes away from the Saxons. I've already decided that Venta Belgarum must do without me, in case I must ride north at a moment's notice. Gronw, or whoever pulls his strings, can stir up spot fires of resistance that will be difficult to root out. Even worse, if I make an example of any credulous fools who raise their hands against me in the name of the Cup, I make them into martyrs and feed the rebellion myself!'

'Galahad is crazed with his god,' Odin offered. 'He'll probably find the Cup, because he'll kill everything that stands between him and his desire.'

'Obsession,' Taliesin corrected.

'Yes, I'm afraid you're right,' Artor agreed. 'I hope that Bedwyr and Percivale will blunt his worst excesses, for obsession has always been a family curse and is not easily deflected. My sister, Morgan, is a perfect example of Galahad's particular form of madness, although he'd probably remove my head for suggesting that they're alike. The difference between them is that she is obsessed with revenge; her gods, if she possesses any, are dark and vengeful creatures who feast on blood and pain. In the meantime, I'm forced to utilize the services of two good men to ensure that Galahad obeys my orders. I don't have enough men like Bedwyr and Percivale, and I can't afford to waste them on wanton stupidity.'

'There's no reason to suppose that they won't survive the quest,' Taliesin reasoned as he moved to fill a cup of wine for the High King. 'But this Gronw appears to be a cunning and vicious adversary. Galahad underestimates him because he considers that all pagans are stupid.'

'His zealotry blinds him, but it also drives him, and therein lies our hope. The Cup must be removed from the game, or we will all be lost.'

Wenhaver lay alone in her perfumed, over-heated room and pleasured herself by imagining what punishments she could rain down on several vulnerable heads. High on her list was Gawayne, who had scarcely acknowledged her existence in recent years. He refused to meet her eyes and scuttled away in the opposite direction whenever he saw her.

'I don't want him, but he should desire me,' she told her pillow. Chagrin filled her eyes with selfish tears of self-pity.

Modred had also displeased her. This very day, after Artor had returned in haste from the north, Modred had snapped at her when she'd asked some trivial question of him. Who did this minor king think he was? A Brigante by-blow, begotten on a slatternly Scotti queen, had no right to censure *her*. Although the court accorded Modred the respect that his station demanded, Wenhaver knew the Brigante was disliked and would never be trusted within the Union of Kings.

His presumption offended the queen, for Modred issued orders in her presence. Her faded blue eyes snapped with remembered anger. If Modred didn't curb that sharp tongue of his, she'd order the guard to snip a little of it off.

'And they'll do it, too,' she comforted herself. 'All those bastard sons of Artor hate Modred like poison for the comments he's made about them and their mothers.'

Wenhaver savoured the most recent insult to Modred's honour that had been delivered by a younger member of Artor's guard.

Modred had been sniping at Artor's old age and the king's fear of the Saxons that had sent him to Venta Belgarum during winter, when all the evidence of the past indicated that the Saxons never attacked in the colder months.

'Our High King is becoming over-cautious in his old age, although I suppose we can never be too safe. Artor is right to fear that his arms have become weak with the march of time. It's a pity that a king can't enter honourable retirement, for our Artor obviously wishes that he could be free to rest.'

'Do you think so, Modred?' Wenhaver cooed, her expression completely unreadable. 'My husband won some stunning battles just this last summer.'

'Yes, I do think so, dear lady. Consider how unpredictable his temper has become in recent months, and how he distrusts everyone around him, even those closest to him. Perhaps my uncle has become a little soft in the head.'

Wenhaver had smiled at the Brigante's words, but the young guardsman who was serving wine was offended and took matters into his own hands. He spilled the full jug directly into Modred's lap.

Modred's fury was icy and controlled. He would have had the young guardsman flogged, but he realized that Artor would consider an attack on his servants to be an attack on himself.

While Wenhaver drifted off to sleep with a smile of satisfaction at Modred's humiliation, Modred himself tossed unhappily in his sumptuous bed, dreaming of retribution. But most of the population within the palace of the High King slept well that night, although Galahad did not sleep at all. Instead, he prayed away the hours until he could begin what he believed would be his life's achievement. The Cup had refocused his life, and driven the irritants of family from his mind. 'Even the blasphemous Bedwyr has no lasting importance, although he insults the Cup by his role in its salvation. It's the Cup that matters. I'll find it, and I'll hold it, even if Hades stands in my way.'

Delusion can be a pleasant self-deception, no matter who practises it.

Bedwyr arrived at Cadbury Tor a week later.

'What's gnawing at the vitals of Galahad, Your Majesty?' he asked as soon as he saw the king. 'He seems taciturn to the point of rudeness. And the look he gave me just now would curdle new milk.'

Bedwyr realized he hadn't bothered with the normal courtesies and flushed under his tan.

'I trust you are well, my liege,' he added pleasantly. 'How may I serve the king?'

'Playing the courtier doesn't suit you, Bedwyr,' Artor responded with a smile.

Bedwyr grinned. 'Am I here at Galahad's urging, my lord? Even before I had time to dismount from my horse, he insisted that I should attend on you immediately to receive my orders. He left me in no doubt that I was to make haste.'

'My kin have always lacked tact,' Artor countered.

'Don't expect me to deny it. I set the forts ahumming when I made my arrangements to return to Cadbury, but you can trust that my warriors are in good hands. Pelles Minor is in command during my absence – and he's near as clever as his father was.' He smiled contentedly at Artor. 'But I'm curious to know why I must be here at such short notice. And why is Galahad so anxious to see me? He's never bothered to acknowledge my existence before, except as a pagan curiosity.'

'Unhappily, I'm forced to ask you to undertake a duty that could be the death of you, Bedwyr. I require you to carry out a mission with Galahad and Percivale. The task is of great importance to the welfare of the kingdom.'

'If you don't mind, Artor, and if you will forgive the presumption, before you give me the details, I would beg your leave to find the kitchens so I can hunt up some wine and a quick meal of bread and cheese. I rode here in haste, without rest, and I'm very tired, not to mention famished, my lord.'

'Assuredly, my friend.' Artor sighed. 'I fail in courtesy. Sit here and talk to me while Odin finds something for my Arden Knife to eat and drink. I'll tell you an astonishing tale.'

Having spent years as a Saxon captive, and having experienced the caprices of a cruel master, Bedwyr knew how to listen. He sat in silence as the king explained the details of Galahad's report. Meanwhile, Odin produced a simple repast with a deft flourish that was rewarded with Bedwyr's customary smile of gratitude.

'Your story goes far beyond any rumours that are afloat, my lord. There have been whispers that the hag, Ceridwen, is abroad. The existence of such artefacts would set the west afire if their origins become widely known and accepted.'

'I don't believe for a moment that the cup is the Bloody Cup of Christ or Ceridwen's cursed cauldron,' Artor stated flatly.

'I agree, but you can't afford to take the risk, can you?'

Bedwyr always seemed to find the heart of any problem. Artor had surrounded himself with such honest men, prizing unvarnished truth above sycophantic agreement. Now, in his quiet apartments, an older Artor almost wished for lying platitudes.

'Galahad is a young man who is ablaze with religious fervour. He's ambitious. If the task is possible, he'll find Gronw and the Cup out of fanatical bloody-mindedness, and will rid me of a great peril at the same time. My only reservation about him is that he may decide to keep the Cup for Mother Church. The prelates are nearly as ambitious as the princelings and kinglets who cluster around the thrones of the west. The

Church creates kings, as Lucius made me, and it then unmakes them if they don't further the interests of Rome.'

'Perhaps Galahad may get himself killed in pursuit of his quest.'

Artor's laughter rasped. 'Perhaps.'

Bedwyr's dry amusement vanished and he sobered immediately. The time for banter was over.

'Percivale is a good choice,' he stated. 'I suppose that faith in his religion spurs him as sharply as it does Galahad, but Percivale is nobody's fool. He'll not form a belief without a strong basis in fact, and he's accustomed to following your orders. On the other hand, Galahad has indulged his personal whims and desires all his life.'

'Indeed. Percivale has his own doubts about the sanctity of the Cup, and he recognizes that such an object would be dangerous to the kingdom if it fell into the wrong hands.' Artor smiled ruefully at Bedwyr. 'At least we can be sure that Percivale is a Celt before he's a Christian.'

Bedwyr nodded in agreement. 'He spent too many years working with Targo to be easily duped. Nor will he react recklessly.'

'I've decided that all three members of this troop shall be equal. Your personal task is to ensure that Galahad doesn't take the bit between his teeth, or you'll be trying to ride the whirlwind. Your personal instructions are to execute Gronw, take back the Cup and bring it to me. If such an outcome is impossible, destroy the sodding thing!' Artor rarely used profanity and his words betrayed the depth of his concern.

'I may have to kill Galahad to obey your instructions,' Bedwyr said soberly. 'Have you considered this possibility? Can

I expect your exoneration from blame if this should become necessary?'

Artor nodded his head. 'I don't like your chances if you confront him, Bedwyr. He's better at weaponry than I was, even before age weakened my arm and slowed my body. You know, better than most, that I still win battles because I think before I act. Galahad doesn't reason, he's all instinct and passion. His rashness and religious zealotry are weaknesses for him and advantages for you, and you must use them to resolve any dispute that might arise.'

'I will carry out your orders to the death, King Artor.'

Impulsively, Artor embraced the younger man. 'You have proved your loyalty over many years, and I honour you for your trust, my Arden Knife. I know what I'm asking, and I deplore the circumstances that demand it. But I'll have no option if Galahad chooses his church over his king.'

Bedwyr knelt and placed Artor's foot upon his neck, just as slaves were forced to do in Saxon households.

Artor was moved beyond words at the significance of this action.

'Protect Elayne during my absence, Artor. She is an old man's last cast of the dice at happiness. She is the future – my future – and I must believe that she is safe before I dare to risk my own life.'

A flush of guilt slid across Artor's cheekbones. Were his private conversations with Elayne really so inappropriate? Of course they were. Would he give up his friendship with her?

'She will be kept as safe as my dearest possession,' Artor vowed.

'Thank you, Artor,' Bedwyr replied, his gratitude showing

clearly on his open face. 'This mission will begin in two days then, my lord. There'll be less chance of talk if we leave at different times and travel in different directions before meeting in Sorviodunum. Perhaps Galahad could leave today, Percivale tomorrow, and myself in two days' time. I'm being selfish, but I long to spend a little time with my wife before I take my leave.'

Artor nodded his approval and they parted, both comforted by their mutual trust.

Later, in any number of places where Modred's spies could eavesdrop if they chose to listen, Artor publicly ordered Galahad to return to Salinae Minor where he would resume his normal duties.

Galahad departed that same night with a noisy flurry of preparation, and the next afternoon Percivale left too.

Bedwyr spent two nights with his wife before leaving the precincts of the court as unobtrusively as he had arrived.

Modred was the only person on the tor who seemed even remotely curious about the separate destinations of the three warriors. The Brigante king asked casual questions and, if he distrusted the answers he was given, then his demeanour revealed nothing of his thoughts.

Winter gave way to a damp and cold spring. Elayne spent her days wearily in the queen's bower, or else she cared for a small portion of land that Artor had decreed should service the needs of widows and orphans. Out in the open air with the other women, Elayne tilled and planted, watered and weeded, and tried to ignore her fears for Bedwyr's safety.

'Why do you work in the sun like a servant?' Wenhaver

asked Elayne some weeks after Bedwyr had come and gone so swiftly. 'Your skin has become quite brown where you've been burned by the sun.'

'Work makes time pass more quickly for me, my lady, and I've always liked to keep myself occupied. I'm poor at weaving and needlework, so I try to carry out those labours that are within my abilities.'

'That a noblewoman should labour in the fields seems very odd to me, my dear,' Wenhaver said with a feline smile. 'But who am I to disagree if such tasks give you pleasure?'

The widows in the fields also found Elayne's actions peculiar. At first they were inclined to be wary, for noblewomen neither looked nor acted like this russet-haired, brown-skinned woman. But her cheerfulness gradually charmed them, as did the gifts for their children that she brought in a woollen bag. Herbs and remedies for fevers, cuts and burns found their slow way into many poor dwellings, as did the occasional worn ladle or pot that had been purloined or discarded from the royal kitchens.

'She's a special woman,' old Eda decided volubly. 'She doesn't make a body feel bad because she has nothing. And she works as hard as me, especially in the weeding and the watering.'

'As if you'd know, Eda!' the widow Hazel murmured. 'You're quick to take a rest to ease your bones when the sun's high. Still, you've read Lady Elayne right. She's like the Virgin must be, if you'll pardon any offence I might give.'

'None taken, Hazel,' Eda replied. 'I wish all the high ladies were like her, but I suppose we should be lucky there's even one of her. She's a pleasant little creature.'

And so Elayne's reputation with the citizens of Cadbury

gradually rose. Despite her homeland in that pagan forest in the wild north, her quality was recognized, and the highest and the lowest of the town curtseyed or tugged their forelocks in respect as she passed by. The older crones remembered the young Nimue and gossiped about her with affection.

'The Maid of Wind and Water was like Lady Elayne in many ways. She was always out looking after the poor with Lord Myrddion's simples and cures. I'd see her abroad finding all kinds of roots and leaves, even before the sun had risen. Lady Nimue was a rare one, just like our Lady Elayne. But the Maid of Wind and Water is long gone.'

The grandam who made this lengthy speech was selling seed potatoes at an open booth near the citadel gates. A portly tavern keeper was quick to agree with her.

'A cook up there told me, private like, that the harpist is the son of Lady Nimue and Lord Myrddion. She told me that he is just as magical as his father, for he plays the harp like it's alive. His harp is shaped like a woman and, when Lord Taliesin plays, her eyes open and the wooden lady sings.'

'Magic has come back to Cadbury at last,' the potato seller said happily. 'The old days have returned.'

'Don't you believe it, auntie. King Artor grows old and there's talk that Druids are out and about in the north. Our lord has no heir, so the kingdom is weak and like to fall.' The warrior who spoke was short and dark, with an open, mobile face that bore no resemblance to his sardonic nature. 'Who's going to rule the Britons when the king dies?'

Through Gruffydd, Artor was fully aware of the people's preoccupation with the absence of a suitable heir. He had been hearing this cry for years, but his own desire for continuity had never become so desperate that he considered elevating one of his bastard sons to the position of heir. Even Artor's strength of character couldn't force a nameless ruler upon the Celtic alliance, for the tribal kings would never accept a bastard.

Half the men who served in Artor's personal guard had the ability and strength to be an effective king, but it would be unconscionably cruel if he raised hopes that could never be fulfilled. The High King's mind worried at the problem constantly, while his eyes searched among his kin and courtiers for *anyone* capable of holding the west together after he journeyed to the shadows.

The twins provided the only simple solution. Artor had tested them in battle throughout the Saxon summer, searching to discover which of the boys had the capacity to rule in his stead. When the quest for the Cup began, Artor still wavered, knowing that his choice would change the lives of the boys, as well as of their mother, their elder brother, Bran, and the people of the Ordovice tribe.

The decision of choosing an heir from the twins was fraught with problems. Could Bran serve under a younger brother? Could one brother forsake the other, without meddling in the affairs of the kingdom? And would Anna ever forgive him for her fatherless childhood if he publicly acknowledged that she was his daughter? Any of the boys would then be eligible for the kingship.

Unfortunately, women couldn't rule unless, like Boedicca, they were warrior queens.

So the twins remained an edge that Artor tucked away for some future usage. The need for an heir could be solved, but which twin should he choose if he had to select one man?

Balan was Artor's natural preference, for the lad was most like himself in temperament. But Balan was kind by nature and, given the choice, Artor would not subject this particular grandson to the fate that he had been forced to endure. Could Balan endure the loss of self – his softer nature, his kindness, his consideration and his gentleness – that the throne of the High King demanded?

Beautiful Balyn was an enigma that Artor could not truly fathom. His excellence in battle made him a formidable opponent, but Balan led the way in intellect. Did Balyn have the prudence and the guile to rule? His pride could be a curse, and impulse ruled his actions; his enthusiasms were passionate and quickly adopted – and as quickly dropped. Moreover, Odin didn't like the boy and Artor always respected Odin's instincts. The time had come to confront Balyn with a real problem and, perhaps, secure an heir to the throne.

'But I can wait a little longer to make up my mind,' Artor murmured to the still air in his room. 'If I choose hastily, I might foist another Uther on my people!'

With a mental shrug, Artor stripped off his tunic and buried himself in his sleeping furs. The warmth eased the aches in muscle and bone that old men feel when death begins to tap their shoulders and remind them that their time is almost over.

Gruffydd had been charged with the task of investigating Otha Redbeard, the newly appointed Bishop of Glastonbury. What Gruffydd discovered gave neither king nor spymaster any reason for complacency, but he found no concrete answers either.

The spymaster returned as spring pushed new growth through the damp, rich soil. He had only been gone three weeks, and Artor marvelled at the arthritic old man's ability to sit in the corners of an inn, ask a few idle questions and milk every gossiper dry of their knowledge, all without stirring his creaking old bones.

'If his brother priests in Venta Belgarum are to be believed, the bishop is a boastful buffoon with little talent and less piety,' Gruffydd reported back to Artor. 'Unfortunately, the man has many supporters, for he is the scion of a wealthy clan in Bremetennacum that is closely connected to the Brigante ruling class. He shamelessly courts approval from persons of influence and has gained many priestly votes for his new position within the Church. However, one of my agents was told by a reliable source that the ancestors of the bishop's father were originally Coritani and they drifted to Bremetennacum from Lindum in the east when the Saxons drove out the last of the Celts. This rumour doesn't necessarily make him false in his oaths towards your kingdom, but the general details of the man's background leave a nasty feeling in my water.'

Artor looked exasperated. 'Do I smell the influence of Modred in this appointment? Or, worse still, the Brigante aristocracy who resent the tribute I demand of them? Or the Saxons from Lindum? Or even both? Modred has the Brigante connections, but the Brigante were unsettled before Modred's reign, and will remain so until I clean out the whole rats' nest of the aristocracy. I can't believe that Modred would attempt to use a man so guaranteed to antagonize my allies. I'd discover the link immediately. I may overestimate my nephew, but I'd have expected something more subtle from Modred.'

'We shouldn't discount the Saxon connection, my lord. But whatever Otha's motives and allegiances might be, I can assure you that he only entered the priesthood for the prestige, the power and the opportunity to feather his own nest. Glastonbury will provide him with years of sanctioned pillage, and I wouldn't trust the man as far as I could throw him.'

'By all reports, Otha's a tub of lard and couldn't be thrown far by anyone,' Artor responded. 'I'll send Balyn on a pilgrimage to Glastonbury and, in the process, we'll discover if the boy's golden tongue can talk Otha Redbeard around in circles.'

Gruffydd pushed back his tangled hair, which had never been quite controllable, even in his youth. His weathered and lined face had the drooping folds and the lugubrious expression of a good hound. Only his eyes were still young and vivid within the deep pouches that surrounded their sockets. He had a horde of grandchildren and great-grandchildren, but his days were fast blurring as his life accelerated into the decay of great old age.

'It's near time I retired, my lord. I've lived for twenty years beyond my allotted lifespan and there's not much more I can give you. My grandson, Trystan, has developed his own spy network out of Kernyu in the north-east of Cymru. I want him away from Cymru, because the damned fool is involved with a married woman, a friendship that could easily catapult him to a premature death. The woman is Queen Iseult, who's married to Mark, the local king. The king is no friend of yours, so Trystan's kinship with me will only harm him further.'

Artor snorted.

'Kernyu is a very small kingdom, lord. It's largely Deceangli in tribal settlement, but some Demetae headed north to settle there in Vortigern's time, and you know what their tempers are like.' Gruffydd paused. 'What I'm asking, Artor, is that Trystan take my place as your spymaster. I'll continue as your adviser in all such matters until the boy is fully settled in but, as I don't want to die on the job, as it were, I wish to leave your employ sooner rather than later. I believe the control of the spy network will probably save Trystan from the revenge of King Mark, as well as providing you with a capable and trustworthy replacement.'

'Mark is a sycophantic, treasonous cur,' Artor grumbled. 'I cannot trust him.'

'Then don't. He's another tribal king who whines continuously about tribute and the cost of maintaining an army. My grandson may be prejudiced against the man, but he has been warning me to beware of Mark for years.'

'I assume Trystan's already on his way to Cadbury, so I'll soon meet this young man whom you obviously admire. Don't blush, Gruffydd. I've known you for near on forty years, and I'll always remember how you first brought Nimue to my court and demanded that I mete out justice on her mother's murderer.'

Gruffydd smiled. 'Yes, I expected that you would approve my choice and the boy is already on his way to Cadbury. I told him that if he is to undertake this duty for you, he should use Caerleon as the centre of his operations. He loves the north, and would be effective in such a place.'

Artor was happy to grant Gruffydd's request; it was the least he could do for a friend who had filled the shoes of Myrddion Merlinus so admirably and who had never asked for favour or reward.

The king smiled reflectively and companionably at his old friend as they toasted their chilled feet before Artor's open fire.

'He's my Ellyn's son – my eldest boy's daughter.' Gruffydd grinned with pride through his bristling white beard. 'And he's wondrously handsome, considering his sire.'

'Didn't I give Ellyn to a Deceangli chieftain out of . . .'

'Castellum Guinion,' Gruffydd reminded his king.

'Yes, that was the place,' Artor said. 'I've an old man's memory, Gruffydd. I'm fading fast.'

'You're twenty years younger than me, young man. Think of the good things that can still be done in the years remaining to you.'

'I doubt I'll have the opportunity, Gruffydd. The wolves are gathering to pull me down, for I'm the stag with antlers so heavy that I can barely lift my head to flee. Still, you have my permission to return to Venta Silurum. Right now, if you should so wish. You've earned a quiet life and one of us should survive the bad years that lie ahead.'

'I've decided to visit Coed Celyddon. I yearn to see those deep woods once more before I die, so I'll go to the mountains nearby and visit Nimue while I'm there. I loved that babe more than my own children, Artor. She wound her fingers around my heart when she was only a day old. And perhaps I'll visit Myrddion's resting place before I die. Your harpist has described the route.'

Silence fell, and in the peace and warmth, Gruffydd dozed off and snored shallowly, while his king watched over him through the night.

CHAPTER XIII

BALYN'S BANE

Balyn was confused. The queen was as gracious to him as ever, so much so that the young man was completely enslaved. To be given tokens of her esteem, such as a rose or a length of fine perfumed wool that she had carried in her sleeve, made his heart tighten with a painful joy.

In his short life, he had never known a woman who was so completely feminine. His rational self recognized that the queen was pampered and idle, when compared with his indefatigable mother. But, in his innocence, Balyn thought that skin such as the queen's could never face the rigours of full sunlight, for he believed that Wenhaver's complexion of roses and cream must be real, like her golden hair. While other women aged, the queen remained eternally young. His brother, Balan, despaired of his twin's ignorance of female deceit.

Balyn wasn't a fool. He was simply young and ardent for the romance of love. Unlike his brother, Balan, who was practical to the point of being prosaic, Balyn had something of the poet's imagination, and so the world of Artor's court was the most graceful and brilliant dream that he had ever contemplated. Within this waking dream, the queen moved gracefully, her lips smiling sweetly and murmuring elegant compliments and witty repartee. If Balyn sometimes sensed deliberate cruelty behind Wenhaver's saccharine words, then he forgave her instantly for what he decided were unconscious lapses.

Balyn had heard the sly whispers that the queen loved Prince Gawayne, and had compromised her honour by betraying her husband with him. But Balyn refused to countenance such slurs, preferring to believe the evidence of his eyes. In his seasons at court, he had seen nothing to suggest a breach of her marriage vows.

For such a youth, disillusion creates an abyss down which he can tumble to ruin. Because he was incapable of temperance, those who Balyn loved must be perfect, or else they were totally flawed. Where Balan expected men and women to be human, with real faults that they constantly tried to hide, Balyn refused to accept that his perfect queen, in this perfect court, was not as he believed her to be.

Early one morning, Balyn rose before dawn and ventured out into the meadows to pick wild flowers for his queen. Perhaps the dew-drenched blossoms were a little untidy, but he planned to present them to Wenhaver so he could bask in the warmth of her smile. When he returned from his small quest, the servants were about their tasks but few of the nobility had yet chosen to stir.

Nothing could have prepared him for what he overheard beyond the corner in a long corridor.

'Gawayne, my love, do I frighten you?' the voice of Wenhaver cooed. She had trapped the prince when he had ventured from his room to use the communal privy. 'I thought you and I were intimates of long standing.'

Gawayne had not lain with Wenhaver for over eighteen months, having managed to avoid her tentacles by regularly escaping to Verterae and Segedunum, and Wenhaver had not forgotten Artor's threat of execution if she did not change her slatternly ways. Between Gawayne's absences and Wenhaver's restraint, the relationship had been permitted to cool but, periodically, with cat-like indolence, Wenhaver strived to fan the dying coals of their illicit affair into at least a glimmer of life.

Boredom had persuaded the queen to wake at an early hour simply to waylay her one-time lover. She wished to make him regret their broken liaison so, knowing how susceptible Gawayne was to bare, ripe flesh, she had donned a flimsy robe that revealed the shape of her body.

'This isn't a suitable time for conversation, Wenhaver! If the servants see you dressed in this . . . thing, the tale will run through the citadel in minutes. Artor wouldn't approve of this meeting, and I . . . well, I promised him.'

Gawayne was desperate to empty his full bladder. Besides, the early light illuminated the network of wrinkles around her eyes and Wenhaver's thinning lips which, even now, pursed unattractively.

'You've seen far more of me than this, Gawayne. On many occasions.'

'I prefer to forget, my queen,' Gawayne responded as sternly as he could. 'The indiscretions of our youth should be left in the past. Please, Wenhaver, allow me to pass.'

As an unwilling eavesdropper, Balyn stood dumbstruck. The flowers, already beginning to wilt, fell from his numb fingers and he felt a sick, dizzying sensation in the pit of his stomach.

'I am the queen, Gawayne, and I order you to explain why you're avoiding me.' Wenhaver's voice was no longer the gentle, melodious invitation that Balyn knew. She sounded almost shrewish.

'Artor is our liege lord, my lady,' Gawayne explained stiffly. 'He's treated me with honour and respect, and overlooked the excesses of my obnoxious family. He's also my uncle, and I know that I'm only half the man he is. You no longer tempt me, lady; my eyes are finally opened, and I'll never again be your paramour. You've never loved me, and I'm tired of being a convenient means of hurting my king.'

Balyn heard the queen stamp her foot in frustration and then came the sharp sound of a slap as she struck Gawayne's face.

'You oaf! You were only ever a convenience to dishonour the bastard I married. He'd kill me, you know, if he thought he could get away with it.'

Balyn felt sickened by the malice that thickened the early morning air.

'Your husband could have had you killed years ago and no one would have cared. In fact, most of the nobility would be overjoyed at your death.'

Balyn heard the sounds of a scuffle and then a thin cry of pain from the queen as Gawayne forced his way past her.

'I hate you,' she hissed. 'How dare you touch the person of the queen?'

Balyn's flowers lay, forgotten, on the flagged floor. Before the queen could see him, he took to his heels, back to the small room he shared with his brother, who was curled up under a fur rug.

'You're back,' Balan muttered and tried to cover his head.

Balyn ignored his twin and threw himself on to their shared pallet. He wanted to sob, to scream or even to kill something. A small moan escaped his lips, causing Balan to open his eyes and look at his brother's tightly curled body with concern.

Balyn sighed brokenly.

'What's happened, brother?' Balan asked. 'And don't try to fob me off.'

'Nothing!' The fur coverlet muffled Balyn's vehement reply.

'Bonehead!' Balan said affectionately. 'I don't care what you've done. You're noise and I'm silence. You're heart and I'm mind. We're one, brother. Our mother explained that to us long ago.'

'You don't understand!' Balyn choked back a sob.

'Try me. I won't laugh or fuss at you.'

Balyn surged up from the pallet, and Balan felt a physical, visceral spasm as he looked into his brother's white face and haunted eyes.

'The queen is false,' Balyn sobbed. 'Everything you said was true. I heard her try to seduce Gawayne – just so she could reject him! They're lovers of long standing!'

Balyn turned his face to the wall.

'But she didn't actually betray Lord Artor, did she?'

'Of course she did! She spoke of it shamelessly, and then Lord Gawayne told her that their liaison was over.'

Balyn was beginning to shout as his self-control unravelled, and Balan clapped a hand over his brother's mouth.

Balyn pulled the hand away. 'She was half-naked! She fawned all over the Lord of the North until he ran away from her. Such insinuations! I felt sick! Are all men and women bare-faced liars in this place?'

Balan struggled to hide his exasperation. 'Most people lie out of laziness, or because of fear of consequences – or even of being disliked. Unfortunately, you haven't learned to dissemble as they have. In any place other than Cadbury, such a virtue would be praised. But here, it's the mark of a fool, which you're surely not.'

'I *am* a fool, for I've danced attendance on a strumpet. How can I face her, brother? How can I pretend I didn't eavesdrop on her?'

'There's no need to lie to her, Balyn. Simply be distant, then you won't be forced to pretend.'

Balyn's face lightened. 'Yes, King Artor is the wounded party here, and I've done nothing of which I should be ashamed.'

Balan sighed. Ever at the whims of his emotions, Balyn must cleave wholly to one side or another, when a cooler head would weigh his allegiances more objectively. Having been exposed to Wenhaver's feet of clay so brutally, Balyn must now turn his ardent, uncritical heart towards her enemy and lay his whole faith and devotion at the feet of the king.

'You must understand that our king is also flawed, despite being the greatest man of his age,' Balan said softly. 'He can't fill the over-large shoes that you would thrust on him. When will you learn?'

But Balyn refused to listen.

Later in the day, Wenhaver chose to summon the twins to her bower. Her invitation was unwelcome; the young men had planned a hunt to allow Balyn's raw and lacerated pride to form a scab and heal a little. But Wenhaver was insistent; her self-esteem had been shaken and her vanity required the balm of Balyn's uncritical adoration.

'Why are you so silent, Lord Balyn?' Modred asked the young man. 'I'd swear you've changed places with your brother. Balan is positively verbose today, while you seem uncomfortable.' Modred's sharp eyes had missed nothing.

'I have had a sick headache all day long, King Modred, and I'm not inclined to converse with anyone at all.' Balyn stared into the distance and made no effort to hide his distaste for the Brigante king.

'You don't fail *me*, my boy, but the queen is looking decidedly put out. She enjoys those pretty flatteries that fall so easily from your tongue.'

'She'll receive them no more!' Balyn retorted unwisely and wandered off to engage Lady Elayne in conversation.

Wenhaver's eyes followed the young man with a mingled expression of bafflement and resentment.

Modred smiled inwardly with suppressed glee. Oh, Wenhaver. You'll hand me the throne yet, you silly old cow!

Then he recalled the humiliating conversation he had had this morning with his most powerful kinsman, and the amusement in his eyes died.

The High King had been striding across the flagged forecourt when he spied Modred sitting in the early sun, looking over to the north and the distant blue tower on Glastonbury Tor.

'Hoi, Modred!' Artor shouted, deciding his ride could wait for a few minutes. 'I meant to speak with you later, so I've saved myself some effort.'

Modred examined the king's tall form, back-lit by the sun,

and he felt a visceral stab of envy. Artor still retained a patina of youth well past his prime. The sun gave his grey hair the sheen of russet, and its shadows hid the lines upon his face and neck. Modred felt his spirits droop and wither.

'How may I assist you, sire? I'm yours to command.'

Artor came straight to the point. 'Do you plan to return to your own country at any time in the immediate future, nephew? You're welcome to remain here, of course, but surely you must be concerned that your throne can be weakened during your absence?'

'Not at all, Artor. As you know, the Brigante have run out of potential kings, and those members of the aristocracy who'd try to take what is not theirs tend to conspire against each other, rather than against me.'

Artor laughed, but there was very little humour in the sound. 'And I suppose you and your supporters control the warriors.'

'Of course, uncle. I've found it always pays to think ahead, and to ensure that the numbers are at my back.'

'How true, Modred. Still, I do pine for my privacy, as should you.'

The High King turned on his heel and strode away, leaving his nephew to wonder if he had been dismissed from court.

Balyn's head ached fiercely as he was forced to watch his hitherto ideal woman through eyes that were newly critical. He hungered to depart from the bower and ride out into the countryside where he could shake the mouldy, clinging comforts of Cadbury from his booted feet.

Elayne recognized the young man's turmoil and placed a hand upon his forearm.

'You must forgive me, Lord Balyn, but I believe you are developing a sick headache that is not caused entirely by the weather,' she began. 'Will you take some advice from a woman old enough to be an elder sister?'

Balyn bowed distantly, but the pressure of Elayne's fingers drew his eyes to meet her gaze.

'The queen is a vain, foolish and irrelevant woman, my lord. She has no power to harm the kingdom, or you, unless you permit her to do so. Somehow, she has managed to put you out of temper and to hurt you deeply. But she acts without thought, and certainly doesn't intend to damage you or to cause you pain. So you must emulate King Artor and treat her with courtesy but without serious consideration. I fear that you wear your heart on your sleeve, and there are those at this court who will pursue you if they believe that you care for her.'

Balyn's forehead knitted with mingled disapproval of Elayne's blunt words and his acknowledgement that she had correctly interpreted his feelings.

'I'm grateful that you would think to spare me pain, Lady Elayne. But I fear your warning comes too late and perhaps would be misconstrued, if eavesdroppers heard our discussion of the queen's character. Perhaps we should both be silent on this matter.'

With a neat, dismissive bow, Balyn excused himself, leaving Elayne with two spots of high colour on her cheekbones and a heart that was burdened with foreboding.

That young man can't tell friend from foe, she thought sadly as she watched his tall form move through the press of courtiers. May the gods protect him.

Through the throng of over twenty persons in the bower,

servants moved in dark robes carrying plates of sweetmeats and confections, liberally sweetened with honey. The queen sat at the centre of the chattering crowd and sipped a cup of fruit juices laced with mead. Her face was frozen and blank.

Shortly afterwards, Balyn was summoned to attend the king in his private chambers.

Balan watched his brother leave the rose arbor with sick dread. He feared Balyn's state of mind would lead him to alienate the king.

Previous experiences heralded an imminent brainstorm.

Heavy roses filled the bower with a scent so sickly that Balan could almost see the perfume clog the air. A trace of corruption lurked under the ripe, sweet smell.

Wenhaver smiled at Balan and the young man felt a tug under his ribs.

The queen is foolish and stupid – and she's dangerous, Balan decided. How could the king have allied himself with such a difficult woman?

Balan observed the full-blown roses, the imported glassware and the finely woven cloth that adorned the ladies, and his common sense told him that the graciousness of older civilizations was aped in this bower, in this palace and throughout the kingdom.

'Rome is dead, just as Artor's kingdom is beginning to die,' Balan murmured to no one in particular as he massaged the insistent ache under his ribs.

'There you are,' Artor greeted Balyn as he crossed his threshold. 'You seem to be a little pale today, my boy.' He smiled into Balyn's dull eyes. 'You may have a glass of wine if you wish, or water if you prefer. Make yourself comfortable, for I have a problematic mission that I need to discuss with you.'

Balyn flushed with pleasure and his eyes became more animated.

Artor saw a boy who was so physically like his youthful self, it was uncanny. He noted the woollen tunic, the leather trews and a simple gold chain around his neck with his father's emblem stamped upon it. The boy had a pleasing appearance.

'I will successfully complete whatever duty you ask of me, Your Majesty.'

Artor laughed and shook his head. 'You should never agree to a challenge until you know what it entails, boy. You might find that my orders aren't to your taste.'

Balyn looked surprised. 'How could I possibly refuse you, my lord? Celts should be honoured to serve the king.'

'Your words are admirable, Balyn, but you should listen to what I say before you agree with me,' Artor stated. 'I want you to travel to Glastonbury and give my best wishes to Bishop Otha. Demand from him the staff that was used to kill Bishop Aethelthred and then return to Cadbury and present it to me.'

Balyn nodded and would have risen to obey immediately, but Artor gestured for him to remain seated.

'The task is not as easy as it sounds, Balyn,' he continued. 'Otha Redbeard's loyalties are in doubt and because this order comes from me, he may refuse to hand over the staff. Your task is to convince him to accede to my demands.'

'By any means, my king?'

'By any means necessary, Balyn, but you should try diplomacy first. I value the prayers of Glastonbury and don't wish to offend the churchmen who reside there.'

'Then I'll take my leave, my lord, so I can be about your business.'

'Take care, Balyn. You are direct kin, and that means you are precious to me. I'm anxious to remove this staff from the hands of Bishop Botha. I don't trust the man so it could be a perilous mission, despite its apparent simplicity.'

Artor pulled the large pearl ring from his thumb. 'You will take this bauble as proof of your status as my emissary. Wear it with pride, for all men know that this ring belongs to Artor, High King of the Britons.'

Balyn felt tears prickle behind his eyes. His emotions were so confused that he almost leaned his head upon the High King's shoulder to weep in gratitude.

'I serve the west, my lord. That is sufficient reason to obey your orders and ride to Glastonbury. Thank you for the confidence you have placed in me.'

'Don't thank me. Sometimes men die when I give orders, good men who do their best with what they have to give.'

'But, lord, nothing you ask could possibly—'

'Please, lad, don't interrupt me when I speak. I have learned that being a king means I have to put aside love and family duty for the larger needs of the country. Do you understand, Balyn?'

Balyn looked at Artor with wide, wondering eyes. 'Yes, I understand, but—'

'I'm sending you to Glastonbury on a delicate mission, Balyn. The repercussions of failure could be very awkward so you will need to keep a cool head and have your wits about you.' Artor patted Balyn's shoulder affectionately.

'I will do nothing to bring shame to the kingdom, or to you,'

Balyn swore solemnly. 'I will return with the staff as soon as I can.'

As Balyn bowed to his king and backed out of the room, Artor felt a tug of anxiety. Almost any one of Artor's retinue could have conveyed this request to the bishop, but Artor must find an heir, so Balyn needed to show his mettle. He was ignorant of Wenhaver's fall from Balyn's pedestal, and had no idea that the boy was a volcano of churning emotions, but something in Balyn's eyes had given Artor cause for concern regarding his grandson's balance.

Balyn bounded through the confusing hive of the citadel to the tiny cell he shared with his sibling. When Balan entered shortly afterwards, he found his brother hurriedly throwing spare tunics into a travel bag, his eyes sparkling with excitement.

'Where are you going, brother? Why the haste? I thought we were off hunting once we could escape the queen's bower.'

Balyn continued to ram items into his leather bags. He paused only to hold out one hand in triumph, to show Balan the thumb where the pearl ring shone dully.

'The King is sending me to Glastonbury on a mission. Me! And he has given me his own thumb ring as proof of my legitimacy. All praise to King Artor. I need not endure the likes of Wenhaver or Modred any longer.'

Balan stared into his brother's earnest face and the excitement that animated his eyes. A niggling sense of alarm gnawed at Balan's vitals.

'Why the haste, Balyn? Let's talk and discover the best way for you to complete your mission.'

'I have no need to talk to you or listen to your advice,' Balyn said loftily. 'I can complete this task alone, thank you.'

'But we've always thrashed out important matters in the past.'

'Not this time. Artor has placed his trust in me. In *me*, not you.'

For one sick moment, Balyn's face was wolfish, and Balan stepped back from the sudden savagery he saw in the eyes of his twin.

'What have I done to offend you, Balyn, that you should be so angry with me?'

Had Balyn paused for reflection, if he hadn't been hurt by his discovery of Wenhaver's true character, if he hadn't been given to fits of intense hero-worship, he might have stayed his tongue. But Balyn remembered the thousand times when Balan had offered sage advice that had later proved to be correct, and he felt a sting of jealousy so hot and sharp that his gorge almost choked him.

Without thinking, he burst into impassioned speech.

'Everybody knows that Balan is the cleverest brother of the twins. Everybody knows that Balan takes care of his elder brother. Well, I'm sick of it! I'm a grown man and the High King has entrusted me with a mission. Not you! So this time you can keep your suggestions to yourself.'

Balan raised both hands in surrender. 'As you wish, brother. Go with God and travel with my best wishes. I'll be here when you return.'

Trying desperately to maintain his anger in the face of his brother's obvious hurt, Balyn buckled his bags and stomped from the room. His back was arrow straight and he resisted the impulse to look back.

Balan watched from a vantage point on the tor as Balyn mounted his horse. He continued to watch as his twin made the circuitous ride through the spiral fortifications. Long after Balyn had vanished on the road to Glastonbury, Balyn continued to stare towards the north-west with eyes that were chill with anxiety.

Balyn had travelled widely since he had sworn himself to the service of the High King. He had seen the Giant's Dance that leered over the flat, green sward with a hovering sense of menace. He had stood on the Heel Stone of the Dance and wondered at its ancient, arcane purpose. He had viewed the wonders of Venta Belgarum, including the square before the king's hall. There, Artor had once battled Uther Pendragon's champion for his life, while Myrddion had plotted to force the Pendragon to accept his unacknowledged son as his heir. But it was Glastonbury, with its fields, its shining expanses of water, and its willing and able workers, that pulled him with its promise of endless peace. To return to the religious enclave was a blessing when his heart was so burdened with disillusion.

Balyn rejoiced in Glastonbury's sense of holiness. Something older than the Christian god seemed to have taken root in these quiet fields. So Glastonbury flourished because it was the heart of Britain. Wiser heads could have told Balyn that many races had come to these isles in search of tin, copper and other commodities over the centuries and these strangers had left behind them layers of culture on which the Celts and the Saxons had built.

Balyn didn't care. His heart sang, the invisible birds warbled in the fruitful trees and the sun shone softly on his tanned face. He was about his king's business: what more could a loyal Celt desire?

The simplicity of the dormitories at Glastonbury, the workshops and even the small wooden church reminded him of his home. The fields were so lovingly tended that he recalled the bone-deep love of the earth that his mother had taught him. Glastonbury eased Balyn's tortured and poetic soul. A youth showed him to a simple room above the stables and with pleasure Balyn entered. He washed himself clean of the dust of his journey and dressed as befitted an Ordovice prince. Then he went to meet the master of the enclave.

Among the peace and harmony, Bishop Otha was an unwelcome contrast. Dressed in magnificent robes and with his fingers encrusted with golden rings, Otha slouched on a heavily carved bench and grunted at his young visitor without raising his head from his meal. His only acknowledgement was to raise his ring to be kissed. Of necessity, Balyn must kneel to perform this mark of respect, and the young man had an uninterrupted view of Otha's greasy face.

'Wine, Master Balyn?' Otha offered disinterestedly as he poured himself a cup.

'Water will adequately slake my thirst, Bishop Otha,' the young man answered easily. 'I have been told that the springs of Glastonbury produce water that is almost perfect.'

'Suit yourself.'

Otha raised his golden cup to his lips and drank daintily, before gesturing to a bench seat opposite his place at the table.

Balyn took the proffered seat.

The bishop sat at a table that could easily have seated half a dozen priests, but he kept himself in isolation, facing other long tables that were crowded with lay brothers and other men of God. The rough, wooden planks were spread with simple ewers and beakers of brown, glossy pottery filled with water. Platters held loaves of coarse, brown bread, fresh yellow butter, slabs of hard cheese and fruit from the orchards. A heavy iron pot of rich vegetable stew sat in the centre of each table, with a long-handled wooden ladle for serving.

The bishop's table could hardly have been more different. Golden platters, a goblet of heavy gold and a real silver spoon were on display. The food, too, was more elaborate. Chunks of meat swam in the bishop's stew, along with greasy slabs of bacon that were sopped up with bread so fluffy that only finely ground flour could have been used in its preparation. Even his eating knife was rich and ostentatious; no priestly poverty or vow of humility were evident in Otha or his meal.

But the bishop was no mincing epicure; his intelligence ranged beyond the circumference of his belly and his desire for comfort. He gazed narrowly at the face of his young visitor.

'So, what do you desire of me, Master Balyn?'

Balyn took his time drinking the cool spring water brought to him by a soft-footed novice. The young man thought the bishop vastly unpleasant and patronizing to one who was a prince of the Ordovice tribe and an envoy of the High King of the Britons.

'The High King offers his felicitations and his thanks for the courtesies that were offered to him when last he visited this sanctuary.' Balyn spoke in his most measured, artless voice. 'He seeks assurance that all is well within Glastonbury, and asks whether the monastery has needs that he could help to fulfil.'

Balyn was thinking on his feet to the very best of his ability.

Otha pursed his thick, moist lips. Balyn felt sure the bishop didn't believe a word of his greeting.

'I thank the High King for his concern, but I can see no reason why he should believe that Glastonbury would be other than well. Care of Glastonbury is invested in Holy Mother Church and is not subject to the reach of King Artor.'

'Excellent news, my lord,' Balyn responded, fighting to hold his temper. 'I shall relay the felicity that my own eyes have seen.'

'Is there anything else, young man?' Otha asked negligently, helping himself to more stew.

'There is one other minor matter, my lord bishop. King Artor has received information that reveals the identity of Aethelthred's murderer, who is also believed to be responsible for a number of other crimes against the Church. King Artor believes the criminal is a rogue called Gronw who is passing himself off as a Druid. The High King requests that the murder weapon, the staff, be loaned to the crown as evidence of this man's criminal activities.'

Otha's eyes were suddenly watchful.

'The staff? Artor requires the staff?'

'That is correct, my lord bishop. I trust you have no objections to assisting in bringing the murderer of your predecessor to justice. He is pagan, and a sworn enemy of Mother Church.'

'No. Not at all. But I should point out that the staff has become something of a holy relic to our community, and you should understand that we would be reluctant to lose it.'

'How could the staff be lost if it is kept in the safe hands of the High King of the Britons?' Balyn countered smoothly.

'Perhaps a trusted brother could accompany the staff to Cadbury to ensure that it is treated with the reverence it deserves.'

Otha was irritating at any time, but he was especially unattractive when he was seeking personal advantage.

He gazed speculatively at his young visitor, his wrinkled brow indicating how little credence he gave to Balyn's assurances.

'That's true. Well ... something might be arranged.' Otha was on his guard, and his agile mind searched for Artor's purpose. 'You shall eat with me this evening, at which time we will discuss this matter further. In the meantime, you may enjoy the felicity of Glastonbury.'

Otha knew the value of delaying tactics when he suspected he was being manipulated. Balyn realized that he was caught at Glastonbury, at the mercy of Otha's ennui. He wanted to grab the priest by his pudgy shoulders and shake him vigorously. Otha was determined to make Artor's envoy await his pleasure, for no better reason than to indulge his sense of his own consequence. For days Balyn was forced to kick his heels. He tried hard to find that calm centre that Balan had always helped him reach – he now bitterly regretted every word he had thrown at his brother with such venomous thoughtlessness. Otha's casual contrariness was insufferable. Like a lidded pot heating over a fire, Balyn's temper rose steadily and began to simmer, until finally it boiled over.

Night after night, the young man ate with the Bishop who believed that his consequence separated him from every other penitent in Glastonbury. Where generations of pious bishops had dined frugally at a common eating table with their fellows,

Otha preferred to dine at a separate table with a novice to serve him.

Balyn was soon offended by Otha's pretensions and was irked by his enforced inactivity.

Under a thick layer of cloying concern, Otha was being particularly offensive.

'You must long for the grand halls of Cadbury after our simple fare, Balyn, although I've heard that the king is a difficult, gruff host.'

The other priests ate hurriedly, as if they were uncomfortable in the bishop's presence. Brother Simon grimaced sourly from a dark corner where he was out of the bishop's vision, and wished that he could plead illness and depart.

Balyn eyed Otha's ostentatious cup and plate distastefully; for all its lavish decoration, the bishop's tableware did not improve his eating habits. His fine wool habit was liberally spotted with grease and food stains.

'Those of us who love the west and value the High King are perfectly comfortable in his presence,' Balyn answered blandly.

Two spots of scarlet appeared on Otha's plump cheeks. His lips pursed.

'I am touched by your loyalties, young sir, but Artor seems to me to be a dour man, one who is lacking in grace or conversation. I speak as an outsider, of course, one who has no personal knowledge of life at court, so I must make allowances for the fact that he has the onerous duties of a relatively small kingdom to plague him. I understand that he is old and well into his dotage.'

Balyn felt his shoulders square. The unnatural pallor of his face was a clear indication of his emotions, but the muscles in his jaw revealed the effort he expended to remain calm.

'King Artor may be old in years, my lord, but his strength and vigour remain, and he is in full control of his kingdom. He is not a dour man, he is simply focused on his duties to his people. His responsibilities leave little room for frivolity, or feasts.'

Ignoring the barb, Otha shrugged indifferently and changed the direction of his probes.

'I have also heard that King Artor follows the path of his cruel father by guarding his throne jealously from any pretender who seeks to weaken his position. I mean no disrespect, but I'm simply repeating rumours that I've heard. If he is truly devoted to his duties, don't you think that he should name an heir?' Otha smiled at the anger that flooded Balyn's face. 'I mean no slight, young man, but King Artor has had a reputation for violence since his youth.'

'King Artor rules a vast kingdom and, at times, all kings are forced to sweep away those who show themselves as enemies.' Balyn smiled thinly at the bishop. 'Your words are unwise as well as offensive.' Balyn's eyes were dangerously flat but Otha was oblivious; he possessed the self-satisfaction of a well-fed hog wallowing in its own mud pit.

'It's common knowledge throughout the land that the king executed a pregnant woman a brief six months ago, and I believe that such actions are an indication of the violence that exists within King Artor's nature.'

Balyn gritted his teeth and threw away his polite words. 'Beware, priest, for you are condoning lies. I was present at the death of the Lady of Salinae Minor and I saw her attack the king with a weapon, as did all those warriors present. The High King did not order her death, his personal guard cut her down as she tried to murder Artor. She had already made one attempt to kill the High King in the early hours of the morning, and her servant was directly responsible for the death of your predecessor.' He paused to allow his words to sink in.

'Bishop Aethelthred was butchered at his altar by a man you appear unwilling to see brought to justice. The pagan who committed this crime was Lady Miryll's servant and co-conspirator.' Balyn spun his delicate eating blade between his fingers. Against his will, Otha watched the small knife flash hypnotically in the light.

'We must agree to differ then, young Balyn.'

'We agree to nothing, Bishop, for your words are lies. You keep me waiting here while you slowly decide if you will obey a legitimate request from the High King. I order you to give me the staff and permit me to be on my way before words are uttered that will offend the king when I repeat them to him on my return to Cadbury.'

Otha was angry, but he attempted to hold his temper in check by saying nothing.

'I don't intend to ask again,' Balyn warned.

'You aren't asking,' Otha snapped. 'You are demanding.'

The other priests in the room, seated at their long benches, flinched at the raised voices at the bishop's table. The novice behind Otha's chair grew pale and recoiled visibly.

'I am demanding in the name of the High King of the Britons! You may refuse if you place no value on your life.'

Still Otha restrained himself from refusing outright.

Balyn rose to his feet and turned to the novice behind his chair.

'You.' Balyn pointed his forefinger at the boy. 'Where is the staff?'

'I don't know, my lord,' he stammered.

'Brother Mark, where is the staff?'

Brother Mark lurched to his feet.

'Do not answer if you value your mortal soul!' Otha roared, his face beet-red with fury.

Brother Mark opened and closed his mouth several times, appalled by the ugly confrontation.

Balyn held up his clenched fist. The distinctive pearl thumb ring was clearly visible to the brothers who sat below the high table.

'I speak for the High King himself! You will bring me the staff!'

Brother Mark fled towards the church, ignoring Otha's shouted threats.

Bearing arms in holy Glastonbury had long been deemed blasphemous, so Balyn had left his weapons in the stable, with his horse. But he had retained the slim-bladed dagger with which he ate in the courtly manner of Cadbury. He gripped the small weapon in his left hand and even Otha realized that Balyn would use it if he was forced to. The bishop subsided into an ominous silence.

Mark's running footsteps could be heard returning to the refectory.

'My lord,' the priest panted as he approached Balyn. 'Here is the staff.'

Balyn took the smooth shaft of aged wood with its ugly

satyr carved at the end. He could see a nasty split in the carving, probably a result of the fierce blows that had rained down on Aethelthred's innocent head.

'You'll regret this insult, you pagan upstart!' Otha spat furiously. 'You're the envoy of a bloodstained, murderous despot and his whore of a wife! Artor is a cuckold who takes his spite out upon anyone who dares to thwart his wishes. Only cowards kill innocent women such as Lady Miryll. He doesn't exact the same vengeance on men who lie with his slut of a wife.'

Balyn rounded on the bishop. 'Traitor! Cur! Artor is the greatest man in Britain, and the church at Glastonbury only exists because of his leadership and courage against our enemies.'

Otha sprang towards Balyn and gripped the head of the staff as if he would wrench the wooden relic out of Balyn's grip.

'You have no right to take what belongs to Glastonbury,' he screamed. 'You rob Mother Church of her rightful possession.'

'This cursed weapon killed your bishop,' Balyn yelled back. 'It doesn't belong to you, but to some assassin who is bent on destroying your Church.' He pulled backwards on the staff with all his strength.

The cracking of wood was loud in the ears of the shocked and silent company as the head of the staff broke away, revealing a length of leaf-shaped iron. The priests gasped in horror as they saw the ugly staff transformed into the head of a short, Roman stabbing spear.

Otha cried out as the ancient blade sliced through his clenched fingers. As Balyn's eyes dropped and he saw the wicked spearhead stained with Otha's blood, his grip on the shaft slackened momentarily and Otha's considerable weight pulled the spear out of the young man's hands. With a hungry little hiss, the blade impaled itself in Otha Redbeard's soft, round gut.

Balyn dropped his hands, his face white with shock. The bishop reeled backwards until he struck the sod wall where he hung, his bleeding hands still clutching the end of the iron spear that had shallowly pierced his gut.

'What have you done to me?' Otha asked blankly, his eyes fixed on the wound in the soft flesh of his belly. Even then, Otha's wound was not mortal, for the spear point had not bitten past deep layers of fat. 'I'm bleeding!' He squealed like a man surprised by some terrible wonder.

Then, he fainted.

His heavy body fell forward and the shaft of the spear skidded along the flagging until it became wedged against the base of the table. Otha's weight drove his body down on to the blade until he hung obscenely over the golden dish and goblet, greasy from his meal. His mouth opened and blood and vomit gushed out of his throat and nose.

The shaft twisted under his considerable weight, and Otha and the spear fell awkwardly sideways on to the sod floor. The bishop, now mortally wounded, mewed in surprise.

Transfixed, Balyn's shocked gaze was riveted on the spear protruding from the bishop's body. The pool of blood at his feet continued to spread. With a short, unpriestly curse, Mark leapt forward, followed by two other brothers who had retained their wits. Carefully, they straightened the body of the bishop until he lay on his back on the floor.

'Dear God,' Mark breathed. 'The bishop dies!'

As Balyn overcame his shock and reached forward to draw out the spear, Brother Mark gripped his right forearm.

'No, my lord! If you remove the spear, the bishop will bleed to death in moments. First, he must be shrived.'

'He bleeds internally,' another brother whispered. 'See? Blood gushes from his mouth. Otha cannot survive these wounds.'

A number of priests hurried to find clean cloth, a soft pillow for the bishop's head, and a golden cross for the bishop to grip while he received extreme unction.

Balyn knelt beside the priests, his eyes blank and his thoughts in tatters.

When Otha's eyes flickered open for a few seconds, he saw Balyn's face hovering above him. He flinched and howled, his bleeding fingers clutching the spear shaft.

'Keep him away from me,' he whispered, his voice full of hate to the very end. 'This man is a murderer, an assassin sent by Artor to remove me from Glastonbury.'

Otha's voice was silenced by bloody coughing.

'My bishop, you must make your confession and ensure that your soul is purified in the eyes of God,' Brother Mark whispered in Otha's ear.

Otha's eyes widened with horror. 'I *cannot* die! I'm the bishop, appointed by the Archbishop of Venta Belgarum. No man of God can be killed by such an unholy weapon as this.'

To Balyn, the drama began to verge on farce.

'Jesus died with such a weapon in his side,' he said glibly. 'Why should you fare better than your god?'

Brother Mark rose and slapped Balyn across the face,

shocking the young man into silence. 'My apologies, Lord Balyn, but your words are unworthy of you. You will be silent!'

Mark turned his attention to the novice, who was weeping hysterically.

'Fetch water, boy, and hurry, for the bishop doesn't have time to waste.'

The novice fled and returned with a bowl of water.

Mark thrust his bloody hands into the bowl and scrubbed them briefly. Another priest brought a white woollen surplice that Mark put on over his plain robe. He picked up the golden cross from Otha's belly.

Balyn continued to kneel beside the man he had inadvertently wounded, while Mark joined him on his knees and began to speak rapidly in Latin. For a brief moment, Balyn's spirit was soothed by the ancient sounds, but when Bishop Otha opened his eyes once again, Balyn flinched away from the malice and terror that sustained the last thread of life in the churchman.

'I will make my confession,' Otha gasped between bouts of bleeding that threatened to choke him.

Two of the brothers raised his torso to ease his struggling lungs, while another wiped his contorted, bloody mouth.

'I affirm that the Lord God is my heavenly master, the Bishop of Venta Belgarum is my spiritual guide, and King Modred of the Brigante is my temporal lord. I have endeavoured to free the west of the pestilential presence of Artor and his slut of a queen so that a true heir, derived from Ygerne of blessed memory might assume the dragon throne and cleanse us all.'

Brother Mark flinched, and seemed to deflate within his

white robe, but the ancient words of forgiveness continued to pour from his lips.

'Do you repent that you placed earthly power above the might of God?' Mark asked in the Latin language of the Church.

'Yes, if I must die without seeing my king on the throne.'

Mark made the sign of the cross over the bishop's flaccid body.

'I confess that I was aware that the murder of Bishop Aethelthred was a plot aimed at Artor. I swear that neither I nor my master had any part in its execution. Nevertheless, I welcomed it—' A fit of coughing choked off the treasonous words.

Mark continued to intone the prayers and signs of forgiveness.

'I confess also that I have plotted against the High King while searching for some weakness in his armour.'

A thick burst of half-clotted blood blunted his words once again, and he panted with the exertion of speaking. Otha Redbeard's eyes were black with malice and ill will.

'I discovered an ancient woman who had worked at the Villa Poppinidii. I am aware that Artor has a daughter and three grandsons – kin that, in his wickedness, he denies. The old woman thought that her confession was protected by extreme unction, but God demands that a Christian should rule, not a soulless demon who worships his Roman gods. I carried out my labours in the name of Mother Church.'

'Who are the grandsons?' Balyn whispered. His eyes were alive once more.

Otha smiled, almost sweetly, as his eyelids drooped. 'You

and Balan, your twin brother. Didn't you know? Bran, the King of the Ordovice, is also a grandson. All three are the fruit of a poisoned tree. You are an heir to the kingdom of the devil!'

Balyn recoiled from Otha's poison. The bishop's words burned into his brain.

'Do you confess to all your sins, great and small, that burden your soul, Bishop Otha?' Mark asked solemnly.

Otha's eyes were smudged black within his white face, as if the fire in them would scorch his skin to ashes. His eyes rounded as he struggled to draw a breath and then rolled back into his head until only the whites showed. A half-breath raised the mountainous belly . . . faltered . . . and then all life stopped.

The priests and novices fell to their knees, and the room was soon thick with the hum of prayer. Balyn's eyes darted from one bowed head to another, but nowhere could he find eyes that would meet his. He imagined that the hunched shoulders and bent backs were reproaches for his actions. His head ached with guilt for what had taken place in this most holy of holy places.

A faint moan escaped his tight lips.

Mark turned towards him and saw the glitter of hysteria in his flat, grey eyes.

'Come, boy, let me find you a glass of apricot brandy. Your hands tremble and you are very pale.'

'The staff. My master has ordered me to bring the spear to Cadbury,' Balyn mumbled, as if trying to retrieve a fragment of reason from his crumbling existence. 'Artor demands that I return to Cadbury with it.'

'Come with me, lord, so I might ease your nerves and help

you to sleep,' the priest murmured softly. 'The High King wouldn't ask you to travel in your unwashed and weary state.'

Balyn's eyes darted from Mark's concerned gaze to the body of Otha Redbeard.

'I didn't mean to kill him, I swear I didn't!' Balyn hiccuped with incipient hysteria. 'He pulled the staff out of my hands. He should have obeyed Artor's instructions and given me the staff willingly. I didn't know it was a spear! How could I? Otha was a traitor, but now I have his blood on my hands.' Balyn opened his palms where blood was already beginning to dry. 'Why didn't anyone tell me? Artor must have known. Why didn't he explain? Otha was unarmed, and now my honour is dead forever.'

'No, lad, no,' Mark said urgently. 'We'll swear that no malice guided your hand. None of us suspected that the staff was a spear, not even Otha. You must come with me and rest.'

'Lad? I'm no boy! I don't know what I am. Did Artor lie? And did Mother lie as well? Everybody seems to know but me, and you're all laughing at me!'

'No. You must be calm, Balyn. The bishop brought his death upon himself by pulling on the spear. Perhaps he torments you with untruths.'

Brother Mark moved back as Balyn suddenly leapt forward in a peculiar, stiff-legged gait. He planted one foot on Otha's belly and wrenched the spear free of its sheath of flesh. The wound made an ugly, sucking noise as if it was reluctant to relinquish its hold on the spearhead, and Balyn felt the weapon twist in his hands as if it was alive.

'I must go,' he repeated to no one in particular. Then he ran from the dining hall, his face set like stone and his limbs uncoordinated. The priests moved out of his path like dry brown leaves in the wind.

Shreds of thought drove Balyn to the stables, to his horse and out into the darkness. As the stars spiralled above his head in coruscations of light that matched the explosions in his brain, Balyn shook his bloody hand, waved the spear towards the uncaring skies and screamed a meaningless curse against the gods.

And he cursed his grandfather.

CHAPTER XIV

THE SKEIN OF BLOOD

Balan surged out of a nightmare like a fish rising towards the light. Dislocated images followed him into consciousness, and he could taste the metallic bitterness of blood in his mouth.

Sweet Jesus! Balan thought, half in curse and half in prayer. His body jittered with nervous tension as his breathing gradually returned to normal.

'What dangers assail my brother?' he asked himself aloud. Over the years, he had become accustomed to nightmares, phantom pangs and emotional chaos whenever his twin was in pain or experiencing turmoil. Balan had come to believe that this strange, symbiotic relationship was at the root of his own caution.

Balyn is reckless enough for both of us, Balan thought disjointedly. Why is it that I should feel his pain, but he never feels any discomfort when I'm in peril?

But Balan didn't begrudge the fact that his twin was free from this particular inheritance of kinship.

The dreary, anxious day became increasingly painful for Balan; he found food tasteless, his head ached insistently and his nerves were stretched to breaking point. He sought relief in the open air, but no number of cooling breezes could soothe the dislocation in his head. He suffered but did not understand the cause of his illness.

The night that followed was full of dreams of blood and death, causing his mind's eye to see the fragmented shapes of dying men and women through a mist of redness. The morning dawned cleanly, but Balan's bloodshot eyes and trembling hands caused his manservant to fear that his master was gravely ill.

Inevitably, several days later, Artor was informed of Balan's malady and the young man was summoned to the king's chambers.

'You're ill, Balan,' Artor began unceremoniously when he registered Balan's ashen complexion and sunken eyes. 'What ails you?'

'I don't know, my lord,' the young warrior replied. 'But I miss my brother ... and I fear for his safety.'

Artor poured Balan a goblet of wine with his own hand.

'Drink, boy, or I swear you'll collapse on my floor. Your mother will pursue me to Hades if I allow you to sicken.'

Balan drank the proffered wine and a little colour stained his high cheekbones. But his eyes remained downcast as he explained the connection between himself and his twin.

'I'm certain that Balyn is in trouble,' he finally admitted. 'I've never missed him so acutely, nor felt the gulf between us to be so wide.'

Artor watched Balan with measuring eyes.

'You possess a strange gift, but it shouldn't be unwelcome, for you reap the benefit of true communion with another person. Few of us can know another soul so intimately.'

Balan shook his head ruefully and finished the wine in his cup.

'Another?' Artor asked economically.

'No, my lord. Where is Balyn? Where is my brother? He told me you sent him to Glastonbury, but that was all. We parted on bad terms . . '.

'He's with Bishop Otha at Glastonbury on my orders. I asked him to recover the staff that was used to slay Bishop Aethelthred'.

'Oh!' Balan could find nothing further to say.

'The task is neither dangerous nor arduous. However, if rumours of Otha's hospitality are true, your brother is in danger of being bored to death'. Artor looked speculatively at Balan. 'Do you truly worry that Balyn has come to some harm? If you wish, I can easily send a messenger to Glastonbury'.

Concern furrowed the brow of the king and Balan was acutely embarrassed.

'No', Balan decided. 'My brother wouldn't thank me if I were to fuss like a virgin aunt. He'd be likely to sulk for days if I meddled in his orders from you. Still . . '.

'Still, you can't help but worry'.

'Aye. Balyn leads with his heart, if you take my meaning, my lord. He is passionate when he should be cool, but his love is true and innocent. In some ways, he's still a child'.

Artor grinned with sudden understanding. 'Whereas you are the reverse. You and your brother are two men who make the perfect whole through separate halves. Aye, you're very fortunate'.

At that moment, a page knocked at the king's door, opened

it tentatively and informed his master that a courier was riding in haste towards Cadbury.

Artor glanced at Balan and recognized the shiver of presentiment in his grandson's eyes. The king had seen such an expression in his own silver mirror often enough.

'Attend on me, Balan, while we await this news at the gates of the citadel.'

Balyn rode into the wilderness with scant concern for his life or for his safety. Sobbing, and retching with distress, all night, he forced his horse on, careless of branches and thorns, and it was only when the beast started to founder that Balyn pulled on the reins and forced the terrified, heaving animal to a shuddering halt.

His head pounded with a crazed refrain.

His grandfather was Artor, High King of the Britons. Did his mother know? Was she foolish? Was she false? And the king had dishonoured Balyn's whole tribe by his silence, rejecting his grandsons and building his kingdom on a lie. In his own twisted fashion, Otha was correct in his assumption that the king was false, which meant the kingdom was also flawed.

Balyn's forehead seemed to be bound by a band of hot iron. All he could see around him was treason, falsehood and pretence. The rot in the west had even contaminated holy Glastonbury, for Bishop Otha had betrayed his vows by serving a corrupt master.

Balyn burned on a pyre of his own making. As his idols crumbled, so did his faith. In the roiling stew of his emotions, he never, for a moment, considered reasons for the choices made in the distant past. If there was no such thing as the rule of law, why should he obey empty words?

He needed rest, food and shelter for himself and his suffering horse. Before this past night of horror, he would have courteously asked for succour at the first cottage that his journey crossed. And he would have been rewarded with hospitality. But he determined that he would be like the rest of the world and simply take what he chose. He was tired; let the cattle serve his needs without chatter or argument.

He walked his sweating horse to a thatched hut surrounded by vegetable plots and fruit trees on the margins of the forest. The night was on the wane and, in a few hours, the sun would rise to create a new day. But for now, deep indigo shadows lurked under the trees and the hut was sunk in deepest silence.

Using the hilt of his sword, Balyn pounded on the flimsy plank door. For a moment, he enjoyed a shameful, visceral thrill that his arrival must frighten the peasants inside.

Within, he heard a faint rustling and the frightened murmur of voices. A face shrouded in purple shadow cast from a dying fire appeared at the opened crack in the doorway.

'I require food, water and care for my horse. Stand aside!'

All that the householder could see was a dark shadow, barred with moonlight, and a pair of pale eyes that glowed eerily in the light of the fire. The man threw his weight against the door to close it, but Balyn had already thrust a foot over the threshold.

A figure scuttled away from him, reaching for a long object leaning in a corner of the hut. Balyn imagined a concealed spear biting deeply into his flesh, just like Otha – so he swung his sword blindly at the shadowy figure in the semi-darkness.

He would hear that scream, as his weapon cleaved through skin and bone, until the moment of his death.

Another form threw itself upon his back and yet another fastened teeth into his sword hand. In a parody of a ritualistic battle dance, the prince stumbled in the enclosed darkness, stabbing, punching and thrusting at nightmarish shadows while his nostrils filled with the hot stink of blood and relaxed bowels.

Then he stood alone in the shadows, panting with terror and exertion.

Tripping over soft forms on the earth floor, he found cut wood by touch and thrust a log into the dying fire. As the wood began to burn, the shabby structure of plaited willow branches and sod slowly became clear.

And Balyn saw what he had done.

The man at the door had taken a sword cut across the side of the throat, almost severing his head from his trunk. The body had almost pumped dry of blood and lay huddled in an untidy shamble on the ground. The man clutched a wooden staff in his still-warm hands.

A woman had leapt on his back and had sustained a sword thrust in her chest. Both hands held the edges of the gross wound together and her eyes had already rolled up into her skull. Her heavy breasts, half exposed in the struggle, seemed pathetically vulnerable.

The bodies of the children were the worst. One child appeared unmarked, except for the strange angle of his neck where Balyn's fist had hurled the child across the room. The boy, for such he had been, stared out of unseeing pupils into the vast spaces of the unknown. He could not have been more than ten.

The girl still lived, but her breathing was already slowing. Twelve-year-old flesh is no match for a sword. And her arm was barely attached at the shoulder.

'I'm sorry,' Balyn moaned as the girl tried to find her mother's hand with a small, grimy paw. 'I'm sorry. I didn't know.'

The girl breathed once more, deeply, and then the hut became silent except for a thin wail from the corner.

Sickened with self-loathing, Balyn saw a plaited rush cradle hanging from a roof rafter. Inside the straw, wrapped in a woven slip of wool, an infant cried weakly.

As if in a dream, Balyn sheathed his bloody sword and raised his hand to touch the flushed, soft face. The pearl of Artor's ring glittered on his hand in a web of wet blood, and Balyn found himself retching uncontrollably.

Guilt rose in his scrambled thoughts in waves of vomit and bile, until his throat was raw and his eyes were filled with tears. Some primal survival instinct caused him to find the hut's meagre store of bread and dried apples and thrust them into his tunic. Then he found a jug containing clean water that he used to fill his water bottle to the brim before taking the remainder to his horse. A small storage area yielded large jars of grain that he gave to the beast.

It shied nervously away from his bloody hands.

Balyn braced himself to re-enter the hut. If he left the infant in this wilderness, it would be dead in a few hours. His essential decency demanded that he find succour for the child.

'How can I look on what I have done?' Balyn screamed at the fading darkness.

The stars had gone down, and the sky was beginning to lighten with the approach of daylight.

He walked through sticky blood in the small, stinking hut, to lift the child out of its cradle with his left arm. Four pairs of eyes seemed to reproach him from the eerie circle of death, while empty, innocent hands mocked his manhood and his honour.

Heedless of the tears that had begun to stream down his face, Balyn pulled a log from the fire and rolled it into the straw pallet where it leapt into harsh, hungry life.

The skin of the unfortunate farmer began to blacken and his hair soon caught alight in a gust of yellow flame. Balyn could gaze on the physical proof of his sin no longer; he left the hut and led his horse into the wilds, heading ever further east.

Artor and Balan waited quietly at the last gate leading to the tor and watched as the approaching horseman passed over the defensive dykes of Cadbury. The rider's passage was slow, but Artor would eventually understand that the reason for his long wait lay in the nature of the steed, a large grey beast with thick fringes of long hair around its plate-like hooves. For a brief moment, Artor remembered a huge, good-natured horse called Plod, and its offspring, Aphrodite, who had endured his lessons in horsemanship so many years earlier when his world was still young. But this horse was old, as was evident in its bony spine and sagging belly, and any farmer would have recognized the rubbed cicatrices in its shaggy coat that spoke of its normal task of dragging a plough.

The rider was equally unkempt. A cloak of stiff sheepskin

protected the traveller from inclement weather. His home-spun clothes and his rough spear, with a point of wood that had been hardened by fire, spoke eloquently of a simple, rustic life.

'Why does a farm boy seek out the High King?' Artor asked aloud as the heavy beast lumbered up to the final gate.

'Will you not see him then, my lord?' Balan asked.

'Of course I'll see him. I must hear the problems of any of my subjects who come to Cadbury,' Artor answered tartly. A vague feeling of unease made his tone brusque and stern.

'At least the common folk know that they have your ear if they need to speak with you.'

Artor sighed. He had learned to his cost over many years that unannounced visitors to the citadel, whether noble or peasant, usually meant trouble.

The farm horse on which the visitor rode was so tall at the shoulder that it almost dwarfed Odin. The Jutlander gripped the horse's cheek straps while the thin shepherd boy eased himself down from its wide back. He shook himself vigorously, stamped his numb feet and tried to tame his tangled hair. Then he recognized the tall figure walking towards him.

'Lord Artor,' he cried brokenly, for the visitor was little more than a youth whose voice was just beginning to change into a masculine baritone. He abased himself full length upon the wet ground.

'Stand on your feet, young man,' Artor stated in his most informal tone. 'You've obviously come to Cadbury for some purpose, so speak out bravely to your king.'

'Sir . . . sir . . . I am Grawryd of Slowwater, half a day by horse to the north.'

The king nodded encouragingly. The boy was so nervous, Artor was afraid he would faint under the strain.

'We ... we ... need help, sir, for we've been set upon by a wild man out of the forest who kills anyone who crosses his path.'

'A wild man?' Artor repeated, raising one eyebrow in surprise. 'What does this man do?'

'He ... kills the people, sir. He butchered Hod Carrottop and his family at their farm near Slowwater. He even slaughtered their children. Then he left their infant son at another farm a few miles from the wood.'

'To kill children is certainly the actions of a wild man,' Artor replied evenly.

The shepherd boy blushed to the roots of his dirty-blond hair.

'The babe died, sir. The wild man couldn't feed it, and the farmer at Longfield was a widower, and his cow died last winter, and ...' The boy's voice trailed away with distress.

'Have you seen this wild man yourself, young Grawryd of Slowwater?' Artor asked gently. 'Have you seen him with your own eyes?'

The youth nodded, his prominent Adam's apple bouncing as he swallowed convulsively.

'Describe him then, young Grawryd.'

The youth looked skyward as if to recall a horrid memory as clearly as he could.

'I was bringing the sheep to the new pasture when I saw a horseman come to my uncle's door, my lord. I'd not have seen him close up if I hadn't heard a scream, so I come running to see what's up. I had my spear, you see.'

Artor nodded, and Balan marvelled at the king's patience.

'By the time I got there, he'd killed my uncle with his huge sword, right beside the animal pen, and was taking my uncle's plough horse, old Fenn here. I could hardly breathe for shaking, but I crawled as close to him as I dared, near the hay rick.' The boy was breathless as he relived the horror.

Artor waited until the shepherd boy lurched back into speech.

'He was dressed in rags. He looked like he'd ridden through thorn trees and branches because his face and arms were cut and scratched. His hair was full of twigs and his eyes were all red and mad. I could hardly bear to look at him.'

The boy searched for an amulet that was strung round his throat on a strip of hide. He kissed the rough form superstitiously, and Artor recalled his first wife's amulet that had hung, warm and comforting, against his own breast until he gifted it to his daughter.

'He was covered in blood – even in his hair. And he stank of it where it had dried on his hands and face. I couldn't make a sound, sir. And him covered in my uncle's blood as well.'

'Yet you're here on old Fenn,' Artor said gently. 'Why didn't he take the plough horse?'

'My aunt came running and she set up such a caterwauling and howling. The wild man drew his sword and I thought sure he'd cut her head off too. But then he sort of shook himself and howled like some beast. After a few minutes, he put his sword away and ran off into the woods.'

'Why did you come here when the villagers could have hunted him down since he was afoot?'

Grawryd gulped, then sobbed. He shivered uncontrollably.

'I took Fenn and rode as fast as I could to Slowwater Village. Straight away, the men found torches and what weapons they had and went after the wild man, even though they only had hoes and hay forks. I tried to warn them that he wasn't some madman or thief, but they'd never seen a wild man before, so they thought five grown men were enough to kill or capture him.'

Tears ran down the boy's cheeks, making runnels through the grime that had dusted his skin during the journey to Cadbury.

'They wouldn't listen to me because they didn't know what he was. I was too scared to go with them, so the headman told me to take care of the women and children. I did my best, my lord, truly I did.'

'I believe you, Grawryd of Slowwater, so speak out bravely,' Artor replied soothingly. The shepherd boy stared up into the face of his king with mingled love and awe.

'I made some of the women take their children into the woods at the end of Longfield, but the blacksmith's wife and her old parents refused to budge. I hid beside the river to watch over them once I got the others hidden. I just knew that the wild man would come looking for a horse, so five farmers wouldn't stand a chance against that sword of his. Within half an hour, I heard howling and screaming, and then it got real quiet. I knew he was coming. Old Fenn was with the women in the woods in case the wild man came after them, so I hid in a tree near the headman's home and waited.'

The boy stopped to ensure Artor understood the gravity of what he was saying.

'He came. Oh, sir, he came!' Grawryd was close to tears. 'He'd killed them all. I checked the bodies later and they'd been hacked to pieces. He'd left them where they fell, all body bits and blood, and had come to Slowwater to take any food and the horse that he wanted. He killed Etta and her children . . . and the old people . . . and he ate his food with those bloody hands on the path outside the blacksmith's house. He seemed to smell the air as if he knew I was watching him. I could hardly breathe, sir, for fear of crying out aloud, but I hid in the leaves and escaped alive. He took the blacksmith's pony when he left.'

Grawryd began to weep in earnest, and Artor gripped his shoulder comfortingly until the boy managed to speak again.

'Then I went and got the women and old Fenn. When I left, they were preparing their menfolk for burial, so I rode here at once. The wild man will kill and kill until someone stops him. His eyes, sir, were red as if they were filled with blood. His face was smeared with dried mud, gore and things I don't like to think about. Whoever he once was, he'd turned into a demon, sir, so twisted up and hating was his face. Even his hair was stiff with blood. I could smell him on the wind. Oh, sir, you must do something, else everyone he comes upon will die.'

The boy was half-fainting with exhaustion and the horror of his experiences, so Artor ordered Odin to take him away and give him food and rest.

'This tale is monstrous,' Balan exclaimed, sickened by Grawryd's story. 'This creature must be hunted down and slaughtered.'

'I agree. But farmers don't carry swords, so this wild man is probably a brigand, or even an escaped Saxon trying to reach the east. Whoever he is, he must be captured. If Saxons are abroad, I must know of it.'

'I beg the opportunity to find him, my king. I'm certain I could capture him and bring him back to be judged for his crimes. I'm half-mad anyway with boredom since my brother went to Glastonbury.'

'Very well. But you must take Gruffydd with you. He's old, and is no longer fit for battle, but he speaks the Saxon tongue and knows the hills and forests like no other person. He must be consulted first, mind, for I promised him that he could leave the court in honourable retirement, but if you hope to find this beast, then Gruffydd is the best man to assist you in your task.'

'Do I take Grawryd with me?'

'Yes. He knows the terrain and he knows the villagers. They will trust him where they would not trust strangers in their midst, especially warriors with swords.'

Artor knew in his heart that this wild man was a rogue soldier so inured to blood and death that the slaughter of a few more peasants meant nothing. Killing was a dangerous habit, one that weakened the barriers between right and wrong. Artor could hear Targo's voice, beyond the shadows, as he reminded his student that warfare had its own particular perils.

'Killing can weaken us', Targo had said, his face sombre. 'Good soldiers kill on demand, without any thought or guilt. They act on orders, like trained animals, and their consciences aren't troubled by the deaths.'

Artor remembered the shadow of the alder tree and how it barred his tutor's face and hid his expression.

'But there seems to be a point where the taking of a human life becomes so familiar that it resolves any problem. I need a horse! He has one! So I'll kill him for his animal! You see, boy? Our morals become stretched out of shape by hard use and, somehow, we become animals ourselves.'

'I won't, will I?' the youthful Artorex had asked nervously.

'Since you're not a soldier, I don't see how,' Targo had answered.

But Artor, king and warrior, had felt the danger of becoming exactly what Targo had described.

Artor and Balan walked side by side on the tooth of rock that was Cadbury Tor, one old and one young, both so alike in many ways. The shadows lengthened around them.

'You must go on the morrow, Balan, although I would prefer to send another warrior in your place. I am too old and too tired to wish to risk a kinsman on a task that gives me cause to worry. It's a sad truth that men such as Modred always sit safely at the hearth while better warriors keep him and his warm and secure. Go with your god, my boy.'

'Thank you, Your Majesty.' Balan grinned engagingly. 'I'll be glad to be doing something useful while I await word of my brother. The concern I feel for him itches at the back of my mind, and if I can't scratch my itch, then I'd lief be about service to the village of Slowwater.'

The High King and his kinsman stood for a long time in their separate silences and watched the far, visible edges of the land turn red and then purple as the sun slipped away.

CHAPTER XV

The Beginning of the End

As the days shortened with the advance of another autumn, Artor remained within the halls of his palace and kept alone, weighed down by matters of state and the ominous silence from his warriors in the north of the kingdom. To add to his woes, the intransigence of Bishop Otha at Glastonbury was causing Artor to endure many sleepless nights, for no word had come from Balyn since his departure. Coupled with these worries, Gronw was an oozing sore in the north where his putrid influence was spreading damaging rumours and talk of insurrection.

And always, above mere personal threats and difficulties, the Saxons hovered on his borders as they sought to gain further toeholds in the west. They didn't attack, but like the ravens and the crows that lived deep in the woods, they waited for carrion.

Artor kept to himself and tried to maintain a commanding, untroubled presence. Nowhere was safe and nothing was certain. Even in Cadbury, his citadel and stronghold, the king's enemies waited patiently for any sign of weakness in its ageing king.

Artor knew he spent too much time alone, but the two men who might have provided company had ridden out with Balan to slay a human monster. Gruffydd had accompanied Balan on the orders of Artor, but Taliesin had volunteered to join them in their quest. The harpist was partly motivated by curiosity and partly by the overwhelming horror of Grawryd's tale.

As for Elayne, Artor could hardly bear the physical and emotional pain that her presence caused him, for he was forced to face anew his loveless existence and the nauseating self-pity that this prompted in him. And Bedwyr deserved his loyalty. Wenhaver's sullen features promised tantrums and held no appeal. Moreover, her company would bring him into the orbit of Modred's sniping, as well as the sweet, tempting presence of Elayne. Artor longed to banish Modred, or to slit his throat, but neither action was politic in such restless times.

Two weeks had passed since Balan had left with Gruffydd, Taliesin and the shepherd boy. The two weeks brought nothing but silence and a sense of numbing hopelessness. Who could say when Cadbury would see his grandsons again? In quiet moments, Artor would wonder whether staff and spear were one and the same, and if he should have warned Balyn of the significance of the staff. Forewarned was forearmed; his duplicity haunted the king.

Artor was already sunk in gloom when he went to Cadbury's gates to view a slow and doleful party climbing upwards towards the fortress. Gruffydd and Taliesin rode together and two horses with wrapped, man-shaped bundles tied across their backs plodded after them.

Tears appeared in Artor's eyes. Those leather-bound shapes were unmistakable.

'I need only to learn how they died,' he whispered brokenly, then squared his shoulders and marched to the gate.

Gruffydd and Taliesin bowed low when they had passed through the final gate and entered the citadel. Taliesin raised his head and his eyes expressed such misery and pity that Artor wanted to run and hide in his private rooms to delay the inevitable news. But, such courage as he still possessed forced him to stand his ground, even when the wrapped bundles were placed on the flagged forecourt at his feet.

'I am heavy of heart, my lord,' Taliesin began.

'I guess at your news,' Artor muttered, his head low. 'These bundles are the mortal remains of my grandsons, Balyn and Balan.'

'Aye, Artor,' Gruffydd replied. His eyes were sombre and direct.

'Let me see them,' the king ordered, drawing himself to his full height. 'I sent them to their deaths, so I should see what I have done with my own eyes.'

Two guards cut the rawhide thongs that bound the wrappings in place, and then lifted away the coarse wool and greasy hide that had covered their bodies.

Balan appeared to be asleep, despite the extreme pallor of his face. His well-shaped lips smiled and his dress wasn't disturbed; the wound in his breast seemed little more than a narrow tear in his leather cuirass. His weapon had been cleansed and placed on his breast where his stiffened fingers gripped it firmly, even though the rigid seizures of death had long passed.

'Balan, my boy, what mischance has killed you?' Artor choked, his eyes shining with unshed tears. He turned to his guards. 'Take him to the chapel, cleanse his body and begin the prayers for his soul.'

As the guards carried away the body of one twin, Balyn's snarling lips were exposed to the harsh morning light.

Balyn's beauty had fled under a thin shroud of caked dirt and dried crusts of blood; his once golden skin had faded to the colour and insubstantiality of ashes. Like his brother, Balyn's hands also gripped his sword hilt, but his sensitive fingers were cut, scarred and fouled with dried blood.

Artor's pearl ring winked derisively at the king from Balyn's thumb.

'Balyn, my grandson, what brought you to this pass?' Artor whispered. 'What curse drove you into madness?'

The young man's clothes had been reduced to bloody rags through which his skin should have shone whitely, had it not been so bruised and bloody. His flesh was covered with cuts, slash wounds and injuries that almost seemed self-inflicted, but he had died from a knife thrust in the belly and another to the throat. He had bled freely and fatally from both gashes. The beautiful young man, so much like the young Artor when he first rode into Cadbury, was now an effigy bathed in blood, or some grotesque sacrifice to a cruel god.

'Serve the same offices to Lord Balyn as to his brother. These warriors were precious to me, so prepare them carefully for the fire.'

A hand touched Artor's elbow from behind.

'I will see to them myself, my king,' Lady Elayne murmured, and Artor felt the tears rising in his eyes until he could no longer stop their flow. Nor could he turn to face her, for he could not bear to gaze on her wise, quiet face filled with the pity that he heard in her voice.

Artor strode away, his jaw set and his shoulders squared, but both Gruffydd and Taliesin recognized the stiff gait and rigid muscles of a man who has been pushed to breaking point. They hastened to follow their damaged king.

Behind them, Elayne looked down at the mortal remains of Balyn. She had dressed for the open with haste, and her hair still hung in long plaits below her waist while her face was flushed and her cloak hadn't been pinned in place. With one hand, she clutched its folds together, while the other gripped the skirts of her robes. The shell of Balyn's ruined beauty tugged at her heart so fiercely that she wept unashamedly.

In death, Balyn's face had aged and mirrored Artor's; Elayne could all too easily imagine that Artor lay there, fresh from some terrible battle, and dead from a multitude of gaping wounds. Her heartbeat faltered, and she realized that more than loyalty lay behind her sorrow; the king had captured part of her heart.

This attachment cannot be, it will not be, she thought fiercely as she walked protectively beside Balyn's corpse as it was moved to the small church at the apex of Cadbury Tor.

Artor would have locked himself in his rooms, but Odin used his body weight to hold the heavy door open and allowed Taliesin and Gruffydd to enter.

'Leave me be,' Artor snarled, thrusting away Odin's arm.

Taliesin scarcely recognized the twisted face of his king;

only one man alive, Odin, had ever seen the face of sorrow and rage that Artor now wore.

'I don't want to know how they met their fate! Have mercy, and don't burden me further! I sent them to their deaths, and can't bear to know how they perished. I can't listen! I can't!'

Taliesin poured a goblet of strong, red wine while Odin forced his king to sit on his curule chair. They coaxed him to drink until colour slowly returned to his ashen cheeks.

Gruffydd sat on a stool to spare his damaged leg and wished that he had stayed at home rather than make this final, fatal visit to Cadbury. Come what may in the years ahead, he would always remember Artor as this shattered, desperate man.

'Please don't punish yourself, lord. You asked services of the twins – simple tasks that should have been quite safe. In truth, Artor, they unknowingly killed each other.' Gruffydd spoke with such conviction and honesty that Artor was forced to listen. He raised his faded, leonine head.

'You are talking nonsense, Gruffydd. The brothers were together all their lives, even in their mother's womb. They knew each other more intimately than husband knows wife, or a mother knows her child. How could they have killed each other?'

Taliesin knelt at the feet of his king. Artor had not the energy to order the harpist to rise, and Taliesin would have refused to listen and remained on his knees.

'Lord, you knew the bond that existed between those brothers. Such a skein of kinship is stronger than iron, even more vigorous than life itself, so that neither brother could resist its pull. Yet the strength of the tie was weakness, for neither brother would believe that he could ever be in a situation where he wouldn't recognize his twin. And so, tragically, they slew each other.'

'Have your way then.' Artor bowed his head in unendurable weariness. 'Tell me the complete tale. You know I have to ask eventually, Taliesin, so perhaps it's best that I listen now while the wounds are fresh.'

'I'll ask Gruffydd to recount most of our experiences, lord,' Taliesin said. 'He proved to be far wiser than I, for it was he who tried to save Balan from his own innocence. Until the moment of his death, Balan wouldn't believe that his brother was the beast of Slowwater. Gruffydd was the only one among us who guessed at the truth.'

'You knew, old friend? How could you have anticipated their fate?'

Gruffydd eased his weight on his painful hips and began the dolorous tale.

'When we arrived at Slowwater in the early evening, we found a village gripped by fear. Slowwater is only a small hamlet, my lord. Of the twenty souls who lived there, less than ten remained alive, and the survivors were too terrified to even draw water from the small well. When we came, the women were securing their huts for the night as if they were repelling a pack of starving wolves.

'The headman was dead, but his wife and youthful son took us into their hut before the light was entirely gone. Neither mother nor son wanted us under their roof, but to leave us outside would have brought more carnage to a village that was already numbed with fear and shock. You have seen such terror, Artor. They were well nigh senseless with its madness, and perhaps they thought we would provide some protection.

'The villagers told us that the wild man came every night, seeking food, and padding between the huts as he searched for a human scent. They told us that they were even more afraid when the wild man took to howling, because they felt that no man born of woman could make such a sound and still be fully human. At first, we thought they were simply superstitious simpletons, so we humoured them as if they were children. We were wrong.

'The wife of the headman feared the scent of heat and fresh meat would draw the wild man to her door, so we ate bowls of cold porridge. Shortly afterwards, we heard an odd shuffling sound. Balan pressed his ear to the door frame, as did I. I could hear ragged breathing and muttering. The sounds were mixed with a nasal, snuffling sound, for all the world like a wild boar scenting for prey.

'I heard the grunts and snarls as the beast fell on the food that the villagers had left out in the roadway to appease the evil spirit. No man ate out there, I could swear, for the most uncouth Saxon does not tear at half-rotten meat as this thing did. For the first time, I knew that Grawryd hadn't lied. Slowwater *was* cursed with a wild man.

'After an hour or so, I believed that the worst was over, but for the rest of that endless night, the beast went from door to door, knocking and scratching at the wood and then howling in mingled sorrow and rage. The sound of the crying was worse than anything I have ever heard, Artor. And if that eerie sound was the voice of Prince Balyn, he had cast off his humanity weeks before we came to Slowwater. Balan didn't recognize the voice behind the terrible sounds. None of us did.

Nor could we see it, for the headman's son had nailed logs, worn-out tools, and pieces of metal over every aperture of the hut, even the hole in the roof where the smoke from the fire escaped. So, lightless, we cowered in the darkness – and we could not sleep for horror.

'But I smelt our enemy, as did Taliesin, who learned his woodcraft from the hill people and his mother. The creature stank of dried blood, vomit and shit – a reek that sickened me to the gut, for even beasts don't allow their bodies to be so fouled. I smelled a rottenness, and my fear grew.

'The creature was gone by dawn without any attempt to disguise its spoor. We could see the footprints clearly in the dust, knitting the village huts together as if the wild man had paced backwards and forwards in its search for something to kill.

'He eventually found some prey. The wild man caught a stray dog and managed to flush a rabbit out from the undergrowth near the vegetable patch. He left their pathetic remains on our doorsteps, and we discovered that he had torn the poor animals apart while they still lived.

'We hunted him for days but, like any wild beast, he was cunning. At night, we slept in trees where we couldn't be taken by surprise. He led us far, in a wide circle, but eventually the tracks returned to where they had started, the forests near Slowwater, and they led us to his lair. It was as if he had led us to it deliberately and wished to be saved from his madness. He had been sleeping in a nest of branches and dried grass not six feet from the bloated, rotting carcass of his horse. Most horribly, he had carved hunks of meat from that corpse, and I nearly gagged to imagine such food.

'The horse had been richly caparisoned, and a spear was still bound to the horse straps. This convinced me that the wild man was no crazed brigand, or a deserter driven to lunacy by old wounds. I tried to persuade Balan, who ought to have recognized Balyn's possessions. God only knows why he didn't do so, but the lad wouldn't listen. Perhaps Balan thought his brother's horse had been stolen. Perhaps he feared that Balyn was the wild man's first victim, for Balan was certainly angry and eager to face the brute. But he could not believe that Balyn could be so lost to reason that he would descend into such bloodlust.

'I began to wonder, too, at Balyn's long absence from court, and when I spoke my thinking aloud, Balan again dismissed my words. He told me, again and again, that he would know if his brother was unhinged. He was insulted by the suggestion, and forbade me from speaking any further on the matter.

'Balan suffered greatly, my lord. When he tried to eat, he was nauseous and could only swallow some stale and mouldy bread. The smell of dried meat caused him to vomit, and he swore that, somewhere, his brother was suffering from a stomach ailment. He made light of his illness, but I could tell that your grandson was deeply troubled during the hunt.

'Having found the lair, we decided to lie in wait for the wild man. Balan told us to hide in the approaches, and he would wait near the lair.'

Gruffydd gazed into the suffering eyes of his king.

'We should have stayed with your grandson, my lord, but he insisted that we obey him. Balan wanted to be alone.

'The night was full of small sounds of violence and looming shadows, so that I saw a monster behind every bush. When I heard shouts from Balan and the screams of rage from his quarry, I was terrified, because I knew I was too old to be of much use to my companions. Still, Taliesin and I returned to the corpse of the dead horse. We could hear the sound of sword blades clashing against each other. I heard Balan cry out his brother's name, just once, and then silence blanketed the woods like a heavy, black shroud. I cursed my bad leg then, for I was slow and feeble, and Taliesin dared not leave me to run ahead in case the wild man came upon me when I was alone.

'Balan had cornered his brother against a rocky outcrop, and Balyn was bleeding heavily from his belly wound. Balyn must have been in agony, but he transcended his pain to stand and fight. At some part of their struggle, Balan either recognized his brother by sight or through the shared pain of Balyn's mortal wound, for he lowered his sword. Then Balyn drove his blade through his brother's breast.

'Balyn was still alive when we found them. He had gathered his twin into his arms and was rocking his brother's dead body as if his caresses could make the cloven heart whole. The eyes that Balyn raised to me were sane, but they were blinded by his loss. Taliesin tried to stop Balyn's blood flow, but I could tell that his labour was pointless, and Taliesin swears that, even if he had survived the night, your grandson would have rotted away from within. Balyn told me that he had killed his brother and I could only nod, like a fool. How could I find words of comfort for him? Then he told me that he did not wish to live, for he had done things that had shamed his mother and father for all time. Again, I could only nod in response, my lord. I didn't know how to offer any comfort.

'I should have known what he would do, my king, for I saw

that shame had replaced the guilt and madness in his eyes. Balyn knew of your relationship with him. He asked me to tell you, his grandfather, that at the very last, he died like a man. Then, without fear, he cut his own throat.'

The burning of the twins took place with much panoply and mourning. Even Wenhaver wept real tears at the thought of such youth and beauty perishing forever on the funeral pyre. Perhaps she felt the first shivers of her own mortality as, clothed in hastily dyed black, she watched her husband consign those glorious young men to the flames.

Artor retreated behind a frozen mask of inscrutability. If Artor felt sorrow, only his intimates knew. The iron doors of duty clanged shut around the High King, and no one was permitted behind the walls of his public face. Even Modred knew better than to foment discord at such a time.

Anna was too far removed from Cadbury to be present for the funeral of her sons, so their ashes were sent to the grieving mother in an urn of golden magnificence, the best that Artor could purchase. Taliesin was dispatched to the north with the reliquary and their swords. In his humility, Artor offered his unacknowledged daughter the greatest boon that he could give, and expressed his fervent desire that they should be laid to rest in Gallia's Garden.

Taliesin performed a song for the mother that was so fair and so tragic that many Ordovice warriors wept as they heard the tale of the doomed twins. Anna remained tearless, for she had been raised in a Roman household and scorned to dishonour their memory with a woman's weakness. After days of funeral celebrations, she took the ashes of her boys to

Gallia's Garden where she had grown to womanhood, then returned to her kingdom to begin the task of rebuilding her life.

On her return, King Bran rode south to learn for himself the reasons for his brothers' deaths. He travelled fast and hard, sparing neither himself nor his horses, until he reached Cadbury at the head of his Ordovice guard.

Even then, with his only grandson standing before him, Artor couldn't reveal the whole truth, although he longed to share the pain he felt with the tall, strong man who resembled his mother so uncannily. Artor told himself that it would be unkind to tell this new and able king that he was now the heir to the dragon throne.

'They killed each other by accident, Bran, and neither could live with the knowledge of what they had done. Cruel chance was responsible for their deaths, but you may be very sure that I'll learn how Balyn came to be at Slowwater in such a condition.'

'Aye, my lord, I'll trust you to sort out the whole, tragic mess. You were forced to sweeten and soften the circumstances of Balyn's crimes for my mother's sake, but I want the unvarnished truth. I ask that you respect me by keeping me informed of what you discover.'

Artor swallowed, and vowed to do as Bran asked. Of course, the High King had no intention of shattering his grandson's memory of Balyn with the exact truth.

Artor marvelled at Bran's height, his glossy brown hair, kept tidy in warrior's plaits, and a face that was comely, masculine and sensitive. The cares of having become King of the Ordovice while still in his teens showed in the furrows that were already carved on his brow and in the air of gravity and purpose that infused his stance and his voice.

Artor felt a stir of pride when he looked up at his grandson as he mounted his horse to depart from Cadbury. Bran's mouth and eyes were vulnerable with sorrow, while care wrapped him in a cloak of unspoken pain. His duty to his people called, so he must put aside personal grief to serve their needs. For such was the Roman way. Anna, her father and her son knew no other way to survive their grief.

In time, when Glastonbury was put to rights, Brother Mark walked up the spiral ramps of Cadbury Tor to tell the tale of Balyn and Otha to the High King in person. Artor heard him out and soundlessly cursed the need for secrecy that had destroyed his grandson's faith. Mark revealed every detail of the death of Bishop Otha, including the priest's confession of his fealty to Modred. Artor raged inwardly that Otha had attacked his grandson through his blood ties with the High King.

For the first time in his long life, Artor bent his knee to a man of God.

'I beg you to hear me, Brother Mark, for I have never confessed my sins. I don't know if your god is real, but something must guide the stars in their long dance through the heavens. I'm an old man and I'll soon know all the secrets of death.'

Brother Mark coloured and then smiled slightly. 'You come to God out of fear of damnation, King Artor.'

'Perhaps I do, I don't know. I believe that something of the soul goes on, the good as well as the bad. I also believe there will be judgement in this life and in the next. Perhaps a long life has simply taught me that what we struggle for in this world of flesh is less than nothing in the face of eternity, a concept that I choose to call God. But you may deny confession to me if you wish, and I'll not punish you for it.'

'No, lord, I would not deny you,' the priest replied.

Artor bared his whole life before this humble man of God. What Mark thought of Artor's disclosures is impossible to imagine, for he did not betray his king to a single, living soul.

'I have one more request, Mark of Glastonbury.' Artor pointed to the source of so much bloodletting and suffering, where it was standing upright in the corner of his chambers. The short Roman spear had been removed from the staff that had concealed it for centuries. It was a plain, utilitarian thing with neither beauty nor grace, and Mark shuddered at the blood it had shed.

'Many of our flock have come to believe it is the weapon that pierced the side of Christ at Golgotha,' he said. 'The common belief is that Joseph of Arimathea brought it to Glastonbury, but he feared its reputation, so he sealed it away in an ancient tower on an island so that it would be safe from the hands of mortal men.'

'Aye, I'm aware of the Christian belief that a Roman soldier used this weapon to wound your Christ. Well, this Roman-raised Celt won't touch such a relic. The weapon is tainted with the blood of my kin and is now cursed by me forever. I beg that you take the Spear and do with it what you will, for it belongs in the hands of Mother Church where it can do no further harm.'

'But didn't you insist that Otha return the relic to you?' Mark asked.

'Yes, I did. And all the deaths that followed were the result of my selfish desire to secure my reign over my people. I have come to realize that the Spear should be in safe hands. Should the relic come into the possession of my enemy, then so be it. I won't risk the lives of more innocents for the sake of a symbol.'

'I mightn't be able to keep it safe from the hands of impious men,' Mark said. 'Perhaps another Otha will be sent to Glastonbury.'

'Perhaps. But I have made my decision. I wouldn't trust Galahad with it, so it's best if it remains among the treasures of Mother Church. I don't care any more.'

At that moment, Artor meant what he said. The twins were dead, Otha had perished and Modred was exposed as having used his influence to force his man into power at Glastonbury. Otha had acquitted Modred of any guilt in the murder of Bishop Aethelthred and the stealing of Lucius's Cup, but Artor now knew beyond doubt that Modred sought a means to steal the throne by stealth. Had Otha remained Bishop of Glastonbury, he could have thrown his considerable influence behind the Brigante king in the event of Artor's death.

Modred must be watched, Artor thought savagely.

Brother Mark saw the sudden menace in the High King's grey eyes. I don't trust you, he thought uneasily. If the safety of your kingdom was at stake, you'd use the Spear just as ruthlessly as any of your enemies, and you'd never count the cost in human life. Now, in your guilt after the death of your grandsons, you want temptation removed from your grasp. But your mood will change soon enough, and then you will call for the Spear once again. Like Otha before me, I'll be forced to refuse you, for motives far removed from Redbeard's foolish dreams of power.

He came to a decision. The Spear must pass out of Artor's reach forever. It must vanish so that men would never again be tempted by its promise. Come not to me again, Lord Artor, Dragon of the Celts, for I'll never give it back to you, Mark vowed.

He didn't voice his thoughts aloud; he simply nodded, and bowed his head low in obeisance to his king.

When he left Artor's presence, he prayed that he would never see the High King again.

Mark hid the Spear where it would never be found and told no one, not even his archbishop, for all men have their price and even a man of God can be corrupted by his own good intentions.

And so a great danger passed out of the ken of the west. The twins became legend before the ashes of their pyre were even cold and Taliesin's song sped them on their way to peace, with a warning and a prayer. In his extremity, Artor thought to cast his body from the tor, anything to ease the mortal hurt that he had suffered. The ghosts of his past reproached him then, and Artor understood that suicide in the face of his enemy was a solace and a cowardice that he could never embrace. No betrayal could harm the west more deeply than his flight into death.

The ravens returned to Cadbury in the autumn. Their shiny, malevolent eyes watched from the fruit trees as Artor faced the coming darkness.

CHAPTER XVI

SEARCHING

'Shite! Shite! Shite!'

Bedwyr was irritated and, like all men of passion who have kept their frustrations in check for months, he was close to exploding with rage.

'What burr has got into your trews?' Galahad snapped, shaking his sodden hair like an angry dog. The prince was supremely indifferent to the fact that he was dripping all over Bedwyr and extinguishing the feeble fire that he had so carefully coaxed into life.

'You're my burr, Galahad. In the name of the gods, stop pissing on the fire. At this rate, we'll freeze before the wood catches properly.'

Galahad moved sullenly further into the leaking shepherd's hut.

'Can't you speak without cursing? We're all wet and tired, but Percivale never whines.'

Bedwyr snarled like his own wolfhound. 'That's because you never piss on him! And if I want to curse, I'll sodding well do it. You'd try the patience of your own Jesus.'

Galahad grunted and turned his back on Bedwyr, behaviour

guaranteed to enrage his companion even further.

'You've dragged us from one place to another, regardless of what Artor's intelligence network tells us. We've chased down every foolish rumour until my arse is sore from hours on my horse for no good sodding reason. You don't listen. In fact, you don't even understand the language. My informants tell us where Gronw is likely to be and where he's been seen recently. Do you take any notice? No! You're too busy saying your prayers.'

Galahad rounded on Bedwyr, his perfect mouth twisted with contempt. 'I cannot imagine why my great-uncle sent me on this mission in the company of a pagan misfit with an exaggerated opinion of his own abilities.'

Bedwyr half rose and Percivale recognized the stance of a man who was about to lose his temper. Hurriedly, he stepped between the two angry men.

'Bedwyr! Galahad! How can we hope to succeed against Gronw and his followers when we can't pull together ourselves? We're doomed to certain failure unless you settle your differences and behave.'

'My thanks, Percivale. Even *you* can see how ignorant this pagan is.'

Percivale flushed at the unconscious insult. 'I am not taking sides, Galahad, but if I had to, I'd say Bedwyr had the right of the argument. You've been high-handed and unchristian!'

'When have I been unchristian?' Galahad demanded, his chin jutting aggressively.

'Right now! Bedwyr is right. He's been trying to start a fire for the best part of an hour while you blithely undo his efforts. Artor sent Bedwyr with us for a reason, and if I have to return to Cadbury to tell the king the cause of the failure of this mission, he won't be amused.'

Sullenly, Galahad retreated to a mouldy pallet of straw in the corner that he suspected had once been the home of a nest of mice, judging by the smell.

'Since I'm responsible for getting our campaign off on the wrong foot, how would you set us to rights, Bedwyr?' he asked pugnaciously.

'Will you listen?' Bedwyr demanded.

'Yes,' Galahad hissed.

'Really listen? If not, I may as well save my breath.'

'I told you so, didn't I?'

'Bedwyr!' Percivale warned.

'Very well then,' Bedwyr said more reasonably. 'Have you heard of a settlement called Bremetennacum?'

'Yes.' Galahad nodded. 'It's a godforsaken fleapit on the edge of Brigante country.'

'We need to detour to that fleapit and frequent the inns for a few days. Mamucium is another possible place where news of Gronw might be found.'

Galahad shook his head. 'We're somewhere east of Deva now, is that right?'

Bedwyr nodded.

'And we've heard nothing of Gronw since we were at Magnis, so why should we continue to the north? Your proposal makes no sense to me.'

Bedwyr resisted the almost visceral urge to grip Galahad by the white column of his throat which was so tantalizingly close at hand. Percivale sighed deeply.

'Everything we hear of Gronw leads us in a northerly

direction,' Bedwyr stated. 'Is that true? Yes. It's true. We know that Modred's Brigante are no friends to Artor and his throne.'

Galahad nodded, albeit unwillingly.

'If I were Gronw, I'd go to a place where I could find eager souls to give me shelter, not to mention credulous fools who might believe I was a Druid who has come to prophesy the fall of the High King. I'd choose a fleapit like Bremetennacum or a greasy hamlet like Mamucium on the Roman road that leads to the north.'

Galahad digested Bedwyr's reasoning slowly but thoroughly.

'Very well then. If we accept your reasoning, what should we do?'

'A Druid preaching treason has to make some noise, so someone will have heard of Gronw. I've a talent for fitting into all types of company, so I'm certain to hear some news of him at the inns.'

Galahad chose to ignore Bedwyr's reference to fitting in.

'I am a reasonable man, Bedwyr, So if you're happy about eavesdropping in inns, it might be best if you get started for Mamucium at first light. We'll await word of Gronw here.'

'Oh, joy!' Bedwyr snarled.

Galahad lay back on the pallet, wrapped his cloak about his long limbs and was soon asleep. Percivale had rarely felt so irritated by the prince's high-handedness.

Bedwyr placed a small pot of water over the struggling fire. 'I'm not going anywhere without food in my belly, regardless of the magnanimity of Lord Holy.'

'Don't antagonize him further, Bedwyr,' Percivale begged. 'He has made an enormous concession to his pride by agreeing with you, so please be content with a successful outcome.'

Bedwyr concentrated on thrusting a skinned, gutted and chopped coney into the pot with a handful of wilting vegetables and tender nettles that he'd collected the previous day. The aroma of cooking meat soon began to overpower the thick fug of wet wool, male sweat and blade oil.

Bedwyr stared out through the flimsy door into an evening made dim with driving rain. The whicker of horses, tethered in a lean-to beside the hut, was comforting and familiar.

'I suppose Galahad can't be blamed for his zeal. His whole family is crazy, except for Artor, and even the king has a fragile temper. But Galahad's certainty in his own great destiny drives me demented with irritation.'

'He's an irritating man, but he's a good one, at bottom,' Percivale said, joining Bedwyr by the doorway.

'Try to keep him here until I return, Percivale. Otherwise, I'll never be able to find you again.'

'I will do my best,' Percivale promised.

Rabbit stew, though without salt, made a warming meal and even Galahad seemed happier with a full belly. Later, while his companions slept, Bedwyr considered their movements during the last months, while his hound nestled at his feet in the straw.

They had ridden far, in all kinds of weather and without the comforts of their station. Galahad was a hard taskmaster and the Cup lured him ever more strongly until he dreamed of its prosaic form whenever he closed his eyes. His zealous obsession made him difficult company.

They had lost Gronw at Farden and had searched the wild hills for days to no avail. Finally, they had followed the wide

Roman road to Deva, trusting that this crossroad township would yield better results. They had been disappointed once again, and so now they found themselves in a shepherd's bothie on an inhospitable hill somewhere between Aquae and Deva.

I wish Elayne was here, Bedwyr thought, and comforted himself by imagining her warm, brown body against his.

Before he had departed on this insane mission, they had spent two days in each other's arms, and Bedwyr had come to realize that women are stronger than men and infinitely more patient. She had understood the need for secrecy that prevented him from telling her where or why he was travelling into the north. But Elayne had wept over his impending departure, knowing she would be lonely, although no complaint passed her lips. Her only thought was for his safety, although Bedwyr knew that she dwelled in a far more dangerous place than he – at court, and surrounded by enemies like Wenhaver and Modred.

'Take care, my darling,' he had whispered when she reached upward to hand him his sword belt, before he rode away from Cadbury.

'Don't fret for me, my love,' she had replied, her eyes glowing softly in the early morning light. 'The only danger I face is the loss I would feel if any harm should come to you. Life would lose its savour without you beside me. I would not have you forsake your honour for me but, please, don't put yourself in harm's way unnecessarily.'

He had bent down and picked her up bodily with one arm. After kissing her, he had buried his face in her loosened hair and drunk in the scent of fresh grass and flowers that was trapped in her tresses. Leaving her had been so difficult that he had spurred his horse into a fast trot to avoid seeing the tears that filled her eyes.

Remembering the perfume of Elayne's hair, Bedwyr smiled as he fell asleep in the straw.

Having spent his youth as a Saxon slave where he was forced to obey the orders of brutes, inexorably bound to the will of others, Bedwyr was essentially a man of action. Consequently, by first light, he had reheated the remains of the stew and had packed his tackle for departure.

'I'll return in fourteen days, if the gods so will it,' he told his companions. 'I suggest you stay put and forage for food to eke out our store of barley but, if you do decide to venture forth, it would be wise to wear unobtrusive clothing.'

'We understand, Bedwyr,' Percivale agreed, eyeing Galahad carefully as the young prince filled a wooden bowl with leftover stew.

'And don't wear your swords. They betray you as warriors and they'll silence any good sources of information you may meet. It's probably best to carry knives like all the commoners.'

'Aye, those are sensible suggestions,' Galahad replied, without looking up from his meal. 'But what if you don't return?'

'You can come after me if I haven't returned within fourteen days, although I'll probably be dead by the time you arrive.' Bedwyr grinned and called his dog to heel. His eagerness to leave the hut made his step light, and he leapt into the saddle like a boy.

With a casual salute, Bedwyr was gone, his dog ranging ahead with the same joy as its master. The hut seemed smaller and more dilapidated for his absence.

'I'm glad to see the last of Bedwyr's mongrel,' Galahad

grumbled. 'That thing eats more than a full-grown man.'

'I like fighting hounds,' Percivale replied evenly. 'Besides, the bitch catches as much as she eats. That rabbit stew was her contribution to our rations.'

'Then I'd better start learning how to trap coneys myself,' Galahad said. 'My father neglected this important aspect of my education, so I'll probably need some suggestions.'

Percivale laughed, dug deeply into his memory of a feckless boyhood and commenced Galahad's practical education in woodcraft.

Winter was coming and even in the more pleasant, gentler climes of Cadbury, the skies were slate grey and cheerless.

Within the king's hall, winter had already arrived, night came early and gloom deflated the spirits of all those souls who dwelt within its walls. Artor was rarely abroad except to hone his battle skills against the younger men of his guard, while Wenhaver's bower was deserted. Chilly winds trapped the ladies within the warmer rooms of the great house.

One small diversion lifted the spirits of Artor's warriors when Trystan, the spymaster of Kernyu, arrived to assume Gruffydd's place in Artor's favour. Gruffydd's grandson was black-haired and slender, second in male beauty only to Galahad, and even his air of effeminacy was no hindrance to the sudden flushes that appeared on the cheeks of Wenhaver's ladies. His skin was the colour of pale honey and was an effective foil for his unusual pale-blue eyes. Some barbarian blood must lurk in his ancestry to create such striking colouring, but any woman who gazed into those sapphire eyes was lost.

Like Taliesin, Trystan was a harpist and his long, slender fingers seemed incapable of lifting a weapon. However, during a short bout of weapons practice, Gareth and several of the more gifted swordsmen among Artor's guard came to realize that Trystan's slim form disguised blinding speed and whip-cord muscles that lay under his soft, white skin. The newcomer was only of middle height, but his lightning reflexes more than compensated for the longer reach of taller men.

'My hands will never be the same again,' Trystan complained after a long day of hunting. His companions ignored him as he pulled off knitted, fingerless gloves and examined his perfectly clean nails. He had killed a boar, afoot and armed only with a long spear, and the other hunters looked at Trystan with amusement at his affectations.

True to form, Wenhaver found Trystan to be an amusing companion. She saw nothing unmanly in his obsessive care of his glossy hair or his passion for finely woven, colourful clothes. While most of the warriors wanted to kick his backside when he complained of non-existent chilblains, Wenhaver took Trystan's maladies seriously and sent her maids scurrying to fetch warmed bricks for his feet and salves for his fingers.

Trystan was an amiable young man with a talent for subterfuge, whom Artor, inexplicably, did not trust, no matter how he tried. Perhaps the king distrusted any man who was so attractive to women that he could pick and choose whose bed he shared. In matters of love, Trystan's effeminacy was soon exposed as another pretty affectation designed to please the ladies. His seductions were effortless and light-hearted.

'Ah, Wenhaver, Queen of Queens, we are so very alike,'

Trystan murmured in the queen's ear as he plied her with wine one afternoon. 'We see the world through the same reflection.'

'What reflection, Trystan?' Wenhaver cooed.

'Why, ourselves, dear lady! Who else?'

Wenhaver's smile wavered slightly as she tried to unravel the young man's reasoning. He lifted her right hand to his mouth and kissed her knuckles, never taking his eyes from hers. The queen blushed a becoming shade of rosy pink.

Elayne watched the private exchange and tightened her lips with disapproval. The queen seems to lack all decorum when she is bathed in the admiration of a handsome man's regard, she thought as she forced her face to remain expressionless.

'I tend to love unwisely and follow my heart when I should take more care,' Trystan confided to Wenhaver's receptive ears.

She tapped him lightly with her spindle, but her giggles betrayed her fascination.

'You're a rogue, Master Trystan. You've turned the heads of my ladies, yet you swear that you passionately love another woman who is very far away. What would she think of your behaviour?'

'Ah, Your Majesty, my lady would weep to learn that I was so perfidious.' He grinned charmingly. 'But I can't help myself when the whole world seems full of pretty flowers to pluck and enjoy.'

Wenhaver pouted. 'Are women such trifles, then, Trystan, that you taste us and then leave us behind?'

'Fair ladies are mere pastimes, my queen, as you must understand. In the game of love, one must take one's pleasures where one can.'

'I refuse to listen to another word, you wicked boy,'

Wenhaver cooed flirtatiously. 'I pity the poor woman who gives her heart to you, for you'll break it before the night is out.'

'Breaking hearts isn't the sole prerogative of males, sweet queen,' Trystan riposted outrageously and kissed her fingers in a most lover-like fashion. 'I'm sure that your charm and beauty could easily break my heart.'

Several ladies winced but most of Wenhaver's attendants shivered with delicious anticipation and jealousy for the liaison that was developing.

Artor was eager to see the last of Trystan for many reasons, so he conducted his business with the young man as quickly as possible. Fortunately, Trystan had a natural talent for secrecy and he gathered up the strands of Gruffydd's network of friends, paid informers and patriots with ease.

'What plans do you have to change Gruffydd's network, young man?' Artor asked gruffly. Trystan's mannerisms set the king's teeth on edge.

'The greatest of the threats within our borders are the Brigante nobles, Your Majesty. So I've already begun to embed spies into the halls of the most vocal aristocrats.'

Artor nodded his approval. 'Anything else?'

'The Picts from Raeburnfoot, deep in the mountains to the north-west of the Wall, are stirring. If they venture into the lowlands of Ituna Aest, we might need to send an Otadini force to chase them back to their hiding places.'

Artor began to feel a stirring of alarm, for enemies seemed to be appearing out of all the plastered-over cracks in his kingdom.

'And, of course, King Mark is no friend to the west.'

'I've heard that the Deceangli tribe are showing some arrogance, in the mistaken belief that the Saxons will never breach the mountain walls west of Deva,' Artor responded. 'If that's Mark's belief, he doesn't understand the Saxons. And that makes him a fool. He doesn't seem to realize that they can approach by sea if the Union of Tribal Kings fails.'

Trystan snorted. 'I don't think Mark really considers much, other than his own consequence. The man is the worst kind of bully. He only makes war on women, children and those who are weaker than himself.'

Despite his prejudices, Artor was impressed with Trystan's knowledge of political intrigue. Here was a clever, adroit young man who might prove to be a most valuable asset. The High King offered Trystan his sword hand.

'Thank you, Trystan.' He smiled. 'Your knowledge of my enemies will be very valuable to me, and I look forward to developing an expansion of the network during the next few weeks to deal with our internal threats.'

'My thanks, my lord, for I live to serve.'

'Not to love then, Trystan?' Artor riposted with a grin. 'I must have been misinformed.'

Two weeks after Trystan's arrival, Artor completed his briefing of the new spymaster and the young man rode away to the north, singing tunefully as he rode. Wenhaver wept tears of self-pity for the loss of her new friend.

'I always seem to be alone,' she moaned to Artor. He forbore to remind her of Modred and a brace of high-born women of marriageable age who had been sent by their fathers to serve the queen and snare a husband. Potential friends surrounded her but, with her usual capriciousness, she pined for young men to charm. Besides, Wenhaver had discovered that she really didn't like King Modred any more.

Modred had fallen from favour during the summer when he had shown his contempt of Artor a little too freely. Like all domestic despots, Wenhaver claimed the privilege of insulting her spouse whenever she chose, but woe betide any person who claimed the same rights. Wenhaver had also looked into her future and had finally accepted that her fate lay with her husband if she wished to remain comfortable and happy. Modred threatened to upset the precarious balance of that comfort by ridiculing her husband, so Modred must be taught to respect the wishes of his betters.

'After all, he is a bastard, and his mother is that very peculiar woman, Morgause, who's my husband's half-sister,' Wenhaver confided to her companions. 'I've only met her once, at my wedding, and I can assure you that she is a very proud and disagreeable woman. And as for Morgan, her sister, she's sharpened her teeth into points. And her tattoos! Ugh!'

The ladies in her bower tittered their amusement and Wenhaver smiled her gentle malice.

At this stage in their lives, Artor and Wenhaver were almost friends, as long as they spent very little time in each other's company. Occasionally, the king even came to Wenhaver's bed and she had no cause for complaint about her ageing husband's performance in matters of physical release, for so Artor treated their infrequent sexual couplings. Out of pride, Wenhaver said nothing to her husband regarding his seeming partiality for Elayne. Nor did she discuss real matters of the heart with her intimates. The one time that Modred tried to draw her out on the matter, Wenhaver's large blue eyes narrowed dangerously.

'You're a sweet boy, Modred, but don't trouble yourself with the private affairs of your superiors. If I've no complaint of the High King's behaviour, what is it to do with you? Lady Elayne is the wife of a vassal lord, not King Artor's leman, so mind your manners.'

'I trust I've caused no offence,' Modred murmured with a lowered head. Venomous dislike filled his downcast eyes. Soon, he thought savagely. If Artor should die, I'll arrange to have your throat sliced open, or you'll be safely locked away in a nunnery where you can cause no further harm.

During that unusually cold winter, the patterns of long habit remained fixed and predictable for those who lived at Cadbury. Perhaps matters would have continued in this fragile balance had a hunt not broken the stasis of the court.

As November aged into December, the frosts held the earth in their iron grip and the shortening days hung heavily on the inhabitants of the tor. Snow began to threaten. When Modred suggested a hunt to break the boredom, the young men of Cadbury embraced the prospect of excitement after weeks of grey days and inactivity.

Artor reluctantly agreed to the plan, especially when Wenhaver proposed that the ladies should accompany the warriors into the field to observe their prowess. Such an expedition involved the same organization devoted to a minor military campaign, for Wenhaver intended to watch the entertainment from a safe distance in a warm, cosy pavilion. Artor might complain that his warriors had better things to do with their time than build her a log cabin on a small rise above the forest, but Wenhaver was determined – and Artor lacked the will to deny the queen her whims.

The day of the hunt dawned cold, clear and brisk. After frantic preparation, a small cavalcade set out from Cadbury, complete with beaters to find game and drive it into range of the hunters' bows, while the ladies of the court kept their mistress amused.

'How pretty it all is,' Wenhaver exclaimed when she spied the simple hut that had been erected from logs, hides and willow just above the tree line of the forest. 'A good fire will keep us as warm as toast while the men are killing things and enacting brave deeds to impress us. Our only task is to admire and comment on their proficiency.'

The cold air had heightened Wenhaver's colour and she seemed almost girlish as she rode on a gentle mare, her skirts gathered decorously around her and her fur-lined cloak framing her flushed cheeks.

Artor grunted a wordless, ambiguous reply but, unenthusiastic though he had been about this excursion, he was beginning to feel his blood stir with anticipation. The muted colours of the many cloaks blended perfectly with the bare trees and a light dusting of snow, and the laughter of the fur-clad ladies created a festive mood.

After an hour in the cabin, however, the ladies were becoming chilled and irritable. The fire in the open hearth burned vigorously, but the hole in the simple roof of the hut not only allowed the smoke to dissipate but it also permitted cold air to swirl around skirts and chill even the most well-insulated feet. Sulkily, Wenhaver discovered that hunting was a long and wearisome pursuit for onlookers. The hides that hung over the walls were an inadequate means of controlling the freshening breezes and the furs on the floor simply sucked the cold out of the ground.

'How can men take pleasure in killing animals in such weather?' Wenhaver complained. 'My feet are frozen and I swear my nose is becoming red.'

'We can't see anything,' one maiden complained.

'When will the men return?' Wenhaver demanded of no one in particular.

'They will have scarcely begun,' Elayne explained gently. 'You will know when the dogs have taken a scent when you hear them starting to bay. The wild animals will then be driven towards us.'

Wenhaver's mouth pursed. 'I suppose you've hunted in Arden and know all there is to know about this manly sport.'

'Not I,' Elayne responded. 'But my brothers were forced to find what game they could during winters when our crops failed.'

Wenhaver wasn't listening. 'I'm returning to the tor,' she announced. Inside her mountain of furs, she looked like a plump, bad-tempered vole. 'We shall allow the men to enjoy killing their beasts, but I don't intend to freeze to death waiting for their return.'

Her personal guard assisted her to cross the freezing ground and mount her horse.

As Elayne straightened Wenhaver's cloak over her horse's withers, the queen eyed the younger woman with a maliciously sweet smile.

'Someone must remain to inform the king that we have returned to warmer quarters. I would send one of my guards, but who knows what dreadful perils we might encounter on the road back to Cadbury.'

Elayne sighed inwardly.

'You're used to these harsh conditions and you're familiar with hunting, so we'll leave you here to let Artor know of our departure. You may use any of my little comforts that remain here after we depart.'

If Elayne was angry at being abandoned on the bare little hilltop beyond the margins of the Cadbury lands, she knew better than to waste her time in fruitless recrimination. She was more concerned by the heavy clouds that were shrouding the blue sky and threatening to bring the first heavy snowfalls of winter.

The hours slipped tediously past. Elayne walked outside periodically to keep her chilled blood moving. Wenhaver had made no preparations to protect the horses from the elements, so out of pity, Elayne led her mount into the hut and felt a moment's amused satisfaction when her roan mare defecated pungently on Wenhaver's dressed hides. 'I wish Wenhaver had to clean up the shit, but no doubt some servant will be ordered to remove any mess.'

Much to Elayne's surprise, she fell asleep before the blazing fire. When she awoke, she was thoroughly chilled and her hands were blue and almost frozen. The fire was beginning to die. She stamped her way to the door and tried to restore some feeling in her numb feet. She had no idea how long she had slept.

Snow was falling in flurries out of a charcoal sky. Within moments, Elayne's eyes were hurting from the bitter cold and the blinding whiteness of the snow that was building up around her. She knew she must find her way back to Cadbury immediately, for the hut provided only meagre shelter and the firewood was almost gone.

Once she had climbed on to her horse with her back to the wind, Elayne felt more confident. But after fifteen minutes of riding, the ceiling of snow cloud began to lower, the darkness deepened and Elayne realized that she had no idea where she was.

The cold bit through her furs and made her skin burn. She was totally lost. She was still close to the hut but she knew she'd never find it again in these conditions. All she could do was set her mare's head forward and hope that the horse would find her way home to Cadbury.

Artor and the other hunters arrived at Cadbury as the snowstorm gathered strength. The High King guessed correctly that Wenhaver would have deserted her vantage point as soon as the weather became nasty, so the hunters returned directly to Cadbury and were soon safely ensconced in the citadel.

When he had bathed, Artor joined his wife to eat a simple evening meal. He was famished, but had barely seated himself when he noticed the empty chair.

'Where's Lady Elayne? I expect she's tired and cold from our little expedition.'

'Wasn't she at the hut?' Wenhaver asked carelessly. 'She wanted to wait for you so you wouldn't be concerned at our absence.'

Artor stared at his wife in disbelief. 'Are you telling me that you left her in that useless little hut? How could you be so uncaring and irresponsible as to abandon anyone in a place like that? You knew we would head straight for the tor if the weather worsened, for that was the arrangement made with your guards.'

'Don't speak to me like that! It's not my fault! She didn't have to remain there!'

Cursing vilely, Artor rose and ordered Odin and Gareth to attend to him.

'Where are you going?' Wenhaver sobbed. 'You'll become lost and die, and then where will I be?'

'You'll stay safe, wife, for it's what you do best,' he snarled at her.

Artor led a hastily arranged search party to the hut. There was no sign of life there, so the men began scouring the area close to the hut, but the snow had covered all trace of hoof prints.

'She'll not last long in this weather, regardless of her woodcraft,' Artor shouted over the howling wind. He split his men into smaller groups to intensify the search. 'If you find her, return straight to the tor and then send a message back to the search party. If you find no trace of her, we'll meet back at the hut in an hour.'

The king's guards raised their gloved hands in acknowledgement and plunged off into the falling snow.

Time dragged by and Elayne remained lost. Artor feared that she would not be found alive. His conscience and his love were twin whips that drove him on, but the horses began to show inevitable signs of exhaustion so, reluctantly, Artor ordered his men to return to Cadbury and the safety of the tor.

'I'll check the hut one last time, then join you as soon as I can,' he shouted to his men.

When Artor found the hut, it was more by accident than design. The flapping of the frozen hide door led him to a snow-swept space that was scarcely recognizable as the cheerful little hut that had been erected earlier in the day.

Snow had blown through the open door and banked against the inner walls. The hut looked as deserted as it had been throughout the long search.

'She's not here. God help me!'

Suddenly, he heard a low-pitched sound. The sound came again, barely more than an exhalation of air, but decidedly human, and it came from within the hut.

Artor discovered Elayne in the corner furthest from the doorway. She had become a human snowdrift, having found her way back to the hut where she had instinctively huddled inside the furs abandoned by Wenhaver's party. She was hovering on the brink of that final, gentle sleep that precedes death from exposure.

Artor knew exactly what must be done. He left Elayne to find his horse. Nothing but snow flurries greeted his gaze and a quick search showed rapidly filling hoof prints leading off into the darkness. No better proof existed that this storm was a killer, for his horse had headed for the shelter of its stables at Cadbury with the inbuilt survival instincts of its kind.

Artor returned to the hut and used his sword and knife to weigh down the hide door.

Then he shook Elayne brutally. When her eyelids lifted a little and he could see slivers of her green-gold eyes, he slapped her hard until they began to open.

'You can't go back to sleep! You'll die! Do you hear me? You'll die! Don't go to sleep!'

'Cold!' she whispered. 'I'm so cold!'

Artor stripped the ornamental furs off the walls and made a nest as near to the cold fire as possible. He picked up Elayne's small form and bundled her securely in the furs.

The king knew that fire was all that stood between them and death. The stools and other items of furniture splintered easily and a basket of cold victuals intended for the hunt party was emptied on to the floor so that the basket could be ripped apart and used for kindling.

Using a flint to strike a fire took Artor far longer.

His fingers were clumsy with cold and he had not been required to make a fire for decades. He was beginning to despair when a feeble flame finally sprang into life. He shielded the flicker with his hand until it finally spread to the split wood and leapt up in tongues of orange and yellow.

A rudimentary search of the hut exposed a neat pile of logs in one corner – albeit covered with snow. A couple were thrust into the centre of the blaze that was quickly consuming the lighter wood and the wicker from the basket. As the blaze continued to grow, Artor could feel the heat beginning to emanate from the fire inside the confined space. Now he must pack snow tightly into gaps in the structure to stop draughts of wind, and then weigh down the inner hide walls with what stones he could discover.

After he had sealed the hut as best he could, Artor turned his attention back to the half-frozen body under the furs.

Elayne's hands were icy, even within her damp mittens, so Artor thrust them inside his shirt. He eased his body down into the nest of fur and wound his body around her small, unresponsive form. Gently, he pulled the furs entirely over their heads so they were cocooned within a dark, soft world of slow breathing and slowly warming flesh.

Artor dozed as the heat rose from the fire. With Elayne in the crook of his arm, a feeling of peace seduced his tired mind. He pressed her face to his breast, and began to knead feeling back into her frozen hands.

He slept.

During the night, Artor woke several times to add more logs to the fire. Each time, he found that Elayne was still deeply asleep, and with a sickening fear that she had ceased to live, he checked her breathing. Exhaustion had sucked her down into the healing darkness of sleep and the king was happy to follow her into its warm oblivion.

When he finally awoke to a stillness that signified that the snowstorm had abated, the fire had become glowing coals in the simple hearth. Only one log remained, so he thrust it into the heart of the embers.

In the furs, Elayne nestled into his arms and twined her legs around his. Her eyes were closed and small veins leapt and pulsed in her eyelids. Without counting the cost, Artor kissed her eyes and felt the first stirrings of an erection. With a great effort of will, he cradled her close to him and tried to banish any thought of her warm softness and the hands that held him under his shirt. She nestled even closer to him in her sleep until they lay breast to breast and thigh to thigh. The king tried to restrain his body with thoughts of Bedwyr but Elayne's warm hands stroked his back and his ribs, until sheer pleasure caused him to groan.

Elayne opened her eyes.

'My lord,' she said simply – and her hands stilled.

'Forgive my familiarity, my lady, but you were half dead from exposure to the cold. I've no wish to compromise you.'

Elayne's eyes were sleepy and mysterious with those thoughts that lie at the heart of all women. His shoulder muffled her gentle laughter, while her free hand traced the outline of his shoulder muscles in the darkness of the furs.

'I don't care what happens on this night, my lord, for I've already died and have arrived in paradise,' she whispered, and he felt the warmth of her breath on his throat. 'I'm no lady, Artor, I'm simply Elayne until such time as I return to life in the morning.'

She freed one hand and gently smoothed the frown lines between his eyes. Then she pulled down his head so his mouth was on hers and Artor was lost in the lingering sweetness of her kiss.

'No, my lady. No! Bedwyr is my friend . . .' his voice trailed away as she closed his mouth with greater insistence.

She stripped his lower clothing and deftly fitted her body to his. Artor felt himself buried in her body as if his sex had a life of its own and cared nothing for friendship, loyalty and honour. Although his reason cried out against the penetration of her body, he was lost in the warmth of her flanks and the silken body that drew him down into a memory of youth.

Elayne was as wanton and needy as a servant girl, and Artor gave up all thoughts except of pleasure in her body. His hungry mouth roamed the unfamiliar terrain of her flesh and he luxuriated in simple sensation until both of them were spent.

They slept again.

When Elayne finally awoke, the passion of the night seemed to be a strange, primal dream. Artor had left the warmth of the furs, dressed in the weak light and now stood beside the partly open door, staring out into the early morning.

Elayne smiled at him contentedly and the day suddenly seemed brighter. Artor frowned and his eyes were hidden in a network of fine lines.

'Don't be troubled, my king. Any sins of the night aren't yours, but mine, done willingly and with pleasure. Nor will I be sad that you have held me in your arms, for my dear Bedwyr would not begrudge me any comfort I could give to my king. You saved my life.'

Artor returned to her side and knelt to kiss her fingers, now rosy and warm.

'I wasn't the High King under the furs during the night. I was just a frightened and lonely man who searched for comfort. I took advantage of you and of your gratitude, no matter how you try to dress my actions in a more charitable light.'

'And I was not Elayne. I made the decision to lie with you, and I willingly put aside my wedding vows.' Then her face dimmed. 'But last night was all we had, because the morning has now come and our rescuers will soon be here. I must become the queen's companion once again, until such time as my dear Bedwyr returns to claim me. And you must assume your mantle of kingship without any care for me. We are friends, not lovers, for circumstances rule our separate duties.'

He lifted her up and cradled her in his arms.

'I wish our lives were otherwise,' Artor whispered, his face buried in her unbound hair.

'Aye. So do I. But you are the High King, and I am the mistress of Arden. Our separate lives are predetermined. But if you ever need a friend, my lord, then I am yours until I die. You need never be lonely, for Elayne will always be yours to command – in all but this.'

Artor smiled down into her eyes, then kissed her deeply, as a lover would, for the last time. When he pulled away from her, he pressed his fingers to his lips as if to retain the taste of her.

Then he rose and bowed low to her. A thousand whispered endearments were compressed into that single moment. Lost in his lambent grey eyes, Elayne drank in a lifetime of companionship and refused to weep for what could never exist.

'Arise now, my lady, for I hear the sound of horses. The time has come for us to resume our separate lives.'

When they were taken back to Cadbury Tor by a detachment of Artor's personal guard, the whole town rejoiced in the salvation of the king. Elayne stood at the fringes of a cheering crowd, smiling ruefully as she watched the king's tall figure engulfed by the assembled warriors, nobles and citizens.

When their lives returned to their even, preordained banalities and the thaw of winter began, Artor ordered that the small hut should be torn down and burned. Some memories are best kept in the heart rather than in the physical world where temptation always provides a keener edge to desire.

The day of the hunt was a memory that Elayne hugged to her breast, although her eyes no longer followed the passage of the king.

CHAPTER XVII

THE TRACE

Bedwyr lounged on a rough bench in a hole-in-the-wall inn at Mamucium. The reek of sour wine, vomit and urine permeated every board of the structure, while the filthy straw over the sod floor crawled with vermin.

The cold bit deeply into Bedwyr's bones, so he wrapped his fleece cloak around him more closely. The hide was untanned and smelled vile, and no one even glanced in his direction.

Nursing a cup of very rough cider, Bedwyr sank his head low and watched his fellow drinkers.

The Blue Boar had a motley clientele. Shepherds, layabouts, the odd carpenter and at least one scarred warrior stood or jostled for a bench seat in the fug of sweat, smelly clothes and stale stew. The floor of the small room was unnaturally warm and Bedwyr guessed that the old Roman baths, now slimy and disused, had a functioning hypocaust that someone had primed with wood to warm the premises. Bedwyr closed his eyes, with one hand gripping his cup and the other wrapped firmly around his purse.

Someone jostled him, so he opened one eye and cursed fluently.

A one-eyed farmer peered at Bedwyr suspiciously as he moved along the bench, grumbling in a half-drunken slur. He closed his eyes again as a heavy rump settled on the other end of the seat. A slouching figure leaned against the wall on his other side. Hemmed in, Bedwyr summoned up a phlegm-coarsened snore.

The men around Bedwyr talked and moaned about their lives. The winter was proving to be harsher than usual, their masters were unreasonable and one man had a brother who had been arrested by the town watch for rape. Their complaints were many and were mostly levelled at the town council and the local king. However, their ill feeling was also directed at King Artor because he was permitting Christianity to flourish within his realms.

One man spat on the straw near Bedwyr's booted foot and the spy barely managed to avoid flinching.

'Them priests be a menace to all right thinking men,' the man complained.

'They spread their milky ways on every soul in sight,' another agreed. 'Who cares about heaven if here and now is so sodding awful?'

'I'll drink to that,' a smoother, more educated voice agreed. 'The sooner the Druids return, the happier I'll be. It was fairer when the Druids gave the laws because they left a man alone, unless he killed or thieved.'

One of the men disagreed, pointing out that Druid law was very similar to Christian dogma, but his friends howled his argument down. They seemed to have a rosy view of the justice meted out by the Druids, and Bedwyr took a brief moment to wonder how long these three idiots would prosper if the old days were to come back again.

They'd most likely end up inside the Wicker Man, he thought.

'At any road, a new order is coming to the west,' the man next to Bedwyr said. 'I heard there's a movement starting up called Ceridwen's Cup.'

'That's a stupid sodding name,' the standing man replied laconically. 'And you ought to be more careful what you say aloud in a place like this.'

Casually, the standing man contrived to kick Bedwyr's exposed ankle. Bedwyr snarled, swore and slumped even lower against the wall.

'He's drunk,' the fat man next to Bedwyr said dismissively.

'Ceridwen's Cup was supposed to have brought knowledge and all good things to the people,' the man with the smooth voice said. 'Like the Horn of Plenty, it can't be emptied.'

Bedwyr snored, causing the three men to remain silent for a short moment.

'It's still a stupid sodding name,' the standing man snapped. 'But I'd like to find out what it's all about. Life with the Cup couldn't be worse than what we have, so how can I find out more?'

The fat man drew in his breath with a sharp hiss, and Bedwyr felt the timbers of the seat shift as the man suddenly flexed his large buttocks.

'All you need do to find other like-minded men is to mention the Cup in passing. They'll know what you're seeking,' the first man murmured.

'So what does the Cup stand for? I've only heard of it in whispers,' the standing man asked, scepticism thick in his voice.

'We're of a mind that the people should decide what the laws are. King Artor is too far away to know how we live, if he even cared. Eating off gold plates won't help him to know much about working people.'

'You talk like a babe at times, Alwyn. Killing Saxons isn't my idea of an easy life.'

'Don't use my name, you shit! Anyways, the Saxons don't follow the Christian ways and they're still true to their old traditions, which are much like ours used to be. Why are the Saxons our enemies? The sodding Romans saddled us with the Jewish god and what good ever came from that cursed race?'

The man beside him stirred his fat rump again and spat.

'I don't know,' the standing man muttered. 'It seems to me that the Romans didn't burn folks alive like the Saxons do. There's nothing wrong with this nice warm floor that we have here and the Roman roads are good for moving sheep to market. Besides, the Romans went away, but there's no sign the Saxons will ever leave.'

The third man's smooth voice interrupted the standing man's recitation of practical Roman habits.

'I'd be careful if I were you, or you'll be judged by the Druid when the day of Ceridwen's Cup comes to our lands. He's got no patience with those Celts who don't know where their future lies.'

'Is that a threat?' the standing man demanded belligerently and Bedwyr heard the grating of a knife as it was eased from its scabbard.

'Why don't you listen before you make up your mind?' the seated man answered in a placatory voice. 'There's a meeting coming for all right thinking men.'

'Where?' the standing man snapped.

'Don't be stupid. This isn't the place to talk about it. The walls in this fleapit have ears.'

The seated man gave Bedwyr a nudge in the side. He grunted and cursed drunkenly.

'You can ask for the Cup at the Lady,' the smooth-voiced man hissed. 'But I should tell you that if we don't think that you're with us, then you're against us!'

The bench groaned as the heavy man moved from the seat alongside him. Bedwyr peeked through one cautiously opened eye.

He saw two retreating backs.

Where's the third man? he thought to himself.

Then the standing man eased his whipcord body away from the wall.

'Did you hear all that, Lord Bedwyr?' a soft voice whispered in the Saxon language. The standing man appeared to be speaking softly to the empty air.

Bedwyr opened both eyes but kept silent.

The man who stood to his right was lean, dark and sun-browned. His black eyes were alert with intelligence.

'Are you Trystan's man?' Bedwyr asked softly. He felt a sudden clasp of strong fingers on his wrist.

Bedwyr nodded his comprehension. He had never met Gruffydd's kin but he knew that Trystan was second-in-command in Artor's spy network.

'Sit! I'm getting a crick in my neck from looking up at you.'

The bench seat moved slightly as the spy slouched down next to Bedwyr. He leaned his back against the wall like any sensible man in such a den of iniquity.

Bedwyr pretended to waken slowly.

He stretched his arms and yawned and, by accident, managed to slap his companion across the face.

He apologized oafishly and shuffled to his feet to buy his companion a mug of vile-tasting cider in atonement.

Once reseated, Bedwyr leaned back against the wall and mimed drinking deeply, although his companion could see that the level of cider didn't seem to be lowering in his rough pottery jar.

'Who are these maniacs?' Bedwyr whispered, although the noise in the small room was deafening.

The spy shrugged. 'Most of those who find their way to the Cup seem to be malcontents. From what I can gather, the Druid preaches revolution and attempts to convince his converts that even Saxons are a better alternative than a southern king who doesn't care about the north. There are other forces at work in this game but, as yet, I can't work out what they are.'

'Humpff!' Bedwyr gave the appearance of sinking into gloom and drink.

'Several of our spies have vanished from the area, which is the reason I've been sent here from Deva. We're playing a dangerous game, Bedwyr, with invisible men who take care that only stupid pawns are exposed.'

'Where is this lady of whom they spoke?' Bedwyr asked quietly.

'It's an inn called the Blue Lady,' the tall man answered softly. 'It's near the abandoned forum. By all accounts, it's a den for thieves, lowlifes and outlaws, so I'm not surprised the Fellowship of the Cup uses it as a rallying point.'

'Then it seems I must go drinking at the Lady. I've always considered blue to be a lucky colour.'

The tall man gripped Bedwyr's forearm painfully.

'Don't be as daft as these cattle. You've been seen, you've come to their notice and you haven't been invited to their little get-together. My presence won't alarm the natives, so I'll go. Meet me by the old stile at the crossroads two nights from now. I'll be there at dusk and I'll pass on to you whatever I discover. For the sake of the gods, don't expose me by blundering into a place where you'll stand out like dog's balls.'

Then, as slippery as any eel, the spy rose to his feet and vanished into the press of malodorous men.

Bedwyr spent two miserable days scratching at bedbug bites and cursing the filth of this northern city. The icy weather made the cobblestones treacherous to walk on and the days were so dark and miserable that Bedwyr huddled in his stinking furs and snuffled like an old man.

He had caught a head cold, but he comforted himself that he'd not been infected with anything worse. For all that it was still a trade town, Mamucium had decayed after the Romans had abandoned the isles. Inertia, or lack of a firm hand, had caused the town to degenerate physically since Luka's benevolent despotism as tribal chief, but now it hunkered down in its rotting, wooden buildings. Remnants of glory lingered in an ordure-stained stone forum and the slimy and chipped mosaics of the abandoned baths, but Mamucium had seen too many armies come and go, while it festered from within.

Two days are a long time when inactivity is forced upon an active man. Bedwyr frequented the coarsest inns and his stomach turned sour from bad wine and worse beer. On the afternoon of the second day, he made his way to a stone monolith situated a little outside Mamucium and set at the centre of the crossroads, as if it marked some ancient, forgotten wrong. Bedwyr had brought his horse, his hound and a full pack, hoping to be on his way at speed once he had concluded his business with the tall spy.

Waiting was tedious, so he sat in the lee of an old oak out of the worst of the wind, where he could watch the stone in comfort.

Darkness came gradually and Bedwyr began to worry. The nameless spy seemed to be a clever man, but he trod a dangerous path and, if what he'd said could be trusted, several men had already perished because they had proved to be overly curious about Ceridwen's Cup.

When a figure came running, Bedwyr did not desert the shadows of the oak immediately. The runner could be anybody, muffled as he was in a long black cloak.

Gradually, Bedwyr became aware of a flame bobbing along behind the fleeing figure. Within a few minutes, two shapes loomed out of the darkness, rimmed by the light of the flaming torch that one man carried high in his left hand. The men wore muffling hoods and the light revealed the glitter of their drawn knives.

The man being followed gave a small cry and summoned up a final burst of speed to reach the ancient rock which he used to protect his back as he turned to face his pursuers. Bedwyr was moving to position himself behind the assailants when the two figures attacked the winded fugitive in deadly, silent combat.

By the time Bedwyr and his dog joined the fray from behind the two attackers, their quarry had already fallen to his knees. Bedwyr closed the gap between them quickly and immediately fell into the stance of the knife-fighter, while his Arden knife hissed in its eagerness to taste blood. His hound leapt at the throat of one man, her great jaws closing over an extended arm. The man screamed and tried to shake the grim beast off him, but her sabre teeth were lodged deeply in his flesh and her jaw was locked. His knife flashed once, then again, and Bedwyr's hound cried thinly like a child.

Bedwyr knew his companion of the road was gone.

The two assassins fought like animals, kicking and spitting to gain any advantage, and Bedwyr blessed his years as a warrior. He rolled and ducked, kicked and then struck from behind, just as they did, but he was a trained killer, and his experience told in the final result.

The man with the wounded arm died quickly and Bedwyr felt a frisson of vengeance as he slashed the man's foolishly exposed throat. His hound was avenged and she would run free in the Otherworld.

The other man was slain ignominiously as he attempted to scramble away from Bedwyr with his hands upraised in supplication. Bedwyr ignored a shallow slash he had taken across his ribs, stepped inside the defences of the retreating man and rammed the Arden knife up through the throat and into the mouth and brain of his enemy.

The night remained silent, except for two sets of lungs that strained to drag air through gaping mouths. Bedwyr retrieved his knife and pulled back the hoods over the heads of the assassins. He recognized neither man.

Bedwyr's hound was dead, her jaws bloodied and her muzzle still raised towards an enemy. With a pang of regret and pride, Bedwyr prayed that when his time came he would die with as much grace and courage as his companion had displayed.

Trystan's spy had collapsed and now he lolled on the frozen ground with his back to the stone. As Bedwyr bent over him, he could see that the man was bleeding sluggishly from a deep knife thrust just below the heart. Bloody froth escaped from the man's lips, and his eyes were half-closed like those of a tired child.

'Bedwyr,' the spy sighed. 'My thanks for your aid, friend, but you've arrived too late to save me.'

'What have you learned?'

'Always on duty, Bedwyr?' the man wheezed painfully. 'I am Glynn ap Rathwyn. Do you remember me?'

'I do, Glynn.' Bedwyr smiled regretfully at the dying man. 'You have little time, and I must have your information. What can you tell me?'

'Gronw, the Druid, is set to move to a ruined and deserted village that sits to the north of Bremetennacum on the road to Olicana. You must be careful, for you will be deep in Brigante country and their king is no friend to Artor.'

Bedwyr looked up and down the crossroads, but the night was silent and deserted.

'I'm sorry, Glynn ap Rathwyn, but I must leave you here while I move these carrion where they can't be found. I must give myself a chance of escape so Gronw remains ignorant of our pursuit. I'll not be any longer than I can help.'

Glynn looked up at Bedwyr with pain-filled eyes. 'You

needn't worry on my account, Bedwyr. I'll be dead soon enough. Leave my body here and, if Gronw's followers care to look for me, they'll believe I've been eliminated. Take care, Bedwyr, and revenge yourself on Gronw for me.'

The words were forced painfully from Glynn's throat, and Bedwyr knew that some major part of the young man's body had been breached. The blood that bubbled at his mouth was filled with air from collapsed and drowning lungs and the blue tinge that edged Glynn's mouth was a sign that the spy was slowly choking on his own blood. Bedwyr knew no remedy that could save the dying man.

'On your way, Bedwyr. You've much to do, and the friends of these mongrels might be curious about my fate.'

When Bedwyr still paused, Glynn's voice became rougher and stronger. 'Get moving, damn you! I'm dying anyway, so don't make it all for nothing.'

The effort drained him, and his head slumped forward.

Bedwyr trudged away, lugging one of the dead men with him across his broad back. He knew he left heavy tracks in the snow and slush, but trusted that the snowflakes now falling would hide his passage. He slung the body over his protesting horse.

The second body was lighter and he soon had it lashed next to the first. Then he went back for the corpse of his hound who would lie, in death, with the creatures who killed her.

Once more, Bedwyr ran back quickly to check on Glynn.

The figure of the spy was already shrouded in a thin cloak of snow. Bedwyr shook the man's shoulder and the spy unwillingly opened his eyes.

'Do you have any messages for your kin?' Bedwyr asked

calmly, for he had seen the face of death so often that it held no dread for him.

'I have no kin. But I ask that you bid Trystan farewell for me. Tell him . . . that no woman is worth his soul.'

Bedwyr had no idea what Glynn ap Rathwyn meant, but he nodded and squeezed the hand of the dying man.

'I feel cowardly for leaving you. Artor's rule has always been that no friend should die alone in enemy hands.'

'Make the killing stroke yourself, Bedwyr. I'd consider it a mercy from one warrior to another. You know what they will do to my body if they find me alive, so I ask that you strike hard and true. I assure you that my shade won't return to haunt you.'

Bedwyr pulled out his knife with its crust of blood along the blade from the bodies of the two assassins. The elaborate carving marked it as a special weapon, and Glynn's eyes widened slightly when he saw it.

'So this is the fabled Arden knife. It's an honour to see it.'

Bedwyr cleaned the blade in a handful of snow so that no impure blood would contaminate either the fine metal or the man who was about to die. Glynn's eyes watched carefully and he grimaced with apprehension in spite of the honour that Bedwyr was about to pay him. Then he closed his eyes, so he couldn't see the thrust that would extinguish his life.

As Bedwyr led his laden horse away from the crossroads, he sighed to think of the waste that Gronw had brought to the west; many more good men would have to die to defeat the Druid and the cause that he espoused.

Bedwyr tipped the two bodies into a sluggish river well outside the boundaries of Mamucium, trusting that they would be undiscovered until spring, if then. He buried his hound in deep snow in the exposed roots of an oak where it would rot in the spring and enrich the ground surrounding the huge tree. Finally, he cleaned the flanks and back of his horse with fresh snow to remove the blood that stained its hide.

With a renewed sense of urgency, Bedwyr rode south at speed.

Dreary days prevailed at Cadbury. The Samhein celebrations had come and gone, leaving Artor sunk in gloom at the absence of the twins. He felt like a straw king, clutching a tin crown with nerveless fingers, and his belief that civil war would burn everything he had striven to build began to turn him into a rudderless leader.

Even the messenger who brought word of a royal visitor failed to rouse Artor from his torpor. King Mark from the west was coming from Segontium, and Cadbury was sent atwitter at the news.

Wenhaver was as excited as a child.

'I know this king is nothing much,' she told Modred, who was still at Cadbury. 'But it will be invigorating to have a new face here on the tor.'

'Mark isn't a very cheerful man,' Modred replied laconically. 'Nor does he travel very willingly. I wonder what he wants?'

Wenhaver smacked Modred's shoulder playfully. 'Perhaps he's bored too, and is seeking pleasure in the larger world. You always think the very worst of people, Modred.'

'And I'm very often right,' Modred muttered.

King Mark had never pretended to approve of Artor as High

King of the Britons and had, many years earlier, raised his objections publicly on the occasion of Artor's crowning. The Deceangli were small, dour and argumentative, and they had taken in those disaffected Demetae tribesmen who chose to reject Artor's division of tribal lands after the battle of Mori Saxonicus. Neither King Mark nor his vassals could be easily appeased by patriotic appeals from Artor's emissaries, for their neighbours were the Ordovice tribe, warriors who enjoyed the sunshine of Artor's approval – and were now their natural enemies.

Eventually, King Mark made his triumphant entrance into Cadbury Town like a conqueror, complete with a retinue of sixty mounted warriors who were armed to the teeth. Although his guards were short and very dark, their black eyes were bright with malice and dislike for Cadbury.

Artor met King Mark at the foot of the tor with his own fully armed retinue chosen from the most impressive men in his bodyguard. Ceremonial gold torcs encircled their throats and the hilts of their weapons were massy with cabochon gems.

Artor, in contrast, had dressed in wintry grey. His eyes, his hair and his rich clothes were sombre, but the gold on his fingers, sword hilt and knife allayed any suggestion of asceticism. As a penance, Artor wore Uther's pearl upon his thumb, having reluctantly accepted the jewel from Elayne's hands, after she had taken it from Balyn's body.

'Welcome to Cadbury, King Mark. I'm honoured to meet you again, and I commiserate with you on the rigours of your journey. Arrangements have been made to accommodate you and four personal servants in state, on the tor itself. Provision has been made for quartering the remainder of your guard in the lower garrison.'

No sensible king would welcome sixty armed men into his fortress.

'My thanks, lord,' Mark responded. 'I've ridden far to meet you, for I need to transact some business with you that I hope will not be unwelcome. But I'd prefer to speak of my requirements later, after I've rested.'

Artor's lips tightened slightly at Mark's presumption.

'You've gained my attention, Mark,' the High King replied silkily. 'I await our discussion with anticipation. As always, I am at the disposal of any petitioner,' Artor continued urbanely. 'But for now you must allow me to conduct you to the tor and to your quarters.'

King Mark was an angular, ageing man whose hair was almost wholly silver at the brow but still black elsewhere. He wore his hair chopped off at the shoulders, and the contrasting locks made him resemble a blackbird with white facial markings. His nose emphasized the avian image, because it was sharply hooked and narrow across the bridge. His lips were thin and colourless, while his black eyes were beady and acquisitive.

Once Mark was ensconced in the best rooms in the citadel, Artor asked Odin and Gareth to join him in his bedchamber.

Artor motioned the two men on to stools and then poured wine for them.

He looked at Odin. 'What do you make of King Mark, old friend?'

'He has a hungry and a busy eye, Artor.'

'What should I know about the man?'

Odin put his large, sandalled feet on Artor's table and drained the wine cup in one long swallow. 'Mark missed nothing of the defences as we climbed the tor. That isn't surprising because all strangers to Cadbury gawp when they see our fortifications for the first time. But I noticed that he made one mistake. He avoided meeting Modred's eyes when he entered our hall, and Modred avoided meeting the eyes of Mark. As Targo would have said, I can smell a large rat in our straw. The Brigante stoat is a near neighbour to King Mark, so they must be acquainted.'

'Mark has never shown any desire to visit us before. Why now? Why would he come in winter? He looks like a person who enjoys comfortable surroundings.'

The three men sank into companionable silence.

'I wish Balan was still here,' Artor muttered sadly. 'He would have had insights into the man. He was a good listener, he had a capacity for stillness.'

'Your Bran is alive . . . and he's a suitable heir, Artor,' Gareth reminded the king. 'He's healthy, he's fully grown into manhood and he's already fathered a successor to follow him.'

'No. I'll not rob Anna of her last son. It's essential that Anna and Bran remain safe after I am dead. While I live, they're vulnerable to predatory claimants to my throne, but this would be as nothing compared with the dangers they'll face once I've gone to the shades.'

Artor sank back into silence, clenching and unclenching his aching knife hand.

Odin looked speculatively at his king, his head cocked to one side. As he aged, he seemed to look more and more like a disreputable bear.

'The winds tell me that you will have another son soon, Lord Artor,' the Jutlander said suddenly. His eyes were veiled and he seemed to be struggling to breach the void that exists between silence and speech.

'I've sired many sons, but they've been born of women whom the tribal kings would never accept. They're good boys, but none of them has the qualities needed to rule our people.'

'Lady Elayne quickens with child,' Odin stated. 'Her maidservant tells me she vomits every morning, and that she's careful with her choice of food.'

The silence that fell was deep and absolute.

'Her maid also informed me, with a little encouragement, that Lady Elayne has not had the moon blood for four months. The lady quickens, as I have said.'

Artor stared at the huge Jutlander with growing horror in his eyes.

'The world will know her to be a faithless wife,' Gareth said regretfully. 'The maids already whisper their suspicions, and it would be foolish to protest that the world will not know the child was sired by the king. Bedwyr has been absent from court for six months and who else would dare to touch Lady Elayne other than the king, given that they were together during a blizzard at the time the child was conceived. The courtiers of Cadbury can count.'

'May the gods save us,' Artor moaned. 'Bedwyr will demand a blood price for his lost honour. And I? I deserve to pay it. But Lady Elayne is without blame in her predicament, and I'll not permit her to become the butt of cruel rumour.'

Odin cleared his throat.

'I say she's without blame,' Artor repeated roughly. 'I am the High King, and my word is law!'

'Should Wenhaver hear any rumour concerning Elayne, the lady will be ruined. Losing your temper won't change her fate.' Gareth's bluntness cut through Artor's rage like a cold knife. The king visibly deflated.

'You're right, Gareth,' Artor said. 'As always, you speak the unadorned truth while I bluster.'

The king became silent as he considered what action he could take. Finally, he turned to Odin.

'Fetch Taliesin. But quietly, understand?'

'Now, Artor?'

The High King nodded distractedly.

Odin found Taliesin quickly, and the harpist soon accompanied the Jutlander into the king's spartan chamber. Artor gave the young man a terse explanation.

'As soon as King Mark has departed from Cadbury, you will accompany Lady Elayne home to Arden. She is in danger here, and I must protect her as best I may.'

Taliesin merely bowed his head in agreement. As a man of medicine, he had already noticed Lady Elayne's flushed cheeks and her loss of appetite. This order simply confirmed his suspicions and concern.

The next evening, Artor and Wenhaver presided over a grand feast in honour of King Mark's visit. The queen had driven the servants almost to madness in her determination that Mark would be struck dumb by the magnificence of Cadbury Tor.

In the halls, perfumed oils burned in flaming sconces and

scented the air, while the best golden platters were laid out ready for the guest's use. The cups were of glass that had come from across the great, inner sea, while amphora and jugs of wine of the best quality were on hand to tempt the most discerning palates.

Wenhaver looked magnificent in cloth of gold and fur. In the secret way of women, her hair was still vivid and any plumpness in her figure was well hidden under her heavy robes. She welcomed her guest graciously and introduced King Mark to the court with natural charm. In such situations, Wenhaver shone. Her performance gave Artor a small, but heartfelt, thrill of pride.

Artor arrived late at his own feast, a slight that forced his guests to cool their heels in small talk and their throats with chilled wine from Gaul. Under his robes, Artor's right leg ached fiercely from an old injury and he would have preferred to read or snooze by his own fire. Instead, he dressed with care and entered the great hall, flanked by Odin and Gareth. Desperately, he tried not to wince or to limp as he strode across the uneven floor.

Mastery of feigned interest and the open, welcoming gaze of friendship is an absolute necessity for all politicians and kings. Artor employed all the hard-learned tricks of diplomacy to conceal his dislike of King Mark, who was resplendent in finely dyed wool, a golden torc, a huge brooch and even an ostentatious crown. Artor was preoccupied by the predicament facing Lady Elayne; as he smiled warmly towards Mark, his thoughts kept slipping away to the lady who was sitting demurely at the end of the table, well below the salt. With a pang of guilt, he realized that a shameful hope was beginning to surge through his ageing blood. Perhaps a son could still succeed him.

The feast began.

'Your earthworks are impressive, Lord Artor. I'd heard of them, but I can see for myself that any siege of your citadel would be fruitless. I congratulate you on their design and construction.'

King Mark's voice made a circuitous route through Artor's ambivalent thoughts. With difficulty, the High King wrenched his mind back to the task at hand.

'It wasn't all my own doing, Mark. Before the Romans, Cadbury was an impregnable fortress, and then it fell into ruins. Myrddion Merlinus planned the new defences of Cadbury many, many years ago, while I merely built it. I might add that his son, Taliesin, is an excellent harpist and he will be singing for us tonight.' Artor paused to skewer King Mark with his eyes. 'Many of our citizens believe that Cadbury will never fall because it has been sanctified with young flesh over the ages.'

Mark surreptitiously made the sign that warded off evil.

Artor considered how small-minded King Mark was in every sense. The puffed-up blackbird, eager to pick at any old bones that came his way, was still frightened that the corpse on which he fed might cause him harm. And he was superstitious, which could be a useful weakness.

King Mark toyed with a piece of chicken on his plate using a jewelled knife. He stabbed at the plump flesh, tearing off thin strips that he impaled on his blade and popped neatly into his mouth.

Artor felt queasy.

'I have heard Myrddion Merlinus is imprisoned in a hollow tree with Nimue, the enchantress. It's said that she uses the same magic she learned from him to cast demonic spells over all those poor souls who come in contact with her.' King Mark picked over what was left of the carcass on his plate and sucked the last of the succulent white meat off its bones. Then he threw the scraps on to the flagged floor like a northern savage.

Artor winced at the King's barbarian manners, while a servant unobtrusively scooped up the mess and carried it away.

'You'd best not speak slightingly of Lady Nimue to her son. He plays and sings like a godling, but he has a wicked knife arm and a slow but fiery temper. And there are many people in Cadbury who have cause to remember Lady Nimue with gratitude. My nephew there, Prince Gawayne, owes the life of his wife and his eldest son to the skills of the Maid of Wind and Water.'

'I stand corrected, Artor,' Mark countered smoothly. 'Peaceful days breed fanciful stories and the marvels of Cadbury are among the most wonderful tales of all.'

'Believe little of what you hear, Mark. Superstitious gossip can be useful to manipulate susceptible men.'

Mark flinched and paled visibly, although Artor had no idea what he had just said that had flustered the northern king. He determined to press home his advantage and smiled conspiratorially at his guest as if they shared a special secret.

Let him make what he chooses of that, Artor thought to himself.

Mark fumbled with his eating knife and managed to drop it.

Taliesin sang his newest composition which related the deaths of Balyn and Balan. When the last chord died, the rapturous approval of the court and the copious tears of Queen Wenhaver washed through the hall.

Throughout Taliesin's performance, in feigned boredom, King Mark continued to eat greedily.

'Those poor, dear boys,' Wenhaver sobbed. 'Balyn was half in love with me, the pet, before his madness took him. It was such a tragic story. How their mother must feel!'

'She has another son,' Mark replied baldly. 'I've met him. He's a large, curly-haired chieftain with grey eyes, and he lacks respect for his betters.'

Artor felt the blood thicken around his heart. Any pretty words he might have offered congealed in his throat. Uncharacteristically, he spat.

Wenhaver looked shocked and spoke hastily to cover her husband's lapse in manners.

'Men can't really understand the loss of children,' she said softly. 'So I'll forgive you for your ignorance on this subject.'

'Bran is a loyal vassal of mine, Mark,' Artor said pointedly.

'Indeed. He's able enough, but he rarely mixes with his equals and he's unwilling to show the deference that is due to his elders. Still, he has a fine look about him . . . much like you, Artor.'

'I've only met the man once, so you have an advantage over me. Of course, his mother Anna is distant kin of mine, but it's many years since I last saw her.'

Wenhaver prattled of trivialities while her husband trod a perilous bridge of words, his mind inwardly seething at the lack of respect and good manners displayed by his visitor.

Displeased, and careless of who knew it, the High King finished his meal in silence. He listened to King Mark and

Wenhaver converse aimlessly of inconsequential matters ranging from the inclement weather to the number of brigands abroad on the roads. When the servants poured more wine and placed great bowls of fruit, nuts and honey on the board, Artor took the initiative.

'I doubt that gossip or good food has brought you to Cadbury, King Mark. We have diverted each other long enough with polite conversation, so it's time you broached the purpose of your visit to my fortress in the depths of winter.'

With studied carelessness, Mark selected a walnut and smashed its shell between his fingers, before dropping the grit on to the floor. If he expected his small show of strength to impress Artor, he was mistaken.

'I come to you because of your dog, Trystan,' Mark said evenly. 'I want him muzzled, and I demand that you keep him away from my wife. I expect your co-operation in this matter, King Artor, and have come to gain your assurances that you will act.' Privately, Mark feared his queen would elope with Artor's spymaster. The public humiliation he would suffer as a result didn't bear thinking about.

'My dog?' Artor queried very quietly. 'I wasn't aware that Trystan was my creature to command. That wilful young man chooses his own path with no reference to me. Apart from carrying out certain basic duties for the throne from time to time, he's master of his own actions. I have met Trystan on only one occasion and I have no particular liking for the young man.'

Mark's thin lips almost disappeared as he chewed on his greying moustache.

'In Trystan's defence, however, I assure you that his loyalty to the Celtic cause is beyond reproach.'

'So you refuse to keep that young seducer away from my queen?'

'You misunderstand me, Mark. I will send a special courier immediately to order Trystan to avoid your wife, but I cannot guarantee that he will take the slightest notice of me. I'm not his kin, and he'll likely tell me to mind my own business. However, it should be easy to take the young man in hand yourself. And perhaps you should keep Queen Iseult away from temptation. I've heard that she is young and impressionable, as well as beautiful.'

'Before you offer marital advice to me, Artor,' Mark snarled, 'perhaps you should—'

'Be very careful what you say in this public place,' Artor interrupted icily. 'Ill-chosen words can be dangerous.'

Mark rose abruptly to take his leave, causing his chair to topple backwards, with a loud clatter. The assembled guests fell silent, for very few visitors had ever acted so imprudently in the presence of the High King.

'Then I will bid you a good night's sleep, King Artor. I hope that all your days are safe and pleasant in the months to come.'

Wenhaver gasped at the threat beneath the words, but Artor seemed unperturbed.

'Naturally, I wish the same future for you, Mark. Tomorrow we go hunting. Please join us, if you enjoy the chase.'

Mark bowed his head fractionally and stalked out of the hall.

Odin bent over to whisper in his master's ear. 'You've given him no reason to love you, Artor. It would be unwise to hunt with him tomorrow.'

The High King patted Odin's arm affectionately. 'You'll be careful enough for both of us, my strong right arm.'

Modred had watched the exchange between the two kings with lively interest. Inwardly, he cursed Mark's ineptitude. The Deceangli king was very foolish to show his hostility so openly, for Artor would now be on his guard.

Outside, the wind dropped and a still, white shroud of mist settled over Cadbury's defences.

CHAPTER XVIII

A CURSE UNLEASHED

The early morning was sharp with frost. The tor was a monochrome of black, grey and pearl-white, but Artor's palace beetled over Elayne like some threatening wooden creature out of legend. Her frightened thoughts created a horse head out of the mists or, seconds later, a leering wicker man writhed out of the low cloud and fog.

She shivered in her heavy furs.

An ostler assisted her to mount, but her horse skittered on the icy flagging. She thought that she might fall as the sky wheeled above her, but a strong arm steadied her shoulders until she was lifted into the saddle.

'My lord!' the ostler gasped, and bowed his head reverently.

'Your Majesty.' Elayne's heart leaped to see him. 'There is no need for you to farewell me. I shall soon be away, and I would be sad to think you had caught cold because of me.'

'Do not fear for my health, my lady, for I don't deserve a moment of your concern. Taliesin? I want you!'

The harpist appeared instantly out of the fog, his long hair beaded with moisture and his mare moving easily with only the pressure of her master's knees.

'Lord Artor, I live to serve.'

'I hold you to your promise, Taliesin. This lady is precious to Lord Bedwyr – and to me. You will stay close to her until her forests fully protect her ... as I cannot.'

Taliesin bowed his head briefly. 'I have so sworn, my lord.'

Elayne felt a lump in her throat that was more painful than the small heaviness in her womb, or the fear that lay heavily on her heart.

'Are there no messages for Arden, Lord Artor?' she asked, although she knew she spoke unwisely. There were twenty mounted warriors close at hand who would act as her escort. If she wished for a message from Artor, he would be foolish to risk being overheard.

Artor swallowed and stood a little straighter, but he remained mute. He took Elayne's gloved hand in both of his, peeled back the leather where it protected the narrow, blue veins on the inside of her wrist and then lingeringly kissed them. Her fingers trembled at his touch.

'Farewell, my lady. There is nothing else to say.'

Elayne's horse moved into the cavalcade of escorts, and her hand was torn from his grip.

'Until later, my lord!'

'Until later,' he replied, and turned away so that no man could see his sadness.

Elayne soon lost sight of his tall figure in the mist. Still looking backwards at the tor, the lady reached the gates of the citadel and passed out of the ken of the west.

Bedwyr rode south with a nasty crosswind making his passage over the icy roads even more difficult than usual. Barely pausing to rest his horse, he made good speed in the poor weather, for urgency provided a sharp spur to his journey.

Gronw had surfaced at last.

The relationship between Percivale and Galahad had not fared well during Bedwyr's absence. Years spent working in the kitchens, followed by the long process of proving his worth to Artor, had inured Percivale to displays of petulance and impatience by courtiers such as Galahad, but the young man had tried Percivale's patience to its limit.

The problem with Galahad, Percivale eventually decided, was that the young man was totally incapable of understanding the needs and feelings of any other person. The bountiful gifts of beauty, talent and good birth had resulted in the development of a personality that was as ignorant of the natural feelings of ordinary men as a dumb beast. In fact, animals were more sensitive than the Otadini prince, for they had empathy and Galahad had none. The prince never raised a finger in the preparation of a meal, or in the cleaning of their cramped quarters, and even stolid, good-natured Percivale had tired of being Galahad's body servant and whipping boy.

'I hate winter. I'm never quite warm and there's too little to do,' Galahad complained on the last day of their enforced inactivity.

'Then perhaps you could make an attempt to turn over the straw. The stench is vile.' Percivale's tone was sharp with frustration, so any sensible man would have understood the dissatisfaction underlying Percivale's complaint.

'I don't do cleaning. I only do things that amuse me.'

'Then perhaps you can kill some defenceless animal that we can eat for our supper.'

Galahad finally realized that Percivale was cross.

'I don't see why you should be so irritable, Percivale. This mission must be a holiday for you, for you'd be at the king's beck and call in Cadbury. I don't ask much of you.'

Uncharacteristically, Percivale swore at the Otadini prince.

'Enough of your shite, Galahad! You've skived away from all menial tasks since we first rode together. I'm no longer a kitchen boy, I'm a warrior in the service of King Artor. I've earned my rank, I wasn't born into wealth and power as you were.'

Galahad's mouth closed with a snap and he made a great show of toying with the straw, a token effort that only served to fill the air with dust.

'Stop it, Galahad! Even this simple task is too difficult for you, so please go outside and kill something.'

And so, when Bedwyr arrived, he found Percivale alone. The warrior had lit a new fire and was preparing a small round pot for cooking whatever delicacy Galahad managed to flush from cover.

'Oh, it's you,' Percivale muttered sullenly.

'I love you too, friend. What's roughened your fur?'

Percivale smiled apologetically at his friend. 'Don't mind me, Bedwyr. I'm homesick and bored. This hut is a malodorous, dreary hole and I'd feign be on our way somewhere, anywhere, rather than remain in this dung heap for one more day.'

Bedwyr watched as Percivale snapped wild parsnips and carrots with his strong fingers.

'I assume that Galahad has been his usual charming self.'

'Don't go down that path,' Percivale warned grimly as he tore leafy greens into strips. 'He never speaks; he preaches! I

435 ✝

know I'm uncharitable to complain about our companion, but I've been driven to distraction in the weeks we've been camped here. I hope you've found the Cup, Bedwyr, so we can leave this pestilential place.'

'I've discovered where Gronw is hiding, but we'll need to ride hard and fast to catch him before he moves on to his next hiding hole.'

At this auspicious moment, Galahad pushed through the door, shaking snow all over the threshold and letting in a frigid draught of air. He was carrying two rabbits, gutted and skinned, and he seemed very pleased with himself.

'You're back! Where's Gronw?'

'No one ever thinks to ask after my health,' Bedwyr joked, but Galahad took him literally and inspected his person from head to foot. 'You look fit and well to me, if a little travel-stained,' he pronounced. 'So, where's Gronw?'

'I've discovered a group of particularly nasty individuals called the Fellowship of the Cup. They've murdered at least three of Artor's servants who stumbled on to news of their foolishness. We're talking revolution here, masters, one that's obviously being funded by someone with a very heavy purse. Gronw, to answer your question, is currently at a deserted village south of Bremetennacum.'

Galahad dropped the rabbits in the straw and began to gather together his tackle and possessions.

'We ride immediately,' he ordered grandly.

Percivale and Bedwyr looked at each other.

'Come on,' Galahad urged. 'Gronw might get away while we're sitting on our backsides, stuffing ourselves with rabbit stew.'

Percivale bent to pick up the rabbits.

'I've just completed a two-day ride, Galahad,' Bedwyr explained patiently. 'My horse will drop dead without food, water and rest. I'm not feeling so alert myself and the thought of rabbit stew sounds tempting to me. Besides, it's getting dark outside, and it's snowing.'

Both companions observed Galahad's internal battle between impatience and practicality and, for once, the latter won.

'Suit yourselves,' he eventually conceded. Then he looked towards Bedwyr's feet. 'Where's your bitch?'

'She's dead,' Bedwyr replied gruffly. He missed his hound; he had hand-raised her from the time she was whelped and he felt incomplete without her.

'I'm sorry to hear it,' Galahad said. 'Shall we leave at first light?'

'Agreed,' Bedwyr said curtly. 'And I suggest we avoid the roads.'

The stew was acceptable and the three men devoured every greasy morsel, using their fingers and then cleansing themselves with fresh snow. Percivale scrubbed the pot with more snow while Galahad and Bedwyr fell asleep on the straw, leaving Artor's man to wonder why he had been sent on this unpleasant journey.

Feeling unappreciated and resentful, Percivale began his nightly prayers. For all his noisy piety, Galahad often forgot to have regular communion with God if he was tired and, uncharitably, Percivale allowed his reservoir of dissatisfaction to intrude between himself and his own devotions.

As he curled into the musty straw and closed his eyes, his

thoughts turned to the Cup. He had decided that he didn't really care whether it was the Cup of the Last Supper or a simple utensil that had been passed from hand to hand by Roman warriors. The object had been blessed during the years it was held by the holy hands of Lucius of Glastonbury, and so it was a blasphemy for the relic to be in the possession of a criminal. That the Cup should be used against the interests of the High King was doubly unthinkable.

Artor is more than a king, Percivale thought ardently. He is an idea, a man who sees beyond birth and status, and into the heart.

Then Percivale considered the plight of the ordinary people whose lives were far removed from the court. One ruler was much like another to them. Artor or some Saxon king – would there be any difference? Wasn't any king just another bubble in the vast river of human history?

He decided that the peasants would regret Artor's passing when he was eventually washed away by time. Goodness, honour, duty and courage all endure far longer in the common mind than in the hearts of kings. Percivale decided that if he must die, then he would perish for Artor rather than the Cup, no matter how seductively it called to him.

At Cadbury, the weather was far milder than it was in the north and, on the day of the hunt, the spring thaw was already underway, so the earth under the horse's hooves was soft and treacherous. In the crisp, pale glare of a watery sun, the hunters were black shapes outlined against the shrinking snow. Artor would have preferred to ease his bones before a fire, but hospitality demanded that he exert himself to amuse King Mark.

The afternoon was largely uneventful. A doe in her winter coat blundered across their path, disturbed by the beaters who slogged through the snow.

Out of courtesy, Artor permitted Mark to make the kill, and the northerner managed a grudging smile of enjoyment as his men dressed the beast where it fell, before slinging the carcass over a packhorse. Artor stared at the steaming entrails that were dumped in the bloody snow and thought of the beauty that had been wasted for something as meaningless as personal amusement.

As the hunters rode back towards Cadbury and warm fires, a flock of large birds rose upwards from deep within a shadowy maze of gorse and trees. King Mark drew his bow and began to fire, followed almost immediately by all the other members of the hunting party. Soon, the air was filled with the hiss of arrows as they arced upwards towards the circling flock. The birds dropped like stones.

Artor took no interest.

Suddenly, something plucked at his cloak and he felt a narrow wire of pain across his side. Startled, he pulled on his horse's mouth and the beast reared in panic. This time, Artor saw a solitary arrow curve past him and fall into a snow bank just five yards away from where he fought to control his excited mount.

'To me! To me!' he roared, throwing himself to the ground to use his horse as a shield.

Within seconds, Artor's bodyguards had surrounded their king.

Odin checked the High King from head to toe before he found the tear in Artor's red cloak. His eyes flared with panic as he swept the material away from Artor's side.

'Find those arrows,' Odin shouted to Gareth, his voice suddenly devoid of its usual heavy accent. 'And mark where they came from.'

'It's nothing but a scratch, Odin.'

Regardless of Artor's assurances that he had taken no hurt, his bodyguard escorted him away from his gaping guests, back to the safety of the tor.

'You were fired on not once, but twice, my lord. Most of the warriors and the nobles of the court, including King Mark's servants, were at the rear, behind the hunters. It would have been easy to hide behind a tree or a snow bank and await the chance for a clear shot. No one would have noticed a brief absence by the assassin.

Gareth joined them, pushing his horse up the last incline with ruthless haste. He carried two arrows in his left hand.

'Not here,' Artor hissed.

He led his two personal guards into the hall and, from there, into his rooms.

Before the king had a chance to speak, Odin found a bowl of clean water and forced his master to strip off his outer clothing to reveal a narrow gouge across Artor's side.

'You were lucky,' Odin grunted, as he smeared one of his vile-smelling salves over the wound, before binding it with a strip of torn cloth.

'Why would King Mark take such risks immediately after an open disagreement with me? I'd expect an assassin to be overly friendly if he planned to kill me. I don't think Mark was involved in this plot.' He turned to Gareth. 'Where are the arrows, Gareth?'

Gareth quickly produced the two arrows and handed them to his king, who began to inspect the shafts.

'Perfectly ordinary, unmarked fletches with nothing to show who might have owned them. They tell us nothing, so we cannot make wild accusations against our guests. We'll treat the attack as opportunistic – some ill-wisher could not resist chancing his luck.'

'Lord, there's more to this assassination attempt than we think,' Gareth said. 'I checked the flight of the arrows against the spot where they fell to earth. The assassin wasn't behind you. He was hidden in a copse of trees ahead of us. He could be one of the beaters, a peasant or even a warrior who separated himself from the other hunters.'

'Trust no one,' Odin said grimly. 'You could so easily be killed, Artor, if you don't take care.'

'I don't intend to live in fear and cower on my stool beside the fire. I'll die as I've lived and shall make no complaint.' Artor grinned recklessly.

He dressed briskly and left his chamber to greet the returning nobles who all wondered at the king's sudden departure from the hunt.

'Forgive me, honoured guests, for I suddenly became faint and my guard panicked.' Artor explained. He smiled at those assembled. 'Old age catches us all in the end.'

Most of the nobles and servants appeared to accept his explanation, but both King Mark and Modred exchanged doubtful, confused glances.

Artor moved among the lords, praising their prowess in the hunt and admiring the birds, snow foxes and, of course, King Mark's deer. The knives are beginning to sharpen, Artor thought, even as he slapped backs and told jokes with guests who could be potential assassins. Someone is tired of waiting and wishes to hasten my departure for Hades. But I'm now forewarned and the reach of my arm is long.

The three searchers slogged through snow-drowned forests, resting frequently to save the horses. They were forced to sleep in a lean-to made from cut branches and they scraped the earth bare of snow inside so a fire could be lit. All in all, Bedwyr had chosen a miserable route for the trio to travel.

'Where are we?' Galahad panted as he attempted to drag his horse out of a snowdrift.

'Just a little to the south-west of Bremetennacum.' Bedwyr helped to push Galahad's steed from behind.

Eventually, the horse escaped the clinging snow with an explosion of muscles, and Galahad and Bedwyr sprawled full length in the snow.

Galahad rose laughing, and Bedwyr could almost forgive the obsessive selfishness that impelled the prince.

'So where is this village of which you speak?' Galahad asked. He carefully checked the legs of his animal.

'From what I was told, it's situated on the Roman road leading to the west. The road travels to the sea and then heads north to Bravoniacum, within reach of the Wall.'

'So we sneak up on this village, do we? What about Gronw?'

'It's not likely we can sneak up on the place,' Bedwyr replied laconically, dusting snow off his leather breeches. 'But I don't think we'll miss the village. Gronw's followers will leave tracks in the snow. He has quite a following now, so it's becoming more and more difficult for him to conceal himself.'

'We must exercise caution from now on,' Percivale warned.

'Yes,' Bedwyr agreed. 'We'll have to be extremely careful when and where we break cover. The Roman road is just beyond the tree line, so we must choose a route where we can ride parallel to it. And we can't light any more fires, so there's no more hot food. Let's not give Gronw any advance warning. I expect enough opposition as it is.'

That night, the three men huddled together in the lee of an oak, while their horses were kept hobbled in places where their soft lips and sharp teeth could find a little dried grass or sweet bark to augment the grain they had been fed. The warriors were uncomfortable and slept little, although they needed healing rest. The Cup burned in each mind like a curse, although each of them desired it for a different reason.

Crazed with dreams of glory, Gronw presided over a growing body of followers. Three times he had passed judgement on spies that had resulted in summary execution, and his decisions created spectacles that brought more potential adherents to his cause. The tattooed Pict gloated over the deaths of his enemies as he sat wrapped in dirty furs in the only sound building remaining among a cluster of four rotting huts.

The traitors had been burned for their sins and their blackened bodies left where they died as object lessons to those fools who still followed the new ways and religions.

Pebr, the phlegmatic, one-eyed warrior, had become Gronw's guide and paymaster, and his link to their anonymous benefactor. Pebr was curt and monosyllabic, and Gronw doubted that this saturnine man believed one word of his injunctions to the people. Not that Gronw blamed him for his doubts, he didn't believe his rantings himself. But any lie that brought harm to either Roman or Celt was acceptable. Revenge had a special taste, like dried blood mixed with salty tears, and Gronw fed on it addictively.

His eyes strayed to the rafter in the corner of the room where he had hidden the Cup. He could feel its power drawing him, even now when he could not physically see it. With his habitual suspicion, he had taken great pains to hide the Cup from Pebr, for Gronw trusted nobody.

Tonight, he would speak of rebellion. He would warn the curious and the true believers alike of the war to come, when Christianity would be cast out and the land would be cleansed of Artor and his kind. Then, tomorrow, he would move further north, to a new location that Pebr had prepared.

Word had spread and messages were passed from mouth to mouth.

Outside, in the forest that encroached upon the ruined village, the three searchers had located Gronw's lair; it was clearly signposted by a wisp of smoke escaping from the conical roof of the hut. They could also smell the remains of the three executed spies. Bedwyr had been the first to recognize the smell of death, that sweet scent that no man or woman can forget once they have experienced it. He wanted to gag.

'Dismount,' he whispered. 'Tether the horses so that they don't shy away from the stink of corpses. Be careful where you put your feet and where you leave tracks in the snow, for we are in danger in this place.'

For once, Galahad did not argue.

Ever cautious, Bedwyr made them crawl through the snow. When they suddenly came upon three bodies, the first thing they saw was the remains of roasted feet.

The executed men, probably Trystan's spies, had been tied to young oak trees that were little more than saplings, but strong enough to resist the frantic struggles of the victims. Oil-soaked wood had been piled around their feet and set alight, so only chalky bones remained of their legs, at least in those places where the animals had left the corpses in peace.

The blackened bellies of the bodies had split open, revealing how the birds, foxes and other carnivores had feasted on the cooked flesh. Even Bedwyr, who had seen the cruelties of the Saxons as well as the carnage of battle, was forced to turn away from this grisly sight. Now that the bodies had frozen solid, the scavengers came no more and the dead men hung stiffly.

'Many feet have packed the snow down hard here around the bodies, and not just when these poor devils were put to death. See? Many gawpers have come, again and again, to view these remains.' Bedwyr spat on to the packed snow.

'That thought is more loathsome than their execution,' Percivale muttered. His face was as white as the snow, except for his boyish freckles that stood out starkly against his pallor.

'Gronw is near, and I'll enjoy killing him,' Galahad snarled. 'These men died hard.' His face showed no revulsion, but anger clenched his jaw.

'Should we bury them?' Percivale asked quietly.

Bedwyr watched as Percivale's fingers traced the sign of the Cross.

'No. I hate to leave the remains of good men to be

desecrated, but nothing would advertise our presence more clearly. We must be invisible until we complete our task, and then we can consider the remains of these men.'

By a circuitous route, the three searchers contrived to crawl to the top of a low ridge line from where they could observe the ruined building which was still emitting smoke through the conical roof. They burrowed into the snow to await darkness.

At dusk, the malcontents began to gather. At first, they came in pairs, and their ragged clothes and filthy, cloth-wrapped hands and feet marked them as farm labourers or layabouts. As the gloom deepened, men began to arrive on horses, their armour clinking in the stillness. Still other men and women wore fur cloaks to conceal their fine woven robes that marked them as wealthy landowners. At least one hundred citizens had gathered by the time a tall, one-eyed warrior left the hut and set alight a large bonfire. The flames rose and danced, washing the faces of the crowd with blood-red colour.

Quiet descended over the assembled group of rebels.

Into this well of stillness, a chanting, unseen voice cut across the whispers of the crowd. Awkwardly, a black-robed form shouldered out of the hut and faced the rapt crowd.

By Galahad's standards, Bedwyr was a pagan. But in recent years he had cleaved to the old religion and had found comfort in it. But if he had expected to hear familiar exhortations and the calm rhetoric of the Druids, then he was disappointed. Gronw spewed out a diatribe of hatred for all things Roman. In the process, he damned those Celts who tolerated Christianity, castigating the long peace of Artor as a coward's concession to the Church of Rome. The crowd devoured his words.

'The Cup!' someone called from within the crowd.

'The Cup! The Cup! The Cup!'

The cry rose out of one hundred throats as if that simple utensil, so jealously guarded by Lucius, was somehow embodied with powers that could crush all civilized life in the west.

Like the charlatan he was, Gronw conjured the Cup out of his sleeve and lifted the battered tin high.

'Behold the Cup of Ceridwen, she who gives all blessings! Hence comes our victory, for the goddess will smite down the Christian gods. She will destroy all the works of Jesus and overthrow the reign of the murderous Artor. Death to Artor, usurper and bastard!'

'Death!' the crowd roared in response, oblivious to the apparent foolishness of worshipping a battered cup.

The ceremony continued.

Brutally, Pebr dragged an unfortunate man out of one of the half-collapsed buildings. The prisoner's hands were tied behind his back and his eyes were mad with terror.

'Ceridwen loves you all,' Gronw screamed. 'But this dog was heard to curse her, while still calling for the Romans to return and bring plenty to the west. He is a spy! He is a traitor! He is a Christian!'

'No, I'm not a Christian.' The man's desperate voice rose in the cold air. 'I was drunk!'

Gronw cast his eyes around the assembled group. 'What penance shall this traitor pay? What does Mother Ceridwen demand of her loyal children?'

'Death! Death! Death!' the crowd screamed.

In any event, the unfortunate workman, for so his dress

447 ✝

proclaimed him to be, was not burned alive. Whipped into frenzy, the crowd snatched the victim away from Pebr and began to pummel and punch him. The body was soon engulfed by the crowd and disappeared from view. Then it reappeared as it was tossed from group to group and torn at with nails, teeth and knives. The bloody meat that was left when the crowd tired of this sport could hardly be recognized as a human being.

Bedwyr shuddered as he watched a woman in a rich, grey hood lick ecstatically at the blood on her fingers. Men danced and spun, others prayed, and some, like Pebr, stood impassively and watched the blood lust boil within the crowd. Some crazed men would have turned on each other, so maddened was the mood of those present, had Gronw not raised his hands and demanded silence.

Eventually he was obeyed, but only because of the strength and authority of Pebr's sword.

'Ceridwen has feasted and has drunk deeply,' Gronw called exultantly. 'She will bless you in the days ahead. But you must be ready to rise up when you hear the call that the Cup has come again.'

The people cheered and stamped their feet in a shared frenzy.

'When this crowd has departed,' Galahad vowed on the ridge line, 'Gronw and whoever remains with him must die.'

'Aye,' Bedwyr whispered. 'The quest for Lucius's Cup may be our primary task, but murder and fomenting revolution are totally different matters.'

'Have you seen men and women before who have done

such vile acts as those we have just seen?' Percivale asked Bedwyr.

'Aye. When people lack a strong, guiding mind to lead them, they can easily revert to beastliness. But these animals aren't worshippers of the old ways. They use religion to justify the vileness of their hatred for the cause of Artor and the west.'

'Perhaps we would be beasts ourselves if we weren't governed by civilized laws.'

'God shouldn't permit anyone to live who can participate in the degenerate deeds we have seen tonight,' Percivale whispered. His face was stark with horror.

The three watchers waited for hours as the more respectable members of Gronw's flock quietly slipped away and the hungers of those men and women who remained turned to sex and the wine they had brought with them. Later, when a light snow began to fall, and the bonfire began to splutter and die, the night returned to a semblance of stillness and the warriors checked their weapons.

Their swords would be needed with the coming of the dawn.

CHAPTER XIX

THE BLUE HAG

King Mark had been gone from the halls of Cadbury for more than a month when the fragile balance of the west began to teeter on a knife edge. On a perfect, early-spring day, when blue skies had finally defeated the grey storm clouds of late winter, one of Artor's oldest enemies came to the citadel.

A retinue of warriors clad entirely in black approached Cadbury Town. The citizens stepped aside and covered their faces when they saw the woman who was carried in much state in a litter of midnight black.

Morgan had come to Cadbury Tor.

Word of her arrival spread through the township, over the dykes, up the spiral defences and into the king's hall.

'The Witch has come', the cry rose, and many greybeards who remembered her name and her deeds prayed to their gods that she would die before she blighted their world with her killing stare.

Artor did not leave his hall to greet Morgan. He waited for her to come to him. The king sat on his throne with his nervous and unwilling wife beside him. No friendly face in the form of Elayne was there, nor was Percivale's calm presence warm at his back.

Four members of Morgan's guard carried her litter into the king's hall. Artor could see that the figure on the litter was shrunken, tiny and was clothed in the deep black of mourning.

Artor rose, permitting no sign of weakness in his ageing body to show. Standing with his feet a little apart and his wide shoulders squared, his vigour must have stabbed his sister to the heart.

She was helped from her litter and moved towards the throne with the bent gait of an old woman. Artor's hooded eyes watched her as she shuffled along, one blue-veined hand clutching a staff carved into the likeness of a serpent. Despite their long enmity, he felt a stab of pity for the loss of her beauty.

Then she drew back her hood with her free hand.

Morgan had endured the pain of tattooing from her hairline deep into the neckline of her robe. Serpents, demons, spiders and other vile creatures crawled in blue woad over her wizened skin so that her features appeared to writhe with unholy life even when she was still. Her white hair had yellowed with ill health, and her lips had thinned over what remained of her sharpened teeth.

'Greetings, my brother,' she rasped in a voice that had lost its musical power to seduce. 'You're still favoured by time, I see.'

Morgan's eyes were still alive, young and glistening with malice. Artor felt an even deeper pang of pity. Morgan had become very like the man she had hated most, Uther Pendragon.

'Be seated, sister, and drink your fill,' Artor replied in his softest voice. 'You've travelled far and I can see that you're not well.'

Morgan's eyes snapped suspiciously at his concern. 'Don't pity me, King of the Britons, for I'll see you in your grave soon enough. But I'm tired, so I'll drink your wine. You, of all men, would never resort to poison.'

A servant fetched a goblet for her and, as she accepted the wine, her forefinger stroked his young hand. The servant recoiled and Morgan laughed at his fear.

'I see you're still striking terror into lesser mortals, sister,' Artor said coldly. 'I thought you'd have wearied of such unworthy charades by now.'

Morgan glared at her brother.

'I'm no Uther to need your charms to hold my kingdom under firm control,' he added. 'Or to retain a memory of youth.'

'No, you aren't, are you?' Morgan replied, and then she turned her baleful eyes on Wenhaver, who cowered under the obsidian glare. 'So, this faded husk is all that's left of the fabled Wenhaver, the great beauty, noblewoman and whore. I haven't seen you since your wedding day. Ah, what a tantrum you threw. I'm sure you've led my brother a nasty dance.'

Wenhaver's mouth fell open at Morgan's attack on her character and appearance, then her eyes narrowed into vindictive slits.

'At least I'm not positively ugly like you are, Morgan,' she retorted and the nobles gasped at her effrontery towards the famed witch.

'You will be silent, Wenhaver,' Artor ordered.

'You must obey your master, Wenhaver,' Morgan rasped. 'You've betrayed him often enough with all manner of men, so perhaps you owe him a still tongue.' She raised one gnarled finger, causing Wenhaver to cover her face with her hands in fear.

Artor laughed. 'Don't try your tricks with me, sister. You aren't able to turn us into toads, or harm us in any way unless we choose to believe you are capable of doing what you claim. I reject your powers utterly.'

It was now Morgan's turn to laugh, a sound rendered dreadful because it was almost girlish.

The smile abruptly left the face of the old woman.

'Enough of friendly banter, brother,' she said. 'I come bearing news of such urgency that I have been forced to travel many weary miles.'

'I didn't think you came because of sisterly love, Morgan, although one of my regrets is that my birth and my sire drove a wedge between us from my infancy. I have always admired your effrontery and your bravery. Speak your news.'

Morgan smiled at Artor without her customary sneer. 'In truth, brother, I might have loved you for yourself if you hadn't been the son of Uther Pen Worm. But if that had come to pass, you'd never have become Artor, the Warrior of the West, would you? Fate is a very odd and demanding master.'

Artor began to feel irritation redden his cheekbones as they played their old and vicious game.

'Enough sparring, Morgan! I believe we've established that we are not loving kinfolk.'

'The news I bring, brother, is that King Lot and Queen Morgause are both dead.'

Artor felt his knees tremble. He resumed his seat before the other nobles should see his weakness.

'When? How?'

'Lot was always a huge man and, in recent times, he barely had the strength to leave his throne. Three weeks ago, he was found dead beside his chair. He must have fallen from the throne during the night. When his body was found, his face was purpled with suffocation, for he had choked on his own weight when he couldn't drag himself upright.'

Morgan displayed no trace of sympathy, but Artor shuddered at the gruesome manner of his brother-in-law's death. The High King could imagine Lot's panic and the slow pressure on his lungs that had ultimately defeated the man as he struggled for breath.

'Lot and I were hardly friends – in fact, our opinions differed on almost everything, but he was a brave and able king. He will be missed.'

Morgan grimaced. 'He'll be missed by some, I suppose.'

'What of Morgause? I cannot imagine her succumbing to grief. How did the queen die?'

'Only one week after Lot perished, and before riders could be sent to inform Prince Gawayne that he was now King of the Otadini, Morgause was poisoned by her maidservant. I can assure you, the assassin told me everything she knew before she died.'

Artor felt his world stop on its axis. 'Explain, Morgan. If my sister was killed in some plot, it is essential that I know the details. If her killing is not avenged, we are all at risk of assassination.'

'Your words are touching, dear brother, but you're a little late. The maidservant was a Pict who had been taken into slavery as an infant, so my sister trusted her implicitly. Morgause never thought to doubt her loyalty, because the woman used her skills with unguents and creams to preserve my sister's beauty. Vanity killed Morgause as surely as the poison that was placed in her face powder. The maid used lead, I believe, and it caused Morgause to die in agony. Such poisoning takes time to kill the victim, many months at least. Had I been at court, I might have recognized my sister's weakness, her aches and her declining appetite. But I was absent.'

'But why?' Artor asked, his head whirling with possibilities. 'What was to be gained by killing the old queen?'

'The plot must have been a long time in the making. I sense the edges of its purpose. Gawayne is scarcely known to his people after spending his youth and middle years in your service. He must return at speed, or there'll be no crown for him to claim.'

Artor turned to Odin. 'Send for Gawayne.'

'The maidservant resisted our torture for a very long time. Hatred is a potent weapon, and an even more effective shield from agony if it has been nurtured for many years. But, with time, even her obsessive enmity was no protection against pain. Eventually, she begged to tell me everything she knew.' Morgan paused to regain her heaving breath.

'She had been swayed by a lover whom she believed was a fellow Pict, but no one in the north has ever heard of him. All I know is that he has one eye, and is called Fydyth. I cannot find him, but I believe he betrayed her, as well as being responsible for the death of Morgause.'

'But I don't really understand why?' Artor muttered. The death of Morgause achieved no practical purpose that he could perceive.

'Don't be a dolt, Artor. The Otadini are in turmoil and will be of no use to you should rebellion threaten your throne. Morgause was respected and feared. She would have steadied the people's resolve and bolstered her son's reputation. Her death is a loss to you and to Gawayne, but of greater importance is the knowledge that she is lost to the Otadini people who have come to believe that she was ageless. I frighten the tribe, but she awed them.' She smiled at the concern that was clearly written on Artor's face. 'I advise you to watch your back, brother.'

At this point, Gawayne strolled into the hall and, seeing his aunt seated before the king, would have taken to his heels if Artor hadn't quickly and succinctly explained the situation.

Gawayne shook his head as if his loss was incomprehensible.

'I must return to my tribe, my lord, and quickly,' he said impulsively. 'I must see to the burial of my parents.'

'Yes, you must depart immediately,' Artor agreed. 'Enid and your brood must be having a difficult time coping with the death of both Otadini sovereigns.' He frowned. 'You must take great care on the roads, for I'm beginning to suspect there might be a plot to deny the throne to any of my kin. You're at great risk of ambush during your journey.'

'You may take my guard with you if you wish,' Morgan offered. 'They're loyal to Lot's lineage.'

Gawayne thanked her and turned to depart.

'You must find a large horse for yourself, Gawayne,' she added conversationally. 'You are getting a little fat; you should remember that you are your father's son.'

'Bitch,' Gawayne muttered. 'You should spend some time with Galahad when he returns. You'd be perfect company for each other.'

She grimaced. 'I am spared that lily-white prig at least, if he is away on your service,' she retorted. 'Gawayne may not be a clever man, but at least he has a talent for blood work. As for Galahad, he's useless. Enid must surely have betrayed her husband when she gave birth to that one.'

Fortunately, Gawayne did not hear Morgan's opinion of his son's worth.

Wisely, Artor made no comment about the young man.

'I beg that you find me a soft bed, brother. I'm weary, and even a crone must rest her bones from time to time.'

'Before you go to your well-earned rest, Morgan, I have one last question to ask you. Are you certain that Lot died by accident? I don't believe in coincidences, and the death of both sovereigns in such a short period of time stretches my credulity. I could believe in chance more readily if revolution didn't threaten from the north.'

Morgan grinned. It was a grotesque sight.

'Yes, the charlatan is causing you trouble, isn't he? But he'll pay soon enough for his blasphemies.' Her baleful eyes narrowed. 'Lot would have been easy to kill, too easy, but only a trusted servant could have approached so closely to the king. Lot was fat, but not stupid, brother. However, taken by surprise, he could have been murdered.'

'I suppose it doesn't matter,' Artor murmured.

'It does matter, Artor!' Morgan snarled. 'If it was Fydyth who killed Lot and Morgause, he did so as part of a greater plot. I won't forgive such a crime, or the reasons behind it. Fydyth, or whatever his name is, will wish he had never been born before I've finished with him.'

'Not if I find him first,' Artor said. 'Thank you for bringing this news to me in person. Given our past history, it's odd that I always value your opinions so highly.'

Morgan rose and bowed. Try as he might, Artor could not remember her ever doing so before.

'Sleep well, brother. The bones tell me you will need your rest.' She turned to the queen and smiled. 'Perhaps I'll tell your future, Wenhaver. When I'm rested.'

Wenhaver barely managed to hide a shudder of revulsion.

The presence of Morgan, even sequestered in the best apartments, dampened the spirits of every soul within the fortress.

Gawayne was gone before dawn and the morning brought news of yet another defection. Modred had departed in the dead of the night. He left behind a servant to inform the High King that he was in mourning for his mother and was returning to the north to offer his services to Gawayne.

Morgan smirked at the news. 'If he thought to avoid my notice, then he failed. He was the slender epicure in black, wasn't he? Morgause was wise to rid herself of that creature. I read the bones when he was born, and I warn you to beware of that young man, Artor.'

'Do you think he'll kill me?'

'No one can completely kill you, Artor. But he's wounded you already. He wants your crown, and he'll tear down every obstacle in his path to achieve his ambitions. He hates you with his entire being and plots to end your reign, so I should be sympathetic to his plans and stratagems. But how could I join with a monster such as Modred? The man is totally unworthy of my regard.'

'You flatter me with your honesty, sister. But you have judged

Modred correctly, for he even rapes children for pleasure. He is indeed a monster while you are merely terrifying.'

Morgan struck Artor's face gently with one gnarled hand. The softness of the blow was almost a caress.

'I never despised you, Artor. If your father hadn't killed mine ... well, there's no point in exchanging possibilities. But our long enmity has always been direct, and both of us have scorned the plots and the machinations of lesser creatures. Modred must never be permitted to rule, for the man's a coward and will, if allowed, become a despot.'

'Modred is more likely to stab Gawayne in the back than give any material assistance to the Otadini', Artor agreed. 'I hope Gawayne is sensible, for Modred can also claim his throne.'

'You must take care yourself, Artor', Odin warned, ignoring the presence of Morgan in his fear for his master. 'Modred has chosen to exert himself, so he's up to something. It's almost as if the loss of King Lot and Queen Morgause has given him his own version of Targo's edge.'

'Of course he's up to something, you Jute clod', Morgan said rudely. 'The man does nothing that isn't in his own interests.'

'I can't afford to worry about the possibility of threats', Artor responded. 'There are a host of real ones that are massing in the north, so I'll send word to the fortresses. The last thing we need is another Saxon summer while our strongest allies are in disarray. The Ordovice are too close to Modred's fist, and as they are the second largest of our allies, we'll really be at risk if they should fall. I'd like to believe they are loyal, but the twins were lost while carrying out my orders. Bran may harbour a grudge over the death of his brothers. And what of King Mark? I'd as lief trust a snake as accept the word of that man.'

Odin agreed. 'Targo always said—'

'United we stand, and divided we're worth sod all', Artor finished for him.

The obscenity sat awkwardly on the king's tongue. Only Morgan laughed at the jest.

The three warriors planned to attack Gronw immediately before dawn, trusting that the Druid would only have a few remaining adherents to protect him. The sun would rise behind their backs, if such a grim night could spawn a sunrise. If they were careful, they might possess the element of surprise.

The three men crawled towards the ruins on their bellies, taking advantage of any depressions that provided conceal-ment. At one point, Bedwyr was forced to slide his body through a pool of frozen blood where the workman had died at the hands of the crowd. He continued onwards, using his elbows to force his body through the packed snow.

They reached the hut, dug into the snow piled against the wooden walls and waited for their prey to emerge.

Galahad had urged a full-frontal assault in the dead of night, but Bedwyr had preached caution. They were still uncertain whether Gronw was alone, in the company of the one-eyed man or protected by some other bodyguard. Percivale reminded Galahad that there had been a number of warriors present at the abomination on the previous night.

'If we were all to die, Galahad, the Cup would stay with Gronw', Percivale argued. 'That outcome would be sheer stupidity on our part. We cannot afford to make a frontal attack without better information.'

Galahad had eventually allowed Percivale to persuade him

but even now, as they lay concealed near the doorway of the hut, Bedwyr watched Galahad with suspicion.

Suddenly, the door to the hut swung open and the one-eyed man strode out into the snow, drawing on fur-lined gloves as he went.

As he walked past, Bedwyr held his breath. Then, in an explosion of snow and muscle, he rose behind the man and used the hilt of the Arden knife to strike his enemy's skull behind the ear.

The one-eyed man had sensed the movement behind him and managed to let out a short-lived shout of warning before the force of Bedwyr's weapon silenced him.

Then Hades rained down on the three warriors.

As chance would have it, Pebr was a cautious man. He had already wakened Gronw and the four warriors who would assist them on the journey they were about to undertake. The soldiers had grumbled, but they had obeyed. Warned by the one-eyed man's cry, the four fighting men exploded through the doorway with drawn swords.

'Shite,' Bedwyr swore and began to turn.

A sword thrust that would have separated his arm from his body at the shoulder whistled harmlessly past his twisting body. Then he was kicked hard in the side and heard the unmistakable sound of his own ribs snapping.

Galahad was upon the warriors, his sword arcing in great, sweeping blows that forced them to scatter. One man went down in a fountain of arterial blood as Galahad struck upwards at his opponent's genitals.

Without pausing to glance at the man writhing in the bloody snow, Galahad went after the others.

461

Percivale darted into the hut, just as Bedwyr struggled to his feet, drawing his sword as he moved.

While Galahad was fending off two huge and very hairy warriors, Bedwyr engaged a third, using every dirty trick he had ever learned in the stews and inns of the northern cities. As he rolled away from a wicked thrust at his vitals, Bedwyr sliced through the hamstring of his adversary. The man's legs collapsed under him and, as he fell, Bedwyr stabbed him with a clean stroke just below the breastbone.

The mortally wounded swordsman hiccuped in surprise and collapsed over Bedwyr in a flurry of blood and snow. Meanwhile, Galahad was still in the process of dispatching the last warrior.

Bedwyr looked up with eyes that were almost blinded by snow and glimpsed a squat figure forcing a passage into a nearby ruin. He struggled to move the corpse that pinned him down.

'Gronw!' he snarled. He struggled painfully to his feet and pursued the fleeing Pict. He had barely reached the gaping hole in a wall of the ruin when a horse and rider exploded out of the darkness within the structure.

Gronw was escaping.

'Galahad!' Bedwyr screamed. 'Galahad! Gronw has the Cup!'

Galahad ceased to toy with his opponent. He sliced the man almost in two across the belly.

'Your horse,' Bedwyr continued to shout to Galahad, pointing to the wood where their horses were tethered. 'Ride after him! I'll join you once I find Percivale.'

Galahad needed no further urging. He ploughed through the snow and disappeared into the tree line.

Bedwyr held his aching ribs with one hand and struggled to

catch his breath. The one-eyed man was beginning to stir, so Bedwyr sacrificed the heavy lacings from his tunic and bound the man's hands securely behind his back. When he searched him, he retrieved a remarkable number of finely honed weapons from his clothing.

'He's no common mercenary,' Bedwyr muttered aloud to the corpses scattered on the churned and bloody earth around him. The sword used by the one-eyed man was decorated with a cabochon sapphire on the hilt and he wore an intaglio ring on one thumb.

The silence was unnerving.

'Percivale?' Bedwyr began to panic. 'Where are you?'

He cursed his painful ribs as he staggered through the doorway of the hut into the Stygian darkness beyond. Percivale must have fallen, for he would never have permitted Gronw to escape with the Cup if he'd been able to wield his sword.

A low sound, half moan and half warning, led Bedwyr to the furthest corner of the room. His companion lay on a tangled nest of hides, his body curled into the foetal position.

'Percivale, my friend,' Bedwyr said softly. 'What has become of you?'

Percivale's helmet had fallen off as he collapsed, but very little blood stained the hides beneath him. The earnest warrior looked like a tired child in the half-light, with his hair tousled over his forehead.

Bedwyr attempted to lift his friend's prone body, but Percivale cried out in such agony that Bedwyr decided to support his head upon a quickly structured pillow of discarded furs. He held Percivale's hand until the wounded man opened tired eyes.

'Bedwyr,' he sighed. 'Gronw escaped me.'

'Don't worry. Galahad has slipped our leash and is after him. If it takes all his life, Galahad will find that sodding Cup, and Gronw as well.'

'You must go after Galahad and stop him, Bedwyr, for Gronw will kill him.'

'Calm yourself, Percivale. We can follow our headstrong companion when you feel better.'

Percivale sighed. 'I'm a warrior, Bedwyr. There's no need to lie to me, I know that I'm dying. Please, you must save Galahad from himself, for that Cup will surely kill him, just as it has killed me.'

Percivale's eyes closed and he appeared to sleep.

Bedwyr left Percivale to take a cooling pot, thick with filthy grease, from a pack that had been abandoned near the doorway. He took it outside and scrubbed it vigorously with snow. Then he filled it with more clean snow and lugged it back into the hut.

The fire was almost dead, but Bedwyr quickly coaxed it back to life and set the snow to melting and heating. Percivale was beginning to stir by the time the water was warm, and Bedwyr helped his friend to drink.

'Are you still here?' Bedwyr had to strain to hear Percivale's thready voice. 'Ah, well. God will decide.'

'How did Gronw manage to wound you?'

'It was my own fault,' Percivale whispered. 'I had him trapped on these hides. He was desperate, so he told me the Cup was on the rafter in the corner.'

Bedwyr understood in an instant. 'You couldn't resist the temptation to hold the Cup, could you? You had to touch it with your hands, just once.'

'Aye . . . and I did hold it, for a moment.' The warrior in Percivale grimaced at his stupidity, but the priest in his soul longed to sing with joy. 'It's such a simple object. It's so plain and so ordinary that you'd find a hundred better in any market. But I felt such peace when I held it in my hands. I believed I could never be happier. I was enchanted. And then Gronw stabbed me in the back. I don't feel anything below the wound, and I'm cold . . . so very cold!'

Bedwyr was distraught. Artor's gentlest and truest warrior was fading before his eyes and he had no means to prevent his death.

'You're not easy to sneak up on, Percivale,' Bedwyr said softly. 'Even when you're distracted.'

'As I fell, Gronw snatched the Cup out of my hands, but it doesn't matter now. I can still feel its power.'

'I'm glad, Percivale. But you must rest and try to sleep.'

'I'll soon be in the deep sleep that will comfort me until the Last Judgement.' Percivale smiled. 'You must allow me to speak while I can, for my mind is clear, even though my body feels heavy and doesn't follow my commands.'

Bedwyr cradled Percivale's head in his lap and they talked sporadically as the warrior drifted in and out of consciousness.

'If you can, you must save Artor from the worst ravages of his fate, for he is my dear and tortured lord,' Percivale begged Bedwyr at one point.

'And I ask that you leave my body to the beasts,' Percivale added later.

Bedwyr could do nothing but nod sorrowfully.

'Galahad will need you soon. He thinks his faith will protect him against the might of pagan savagery. But he's young. I should have waited for you and Galahad to share the Cup and any goodness that dwelt within it. But I was captivated, and my selfishness has brought me to an ignoble end.'

'That's not true, Percivale,' Bedwyr responded. 'You're the truest and most perfect warrior I have known in my lifetime. You're among the very best of men.'

Percivale clasped Bedwyr's hand weakly.

'I was at fault, Bedwyr.' He sighed. 'The curse of the Cup is that it seeks out our deepest longings and our greatest flaws. Artor mustn't have it. And neither should any other man, unless he has a soul that is as tested and as pure as the spirit of Lucius of Glastonbury.'

Time passed and Bedwyr listened to the fire crackle. Percivale was silent but still breathing. Suddenly he gave a sharp, high cry.

'Save her! Save her! Save the babe!'

Bedwyr understood that Percivale was caught in another time and place, but then the dying man's eyes cleared and seemed unnaturally bright.

'Tell Nimue I loved her truly, nearly as much as I love God. Tell her.'

'I will, Percivale. I swear I will!'

Then Percivale smiled sweetly and died.

Bedwyr had no time to weep and no leisure in which to feel regret for the loss of a companion of the road. Percivale had been the best warrior of them all, and Bedwyr had disobeyed the wishes of his king to sit through the long vigil while

Percivale died. But now the dogs of Hades were snapping at Bedwyr's heels.

A cold, merciless anger embraced him. He strode out of the hut and into the killing ground before it, his fury seeking an outlet.

And there, like the answer to a cruel prayer, was the prone form of Pebr, conscious and angry within his bonds. The one-eyed man glared balefully at him, his lips pressed together tightly as if daring Bedwyr to force him to speak.

'I don't intend to waste time on carrion like you. You'll tell me who your master is, and Gronw's destination.'

The one-eyed man spat up at Bedwyr's face.

The Cornovii wiped the spittle away reflectively. 'The noble Percivale would have forgiven you for that particular insult, but I believe in an eye for an eye. My friend lies dead at the hands of Gronw. I intend to obtain my revenge for his suffering from you.'

'Do your worst, pig!'

Bedwyr began to collect dried wood from the hut. 'You must be cold, sir. Had I the time, I'd build a proper fire and a long, wooden spit, and I'd warm you slowly, as the Saxons once taught me to do. But I'm in something of a rush.'

The one-eyed man sneered at him.

Bedwyr built a good-sized mound of wood over the feet of his prisoner, but not before he had tied the man's thrashing legs together. Struggle as he might, Pebr couldn't dislodge the heavy logs.

Bedwyr set the wood alight.

Because the one-eyed man lay prone, no blessed smoke rose to choke his lungs and give him a kindly death – or unconsciousness. Bedwyr hardened his heart against the man's screams and he sat in the doorway of the hut cleaning his nails with feigned nonchalance.

The one-eyed man was strong, but no one can endure the pain of burning. When Pebr could no longer feel his feet, Bedwyr stoked the fire higher up his legs. He felt neither shame nor qualms at his use of torture.

Eventually, crazed with pain, the one-eyed man admitted that his true name was Pebr, although he had used many names in the service of his master, including the Outlander name of Fydyth.

'Well, Pebr, you have my word that I will douse the fire if you wish to speak to me. You have only to ask.'

Between screams, Pebr begged.

Bedwyr doused the fire with snow. Pebr whimpered and stared at his blackened feet and legs. He would have fainted if Bedwyr hadn't slapped him back to consciousness.

'I'm now going to ask you nicely. Just once. Where is Gronw going?'

'He'll follow the river to the sea and then he'll take the old Roman road north towards Bravoniacum. Friends will meet him and guide him along the journey.'

'Well done, Pebr. I've one more question. Who is your master? Who provides the gold?'

Pebr's single eye flared wildly. 'I serve no master! I have my own means!'

'Oh, dear. And we were getting along so well. I shall have to collect more wood.'

'No!' Pebr screamed, but Bedwyr began to trudge back towards the hut. 'The Brigante king pays me! I'm Brigante, and Modred is my master. I'm his servant.'

Bedwyr turned, his face showing his contempt. 'So you're a mercenary as well as a traitor. I suspected as much. Only a man who's been bought and paid for could countenance Modred as his master.'

'No, I am a patriot. Artor killed my master, Lord Simnel, and left his body to be eaten by the crows. Simnel was the true Brigante king, and I swore an oath that I would revenge him.'

Bedwyr spat into the snow near Pebr's tortured face. 'Your master stole the throne from King Luka. What did you expect Artor to do?'

'I was oath bound, as are you. What would you do in my place?'

This final plea rose to a scream as Bedwyr placed a log carefully across Pebr's genitals.

'What other devilry has your master ordered you to complete?'

Pebr answered in a rush, barely pausing for breath. 'It's all done and the pathway towards the throne of the west is prepared. That evil bitch, Morgause, is dead. I tricked one of Morgause's maidservants into placing a poison in a face powder that her mistress used every day. It took months for her to die. I also tipped King Lot out of his throne when he was alone. He couldn't rise to his feet so I left him to die like the pig that he was.'

Bedwyr felt his stomach roil with the scope of Modred's planning. 'What was the purpose of these crimes?'

'My master wanted to ensure that the Otadini don't come to Artor's aid when Modred eventually commences his revolt against the High King. The claimants to the Otadini throne will be fighting amongst themselves to determine the succession. Their self-destruction will truly be a just punishment, for they didn't lift a finger to help my master when he was their ally and needed their assistance.'

'God's teeth,' Bedwyr cursed. 'You believe you've done your liege lord a great service, but all you've achieved is to raise a storm of opposition against him. Modred will die for his treasons. How could he be so depraved that he kills his own mother?'

'But Artor and his kin will also be dead,' Pebr wailed. His muscles began to spasm and he began to weep hoarsely in pain.

'I know what I've done. I've murdered my honour to fulfil my oaths to Modred. I've killed in the dark like a felon. But the gods will understand that I've been a tool, forced to become as base as the masters who own me.'

Even though he was angry and heartsick at Percivale's death, Bedwyr felt a shiver of pity for the Brigante warrior.

'You always had a choice,' Bedwyr stated baldly. 'The strongest of oaths is secondary to the laws of the gods and of the land, but you allowed your vanity to bring you to this pass.'

Bedwyr left Pebr and returned once more to Percivale's corpse, even though reason told him that he should depart at once and go after Galahad. But he couldn't leave Percivale's mortal remains for the scavengers to feed on. He spent a precious hour stitching the corpse into a hide shroud, and still more precious energy collecting the two horses from the woods.

More time and further depletion of his strength was expended as he lashed the man-sized bundle across the back of one horse. Then, with his ribs screaming in protest at every stride, Bedwyr mounted his own horse to follow Galahad's tracks through the churned snow.

The crippled Pebr screamed at Bedwyr as the horses moved past him. 'You can't leave me like this. I'll be eaten alive! Artor has determined many times that even the worst of monsters should be granted a clean death.' Pebr's voice was hoarse with terror.

Bedwyr drew Pebr's own knife from his belt and cast it into the snow, just within reach of the tethered figure.

'You're right. Artor would grant you a speedy death with his sword.'

Pebr gritted his teeth.

'But I'm not Artor, and I live by the rules I have been taught. Since you are Celt, I'll allow you a frail chance at survival, for to be devoured by wolves while still living is not a fit death for any true warrior. The knife is within reach of your hand, if you care to strive for it. You can cut yourself free, or defend yourself from the wolves, or slit your own throat. Do as you choose, Pebr. You might even call for Modred, but I doubt he'll hear you. But be sure to disappear, Pebr, for the west can no longer support the touch of your feet on this land – assuming they ever walk again.'

Bedwyr kicked his steed's flanks and rode off through the gloom, his spare horse following docilely behind him with its gruesome burden.

He could still hear Pebr's screams long after the ruined village disappeared from sight, but Bedwyr consigned his piteous cries to the winds and the cruelty of the times.

CHAPTER XX

THE WIDOW MAKER

Gronw was no woodsman and Galahad was scarcely better, although he could ride for days without tiring. Both men were many hours ahead of Bedwyr and the Cornovii knew that he had no chance of catching them.

But Bedwyr was familiar with the land, so he knew that Bremetennacum was situated on the banks of a swift river. Instead of following the tracks of Gronw and Galahad through the wilds, he headed south towards the river itself.

Luck favoured him, or the blessings of the gods were still with him.

At best speed, he made his way to the riverbank and, by chance, to a small hamlet downstream from the town. Three brothers and their families dwelt there in a cluster of conical huts at a place where the current was slowed by a long bend in the river. One of the men farmed the river fields, another worked as a smith, while a third brother netted fish and salted them for sale in Bremetennacum.

'Your river is fast-flowing,' Bedwyr observed to the fisherman, who was gutting his catch from the previous night before spitting them on a timber frame for smoking.

'Aye,' the fisherman replied warily as he cautiously eyed Bedwyr's body armour, the hide-wrapped corpse and the two huge horses.

'It moves faster than a horse can gallop.'

'Aye, my lord,' the fisherman muttered. 'A horse needs rest. The river doesn't need to sleep, and she's always busy, whether it's the flood tide or the ebb tide.'

'So your coracle could take me downstream to the mouth of the river very quickly?'

'Aye, if I was foolish enough to give it to you.'

Bedwyr stripped a golden ring from his finger.

The fisherman's eyes opened wide. 'I can't eat gold. I need my coracle to fish.'

Frustrated, Bedwyr hunted through Percivale's purse and found one gold coin, two of silver, and a handful of base metal scraps.

'I wish to use your coracle for a short time only. If we can make an agreement that meets your approval, I'll leave my horses with you until I return. I can pay for the use of your vessel.' He thrust Percivale's coins into the hands of the fisherman.

The fisherman grinned and exposed two brown fangs and a gaping hole where his front teeth should have been. He could make another coracle in a day, as any fisherman knew. The great ones could be very strange, but if they gave him buttery, yellow gold for very little, they could be as mad as they chose.

'Do you know how to steer a coracle?' the fisherman asked. He removed his nets from the circular vessel and carried it towards the river, upside down and above his head.

'I'll soon learn.'

In truth, Bedwyr hated the water, and the thought of spinning out of control in a tiny, hide-covered construction of bent branches made him feel ill.

The fisherman gave him a cursory explanation of how to control the small boat and showed him how a flattened paddle could be used as a makeshift rudder.

Cursing vilely to hide his terror, Bedwyr splashed into the craft, which spun wildly as if with a mind of its own. Clutching his paddle in both hands, he struggled to control the contents of his stomach.

'What if you don't come back?' the fisherman yelled as Bedwyr pushed away from the riverbank.

'Keep the horses, and send the body of my friend to his ancestors,' Bedwyr bellowed in reply over the rush of the water.

The current soon had the coracle in its powerful grip, and the boat was swept away downstream. Straining his muscles to hold the coracle level, and gasping with pain from his broken ribs, Bedwyr managed to keep the coracle in the main channel. Small villages and single huts rushed by him at a dizzying speed. Nausea threatened to overcome him, but he managed to defeat the motion sickness by concentrating on the horizon and maintaining a small semblance of control over the boat.

At breakneck speed, the coracle spun and twisted through the water, zigzagging from bank to bank in a drunken reel. Bedwyr and his craft eventually reached the mouth of the river where the broad, slower waters pumped into the grey sea. Wet, cold and miserable, he came to journey's end on a broad sandbank that allowed him to wade through knee-high water to dry land, lugging his craft with him.

Bedwyr had lost all track of time in his madcap voyage down the stream. Two hours or five could easily have passed. The stars wheeled above him and the white water of the river had a ghostly gleam to his tired eyes. He found a small tangle of stunted bushes, wrapped his worn cloak around his chilled body and slept on the bare, sandy ground.

Early morning came dimly with a wintry sun. Angry gulls wheeled and fought as they snatched shells from the pebbled beach before dropping them, again and again, until the flesh inside the molluscs was exposed.

Even the birds are killers, Bedwyr thought. He had never tortured a man before and the sound of the gulls calling on the wind echoed the screams of the doomed Pebr.

The beach was empty and unmarked by the tracks of either men or beasts. The old Roman road crossed a narrow section of the river where sandbanks created a series of shallows, and only a few narrow channels of deeper water led towards the grey sea to the west. A bridge had once spanned the deeper channels and the ruins still remained, but a horse could easily swim across, especially on the ebb tide. From the river, the road ran north, skirting hills and small forests before heading directly to Bravoniacum.

After retrieving the coracle from the riverbank and carrying it to higher ground beside the derelict Roman bridge, Bedwyr settled down to rest and wait, still marvelling that he had managed to outstrip two men on strong horses who had a head start of almost a full day.

In fact, Gronw had arrived during the night. The Druid had found the place where the promised guides would meet him, and he had built a telltale fire. Bedwyr saw the thin plume of smoke as it rose against the greyer sky, upstream from where he waited.

Gronw may have caused much trouble for Artor, but the man's a fool, Bedwyr thought incredulously. Only an idiot would light a fire when he's being hunted.

On the silent feet of a born predator, Bedwyr moved further upstream and scouted around Gronw's camp in an effort to find Galahad. If they were to capture Gronw and obtain possession of the Cup, the Pict must be taken before his guides arrived to protect him.

A twig snapped ahead of him, and Bedwyr fell into a fighting crouch.

'Lord blight him, where is he?' a voice growled huskily, and Bedwyr realized that Galahad had managed to track Gronw through the wilds successfully, more proof that Gronw was inept in the woods.

Bedwyr was beside Galahad before the prince was aware of his presence. Galahad's first inklings of danger occurred when a shadow became solid at the same instant that invisible fingers were clamped over his mouth.

'It's only me, Galahad,' Bedwyr hissed into his ear. 'You couldn't possibly make any more noise than you're already doing. Gronw is camped only one hundred yards away, and the noise of your stumbling about will carry to him.'

'What are you doing here? Where's Percivale?' Galahad hissed.

'Percivale's dead. He was slain by Gronw, stabbed in the back when he took the Cup. Your grandparents are also dead. They were both assassinated on the orders of Modred, and we now have proof that he's the guiding force behind Artor's troubles.'

Galahad's eyes narrowed with emotion.

'Keep quiet, please,' Bedwyr ordered before the prince could speak. 'I'll circle round behind Gronw's fire and we can approach him from two sides. I'll gain his attention first, then you enter his camp.'

Without waiting for Galahad's agreement, and taking shameless advantage of the tragic tidings dumped unceremoniously on the prince, Bedwyr slid away into the sparse cover.

Galahad swore under his breath and tried to make his way silently towards the plume of smoke. He pushed all thoughts of the murder of his grandparents and Percivale's sad death to one side and focused on his vision of the Cup. Soon he would earn his place in history. He realized that his feet were numb with cold within his damp boots, but he cared nothing for personal discomfort. If this path led to his heart's desire, he would gladly walk through freezing water for hours.

Quickly he reached a small clearing. Within it, the figure of Gronw hunched like a miserable black lump that blocked Galahad's view of the fire. His horse was tethered to one side. If the jumble of soft sounds was any indication, the fugitive was talking to himself and rubbing his tattooed hands together.

Gronw thrust his hand into his robe and drew out something that glinted in the early morning sunlight.

'The Cup!' Galahad breathed.

Blinded by the sight of the vessel and deaf to the orders given by Bedwyr, Galahad drew his sword and strode into the clearing. Gronw's eyes widened and then darted from side to side as he sought a means of escape.

Then Bedwyr stepped into the clearing behind Gronw. The

Pict turned in alarm, and his face twisted with a fury and loathing so intense that Bedwyr almost stepped back. A wall of malevolent hatred flowed out from the troll-like form.

'You're both dead men . . . and your master will soon follow you!'

Gronw moved sideways in an attempt to keep his enemies in view.

'As is that other thief who tried to steal Ceridwen's Cup from me. Nothing you can say, or do, will save you from the fate that is soon to befall you, for you still can't smell the scent of innocent blood upon your hands. Ceridwen will have her revenge, and she'll devour your souls.'

'Keep back, Galahad,' Bedwyr warned. 'This charlatan carries at least one knife, and its blade is still stained with Percivale's blood.'

'You think to steal Ceridwen's Cup,' Gronw hissed. 'Never! Ceridwen will strike you dead, just as she destroyed your comrade.'

With an oath, Galahad raised his sword, but Bedwyr shouted for the prince to halt.

'He's baiting you, Galahad! He's trying to draw you towards him. This Pictish dog is incapable of fighting a man face to face unless his opponent is old and unarmed.'

Bedwyr moved closer, his right hand holding his sword loosely before his body in the warrior's fighting crouch, the Arden knife in his left hand, tucked in close against his body.

Outnumbered and cornered, Gronw struck like the serpent he was. One hand darted out, gripped the pannikin heating over the open fire and threw the boiling water over Galahad. The other hand hurled a blazing log at Bedwyr.

Galahad cursed loudly as hot water scalded his left hand and forearm. Bedwyr was more fortunate, and was able to deflect the log with his forearm.

Seeing his chance, Gronw made a desperate break towards freedom, but Bedwyr had anticipated his movement and took a single step towards him, slicing at the knees of his quarry. Gronw howled and dodged, thrusting out his staff so that it caught Bedwyr across his wounded ribs, momentarily blinding his vision with pain.

Galahad ignored the throbbing agony in his burned flesh and moved faster than Gawayne had ever managed, even in his prime. One moment, Gronw was beginning to run; the next instant, his head leapt from his shoulders. His torso staggered on nerveless legs for half a step and then fell, spraying blood over Bedwyr's legs and feet.

'Shite!' Bedwyr swore.

Galahad bent over the headless body and ripped the Cup out of Gronw's robe, his face transfigured with evanescent joy.

'So that's what all the fuss has been about,' Bedwyr marvelled. 'It's not much, is it?'

Galahad simply cradled the Cup with awe.

'May I hold it, Galahad?' Bedwyr asked. 'I'd like to know what it is about that thing that made Percivale believe was worth his life.'

'No! Get back!' Galahad snarled, his handsome face contorted in anger. 'You're pagan, you've no right to touch the Cup. Back away!' He clutched the Cup to his heart with his reddened, blistering left hand, while his eyes glittered with manic suspicion. He swung his sword slowly until it pointed at Bedwyr's chest.

'I'm Bedwyr, Galahad. I'm not your enemy, and I don't want your sodding cup.'

'If you value your life, heathen, stand back. I, Galahad, have won the Cup, I have achieved Artor's quest. The triumph is mine alone. Go back to your forests and your pagan Druids.'

Bedwyr held his open hands away from his body and slowly backed away from his companion.

'Whatever you decide, Galahad. But what shall we do now?'

Galahad's face was transfigured by religious ecstasy. Bedwyr had heard of the condition but he had never believed that a man's reason could be lost over a religious experience. Yet what else explained Galahad's behaviour?

Galahad began to walk towards the sea. 'I'm going back to Cadbury. You can go your own way to your Satan.'

Bedwyr looked at his companion's retreating back in bemusement. 'I'd rather stay with you, my friend. I need your protection.' Bedwyr padded past the prince so he could face him. 'How will we get to Cadbury? It's many weeks of riding.'

Bedwyr realized that he was talking to the prince as if he was a small child.

Galahad continued to walk, clutching the Cup to his chest. Bedwyr was forced to jog beside him.

'My horse is dead, so I must walk,' the prince replied evenly.

'You're going the wrong way, Galahad. Let me show you the shortest route to Cadbury. We can use Gronw's horse – it's back in the clearing.'

Galahad took no notice.

'Stop this nonsense.' Bedwyr shouted, standing directly in Galahad's path.

Galahad struck Bedwyr across the head with an absent-minded, but numbing, left-handed blow. The blistered skin on the prince's hand broke open but, if he suffered any pain, he gave no sign.

Bedwyr fell and rolled away from Galahad's dangerous feet.

He shook his head to clear it and then launched himself painfully at his companion's knees, bringing Galahad down, face forward. The Cup flew out of Galahad's hands and rolled on to a tussock.

'So you want to steal the Cup?' Galahad snarled, and threw himself at Bedwyr's sprawled body with vicious, murderous intent. He clawed at Bedwyr's eyes and sought to find his throat with his iron thumbs.

Bedwyr twisted and turned, punched at Galahad's genitals and tore at his companion's long braids, anything that would keep those powerful fingers from obtaining a death grip on his throat.

He fumbled for the Arden knife in its scabbard at his waist and managed to find the hilt of the weapon. Somehow, he contrived to drag the knife free and drove the keen blade up into Galahad's body between the side lacings of his breast-plate. Galahad didn't loosen his grip on Bedwyr's throat as the Arden knife pierced muscle and flesh, so Bedwyr twisted the blade.

Galahad's body slumped and the prince rolled away as abruptly as he had commenced the attack.

What have I done? Bedwyr thought as he fought to drag air into his aching lungs.

What have I done? Galahad wondered, as he felt an almost peaceful weakness wash over him.

'Sweet Jesus!' Bedwyr swore when he had caught his breath.

His broken ribs made him gasp and his throat and neck pulsed with dull pain.

He used his elbows to slowly drag himself to Galahad's side, the Arden knife ready for use in his hand.

'Oh, Galahad!' he moaned. 'Why did you make me do this thing to you?'

'I think I've been a little mad, Bedwyr,' Galahad whispered painfully. 'I've been obsessed with the Cup, for I can't remember a night when it hasn't been part of my dreams. I thought you intended to steal it from Mother Church.'

'I'm so bitterly sorry to have harmed you, my lord,' Bedwyr whispered. 'We must search for a healer to mend your wound.'

'Help me to my feet, Bedwyr,' Galahad ordered. 'We must put the Cup in some safe place, for only holy hands may dare to hold it.'

Gingerly, Bedwyr scooped up the Cup with a scrap torn from his tunic. It was made of base metal and appeared quite battered. To Bedwyr, it was valueless, yet it had caused the deaths of many good men. He thrust it into his shirt. Miserably, he wadded another piece of his tunic to stem the blood from Galahad's wound. Then he helped his companion to his feet.

'Your wound need not be mortal, Galahad. Cleansing, bandaging, rest and care may yet see you well.'

'If it's God's will that I'm to die in this quest, then so be it,' Galahad replied in a monotone. 'But first, I want to cleanse myself from sin in the sea.'

'We waste time, my friend. You needn't perish. For the sake of your God, you must see sense!'

'Don't be an ass, Bedwyr,' Galahad replied in his usual

superior tone. Unaccountably, the prince's scorn made Bedwyr feel a little better.

With the help of Bedwyr's shoulder, Galahad began to walk, his steps becoming firmer as he slowly gained some balance. The two men retraced their steps past Gronw's corpse towards the saddlebags that were lying beside the dying fire.

'How did you manage to reach Gronw so quickly?' Galahad asked painfully as they struggled towards the river edge.

'I used a coracle. I've never paddled one of the infernal things before, so I'm lucky to be alive to tell the tale. I can't swim.'

Galahad tried to laugh, but he coughed and spat blood into the grass. Bedwyr averted his gaze in shame.

'Your coracle will suit my purposes admirably.'

Eventually, Galahad eased himself on to a large stone that had fallen from the Roman bridge.

'The Romans were great builders,' Galahad said softly as he looked in appreciation at the stonework of the structure above him. 'It's one of the reasons that King Artor has been so successful, for he's always tried to retain the best that they left behind.'

Bedwyr was surprised by the sensitivity of Galahad's words, for the Otadini prince was hardly an introspective man.

'I'm beginning to think that he could do without the bad influence of Lucius's Cup,' Galahad went on. 'I won the Cup in fair combat, so I think I should be the one to determine its fate.' He smiled at Bedwyr with a hint of pride. 'You may return it to me now.'

'You won't try to kill me again?' Bedwyr asked carefully as he drew the relic out of his tunic and handed it to the prince.

'I don't think I have the strength to try,' Galahad replied ruefully. 'It will be coming with me on my journey, so there'll be one less temptation for evil to use.'

Bedwyr stared into Galahad's stern, beautiful face. 'Where are you going?'

'I'll head for Mona Island in your coracle. The holy men there will cure me if I survive the journey. If the Cup of Jesus should reach the priests of Mona, they will protect it with their lives. If not, the sea will take it and keep it safe from the impious hands of mortal men until the Last Judgement.'

'You can't reach Mona in a coracle,' Bedwyr stated, aghast at Galahad's intentions, for the crossing could take many hard days.

'With God's grace, I shall complete the journey. But you mustn't look for me among the courts of men, for I've lost the right to stand beside my fellow warriors.'

Bedwyr was stricken. 'I'm the only person who knows about your lapse, and I won't tell anyone, because I'm the one who has sorely wounded you.'

'For the sake of my resolve, Bedwyr, I beg you to be silent. Help me into the coracle and then I'll be gone. If you won't assist me, I'll launch it myself.'

Bedwyr realized that Galahad was in deadly earnest.

'I won't stop you, but you must have fresh water if you're to survive the journey. Isn't suicide a mortal sin in your faith?'

Bedwyr ran back to Gronw's camp to snatch up a leather bladder of water and then hurried back to Galahad. With regret, he helped his companion to the water's edge and dragged the coracle with his free hand.

He stood knee-deep in the water while he loaded the water

skin and the remainder of their rations. Galahad sat quietly through the operation, the Cup held loosely in both hands.

'Why didn't the Cup betray you, Bedwyr? Why could you hold it, and yet it had no power to touch your heart?'

Bedwyr held the frail boat steady with both hands and frowned.

'My eyes saw the Cup as a fragment of old metal and nothing more. Lucius of Glastonbury used it to hold clean water, the purpose for which it was first fashioned. It may have held sacred blood, or poetic inspiration, or the hopes of good men, but its value was always in the hands that held it. I'll not revere an object, and nor will I kill, or die, for such a thing. But I would be prepared to die for Lucius or Percivale. I would even be prepared to give my life for you, Galahad. Yes, I'd die for human hands and hearts, but not for that thing. I've seen too much death and sent too many men to the shadows myself to give a damn for any object, regardless of its power.'

Galahad was silent, as if sunk deeply in thought. Then he rose painfully to his feet.

'Farewell, my friend,' he said as he struggled into the flimsy vessel that Bedwyr held steady for him. 'I hope to see you in my heaven one day, even though you will always be a pagan. You've proved to be a far wiser man than I shall ever be.'

He gripped Bedwyr's wrist in the time-honoured sign of friendship.

'When you speak with Artor, perhaps you shouldn't tell the whole truth of the Cup. Some tales are best embroidered if the truth can cause harm. I ask only that you tell my father that I achieved my avowed task.'

'Is there nothing else I should tell him?' Galahad had made

no mention of messages of love or regret, even to his mother.

'There's nothing more to say', Galahad replied.

Bedwyr would remember the Otherworld calm and the eldritch glow on the face of the prince for many years to come, and would wonder if the sacrifice of such an extraordinary life was necessary to expunge a momentary lapse of honour.

Then the fast-flowing current gripped the coracle and its passenger, and Bedwyr began to weep for the loss of his companion.

When he reached the hamlet where he had left his horses and Percivale's body, the fisherman wondered at his ragged dress and the lines of pain and grief in his face.

Bedwyr dismounted and apologized for losing the coracle, but the fisherman simply jerked his head towards the river where a new coracle rested, upside down, on the grassy bank. Bedwyr grinned in amusement, a response that convinced the fisherman that this scarecrow was daft.

'Keep this horse in lieu of your lost vessel, my friend. I've no further use for the beast and I hope you have better luck than the last man who owned it. I'll simply take my property and leave you in peace.'

'We put the corpse in the shed, so the snows will have kept him fresh. I hope it worked.'

'I'm sure you did your best. Does your kindness extend to providing me with a meal and a store of grain for my horses?'

'Aye, I'm no thief. For such a beast, you can take whatever grain and fish you need. A horse will make the ploughing easier.' The fisherman peered between the beast's legs and grinned with real delight. 'He's a stallion too. Shite, he's worth a jug of cider, if your lordship isn't too proud to drink a poor man's tipple. Aye, this big boy will pay his way with the mares around these parts. It were a good day for me when you bought my old coracle, my lord.'

When Bedwyr departed for Bremetennacum, he left with a large bag of grain, and a supply of smoked fish and meat that would last through his journey. He had developed a liking for these laconic peasants and their untroubled approach to life's tragedies and unexpected windfalls. He wished them well.

At Deva, Bedwyr rejected the main route leading to the south in order to visit Lady Nimue at Caer Gai. Dragging his friend's corpse all the way to Cadbury was impractical, so Bedwyr decided to ask Nimue if Percivale's remains could lie in peace close to her home.

Little more than a goat track snaked through the tall, grey-black mountains to the eyrie of Caer Gai. The route was cruel and Bedwyr was forced to lead his horses on foot to spare the beast's hooves from the flinty and treacherous terrain. His own feet suffered too, for his boots had split apart through hard usage and water-damage.

'Who'd choose to live in this desolate place?' he asked the wind, in the absence of any living companion and to break the cold, aching silence. Above him, the mountains frowned down on the bare track and an occasional hawk circled in the thin air. Sometimes, out of loneliness, Bedwyr caught himself speaking to Percivale whose corpse should have long since been buried.

Eventually, he arrived at a remote village in a fold of the hills and he recognized the influence of Myrddion Merlinus. The people were hardy and stunted, like the trees that set their roots in barren earth, but they were well fed and clean. They had probably dwelt in this isolated, unforgiving place for generations beyond counting. Bedwyr noted the cunning irrigation that fed their crops and explained the prosperity of the village. What arable land existed had been ingeniously put to work, and well-fed goats and sheep were penned where they could be protected from the extremes of weather.

He asked for the whereabouts of Lady Nimue from each person he met, but every villager steered him unceremoniously towards the headman of the village. The farmers regarded him with suspicious, unfriendly eyes, while large-eyed children clutched their mothers' skirts and sucked their thumbs. The obvious evidence that the stranger carried a corpse made him fearsome to these simple folk, and Bedwyr noticed that several of the women warded themselves and their children from the curse of evil magic.

'I mean Lady Nimue no harm,' he told the headman. 'Her son, Taliesin, is well-known to me. I bring news ... and the body of her friend.'

The headman continued to shake his head, as if he feared Bedwyr would spirit the Lady of the Lake clean away when their backs were turned.

'Please, sir, I have travelled for many weary miles afoot to deliver a message from the dead to the Lady of the Lake. Do you dare to anger a shade because you stood between his desires and the lady whom he loved? I know the lady will be glad of my arrival.'

So Bedwyr alternated between cajoling and threatening until the headman's fat, squat wife bade him send the lordling to the mistress; she would know immediately if there was any wrong in the intentions of her visitor.

Aided by sketchy directions, Bedwyr eventually found the lake, still partly frozen and pearl-grey under warming skies. From there, he travelled to a strange hilltop villa that sprawled around and above the trunk and roots of a riven oak.

'The legends live on, I see,' Bedwyr grunted to the corpse of Percivale as he stumbled on bleeding feet towards a metal-bound, oak door. Like the beggar he resembled, Bedwyr longed for warmth, fresh bread and, desperately, for sleep.

He used the hilt of the Arden knife to pound upon the heavy door. When it was opened, a vivid, smiling young man stood on the threshold. His eyes opened wide as he saw, and smelt, Percivale's remains.

'Rest, friend, for exhaustion covers you like the shroud that your companion wears. Let me take your horse – and his mate, who carries his burden with growing unease. I'll feed, water and curry their coats until they are content. My mother waits in the great room for you.'

The young man slipped past Bedwyr, leaving him to enter a short, flagged passage that opened into a room full of colour, strange weavings and the scent of sweet wood and dried flowers. A fire blazed in a stone hearth in the centre of the room and several huge, shaggy mastiffs sprawled on the warm stone floor at its base. They lifted their heads as he entered, and Bedwyr saw their noses catch the smell of death that he carried with him. They would have growled to match their raised hackles, but a crisp voice hushed them, and they dropped back into their warm sloth.

'Enter, friend,' a woman's voice greeted him from the corner of the room where a great loom stood. 'I don't remember your name, but your face is familiar. You are one of the men who fought with Myrddion and Artor at Mori Saxonicus, aren't you?'

Although the ceiling of the room was tall and the fire smoke was dissipated by cunning use of hide flaps, the air was dim and glittering with dust motes so that Bedwyr's tired eyes were almost blind. Then the woman moved towards him and Bedwyr immediately recognized the Nimue he had first glimpsed at a distance, so many years earlier, for what man could forget her silver hair or her pearl complexion? But now her beauty seemed incandescent in the filtered firelight. Her simple robe of unbleached wool moved around her with a memory of life. Her hair shone on her shoulders and back as she slid into the light.

Bedwyr fell to his knees in exhaustion and superstitious dread. He lowered his head in supplication.

'My lady, I bear a message to you from the dead, and I beg your forgiveness for the sorrow that I bring. I ask that you bless my friend and give him peace and a final resting place.'

Her breath caught in her throat. 'Taliesin! My son, Taliesin. He's not your dead companion, is he? Do not fear to speak the truth, for I'll not harm the bringer of bad news. But tell me quickly, for I can scarcely think for fear.'

'No, madam. I'd not bring your son to you unheralded. I swear to you that Taliesin was hale and happy when I left Cadbury.'

Relief showed clearly on her face.

'Come, my lord, rise. I'm not a woman of worth or power, and my sons would be amused to see a man on his knees at my feet.'

An unobtrusive servant woman knocked at the doorway.

Nimue instructed her to bring food and wine. Then Nimue led the exhausted Bedwyr to a heavy bench. Only then did she notice the blood that caked his rag-covered feet.

'Your poor feet!' She exclaimed. 'They are in sore need of attention.'

She knelt to unwrap the crude bandages and examine each foot, toe by toe. Bedwyr protested that one of her servants could dress his cuts and blisters, but Nimue ignored his suggestions. She clucked over deep, half-scabbed gashes and sniffed at the wounds to assess whether infection was present. Then she left him to fetch what she needed.

The warmth of the fire slowly seeped through to his bones. As he leaned back against the stone wall, his eyelids drooped. His tired mind reminded him dimly that his tasks were not yet completed, but the luxury and comfort of his surroundings lulled him as if he was a babe. His head nodded on to his breast and he slept.

He awoke when Nimue returned and forced him to endure having his feet washed in bowls of warm water. The filth and corruption that soon stained the water embarrassed Bedwyr. He protested and would have pulled away from her touch, but her clear blue eyes stilled him.

Nimue found an unguent on her shelves that smelled of sheep's fat and smeared it over his wounds. It soon began to dull the throbbing ache of his sores. Then she bound his feet firmly with clean rags.

'These poor, abused feet have carried you many miles to my door. What is your name, master, for I find I cannot remember.'

'I am Bedwyr, whom Artor called the Arden Knife,' he replied slowly. 'I have walked and ridden from Deva and, before that, from Bremetennacum.'

'You have come far then,' Nimue replied. She waited with perfect stillness

'Forgive me—'

'My son says your second horse bears a corpse,' she interrupted, her forehead furrowed.

He sighed. 'The body is all that remains of my friend, Percivale, warrior and favourite of the High King and all who knew him.'

'Percivale? My Perce is dead?'

'Aye, my lady. He fell beside me at Bremetennacum in the service of the High King.'

Nimue's eyes filled with tears. Mutely, she folded her hands in her lap and allowed her sorrow to flow without check or shame.

The silence in the room was profound; Bedwyr could hear the evening wind outside the walls.

After a time, Nimue spoke.

'Long ago, when I was a babe in the kitchens of Venonae, he was my brother in all but blood,' Nimue explained. 'He saved me from scalds and burns more than once. He dried my tears and told me wondrous stories of pigs and sheep on the farms. And at Cadbury Tor, he served the ancient Targo with all the purity of his love, risking his life with me when plague struck the citadel. Why would Fortuna desire the life of sweet Percivale?'

Bedwyr had no sensible reason to offer her. 'Percivale asked me to tell you that he always loved you. Perhaps his declaration seems simple, but Percivale was a true warrior whose heart was ever innocent and pure.'

'Yes, he was always so. But has he no wife or children who long for his presence? Why have you brought him to me?'

Bedwyr fiddled with his ragged tunic. Lady Nimue did not know she had been Percivale's only love. Should he burden her further, for truth isn't always kind.

'You must tell me, Bedwyr,' she pleaded, as if she could read his mind, and the warrior knew there was nothing he could deny this woman.

'Percivale never wed, for his heart had long been lost to you, my lady. But you mustn't frown or weep over his choice, for my friend understood that Lord Myrddion was the only man you ever desired. One's heart feels what it chooses, whether we desire it or not.'

The lady wept softly. Her son entered the room and came swiftly to comfort her with strong arms and a full heart, while Bedwyr sat by the fire, cloaked in his own misery.

Suddenly, in the way of this magical place and the family who seemed to have no need for words, soup appeared before him on a small table and wine came in an earthenware cup. A servant pressed him to eat and drink and, by his side, Lady Nimue sat quietly until he was finished.

'My son, Glynn, will take you to a warm pallet where you may sleep.' The storms of her sorrow had been washed out of her extraordinary eyes. 'You have carried your burdens like a true warrior and I fear you will bear many more before you reach the final darkness. When you have rested, I wish to hear more of my Perce and how he died. And then we will consign Percivale's body to the fire.'

✟ ✟ ✟

The sun revealed the dust motes that danced through the shafts of light stealing through the shutters. Bedwyr watched the light, his eyes still cloudy with sleep.

Instantly, Glynn was beside his bed.

This whole family seems able to materialize at will, Bedwyr thought remotely, his mental processes slow and heavy. She drugged my wine, I suppose, for I have slept far too long.

He found that his feet were so swollen that they could barely support his weight, but a short staff stood beside his pallet and Nimue's son helped him to his feet and supported him, until he could bear the pain of hobbling.

'Mother has laid Percivale out in our drying room. She has washed his body and has dressed him in fine clothes. Would you like to see him one last time before the burning?'

Bedwyr looked up into the eyes of the tall young man. 'Yes. I would like to see Percivale once more. Your mother must be made of stern stuff, for he was two weeks dead at least when I arrived at your home. I've lost all track of time, but corruption must have ruined his face and body, even though he was near frozen.'

The boy smiled. 'You will come to know that Mother is a remarkable woman. The hill people will also attend the burning of Lord Percivale out of their love for her. Those lucky persons who are loved by the Lady of the Lake are considered near to sacred in these mountains.'

As they talked, Bedwyr found himself being led out of the strange, sprawling building and into a low, stone outhouse where herbs, smoked meat and dried fish hung from the ceiling in a miracle of good housekeeping.

A low bier had been hastily constructed from timber and

placed in the centre of the room. On it, like the marble effigy of a warrior, Percivale lay in state.

Nimue rose from Percivale's side as Bedwyr entered the room.

In death, Percivale appeared grimly pale. His lips were livid, but were parted slightly as if he was about to speak, while his closed eyes, sunken and purpled as they were, still retained their long lashes. Percivale's hair had been washed thoroughly and lay, unplaited, around his shoulders. He had been dressed in a white woollen robe that was a little too long for him, and Bedwyr guessed that from beyond the grave, Myrddion Merlinus had provided this last gift to a brave old friend.

Unassisted, Bedwyr hobbled forward and caressed the sweet-smelling, silken hair.

'It feels alive,' he whispered, forcing back his tears.

Nimue touched Bedwyr's outstretched hand respectfully.

'I choose to believe that nothing that has lived is ever truly dead. We change, as Myrddion would have said. Our bodies transmute into ashes or earth, and then enrich other living things. Perhaps the flowers themselves are really the faces of the long dead and the tall grasses are their hair.'

Bedwyr swallowed. 'Such a pretty concept, my lady, and one that gives comfort to those of us who remain. But this shell is not Percivale – not to me, anyhow. His essence fled on a long journey and he now dwells in a place that is beyond our comprehension. I hope he's found his heaven.'

Nimue smiled and the little room seemed warmer.

'If anyone could be assured of immortality, it would be Percivale.' She looked with love at the body of the departed man. 'Dearest Perce, you were truly my brother.'

Then she did what Bedwyr could never have done, for she kissed the open mouth of the corpse with lingering sweetness. She stroked Percivale's hand one last time and then led Bedwyr out into the clear morning sunshine.

'My sons are gathering the wood for Percivale's pyre and, at sunset, we'll set the mountains aflame as we speed his soul towards his heaven. But, while we wait, you must tell me how my Perce died.'

Bedwyr explained the history of the Cup, what was known of its enigmatic journey to Britain and the bloody carnage that had followed its theft from the tomb of Bishop Lucius. He described how Percivale had perished and the role that the Cup had played in his wasted death. When he had nothing further to say, Nimue gazed at him, her head on one side like a neat grey bird, and considered what she had heard.

'Whenever a symbol is turned into something more important than reality, it becomes dangerous. Percivale's momentary obsession killed him, and the same flaw mortally wounded Galahad. If he has died as he sailed across the sea, then let us pray that the Cup lies in deep water where men cannot search it out.'

'Whenever I held the relic, I always saw an old, battered cup, and nothing else,' Bedwyr said reflectively. 'It meant nothing to me.'

'You are fortunate that you don't desire what the Cup promised to the others. You are a plain man, Bedwyr, and, at bottom, you believe in little beyond your forests and the people you love.'

'How faithless I sound,' Bedwyr replied ruefully.

'Not faithless, Bedwyr. Your beliefs lie in the slow patterns of the seasons, in the beauty of the forests, in the wonder of the stars and in your loyalty to Artor, don't they?'

'Aye, they do. Forests and stars rarely betray us and if some god or gods reside in the spirits of the earth, then I am content to believe in them. I've not been Christian since Caer Fyrddin. I'm not even a pagan any more, so I suppose that makes me nothing.'

Nimue pressed his hand and captured his eyes with hers in a long gaze. Bedwyr felt her urgency.

'You are very far from nothing, Bedwyr. You'll be remembered down the centuries for your truthfulness and sincerity. In days to come, when your faith is tested, you must remember the pursuit of honour and the obsessions displayed by Galahad and Percivale. You'll remember then how frail we are – and you must be kind.'

Bedwyr wondered what lay behind her words and the urgency that threaded them together.

'My Percivale is the reason that we have met again,' Nimue said, her tone lighter, 'so I'm grateful to find some small grace on such a sad day.'

Bedwyr nodded in heartfelt agreement.

And so the warrior and the widow sat companionably in the sunshine, eating and drinking as they wished, while Nimue's sons and several villagers raised Percivale's pyre on the highest point of ground overlooking the valley.

At sunset, Nimue excused herself. When she returned, she was clad in a grey-green robe and she was wearing her electrum necklace, for she wished to honour Percivale as best she could. The corpse had been placed on top of the pyre, and the villagers gradually struggled up to the knoll to watch the ritual cremation. They were excited at this brief holiday from the tedium of their usual lives, and the women carried what little bounty in foliage and early buds that the terrain permitted.

Nimue's son poured oil over the lower levels of the pyre and Nimue began to sing a strange, haunting song extolling the life and death of a brave warrior. Her voice was high and not overly strong, but because of the silence of the small crowd, her unaccompanied voice echoed over the knoll.

She sang of the farm where Percivale was born and of the kitchens where he worked, how he had braved the anger of a king to go to court, and his humility in service and sacrifice for his friends. When her song ended, many villagers wept without shame.

Bedwyr also wept when he showed the crowd the sword of Percivale, a plain but beautiful weapon that had been crafted by a master blacksmith. Then Nimue's second son climbed the pyre and rested the sword hilt under Percivale's folded hands.

Bedwyr lit the fire.

The flames rose high in the air from the oil-soaked branches, and the smoke melded into the grey of early evening. The women wailed as if they were professional mourners, but Bedwyr realized their cries were marks of respect given to a figure who was less a man than an effigy of valour who had come to them from another world.

So this is how gods and heroes are created, Bedwyr thought to himself.

Percivale's ashes, mingled with the remains of the pyre, were permitted to disperse with the onset of the early spring rains. Only his sword was recovered, although the hilt was badly damaged by the heat of the flames. Nimue would have given it to Bedwyr, but he refused to touch it.

'No other hand but Percivale's should care for his sword. Let your son, Rhys, turn the weapon into ploughshares, for such were Percivale's beliefs. Or reforge it into another blade for some other good man who might have use of it.'

Nimue smiled sadly. 'Not all men have Percivale's purity of heart, and kings cannot always travel the straight roads that he chose.'

'My lady?' Bedwyr was still thinking about Percivale's sword.

'Tomorrow, and in the days to come, Percivale's ashes will begin to enrich the earth. He will be gone and will be remembered only by those who knew him. Such a gentle fate is not permitted to all men. Remember, when you stand in your forest, that we are all fallible creatures who search for forgiveness.'

'I'll remember, even if I don't understand,' Bedwyr promised.

'You will,' she said and Nimue's eyes were suddenly hard, like mountain stone.

When Bedwyr's health was restored, he rode away from Caer Gai, taking nothing but provisions, a letter for Taliesin and a memory of quiet sweetness. In the war that was to come, the House of the Oak Tree was often in his thoughts when the rest of his world was filled with brutality, betrayal and pain.

CHAPTER XXI

COMRADES IN BLOOD

Mother,

I write in haste, south of Deva, as we head north to meet the Brigante and their allies in the field. An old hill man has promised to deliver this message in exchange for sanctuary, but I cannot predict if you will read my words before we meet the enemy.

Artor is in pain and I am afraid that he expects to die in the coming conflict. He refuses to speak of his fears, and has chosen the ground for the battle, just as if he believes his luck is unchanged. I tell him – whenever he will listen – that luck will not win him the field in this conflict. He has a need for better strategic planning and improved tactical ability from his commanders. More importantly, he needs to have belief in himself, a truth he knows in his heart. But he is very tired and sickened by guilt and grief for those who must die.

I intend to fight bravely if I am forced to do so, but I would prefer to use my skills to help the healers. I wish now that I had listened more carefully when Father tried to teach me his secrets, but my mind was full of music at the time.

However, if it is my fate to die, I must pass on a secret to someone who will not speak of it. That person is you, my mother.

Lady Elayne, wife of Bedwyr of Arden, has birthed Artor's son. Lord Bedwyr knows, for Artor is too honest to tell falsehoods or to leave the lady to take any blame alone, but Bedwyr is angry and avoids the king. Should both Bedwyr and Artor fall in battle, I ask that you watch over their child. Elayne has birthed the boy in Arden, and the child would be a powerful prize for those kinglets who covet what Artor has won, for it may be that others will ferret out the truth from Bedwyr's anger.

I know my messenger will not read this secret. Even now he scratches his head over my Latin and calls it 'chicken tracks'. I chose him because he is illiterate and has developed the coughing disease, so his usefulness as an archer is finished. I have been ministering to his illness and his loyalty to me is beyond question. Care for him, Mother, and give him work.

I love you, as I also love my brothers.

Should I return, I will spend my life creating song and beauty. Should I die, I ask that you mourn me for a short time, and then live on as if I was coming home in the spring.

Taliesin

Taliesin sighed as his messenger slipped out into the night with his precious letter. Taliesin slept in a small leather tent with the other men who would soon tend to the wounded and the dying. The tent was crowded, so any movement disturbed the sleep of the other healers. Taliesin discovered he couldn't rest inside the stuffy tent, even after completing his duty to his mother.

The past six months had been dreadful in the number of tragedies and disasters that had beset the court of King Artor. Even the most optimistic of his warriors felt the weight of suspicion and old enmities that seethed under the veneer of courtly manners. Change, when it finally shattered the stasis of Cadbury, was curiously welcome after months of anxious waiting.

Bedwyr had returned to Cadbury Tor to recount the loss of his companions and to reveal the scope of Modred's treasonous ambition. Artor insisted that the whole court, even the servants, should gather to hear Bedwyr's dolorous account of the quest for the Bloody Cup. In a quiet, measured voice, Bedwyr recounted the corrosive influence of the relic that some Christian warriors now called the Sangraal.

The loss of two heroes captured the public imagination and focused the hatred of the common people on the guilty head of the Brigante king. Their rage grew slowly, but at a time when peace seemed only a thin skin over the roiling ambitions of faithless men, their anger grew deeply and inexorably.

The death of Percivale was a crushing, personal blow to Artor, not least because he had insisted on his friend's presence on the quest. In an effort to mitigate the loss of confidence that Galahad's death would mean to his warriors, Artor asked Taliesin to weave a fanciful, heroic tale concerning the Cup and its capture by Gawayne's son. In fact, Taliesin changed the heroic epic very little, for he had learned that fact becomes myth with the addition of only a few flourishes.

But Artor had more pressing problems than the death of a close friend or the loss of the Otadini prince. Knowing that Bedwyr would soon discover his king's perfidy when he joined Elayne in Arden, Artor summoned him to his private apartments and confessed the truth to his vassal. White-faced, and shaking with anger, the Arden Knife left Cadbury at a mad gallop, without a word of explanation to anyone.

After Bedwyr's departure, Artor drank himself into a stupor in his rooms, safe from prying, speculative eyes.

Artor had barely recovered from the death of Percivale and the loss of Bedwyr when a courier from King Mark delivered the head of Trystan to Artor's court. The dark warrior dropped the leaking, odorous bag at Artor's feet in the Judgement Hall with arrogant disdain, and Odin would have killed the insolent messenger out of hand had Artor not stayed his servant's hand. Mark's envoy informed the High King that Queen Iseult had left her husband's bed to cohabit with Artor's spymaster, so her lover had finally paid the highest price for underestimating the consequences of betraying a king. When the warrior had finished smirking his way through Mark's insulting message, Artor fixed his hard, grey stare on the young man until the Deceangli nobleman flushed, and dropped his gaze.

'You may tell your king that we will meet again in some future place of my choosing. He may count himself fortunate that my friend Gruffydd is too old to exact a blood price from King Mark ... although Gruffydd's kin may have other ideas.'

Mark's courier was dismissed with scant courtesy.

Artor felt no guilt over the execution of Trystan, for the young man had been clearly warned of the possible repercussions of his illicit love affair. But Artor's network of spies had been seriously compromised. Even when Gruffydd answered his old master's call to take up the reins once more, Artor's captains suffered from a serious lack of good intelligence.

Cadbury settled down nervously, as the population waited

on news from the north. Artor's court didn't have to wait over-long. Before the first summer winds had come, Modred and his Brigante horde poured out of the north and cut a deep swathe into Cornovii and Ordovice territory, smashing the old treaties under the marching feet of his warriors. The speed and ferocity of the attack was unexpected.

King Bran of the Ordovice rode at the head of his army to impede Modred's advance into the fertile lands of the south. Bran knew that Modred's horde was numerically superior, for the Brigante had ignored Artor's levees of men for the border forts for a decade. Bran also understood that the warriors he would face were well trained and motivated by old resentments. Modred's nobles had neither forgotten nor forgiven Artor's revenge for the assassination of King Luka. As his grandfather would have done, Bran assessed his enemies with cold detachment, realized that he would need great luck and a good exit strategy, and then led his warriors into the north.

Artor learned of the gravity of the situation when an Ordovice courier arrived at Cadbury Tor four days after the attack. The young messenger had suffered a calf wound that had been hastily bandaged with a strip of dirty cloth. The dark brooch on his tunic proclaimed him as a warrior of the Viroconium Ordovice.

After a cursory obeisance, the warrior formally introduced Bran's message. He had learned the words by heart, and Artor was cheered to hear the authentic sound of Bran's vocabulary in the courier's memorized speech. His grandson was still alive.

Greetings from Bran, King of the Ordovice, and from Anna, matriarch of the tribe.

The people need the help and the strong right arm of their High King, for treason has come in the night, like a thief or a scavenging dog, in the person of Modred, King of the Brigante, and his warlords. They have committed heinous crimes against the civilian population of Deva and must be called to account for their atrocities.

'You may speak, friend. And welcome. I can tell that you bring serious tidings.' Artor spoke with ceremonial gravity, although a corner of his mind rejoiced that the terrible waiting was over.

'Lord, word came to my king that the port of Deva had been taken by force, late at night, by disguised Brigante warriors who had entered the township over several days. They captured the local magistrate and took his family hostage, then opened the gates and permitted Modred's forces to enter the town. When the magistrate refused to hand over the chest of municipal gold, he and his family were killed and their bodies were nailed on the town gates to teach the townspeople the futility of resisting Modred's orders. My lord, two little girls were left to hang alive until their eyes were attacked by ravens. The sight of their tiny, abused bodies will linger in my memory for the rest of my life.' The courier's voice broke and he gratefully accepted a mug of wine from a servant.

'Bran gathered the guard together at Viroconium and sent a demand to the frontier forts for more troops but, by the time he reached Deva, it had already been sacked. We were enraged by the carnage, my lord. Everything of value had been stripped from Deva, a town that has been open to all the tribes for peaceful trade. The Brigante army had been let loose on Deva's population, to rape and loot at will. Old men and women, even children, were put to the sword for no reason other than to break our spirit. King Bran became very quiet when he saw the heaped bodies and burned churches, then set out to follow the Brigante spoor as they killed and ruined everything in their path. All we could learn from captured Brigante warriors was a chant that the "Cup has come".'

Artor stirred with disgust. 'The Brigante king is a liar, for the Cup cannot have come! The sainted Percivale and holy Galahad both died to capture it, and Galahad has risen to the Christian heaven with the relic. If any man should doubt my words, the body of the Pictish Druid still lies, headless, where Bremetennacum's river meets the sea.'

The courier gazed at Artor with a flush of superstitious awe. Hesitantly, he continued with his report.

'On the hills to the south of Aquae, Modred was waiting for us. Bran realized that the Brigante had gone to ground, so he sent outriders to scour the foothills for any signs of the host. When his scouts failed to return, my lord knew that Modred's forces were close at hand.

'The curs attacked us during the night, setting fire to the woods to light their path. Flames leapt up where the winter grasses were dry, and a wall of fire met us and burned the unwary inside their armour. Modred followed fire with cavalry attacks from the front and from behind, for King Mark has broken his oath to you and joined Modred with a small contingent. We lacked Modred's numbers and my king knew that we couldn't prevail, so we fought our way through the

Deceangli and Brigante lines until we reached open country where we could speed our withdrawal. My king was sorely wounded in the retreat as he attempted to delay the Brigante cavalry and protect our wounded. He lies at Vernemetum under the care of Queen Anna and his personal physicians. We pray for a speedy recovery from his ailments.

'In spite of his wounds, King Bran has fortified Vernemetum. From his sickbed, he has sent out messengers to strip his land bare of all men who are old enough to fight. When you come, we will follow you to death or to ruin, for our blood has been spilt on the earth of the west and we must have our revenge for Modred's treachery.'

Artor grunted his understanding. The road to Cadbury lay open for Modred's forces if they had the wisdom and the courage to press home their advantage.

'Whatever comes, the Ordovice tribe has behaved as loyal warriors should. There can be no shame if a stronger force defeats your warriors. You may rest, eat and drink and then return to your royal master with my thanks, and my oath that we are coming to your aid.'

But the courier had not quite finished.

'The enemy pretended to be Picts, my lord, although perhaps there were Picts among them, for they aped barbarian habits by painting their faces with blue woad. We didn't fear their paint, but fire and siege machines broke us. They pelted our warriors with the heads of the citizens of Deva to sap our spirits. That Celt should fight Celt in such a manner is an abomination, and I live to punish the Brigante warriors for their crimes against their own race. I just cannot understand . .'

The courier crumpled as his wounded leg folded under him and exhaustion robbed his body of strength. With two quick steps, Gareth supported the young man.

'See to his wounds, Gareth, for he has ridden far to bring us this intelligence,' Artor ordered. Then he turned back to the courier.

'Avarice is a powerful weapon, young man, and it can be used to lead simple people astray. I recall that the tribes unhesitatingly followed my father, Uther Pendragon, until his death, even though his decisions were dangerous and wicked towards the end of his reign. A strong hand and the willingness to use power for its own ends can often convince quite reasonable men to act unreasonably. The Brigante warriors follow Modred for the simple reason that he promises them much, and will permit them to indulge in any brutality they may desire. Rest now, my boy, and accept my gratitude. No shame attaches to you.'

'When did you know that Modred lusted after your throne and that he was the architect of the Bloody Cup, the Otadini murders and the slaughter of Bishop Aethelthred?' Taliesin asked later, and immediately reddened at the presumption in his hasty words. Who was he to question the High King?

Artor gazed steadily at the son of his old adviser, his grey eyes unreadable.

'I suspected that Modred was behind the murder of Aethelthred. Otha Redbeard was his creature, and once that relationship was proven, the Bloody Cup and Gronw had to be part of his web of lies. But I was only guessing until Brother Mark told me of Otha's confession.'

Taliesin was incredulous. 'You knew?'

'I *suspected*.'

'So why didn't you kill Modred when you became aware of the plot? You didn't spare his kinsman, Simnel, for the less heinous crime of the assassination of King Luka. You decimated a whole troop for the sake of my mother, and Lady Miryll died for her sins at Salinae Minor. Gods, Artor! Modred was *here*, in your house, at your mercy! His death would have saved the lives of thousands . . . all the innocent dead of Deva. Now you must meet him on the battlefield, and the gods alone know who will win!' Taliesin was angry, Artor knew, and the young man paced back and forth across Artor's comfortable room with his robes hissing over the wooden floor with a nervous, irritable susurration.

'Have a little faith in my abilities, harpist! When Balyn and Balan perished, my rage and sorrow were sharp enough to kill Modred out of hand. But what would I have gained? In hindsight, Lot and Morgause might have lived, although it's unlikely that Pebr would have been deflected before his goals were attained. Nor would Gronw have changed his course of action, even if Modred had been killed. My nephew has created a plot that exists almost independently of him. At any rate, I made a choice and I must live with it.'

'But why? I still don't understand.'

'I found myself unable to assassinate Modred in secret, and he took great care to do nothing wrong within the confines of my court. How could I dispense justice with any validity if I ignored my own rules? We Celts are either civilized, or we are not. If the Unity of Kings was to be broken, then Modred must be the one to cause the fracture, not me, or else my whole reign has been a lie.

'I have cursed the darkness, night after night. I have wept when no man could see me, Taliesin, because Modred has cost me everything – *everything*. My grandsons, my friends – he must feed on everything that is mine while I watch, wait and pray that my arm can still lift a sword when he comes knocking at the gates of my kingdom.'

Odin stepped forward and kneeled before his master. 'I understand, my lord. But we must now be about our business, which is the destruction of Modred. After which we shall all feel very much better.'

Artor laughed and clenched his fist as if it clutched at Caliburn, his sword.

Wenhaver was aghast at Artor's turn of fortune, and gazed about her gilded rooms like a child who has had a favourite treat withdrawn.

'But why must I go to the nunnery at Tintagel, Artor? Modred would never hurt me. We are friends, even though he's been perfectly beastly to all of us since he left Cadbury like a thief in the night. Still, he'd never hurt me.'

'Of course he would, Wenhaver, because you're my queen. If he wins, I will be dead and he'll kill you in a heartbeat. As the High Queen, any claimant to the throne must have your blessing. Will you give it willingly? Or will he slit your pretty throat – and smile while he carries out what will, for him, be a very trivial task? He doesn't hate you. He doesn't even think of you very much, except as an obstacle that stands in his way. Perhaps you'll welcome him. I'd not blame you, for we've never been particularly happy, have we?' Artor's voice was thick with bitterness and regret.

'But you'll come back! You *always* come back! Why must you be so contrary, Artor? And why are you so insulting? I am the queen, your queen, and my position is important to me.' Wenhaver raised herself to her full height. Ironically, dressed as she was in her daily, plain-woven robes and bare of most of her usual ornamentation, she had the bearing of a queen. And now she focused on the most pointed of Artor's insults.

'How dare you suggest that I'd countenance Modred as High King? You've always been a selfish bastard, Artor, but you've really hurt my feelings this time. I may not have given you sons, but I know where my duty lies! By the laws of God and man, you are the rightful king of the Britons.'

Artor lifted one of the queen's plump hands and kissed her fingertips. Wenhaver blushed.

'I'll remember your loyalty, and will always be grateful for it. But you're still going to Tintagel. I must take every precaution to keep you safe, my lady. The queen must be protected, no matter what may come. And I will send my crown with you into the care of Mother Church, for there, I know, it will be safe.'

Wenhaver still refused to accept the truth of her situation, and only when Artor ordered his guards to carry her away bodily did she summon her maids and her dignity and prepare for an orderly departure.

'The nuns will soon put her to work,' the king told Taliesin when she had departed for the haven of the convent with an armed escort for protection.

'At least there'll be few handsome young men to distract her in her new abode.'

'It's more likely that she'll choose to rule the roost herself,' Odin interjected dourly and Artor laughed.

'Perhaps you're right, Odin. She has a talent for getting her own way, by fair means or by foul.'

Taliesin saw a flicker of affection in the grey eyes of the king.

'The queen is who she is, regardless of what I might have desired. There's no point in wondering what might have happened if circumstances had been different.'

His mind ranged back to Gallia, as it did so often now. His face softened and his gaze was unfocused.

Taliesin and Odin recognized the signs. Artor's thoughts had turned to Gallia for comfort with greater frequency during the past year, and it alarmed them. They both knew that when a man's thoughts settled into the past, he was cutting the ties to any possible future and consigning himself to death.

Abruptly, Artor straightened his back. 'I must deal with Modred and see to my succession. Then, and only then, may I rest peacefully.' He looked at the concerned faces of Odin and Gareth. 'My old friends, I acquit you of any obligation to ride with me on this last campaign. With luck, I'll be back when I've put Modred under the earth where he belongs. Whatever happens, my successor will need your wise counsel.'

The two old men launched into angry protests. They wouldn't stay behind; he insulted them if he thought they were too ancient for battle; they would follow him anyway, whatever he said.

'You shame us, Artor,' Odin said, 'for we made oaths, and if we break our vows, all that will be left for us is the funeral pyre. What is safety and peace, anyway? It is the refuge of old men who sit by the fireside and dream of what might have been.'

Artor said no more, for in his deepest heart he was glad to travel with his old friends. The campaign was certain to be harsh and costly.

The first blow came quickly, as Artor marshalled the soldiers of the west to march in his wake. Gawayne could not come to their aid. A courier, a dour, scowling man on a failing horse who had picked his way carefully through the enemy lines, brought a message from Enid, Gawayne's wife. Artor remembered her soft brown hair, luminous eyes and a willowy form that was as inflexible as a sword blade.

From Queen Enid of the Otadini.

All praise to King Artor, rightful High King of the Britons and the Warrior of the West.

I speak for your nephew, Gawayne, King of the Otadini, who is hunting pretenders to his crown at Trimontium in the north.

We are desolated that we can send no troops to fight by your side in the legitimate war against Modred the Matricide. Our warriors are locked in a deadly struggle with several claimants to the Otadini throne, and my husband is stretched thinly to pursue traitors from one end of his tribal lands to the other. However, I am obliged to tell you that the barbarian Picts are moving out of the mountains. War parties have been sighted at Magnis and Camboglanna on the Wall. We must deduce that they travel south to join the Matricide in his unholy war.

Be assured that the Otadini will come in honour of our treaties as soon as our situation allows, although I cannot predict the day. Only then can the spirits of King Lot and Queen Morgause sleep peacefully in the early graves to which the Matricide has sent them.

May the gods protect you.

Your servant,

Queen Enid

The Otadini warrior repeated his memorized message without a pause, but what the man had actually seen for himself was of far greater interest to the High King. After a few well-chosen questions, Artor was able to determine the size and effectiveness of Modred's army.

'They lack a firm hand,' the warrior growled with a typical Otadini scowl. 'I could smell them long before I saw them, filthy creatures that they are. I didn't think their captains were up to the job. Aye, and they're fair slow with their movements, almost at odds with each other as to who's in command when they're taking up positions in the field. But that sodding, mother-killing bastard Modred has amassed a huge host, and he's rat-cunning and cherishes his own skin. That turncoat, Mark of Canovium, has joined him. My old king, Lot, never trusted that jumped-up bag of piss and wind. He'd sell his own mother for a good purse, so I wasn't surprised to learn that the Matricide has promised him the Ordovice lands on your death.

'I heard some of their sentries talking as I moved through their lines. I ditched my horse, temporary like, and climbed a tree, because I knew the sodding fools wouldn't look upwards. I soon discovered they reckon you'll be too angry to think straight and will come charging north at speed. They imagine you'll be caught between their two forces.'

Artor scratched his chin where Odin had missed an area of white stubble when he'd shaved him that morning. The king's fingers rasped over the bristles.

'Thank you for your news,' he said. 'How can I recompense you?'

'Don't lose to Modred!' the warrior responded economically. 'My master has enough problems without a hostile neighbour perched on his borders. The Matricide will cross the Wall to attack us if he's made a treaty with the blue Picts.'

When the Otadini had been led to good food, beer and warm quarters, Artor turned to his intimates to refine his plans.

Artor felt an enormous sense of relief on the day he finally left the tor. His halls, the spiral fortifications and even the fertile fields that surrounded Cadbury all reminded him of his lost opportunities. The shadows of Balyn and Balan laughed in the corridors, and Percivale looked up from sharpening his sword whenever Artor prepared to leave his apartments. Cadbury was full of ghosts – Targo, Myrddion, Luka, Llanwith, all his beloved dead – and he couldn't bear to look on them any longer.

Will I see fair Cadbury again? he wondered, with very little regret for what he had built.

A raven swore maliciously from an oak coppice as Artor passed, causing Taliesin to shiver in his woollen cloak. Behind the cavalcade, splendid in scarlet, green and gold, the tor and its villages seemed like a dream of order and plenty. Women threw flowers under the horse's hooves, children gaped and old men were awed anew by the High King, despite their familiarity with Artor at the hunt, riding with his troops or dispensing wisdom in his Judgement Hall. Their lord had the mien of a god, so calm and so focused was he on the cleansing of his realm. Instead of the golden crown, which had gone with the queen to Tintagel, Artor wore a diadem of oak leaves created by Taliesin's nimble fingers. Artor had laughed at the affectation at first but, when Odin placed the coronet over his grey curls with all the seriousness reserved for a true coronation, Artor acquiesced.

When the king looked back several hours after they had left the citadel, he saw the hill rising through the woods, as if Cadbury, too, wore a diadem of oak leaves.

CHAPTER XXII

EΤ FĪNĪ

May God grant to the living * Grace
To the departed * Rest
To the Church & the World * Peace & Concord
And to us sinners * Eternal Life
  (Stone on the outer wall of Westminster Abbey)

The Dragon wound its way northward. Like a ponderous and muscular beast, it slid and clawed its way across ground that could accommodate its girth. Artor's army moved faster than most hordes but he wished that it could grow dragon wings and soar over the hills and rivers, so that he could seek out Modred quickly and rend him with the vast claws of his creature.

Uncharacteristically, Artor chose to bypass Aquae Sulis and the Villa Poppinidii as his army marched northward. In past campaigns, Gallia's Garden had offered physical proof of the beauty of the west and had encouraged Artor to drag himself above his many weaknesses. But almost everyone who had known the youthful Artorex was dead, and the villa's former comfort and companionship had vanished with the inexorable march of time.

The cavalry, a dozen mounted men across, moved at the head of the army. Behind the cavalry came the archers under the vivid battle standards of their masters and the flag of their commander, Pelles Minor of Ratae. Like their leader, the archers wore gay colours, for they rarely stood at the forefront of the battlefield and were not at risk of being singled out by the enemy. Their blues, greens, scarlet and gorgeous yellows enlivened the more sombre hues of the cavalry.

The foot soldiers followed, drawn from the peasantry. Trained in the old Roman styles of combat passed on to their elders by Targo, they marched with dignity in compact companies that moved with the mile-devouring steps of disciplined infantry, carrying all their gear lashed to their shields or on their backs, and bearing long spears and short swords. As the foot soldiers always felt the full force of the enemy in any engagement, their pride was a living testament to their loyalty and honour.

The rear guard consisted of heavy wains drawn by teams of white oxen. In the wains, parts of siege machines, weapons, supplies, food and a team of healers with the tools of their craft kept pace with the foot soldiers. Armies must travel with vast provisions, or warriors starve on land burned black by the enemy.

But armies are more than just those men who fight and die, even a well-oiled machine like Artor's. The camp followers brought up the rear, some on foot and some horsed; some were dressed in rich tunics that had been won for them by their men, while others walked in dun-coloured, practical leathers, leading children and pack animals with their few possessions. Ragtag, hopeful or inured to the rigours of the march, the women followed their men into danger.

Each night, in his leather tent, Artor drank his beer and pored over Myrddion's old maps as he sought a battleground that would give him an advantage in the coming conflict. Like his warriors, Artor renounced his usual draughts of water when on the march, for only fools drank from streams and rivers when they were ignorant of the cleanliness of the water sources. Foul water killed more warriors than swords, if the troops were unwary, and each man had a supply of brewed beer and ale to drink.

As the army made camp on a Roman road to the east of Viroconium and north of the Forest of Arden that would later be called the Ryknield Way, Artor received news that Bran was approaching the bivouac.

Bran's small cavalcade joined the vanguard of the army at sunset. By the light of the long, golden dusk, the High King saw a troop of Ordovice warriors riding as bodyguards to a tall, raw-boned woman mounted on a large bay horse. She travelled beside a litter being carried by six muscular servants. The woman's hair burned in the last light with the colour of rust and dried blood.

King Bran was carried to Artor's tent on his litter, irritably accepting that his wound precluded him from presenting himself on horseback. Even now, after rest and care for several weeks, he was waxen and grey from the relatively short journey from Vernemetum by wagon. But his eyes still snapped with confidence and determination, and Artor's heart lifted to see that his grandson's spirit was unbroken by his losses on the battlefield.

He was less confident when he gazed into Anna's face, for

so he now thought of her. This hazel-eyed woman whose high cheekbones had been hollowed out by sorrow had subsumed Licia, his joyous child. In her eyes Artor saw an emptiness, an aching void that could never be filled, and his heart was wrenched to see how the loss of her beautiful twins had extinguished her. When he bent to kiss her hand, his longing and regret threatened to overwhelm him.

Artor had not set eyes on his daughter for over twenty-five years, but he would have recognized her face anywhere, for something of Ygerne and the twins hid in the curve of her upper lip and nestled in the curls at the nape of her tender neck.

'Little Anna, your beauty has scarcely changed,' the king murmured. He longed to embrace his daughter and confess her parentage at last, but such desires were selfish and the time to submit to them had passed.

'You have a smooth tongue when you choose, King Artor,' Anna replied bluntly, but her sad eyes twinkled. 'Time has been more generous to you than it has to me, so your polite compliments do honour to neither of us. I'm an old woman, my lord. We could be siblings, if we weren't separated by twenty years or more.'

For a moment, Artor's heart stuttered in his chest. Did Anna truly believe they were brother and sister, as the old lie had suggested?

'Lord?' Bran asked. The Ordovice king was acute and he realized that something lay between his mother and the High King. He had struggled to his feet from his litter and his face showed the cost.

Artor smiled and embraced him, king to king.

'Welcome, Bran. Sit, my good man, sit! You're very pale and it's obvious that you've over-taxed your strength by greeting me in person. Forgive me, I should have come to you, but the north calls me urgently.'

Bran's smile was broad and Taliesin caught his breath to see the reflection of Artor and Balan in it.

'Your words are courteous, lord, yet they pain me since I cannot ride against Modred with you. The remnants of my army await you on the ridge line with orders to follow you. I've called every Ordovice tribesman who can lift a sword, whether noble or peasant, to stand behind you. They came with joy, my lord, and fierce determination, having sworn that no rebellious Brigante will be allowed to remain on Ordovice soil unscathed.'

Artor noticed that Bran's hand trembled, although the young man struggled to disguise his exhaustion. A simple glance from the king to Odin sufficed, and the servant produced a cup of strong red wine that he pressed into Bran's hands.

'Thank you.' Bran smiled at Odin with natural courtesy, and the old Jutlander's heart was lost to this fine young man.

Bran drank and colour returned to his face, although he grimaced a little at the strength of the wine. 'When you defeat Modred, as is inevitable, Your Majesty, permit me to punish the Deceangli tribe. I will enjoy selecting a suitable punishment for Mark and confiscating his treasure for your use. In fact, I believe the loss of his wealth will punish that miser worse than his death. Perhaps I'll let him beg for food for a month or two, before I have him executed.'

Artor and Bran both laughed.

'At the end of this campaign, when Mark goes howling back to his court like the mongrel he is, take his lands and treasure with my blessing', Artor said. 'Your loyalty is unquestioned and I value it more highly than you might believe.'

Bran bowed his acknowledgement.

'I also ask that you accept my eldest son as an observer of the coming battle. His name is Ector, in honour of my grandfather. He is only ten, my lord, but it's time he learned what it is to be a man – and a king.'

In a silence so deep and charged that the air shivered, Artor cleared his throat lest his voice reveal the pain he felt when Ector, his dearly beloved foster-father, was honoured as Bran's kin while he was not now – nor could ever be.

'He is welcome, and Gareth will protect the boy with his life, if necessary, but are you sure you want him to see the brutality of war? Killing is an ugly trade, and he will be changed by what he sees.'

'Thank you for your consideration, my lord. But my heir must know what his duties and responsibilities entail.'

With that answer, Artor was forced to be content.

Bran had aged in the last few years, although he had a young family and a handsome, spirited wife. Trouble, responsibility and loss had engraved heavy lines from Bran's nose to the corners of his well-shaped mouth.

'You've done more than your duty requires, Bran. In fact, you've done far more than any other king of the west. Your paternal grandfather, Llanwith, would have been proud of you.'

Bran flushed darkly across his high, pale cheekbones, but Anna nodded her head in agreement and approval.

Both Bran and Anna had an instinctive grasp of military

strategy, and Artor warmed to their advice as they discussed the possible outcomes for the west once the usurper had been defeated in battle.

Ever the realist, Artor did not shy away from addressing the consequences of defeat on the battlefield.

'In the event that I should fail, it will be your duty to withdraw beyond the Roman road leading to the north,' Artor stated bluntly. 'You must hold all the land from Pennel to Viroconium, and from Deva to Glevum, so that the remnants of the Celtic tribes might have a final sanctuary. If I fail, the Saxons will fall on us like a huge, drowning wave once our internal fighting begins, so you are ordered to unite what is left of our forces, bring Mark to justice and preserve the values of the Celtic people. Don't attempt to take the throne, no matter what promises are offered to you. But it is my wish that young Ector be trained to become my heir.'

'The lands of the Ordovice will not be relinquished to the Saxons while I, my sons and their sons still live,' Bran vowed, his voice steady and restrained. 'Ector shall become yours when you return from the fields of battle.'

'I also make this promise to you, Artor,' Anna said.

Taliesin shuddered inwardly at the iron in her eyes. Saxon bodies would fill the rivers to the brim before this oath would be broken.

'It's time for you to go to your beds,' Artor said. 'You are weary, Bran, and need to preserve your strength. I'll not see you again until I return from the north, for I depart at first light. May Mithras stand at your shoulder and heal your wounds.' He smiled his regrets at their parting.

Artor would have risen, but Anna pushed him back into his

campaign chair with work-hardened hands. She bent over him and kissed each eyelid with lingering sweetness.

'I remember talking to you a long time ago in the Villa Poppinidii, dear Artor. My brave father, as you described him, had died – or so you told me. I'll pray that you sleep gently throughout eternity, if it is Fortuna's plan that we never meet again. If you return, you may have my first grandson with my blessing. Your Licia remembers everything, my lord, and she forgives you for everything, even your silence. Licia always knew, and she understands the reasons behind the lies she was told.'

Artor had no words to express his feelings. He kissed her hands on each palm and closed her fingers over the place where his lips had rested.

After Anna and Bran had gone to the soft pallets prepared for them by the king's servants, Artor slumped in his chair.

'She knows. She's known all these years,' he whispered, his mouth dragging with regret at lost opportunities.

He spoke no more, and maintained his own counsel throughout the long night.

On the long march to the north, Artor seemed to become stronger and younger. Every mile covered saw the marks of time drop away until the old man's spine was straight and strong, and his face shone with the ferocity and piercing intent of a snow hawk.

Once Deva was behind them to the west, the ranks of Artor's army swelled with Cornovii archers and cavalry under the command of a thin and careworn Bedwyr. Artor greeted him warmly but cautiously.

'I'm grateful that you have come freely, Bedwyr, for I didn't have the effrontery to ask it of you,' the king admitted, once the army was in bivouac. 'Many men in your position would have abandoned me to my fate.'

Shamed to his soul, the High King's eyes dropped to his booted feet and his shoulders sagged.

'You must know that Queen Elayne has given birth to a son. He's a strong, beautiful child and is likely to grow very tall. She has named him Arthur.'

Bedwyr's eyes were fixed steadily on his king. Artor couldn't turn his gaze away, even as he felt himself colour with shame.

'Do you have a message for my wife?' Bedwyr's sharp-edged voice demanded.

Odin's chest rumbled warningly.

Artor continued to meet Bedwyr's accusing eyes. 'I wish your lady long life and health for the kindness she offered to an old man at a time when his life was in tatters and he had need of a true friend. As for the babe, may he grow strong and true in the forests of his father, the honourable Bedwyr.'

'His father?' Bedwyr sneered. 'Plain speaking might be best between us, especially in private.'

'Taliesin, Gareth and Odin are the only living souls who know the truth of what lies between us,' Artor replied. 'I'll not complain if you seek satisfaction.'

Bedwyr heaved a deep, exasperated sigh.

'I've persuaded myself that Elayne was guiltless in this matter. The gods placed you both together for a purpose, so I will accept the decision of fate. I've learned that nothing is absolute – not pride, nor loyalty, nor honour. I am angry, but what has happened, has happened. The quest taught me too much about my own flaws to dwell upon the weaknesses of other men.'

'You're generous, Bedwyr,' Artor acknowledged. 'I'm grateful for any forgiveness that you can grant me.'

'I can never believe in you as I once did. But I'll always love Elayne, and I can understand why you would care for her. Let peace be between us, now that Modred launches himself at our throats.'

Artor stripped the pearl ring from his thumb. 'This ring should be given to young Arthur after my death. But if you love Elayne and the child, it might be best if you didn't tell the boy the full truth of his parentage. He's too young to sit on my throne. But the final decision must be yours.'

Artor pressed the ring into Bedwyr's unwilling hands. His vassal nodded, but still refused to speak.

'If I should die, give the dragon knife to Elayne for your son, for I hope he will always believe that he is your child. The dragon knife is most truly mine, for the blacksmith, Brego, wrought it for me when I rescued his son a lifetime ago. It was gilded at Glastonbury, and Caliburn was made in its likeness, but the knife represents Artor and all that he was. You may explain the gift in any way that you choose. Caliburn must go to Lady Nimue, who will decide what must be done with it. Like Uther, I trust no man with Caliburn. To obey the demands I place on you, I insist that you live through the coming conflict at all cost. You must heed my wishes, Bedwyr, for my sword mustn't fall into Brigante hands. I entrust you with the physical symbols of my kingship, for only you, my Arden Knife, will comply with my orders and obey them without question.'

Bedwyr nodded his assent once more and, with obvious deliberation, bowed his head in grudging respect.

In Caer Gai, Nimue hastily packed a leather satchel and tied it across the broad back of her roan mare. For hours, her sons had tried to dissuade her from this imprudent and dangerous journey.

'The king needs me. Your father would not forgive me if I did not go to Artor. Nor would I forgive myself.'

'What can you do, Mother, in all common sense?' Rhys pleaded, while his brother nodded in agreement. 'Or are you planning to wield a sword in the coming battle?'

'I'll consider that your sarcasm is motivated by fear for my safety and not impudence,' Nimue replied stiffly. 'I've made my decision, so kiss me and I'll be off on my journey.'

'At least let one of us accompany you,' Rhys persisted.

'No. I'm safe in these mountains.'

Defeated and baffled, the boys stepped out of the path of their mother's horse and Nimue rode away in a spray of flint shards. She didn't look back.

In Viroconium, King Bran was using the same fruitless arguments with his mother.

'But Artor only left Letocetum a week ago,' Bran stated. 'What's so urgent you didn't tell him then? Are you moon-mad, Mother? The king will not welcome you trailing after him towards a battlefield.'

Anna ignored her son and, once she had made her preparations, ordered two trusted warriors to accompany her on her journey. As she left the shelter of the city, she sighted Nimue following the riverbank that led down from the mountains, so she waited for the stranger to reach the city. Once Nimue had joined the Dowager queen of the Ordovice, the two formidable women met and sized each other up through narrowed eyes. Nimue broke the impasse first with laughter. She embraced Anna and dismounted from her weary horse, reminding the Ordovice queen of the rules of hospitality. Anna led Nimue back into the city, as the two women spoke of the compulsion that had prompted them to leave their homes.

Bran arranged for a fresh horse to be provided for the widow of Myrddion Merlinus. If the young king believed for a moment that Nimue's arrival might convince his mother to change her mind, he was quickly disabused of the notion.

Bran seemed immune to Nimue's charmed aura; he treated her with all the deference owed to an elderly lady but was in no way in awe of her.

'Your son does you credit,' Nimue told Anna. 'He's a man unlikely to be seduced by his senses. He will become a great king.'

Anna flushed. She had never previously met the famed Nimue but, already, she could believe that all the stories she'd heard were true. She sensed that Nimue's eyes saw through flesh and bone, deep into the soul.

'It's kind of you to say so, my lady.'

'Myrddion spoke of you often. He also spoke of Gallia, your mother.'

Widow eyed widow with mutual respect and understanding.

'Men!' Anna dismissed the opposite sex with causal, affectionate contempt. 'Artor spent most of his life protecting me from what I already knew. But I suppose he couldn't have known that Livinia Minor let his secret slip decades ago.'

It didn't occur to Anna to question how Nimue could know she was aware of the truth of her birth. Most strangers were fearful of Nimue's sudden insights, but Anna felt no such uneasiness in her presence, and Nimue, for her part, was glad of it.

No more was said on the subject.

'We must depart, my lady.' Nimue eyed the noon sun that hung almost directly above them. 'We must be in Mamucium to meet Queen Enid within the week, for Artor's destiny awaits him.'

'Then we'll leave immediately, although you must be weary. I've sufficient provisions for us all, in spite of my son's efforts to divert me from my duty.'

'I can sleep when my journey is done,' Nimue said flatly. 'If Queen Enid can turn her back on the rebellions in the north, then I can survive for a few days without sleep.'

Anna nodded and the two women began the long ride to the north.

Sooner or later all roads meet at one point in each man's life, Taliesin reflected, as he stood on a small rise that overlooked Artor's army. And when they do, the sum total of his existence becomes plain to him. This is Artor's time. He's finally arrived at a nameless river outside a filthy, half-Roman town, a place where he'll meet his final test of strength.

The countryside was soft and sweet-smelling. Winds came fresh from the unseen sea in the west, and the low, undulating fields were green and golden with long grass, field flowers and gorse. On the nearby hills, heather flowered in pale drifts of pink and lavender and the wide river glinted in the perfect summer weather. The army could have been about a pleasant visit to an amicable ally, so lightly did the impending war touch the warriors as they made their bivouac.

Taliesin gazed at the far bank of the river and thought of Galahad's obsessed pursuit of Gronw and the Bloody Cup. Both men were gone now, and part of the harpist's reason hoped that the west would not see their like again. But Percivale's wrapped corpse had also passed this way, and the wound of his absence was slow to heal.

With his usual skill, Artor had arranged his army on the river flatlands in the form of a deep crescent. Foot soldiers were spread thinly on the horns of his formation, covering a strong centre with ranks that were at least ten men deep. Artor's strategy for this battle was to use the ancient Roman tactics of concentrated force, coupled with the defensive lessons learned at Mori Saxonicus. He expected the men at the centre to hold their position in the line or die. The infantry ate, practised and took their rest in their fighting ranks along the line. Artor's troops could rise from their cooking fires and assume their defensive formations within minutes if necessary. Behind the horns of the crescent, the cavalry had set their picket lines.

There was a festive mood throughout the ranks. Perhaps the deep grass, the sweet air and the clear blue skies lightened every heart. Perhaps Artor's troops were glad to be about the business they knew so well, the terrible and exacting business of killing.

Taliesin started in surprise when he realized that Odin had

materialized at his side. For such a large man, the Jutlander was as quiet as a cat, even in old age.

'You caught me out, Odin. How do you do it?'

Odin shrugged. His broad, craggy face showed no emotion at all.

'I thought I was alone,' Taliesin murmured. 'A time to think, perhaps, before the battle begins.'

Odin shrugged again.

'Aren't you afraid?' Taliesin asked. 'You're an old man, Odin, even older than Artor. How can you face another battle?'

The huge Jutlander rested an arm on his double-edged war axe.

'I started fighting as a boy, song-master. It's what I do. I'm a weapon. I'm a knife that is fitted to my master's hand. The knife knows what it is, but it doesn't choose its purpose. The master sets the knife to work.'

'You give a grotesque explanation of your purpose in life,' Taliesin muttered. 'One that implies that you have no free will.'

'Why do you insult me?' Odin thrust his head forward aggressively. 'What has free will to do with warfare? I've always been Artor's man, and I thank the gods in Asgaad that my master is the greatest warrior in all these lands, even in his old age. How many warriors have been fortunate enough to live as gloriously as Odin? How many warriors earn such a good death as the one that will soon come to Odin, fighting with the greatest warrior of the age?' He looked down at the young poet.

'Targo and me, we were made from iron, and Artor fashioned us into his knives, even when we thought we were making him. Targo swore that he had been born to train the young king. Every wound he suffered in his youth and every hardship he endured was designed by his Mithras to help him shape the future king. In thanks for his honest labours, Artor lifted Targo up. Old Targo saw the whole world, and not just his little slice of it. I am the same. I have no wish to live if Artor is dead, for my world would be narrow and I would have no purpose.'

'I apologize for my stupidity, Odin,' Taliesin admitted with humility. 'Will you accept my hand in friendship?'

Odin extended his sword arm, letting his axe fall unheeded. He gripped the wrist of Taliesin's sword arm and the two men stood for a moment, entwined as one.

At noon, Modred's army arrived and began to set up camp on the far side of the shallow river. The disciplined ranks of older Brigante warriors, who had served in Artor's wars, were in stark contrast to the younger members of Modred's force, a whooping, shouting, ragtag drizzle of men. A solitary horseman in black attempted to impose some discipline on the camp.

Artor and his captains watched the enemy from a small knoll.

'This is an army with three heads,' Artor commented. 'One head is Pictish, one is Deceangli and the biggest is Brigante. The heads barely understand each other, which is an advantage for us.'

'That may be so, my lord,' Bedwyr responded, 'but Modred has collected an enormous horde of men to fight this battle for him. A whole contingent of Picts has just joined them on the left flank, and there are disciplined warriors among them.'

The arrival of the Picts sent a frisson of fear through the Celtic ranks. Although those bitter warriors had been driven out of the west many years earlier, the Celts had a healthy respect for the blue tattooed maniacs who rarely surrendered in battle, and who hated the Celtic invaders with a passion that was undimmed by the passage of many hundreds of years.

'If Modred's forces don't cross the river,' Artor said slowly. 'I wouldn't consider taking the battle to them.'

'Of course they'll come,' Pelles Minor snapped. 'Look at them.'

Several pairs of eyes turned accusingly and frowned at this discourtesy.

The short, dark archer was dressed in a gaudy tunic of yellow wool with a cloak of a particularly virulent green. Artor surveyed his vassal's dress sense and wondered if Pelles was colour-blind.

'I spoke roughly, my lord,' Pelles apologized. 'Hades, I'm a rough man! But how do you suppose such a rabble will hold together for an orderly approach?'

'I don't believe that Modred intends to cross the river at all. He wants to force us to go to him, where he holds a strong defensive position.'

Bedwyr's jaw worked. 'Surely not! Not even Modred would be so foolish as to believe we'd willingly put our heads in a noose. We'd starve him out.'

'I'm not so sure, Bedwyr. If they simply sit where they are, and we sit here on our thumbs, we have an impasse. We'll run out of rations, but he'll receive supplies from the Brigante people who are at his back. What then? How long would we be prepared to camp on this riverbank? Weeks? Months? Passivity has always been Modred's way, and he'll use it until we starve or choke on our own shit'. Artor dragged his hands through his hair.

'We must offer him an attractive target. We'll feint a cavalry charge across the river and present him with an irresistible prize. I'll let Modred think that I'm as stupid as Glamdring Ironfist was, that I'll advance from a safe defensive position in response to taunts from my enemy. It worked for us at Mori Saxonicus. Perhaps, in reverse, it will work again'.

Across the river, Modred's army settled down for the night around cooking fires, to eat, drink and hone their weapons. The dusk came to life with the firefly glow of hundreds of small cooking fires while the sounds of laughter and talk wafted across the river on the night air. By comparison with Artor's quiet, disciplined bivouac, the Brigante and their allies were loud, raucous and over-confident.

In the centre of the camp, barely visible in the fading light, a huge blue tent was raised by a team of grunting, cursing warriors. Its grotesque size marked it as Modred's resting place.

'Modred is, as always, ostentatious', Artor noted. 'All he lacks is a sign that says, here lies the king of the traitors. Please fire your arrows here!'

Artor turned his back on Modred's army dismissively.

'That huge army does not rest, does not sleep. They drink, dance, boast, gorge and even squabble in their separate companies. How can such a huge, undisciplined body of men fight together? There is our edge'.

At first light on the following morning, Bedwyr, Pelles and the other captains of the western army joined their king on the same low knoll. Across the river, they saw an ant heap of furious activity that made the High King shake his head.

'Squabbling warriors eating red meat in the mornings, women in the bivouac with the fighting men, children running through the cooking fires. Modred's army is a rabble.'

Bedwyr looked upstream and saw a small contingent of Brigante warriors washing in the shallows, collecting drinking water and even relieving themselves in the river without concern.

'They're fouling their own nest!' he exclaimed.

'Yes, and ours. Warn the men to avoid drinking river water.' Artor's face appeared almost serene under his oak-leaf crown. Uncharacteristically, he was dressed in gilded armour and he was carrying a brilliant scarlet shield, whose golden bosses and ornamentation glinted in the rising sun.

Artor faced his captains. 'We spoke last night of a feint across the river to tempt the Brigante to attack us in force, and that is what we shall do. I intend to lead my personal guard in the feint, for Modred won't stir off his arse for anyone but me.'

'So that's why you're tricked out like a fairground whore,' Bedwyr said. 'You wish to make yourself a colourful target.'

'Exactly. He must recognize me.'

'But you'll be in deadly danger,' Pelles protested. 'Allow me to take your place. I'm partial to golden armour, you mustn't be at risk. It's an audacious plan, and it could work, but not if we lose the Warrior of the West.'

'I thank you for your offer, Pelles, but my mind is made up. Modred will not risk himself for anyone but the High King, of that I am sure. Even golden armour couldn't disguise the fact that you're close to a foot shorter than I am. And I shall need you with your archers. I predict that Modred's undisciplined rabble will pour over the shallows to become part of the kill, once they have me on the run. Each of his warriors will want to capture me as their prize, alive or dead, and collect the price that Modred has put on my old head. A hail of arrows from your archers, Pelles, will add to the chaos and increase my chances of survival.' He smiled at his companions. 'Then, my friends, Modred's forces can be crushed utterly. Once Modred's men cross the river, our positions are reversed and his force will be vulnerable.'

Taliesin heard the thin, high cry of a bird and looked up. A barred peregrine hawk hovered high above Artor's camp. The bird still wore its winter raiment, and its outspread wings were scarcely moving in the light breeze. Taliesin felt a cold sensation on the back of his neck, a superstitious recognition that the peregrine was the symbol of kingship. He raised one hand to shield his eyes from the sun, wondering if the gods had sent this bird as proof that Artor's cause was just. But when he looked again to where the hawk had hovered, it had vanished.

CHAPTER XXIII

THE ONCE AND FUTURE KING

The day glittered with a thin dusting of heat over the sky. The warmth wasn't unpleasant, even in heavy armour, but men felt sweat bead lightly on their brows as they set about the many tasks that armies require to thrive. Foragers were about, seeking out game to augment their rations; other warriors cut grass for the horses or filled wooden pails, downstream, to water the beasts; wood must be collected for cooking fires, and for miles around the bivouac, the land must be forced to give up its bounty for the belly of the beast. The mundane task of digging latrines was so critical to the health of the army that a team of men was tasked with doing nothing else but oversee sanitation.

Artor's captains, however, had other preoccupations. One by one, they volunteered to take Artor's place as decoy. The High King simply smiled and shook his head.

'You all have a role to play in this, and you must stay with your men. I could find a warrior to match me in build and height but the man in charge of this raid must think on his feet

– or his horse – and I am that man. I don't intend to sacrifice myself for Modred's pleasure. We only have to engage and hold for a count of ten.

As always, Artor was coolly practical. His personal guard, consisting of fifty superbly trained fighting men, was utterly loyal to him, if for no other reason than their familial relationship with him. He had no illusions about what his planned feint would cost in the lives of his bastard sons. They were dear to him and he grieved at the sacrifice to come, but the cruel circumstances of civil war demanded implacable and unpleasant decisions. Besides, when he died, any new king was likely to kill all of his kin, illegitimate or not, to secure his position.

Artor gathered his captains in the campaign tent, and they were soon bent over a large vellum chart, scanning every detail of the strategy that Artor had devised.

A small scratching announced the presence of a red-haired boy in the tent's entry.

'Ah. Ector Minor.' Artor smiled indulgently. 'Come forward, young master, and join us. As we talk, I'll explain to you how a map works.'

Bran's son was a tall, sturdy boy who was blessed with a powerful upper body inherited from his paternal grandfather, Llanwith pen Bryn. His carrot-coloured hair curled in wild spirals and he possessed brilliant green eyes that seemed to see clear through anything, or anyone, that caught his attention.

'I can sketch the position of the enemy companies on this vellum as if I was a hawk flying high above them. Can you see how a map gives us an advantage?'

The boy gazed at Artor with cool intensity. He nodded, and

Taliesin knew the lad had immediately understood the concepts involved.

'A map allows a war chief to plan what he might do', Ector said. 'He can see where everyone is, on both sides, and he can change his mind if his enemy does something unexpected.'

Artor grinned delightedly. 'Excellent, Ector. A leader need never be taken by surprise on the battlefield if he is clever.'

Artor introduced each of his war chiefs – including Bors, the dour Dumnonii king, who rarely smiled under his shock of thick black hair. He had strange, lambent grey eyes. Having only recently inherited his throne, and as a man who had avoided the courts of power, Bors was something of an enigma. Artor explained the histories of his captains to Ector, and acknowledged Bors as kin through the High King's mother, the fabled Ygerne. Each man bowed seriously to the boy, as if he was an equal.

Ector blushed, but his eyes never dropped as he politely greeted each king and war chief by name.

Artor's plan could be a triumph of calculated risk, Taliesin decided. Artor saw the whole pattern of the game, like the hawk, while his captains only understood their part upon the board.

Little happened during the course of that afternoon.

Across the ford, Modred's large, sky-blue leather tent drew every eye but, other than exchanging catcalls and scornful insults, the enemies did not engage.

At dusk, all but the sentries were stood down to take their rest. Stars filled the clear velvet skies with little pinholes of white light, like holes stabbed in a blackened curtain.

'For the time being, we'll leave Modred to wait and worry,' Artor explained. 'Even that cold-blooded traitor is capable of anxiety while he waits for his destiny to unfold.'

Wrapped warmly in thick furs, the king fell asleep sitting bolt upright in his campaign chair. Ector slept in a pile of furs near the tent flap, while Gareth watched over him.

Gareth's silver, uncut hair was bound with bands of plaited brass, so that it hung below his waist in a thick rope. His face was a little lined under his deep tan and his body had stiffened so that the limber elegance of his youth was a lost memory, but his appearance was deceptive. Like his grandmother, Frith, Artor's first foster-mother, whom he now resembled, Gareth was as strong as an oak tree. And as watchful and wise.

Earlier, Artor had charged Gareth with his new and difficult duty.

'You cared for Licia when our world was young, Gareth, and you still have some years left to you.'

'Aye, King Artor, my god continues to spare me.'

'I am entrusting my great-grandson to your care. In the years ahead, Ector will need you to guard his back and offer him sound advice. His relationship with me, should he become High King, will put him under threat, so he will need someone who knows and understands the corruption of court life. He's not a playful boy, so he needs someone who will treat him seriously, but love him for himself.' Artor gripped Gareth's shoulder affectionately. 'Besides, you know all the old histories. You lived through them, so who better to make Ector into a man.'

'But Artor, shouldn't his father fulfil that duty?'

'Of course, but his father will be too busy saving his lands to guide the boy's path. Promise me that you will serve me for the rest of your life in this matter.'

Gareth had bowed his head in acquiescence.

Few Celts slept deeply that night.

The morrow promised blood, and any warrior who could count knew that Artor's army was vastly outnumbered. Yet the air was sweet with the scents of early summer, and the rain that fell before dawn was light and soft. The warriors were convinced that they were embarked on a war hallowed by God, whoever that deity might be.

Artor rose before dawn stained the sky and was soon dressed in full battle gear. He immediately called on Odin to prepare for a special mission to humiliate and goad the enemy forces into taking precipitate action. Warriors began to wander just out of bowshot range and performed sundry crude actions towards the Brigante camp. They bared their backsides, or their privates, made rude gestures and shouted complicated descriptions of their enemy's mothers.

The army of the west waited stiffly, utilizing the discipline of well-trained troops for most of that day until, late in the afternoon, a large Brigante warrior rode out into the shallows of the river and shouted out that he was the appointed envoy of Modred.

'Find out what the Matricide wants, Bedwyr,' Artor ordered crisply.

Obediently, Bedwyr trotted his horse over the dried grasses and broken reeds on the margins of the river, until its hocks were buried in green water. A gentle breeze played through the bulrushes and disturbed the dragonflies as they skipped out from the waterweeds.

'Bedwyr stands for Artor,' the Cornovii shouted. 'So talk.'

The Brigante warrior was large, hirsute and humourless. Bedwyr noticed that his battle gear was clean and well-oiled, and he wondered where the warrior had received the scar that cut across his cheek and distorted his nose.

'My king, Modred, demands that Artor relinquishes the field to a younger man. He insists that the High King must retreat from our lands, or else he'll be humiliated and killed in battle.'

'Words, words, words!' Bedwyr shouted back derisively at the Brigante warrior. 'If you're so confident, come and fight, traitor! We're here! We're ready to fight you! The murdered citizens of Deva call out for revenge.'

'Your men are cowards who hunker down by this river,' the Brigante warrior countered as he jerked on his horse's reins. The animal bridled and snorted. 'We challenge you to come over and fight!'

'Perhaps when the Brigante tribe finds its nerve you might come to your High King and give your justification for your treachery and betrayal. You murdered fellow Celts! Artor demands an explanation; we demand to hear a reason to justify such a crime! You outnumber us, so the gods of war will surely stand with you if your cause is just.'

Then, as an afterthought, and because the Brigante's voice was familiar, Bedwyr threw out one last barbed challenge.

'I know you, Brigante! You stood with Artor at Mori Saxonicus when we were all young. How have you come to this pass, to serve a man of Modred's mettle? We who stood and died at the shield wall were true brothers. How could you betray us?'

A red stain of embarrassment flushed the warrior's face, causing the scar to stand out like a fresh white wound.

'I am Brigante, and Mori Saxonicus was a long time ago!' The warrior spat, and then raised one clenched, armoured fist. 'Look for me in the coming battle, Arden Knife. My name is Cadwy Scarface, and I remember the past, and old sins, as if it were yesterday.'

Bedwyr cursed and lifted his sword so it flashed in the afternoon light.

'How could you forget the blood of King Luka, hero of a hundred Brigante battles? How can you ignore that Celt will fight Celt on these fair fields because of your king's greed? Modred does not have the endorsement of the Council of Tribes, and he isn't even a legitimate heir. Your forces killed the peaceful, neutral traders of Deva just to lure out the Ordovice king. How can you justify what you have done?'

Cadwy Scarface flinched as each word pierced his armour of arrogance.

'Will you ask King Bran to allow you to settle in his mountains when the Saxons come knocking on the walls of your towns and villages? Or will you take ship for Hibernia? Better still, will you grovel and promise to serve the Pictish kings, your allies, when you flee over the Wall? If these horrors come to pass, remember that Bedwyr, King of the Forests of Arden, warned you that there are consequences for treason.'

Bedwyr laughed at Cadwy's flushed, angry face, then wheeled his horse and cantered back to the High King. His mouth smiled, but his mind wept for the warrior he had stood with in the shield wall at Mori Saxonicus, although all he remembered of Cadwy in those bloody days was a pair of grim, brown eyes under a battered, iron helm.

'Their ragtag rabble are all huff and puff, without substance,' he reported to Artor. 'Modred is posturing for the benefit of the Picts, but they won't attack us, regardless of their rhetoric. Cadwy Scarface was used for parlay only because he is a warrior with a stern reputation, but the words of Modred are base coinage. Many of his men have fought and bled alongside us as brothers in our cause and my heart shudders at the thought of slaying fellow Celts. But Modred has left us with no other choice.'

'We'll wait for another day,' Artor decided. 'Let their nerves stretch a little. Tomorrow we'll rest, for I'll wager my crown that Modred will sit in his blue tent like a lump of wood. The day after, in the early afternoon, we will begin our attack, just when they are most comfortable over their cooking fires. Instruct the captains to explain my decision to the men. This waiting is hard on everyone.'

Bedwyr nodded his understanding, wheeled his horse again and trotted off towards the left horn of the crescent where Bors of the Dumnonii waited like a huge, hulking bull.

'So, it's about to start, Bedwyr,' Bors growled. 'Artor's plan is risky.'

'It is, but that's how the High King wins. He'll succeed in this battle, as he always does.'

'We live in extraordinary times,' Bors responded and turned away.

In his campaign tent, Artor instructed Taliesin to find Pelles. 'Tell him he is to target Modred's tent with flame arrows when we ride over the ford. The colour offends my good taste, and I find its destruction irresistible.'

Artor turned to his bodyguard. 'Odin, do you suppose that you can find a small group of volunteers who'd enjoy insulting the Picts and Brigante all day? Yesterday's group was very colourful, but today I want you to find warriors who speak Pictish. It's time to plant some burrs under woad-covered arses and place them in a fit mood to meet us.'

Odin grinned. 'I'll have more volunteers than I'll ever need.'

Taliesin bowed briskly and left with Odin, whose shoulders were shaking with laughter. Taliesin trotted off to find Pelles Minor, son of the one-eyed Scum captain who had served as Artor's loyal mercenary for many years, while Odin was engulfed by foot soldiers who soon became loudly amused at the orders issued by the Jutlander.

Pelles had erected the tents of his archers behind the broad flanks of Artor's army. Taliesin noted the neatness, the cleanliness and the efficient purposefulness of Pelles' command. Taliesin had heard tales of Pelles Major, a one-eyed ruffian with a talent for survival. His son appeared to share many of his father's gifts.

Pelles was checking barrels filled with arrows and a supply of sheep's fat that was to be used for incendiaries. He certainly looks disreputable, Taliesin thought. But at least the son has two good eyes.

Pelles Minor was obviously not a Celt by race, even though he had been born within the isles of Britain. His father had been small, slight and very dark, a typical Roman mercenary, but his son stood taller, close to five feet and seven inches, which made him a veritable giant of his race. Pelles Minor was

545 ✝

burly where his father had been all whipcord and sinewy muscle. Pelles Major had possessed a scarred, unprepossessing face, but his son was almost handsome, except for the closeness of his green eyes.

'Greetings, Taliesin,' Pelles Minor said in an unexpected baritone voice that was particularly loud in volume. 'Don't look so surprised, song-master; we have all heard of the son of Myrddion.'

Taliesin blushed. 'And I have heard of you, son of Pelles who was the last of the Scum. My father spoke of your sire with affection. But enough politeness, for I have little time to waste on ancient history.'

He smiled at the archer to rob his brusqueness of insult. Pelles smiled back like a pike, all teeth and thinly disguised hunger.

'The High King requires the particular skills of your archers.'

'The battlefield will be won by the cavalry, but I agree that my arrows tend to even up the numbers.'

'As you know, Artor plans to make a feint across the river with his personal guard. If the strategy works, Modred's main force will charge across the shallows of the river in the hope of capturing Artor's head. But their response will make them vulnerable to our cavalry and your archers.'

Pelles was becoming irritated by the harpist's tone and manner.

'I was there, harpist, I heard the king's plans at first hand. I've been up here working out the details. No offence, Taliesin, but as a song-master, you know bugger all about battlefields.'

'I meant no insult, Pelles . . .'

'Pa always said Myrddion's only sin was that he liked the sound of his own voice.'

In the small silence that followed, Taliesin digested the insult.

Pelles pointed to small knots of men at the rear of Modred's camp. 'The flaw in Artor's plan is that Modred also has archers, and he'll pincushion Artor, and his guard, before they leave the river. Artor will depend on my men to even the odds a little in the initial feint attack, especially when he begins his retreat. His unprotected back will be a tantalizing target for Brigante arrows. There'll be no difficulty in supplying an arrow storm, but the bolts will fall where they fall and, if we miscalculate, some arrows might kill friend as well as foe. But if the High King commands us to fire our weapons, we'll do so, even if it seems a crazy idea. My pa always said that Artor was crazy like a fox.'

'At the risk of offending you further, Artor would be grateful if you could remove Modred's blue tent with some flaming arrows at some convenient time after the feint attack commences. I would only add that Artor chose me to deliver his orders because I happened to be the nearest warm and breathing body.'

'No matter, Taliesin. Does the colour of the tent annoy my king as much as it does me?'

'He doesn't like its shade or its size but its owner offends him most.'

'I'll shoot that arrow myself,' Pelles rumbled, his dark brows bristling.

Taliesin nodded. 'I fear that the High King courts death by placing himself in harm's way, but I hope I'm proved wrong.'

'Ask the king to dress in armour over a sturdy ox-hide shirt. Or a pad of iron at the back. He'll need it!' Pelles laughed and slapped Taliesin's back so hard that the harpist almost overbalanced. 'Stick to your harp, Taliesin. Artor has made up his mind and he knows what he's doing.'

The two men parted amicably and Taliesin returned to the High King, rubbing his shoulder where Pelles had clapped him on the back.

The day ended and night fell. Artor slept like an innocent, certain that he had considered everything that could affect his control of the coming battle. Gareth told Ector stories about Anderida and Mori Saxonicus until the boy fell asleep, his dreams full of heroic battles, staunch courage and cruel death. Later, Taliesin listened in the shadows as Gareth and Odin talked as old friends do, of times long past. When the old men slept, Taliesin stayed alert, as poems formed and swirled in his mind.

Eventually, he could no longer bear the enclosed space of the tent and stepped out into the soft night air. The many fires of the great encampment had burned low, providing a soft light that gently limned the outlines of sleeping men. As he walked between the campfires and made for the longer grass near the picket lines, he heard a tuneless whistling that carried on the slight breeze. A soft voice challenged him, and a mounted cavalry officer loomed up out of the darkness like a wraith. Taliesen responded with his name and his purpose in being abroad, and felt oddly comforted. Armed men prowled the fringes of the camp, alert to the smallest sound or untoward movement.

✝ ✝ ✝

Shadows were lengthening the following day when Artor strode from his campaign tent in his gilded armour and mounted his horse.

His personal guard appeared like smoke from the body of the army.

'We ride,' Artor called, eager to retain the advantage of surprise.

'We ride,' fifty strong throats shouted back.

In disciplined lines, the guard moved their horses from a walk to a trot, then to a canter and finally to a full gallop through the shallows of the river as they maintained their impetus towards the enemy lines. As the Brigante and the Picts deserted their cooking fires in sudden panic, Pelles unleashed his archers. A volley of arrows sailed over the heads of the guard and fell on the enemy. Among them were several fire arrows, aimed at Modred's brilliant blue tent.

Taliesin watched from the small knoll where Artor had first voiced his intention to draw out Modred.

Artor's horse gained purchase on the muddy shingle of the riverbank and the red-cloaked figure charged towards a running huddle of Picts. His arm was upraised and the remnants of the sun's direct rays turned Caliburn into a flaming brand. The guard ploughed through the Pict defenders with a loud clang of metal against metal and wheeled to destroy any man still standing.

Another flaming arrow arced out of the rear of the Celtic lines and, this time, it met its target. The blue tent erupted in flame.

Taliesin smiled to see it.

But the Brigante warriors had served under Artor's command for decades. They were familiar with Artor's tactics and his penchant for lightning-fast attacks, and their grizzled officers had anticipated this tactic. Although the afternoon light was in their eyes, they knew how to respond. In ordered rows, they fell into a defensive stance with their spear points at the ready, and taunted Artor to attack them in a full frontal assault.

'Ride back, Artor!' Taliesin shouted uselessly. 'You'll be cut to pieces if you continue!'

His pleas were as useless as dried leaves against a sudden, freshening wind.

Artor hit the waiting phalanx – and his attack was blunted by the shock.

Taliesin winced as the force of cavalry struck at the massed foot soldiers. Shield screamed against shield, spears pierced the breastbones of horses, and warriors were flung headlong on to the hoof-churned earth.

'Ride back, Artor!' Taliesin called to his king once more. 'Ride back!'

But Artor knew that the Brigante wouldn't follow unless they believed his attack was a complete failure and, for the feint to work, many of his personal guard would have to be sacrificed. At the rear of Modred's lines, Taliesin could just make out some sudden activity as the Brigante cavalry released their horses from the picket line.

'God help them,' he muttered.

In a moment of clarity, Taliesin understood that Artor's personal guard must be chopped to pieces, for nothing else would cause the Brigante to lose their heads and commence a full frontal attack. Artor could not have sent another man in his place, for the responsibility for the death and destruction of those men, many of them his own sons, must rest on the broad shoulders of the High King.

A high, thin wail rose above the sounds of battle. Taliesin turned and saw Ector, perched upon Gareth's shoulder, his face as white as newly washed wool and his right hand pointing towards the battlefield. The boy's green eyes were dark and terrified.

A fragile hope whispered in Taliesin's heart that Percivale's god would not permit such fine men to die so wastefully. In desperation, Taliesin began a fervent prayer to the Christian god.

From above, battlefields are silent, strategic board games, where the action is clear in its entirety. But in the heart of the fray, the battle is a confusing cacophony of clashing armour, thundering hooves, and screaming men.

Slurries of mud and blood threatened both horsemen and foot soldiers. Wounded horses lay in their own gore and entrails, kicking out at friend and foe alike, while warriors slid and cursed amid the thrusts and screams of a terrible chorus of death. Riderless horses further impeded the field and struggled to survive the conflict.

A man appeared out of the fray beside Artor and, for a moment, the High King thought he saw a younger version of himself, maddened, and with upraised sword, smashing a Pictish face into bloody pulp. Another mirror image, but achingly young, screamed shrilly as he pushed his body down the shaft of the spear that impaled him to kill the warrior who held it. Around the High King, in a grim, bloody display, Artor saw himself killing and being killed, over and over again.

Artor had retained his horse, although blood steadily seeped from a long, shallow sword cut across its flank where a Pict had narrowly missed a gut-splitting blow. Fought almost to a standstill, Artor wheeled and turned his horse by the pressure of his knees alone, swinging his sword in wicked, scythe-like arcs that protected him inside a circlet of steel.

One tattooed Pict leapt up on the back of the king's horse, forcing Artor to drop his shield and employ his dragon knife to dislodge the blue-faced warrior. The king was not unscathed in the encounter. Reckless with hate, the Pict found a chink in Artor's armour near his sword belt, and drove his knife home.

In the heat of the conflict, Artor scarcely felt the wound. His eyes scanned the rear and saw the cavalry forming. Around him, red, russet and tawny heads bowed under the intensity of the struggle, while wounded and maimed warriors from both camps lay sprawled in the mud. Barely half of Artor's force remained on their horses.

Odin appeared out of one cluster of warriors, casually sweeping enemy soldiers from his path with his bloody, brain-spattered axe.

'It's time for us to leave, Artor,' he shouted. 'Our men can't hold much longer.'

'If they still live, pick up the wounded that are afoot,' Artor screamed to his men. 'Retreat! Retreat! Retreat!'

Such was the discipline of his men that Artor's orders were obeyed as if in slow motion, and without panic. Where a rider still had a whole beast, he reached down and assisted a companion who was in peril. Slowly, ever so slowly, Artor's troops wheeled, disengaged and retreated back along the route they had come. Taliesin watched as the red-cloaked figure of the king tarried at the rear of his departing warriors to slow down the enemy advance.

As the personal guard galloped into the river, Pelles ordered the archers to resume their relentless rain of arrows.

The Brigante cavalry arrived on the scene with a great thunder of galloping hooves. The enemy phalanx parted to allow the horsemen to engage the Celtic stragglers, while Artor roared defiance as they advanced. The small mountain ponies used by the Brigante were swift, for all that they were shaggy and unkempt, and Artor and Odin were in danger of being cut off. Then, just as Artor at last began to retreat from the field, Modred finally remembered his own archers, and Artor's escape route was suddenly filled with flights of arrows.

Artor had dropped his shield. One bolt struck his horse, but the thick armour of ox hide protected the poor beast from a fatal wound. Several arrows fell away harmlessly from Artor's mailed back, but his red cloak was now the prime target for every one of Modred's archers. Every eye on both sides of the riverbank was focused on the figure in the red cloak.

Odin turned, summed up the danger to his king with a single glance, and abandoned his own wounded horse in the water. As Artor's beast swam past, Odin scrambled on to its blood-streaked back behind Artor and clutched at the king's belt like a limpet. Unaware that his old servant had deliberately relinquished his horse, Artor used one hand to grip Odin's leather coat and drove his beast on. As the horse's legs gained some purchase on the gravel of the riverbank, Artor heaved a sigh of relief and slackened the furious pace.

He turned his horse to face the enemy. Had Modred's men taken the bait? How long could he stand here, exposed to enemy fire, to tempt the Brigante to leave the safety of their bivouac?

The air around him hummed and buzzed with arrows from both sides. Artor stood his ground until Bedwyr drove his horse at breakneck speed to Artor's side and lifted his own shield to protect the body of the king.

Artor was quick to assess the fruits of the sacrifice made by his personal guard. The Brigante cavalry had scented blood and were already in the shallows as they chased the remnants of Artor's attacking force. The Pictish foot soldiers followed their cavalry across the shallows in hot pursuit, screaming and whooping battle cries as they ran.

The Brigante phalanx was the only enemy unit with the discipline to hold its position.

On the far side of the shallow river, already alive with Modred's horsemen and the first foot soldiers holding their weapons above their heads, Artor could see the Brigante king on a white horse as he waited at the head of his troops. Now that Artor's force had retreated to their own side of the river, the Brigante king was belatedly playing the role of a leader of men.

Fronting the phalanx, Modred appeared to argue with a Brigante warrior. Bedwyr could just make out a white scar under the shadow of the officer's helmet. Cadwy Scarface!

'Come away, Artor,' Bedwyr shouted, the whites of his eyes clearly visible. 'Or we'll both be trapped.'

'A moment!' Artor ordered.

The High King watched the pantomime of Modred striking the captain of the phalanx with his open hand. No words were needed to show that a dispute was taking place in the enemy encampment. The hands of the grizzled warrior rose momentarily towards his sword pommel and then rejected the hasty action. With some slight gesticulation, the captain's orders set the phalanx on the march towards Artor's positions.

Finally, Artor wheeled his horse and galloped towards his own lines.

'The Brigante are coming!' Artor shouted in a stentorian voice. 'Prepare! Prepare! Back to your position, Bedwyr. Our strategy is working.'

Gareth intercepted his king as soon as Artor reached his foot soldiers.

'Order your men into position, Gareth,' Artor yelled. 'Prepare to repel a cavalry charge.'

Like deadly puppets, Artor's troops formed into battle lines. The front row of soldiers dropped into a uniform crouch, anchored their shields firmly in the earth and positioned their spears so that the points formed a hedgehog of metallic quills. The second row used their shields to partially protect the front row so that a wall of iron confronted the charging horse soldiers. A third row consisted of reserves ready to fill the breaches made by the attacking cavalry.

Artor wheeled his horse and headed for the knoll, followed by Gareth.

'Lord, you must permit us to care for Odin,' Gareth shouted, his white hair streaming back from his face in the breeze. The boy, Ector, followed Gareth on his hill pony, his face strained and pale, his right hand clutching at a short knife at his waist.

555

Artor shook his head slowly, like an old bull tormented by arrows he couldn't deflect.

'What did you say, Gareth?' Artor asked. 'Is Odin hurt?'

'Aye, lord.' Gareth nodded. 'He is sorely wounded.'

Then Artor saw a cluster of men running towards him, accompanied by Taliesin with a leather satchel in his hand.

'My lord,' Gareth pleaded, 'you must release your hold on Odin.'

Artor did so and the healers lifted the old warrior down. His body fell slackly once Taliesin forced Odin's hand to release its death grip on Artor's sword belt.

Artor's old friend was dead before he reached the ground. A dozen arrows had pierced his leather shirt between the heavy bands of iron that strengthened it.

'Odin!' Artor murmured brokenly within his helmet. Something shattered within the consciousness of the High King. Odin had taken every arrow aimed at the broad back of his master.

'We shall wade through a sea of blood, old friend, to avenge you,' Artor vowed. 'For Death! For the Celts! For Artor!' he roared as the Brigante horsemen began to close in on his defensive position.

The enemy cavalry struck and the force of the impact juddered through the bones of both men and beasts. Horses screamed with the high-pitched sounds of women's wailing, and oaths, cries and prayers were melded into a cacophony of noise. Artor's eyes did not leave the front line, but the king's mind was slowed, so that the carnage he observed around him seemed to be the exaggerated gestures of play actors. Odin couldn't be dead! The sun still shone, and the grass still grew.

His own heart still pumped, and his eyes still saw.

Odin couldn't be dead!

The enemy wheeled away and struggled through the tangle of fallen men and horses. Once again, they charged the Celtic lines and Artor watched numbly as Modred's men fell under the weight of their horses, only to be replaced smoothly by other horsemen from the rear of the attacking force.

For a third time, the Brigante cavalry retreated and then, out of the chaos, Artor's warriors saw a wave of armed infantry rushing towards them.

'Death to the traitors!' Artor screamed. 'Death to all men who attack their own!'

'Death to the traitors!' echoed from hundreds of throats.

Gareth used a polished plate of silver to catch the sun high above them to send a signal to the commanders who were on the tips of the crescent formation. Within a few heartbeats, Artor saw Bors and Bedwyr on the move as their cavalry swept wide to encircle the whole field and enclose the Brigante and Pictish warriors within a net of death.

'Death to the traitors! Death to Modred!'

The sounds of battle rose and swelled. The ground, the hill and the sky seemed to echo the cries across the field as seasoned warriors turned on each other in a carnage rendered more terrible because it was personal, hand-to-hand combat.

The depleted lines of Celtic warriors began to step forward smoothly under the orders of their captains, with the men at each end of the line curving visibly inward. The king spun on his heel, grasped Gareth's hand in his mailed fist, either in commiseration or farewell, before remounting and spurring his horse back into the fray.

Gareth followed slowly, his shoulders slumped. Behind him, Ector was left with three survivors of Artor's charge. The boy's huge eyes reflected the horrors he had seen.

In the distance, Artor caught a flash of blue. Ostentatious as ever, Modred had ridden with his household cavalry to enjoy the rout of the Celts from a position of relative safety. Artor headed towards the patch of colour, his red cloak streaming behind him like a pennon. Foot soldiers and horsemen made way for his passage, for Artor's shark eyes were set inexorably upon Modred's blue cloak.

Odin's death, the loss of the twins and the tragedy of the Cup all fused together in the king's mind to find expression in a ferocious charge at the Matricide. Artor drove his horse into the beast ridden by Modred, forcing the animal back on its haunches where it scrambled for purchase on the churned earth. Modred screamed shrilly and parried Artor's vicious overhead blow with his own sword. Muscles cracked under the strain, but youth and desperation won, and Artor found himself unseated.

But Modred's beast lost its footing. Falling backwards and screaming shrilly, Modred and his horse both landed heavily.

Artor was in the guard position immediately, although every bone and muscle shouted an old man's pain.

'Defend yourself, Modred!'

'You're bleeding, old man,' Modred scrambled to his feet and recovered his sword. 'When will you admit that you're past all this effort?'

'When you are dead!'

The blade of the dragon knife purred as the king drew it from its sheath.

As soon as Modred was on his feet, Artor feinted and then changed direction. Modred's talent was for subterfuge, not in the use of arms. The younger Artorex would have spitted him on his sword like a fish. But Artor was old, and he was slow. His muscles screamed with weariness and only his unconquered will kept him on his feet.

The king's thrust went wide.

Modred countered with an underhand, scything sweep designed to keep Artor at bay more than anything else. Artor stepped inside the sword blow and dashed the blade away.

Modred's chest was exposed. The dragon knife clanged against Modred's blade and slid down and across, finding an easy passage through skin, bone and muscle before Artor twisted the knife and wrenched it free.

Modred stared at his own blood on the blade. Artor's strike had missed the Brigante's heart, but the High King's sword was now moving in for the killing blow. Modred clearly saw Caliburn as it came at him, as if the passage of time had slowed.

He shrieked in horror.

As the king's sword sheared down towards Modred's shoulder, it angled across to sever the carotid and jugular arteries. As Artor struck, Modred used his own long knife to strike upward at Artor's abdomen. The blade skidded along the High King's mail with a spark of fire before finding a break in his armour and gashing him over the wound inflicted earlier by the Pict warrior. The cut wasn't overly deep but it was bloody.

Caliburn smashed through Modred's armour, flesh and bone.

Modred's head was almost severed from his body by the

force of Artor's blow and fell grotesquely on to his right shoulder. His mouth filled with blood as he fell, and the bright scarlet fountain splashed over Artor's feet.

Modred was dead and Artor still stood, although the blue sky reeled about him and the earth felt as insubstantial as thistledown.

Faithful Gareth was at the High King's side in an instant, although he, too, was bleeding from half a dozen wounds.

Wearily, Artor leaned against his servant and watched the battle swirl around him.

The Picts fought on until every warrior was dead, but they reaped a deadly harvest of Celts as they fell. Without a master, the Brigante began to run when they realized that King Modred had perished.

'Permit them to leave the field,' Artor ordered. 'Their tainted king is slain, so let the tribe bear the shame of treason forever. They can run until their legs are bloody stumps.'

Taliesin was called to the king's side as soon as Artor could be persuaded to rest. The army was mopping up the enemy wounded, gathering the bodies of comrades for cremation or tossing the enemy corpses into the river.

'Let the sea consume their flesh,' Artor had ordered, and his instructions were followed to the letter.

In his tent, with his armour stripped from his body and clean rags applied to his wounds, Artor could finally relinquish his iron control.

Taliesin thrust his way past Artor's captains and knelt beside the pallet of the High King. He fumbled for his healer's satchel.

When Taliesin saw the awkward slash over a deep triangular

wound that scarcely oozed blood, he knew that Artor had suffered a mortal blow.

Three women rode through the closing afternoon light over the low flatlands below Mamucium. One had hair so blond that it was silver; one was brunette, as dark as a raven's wing upon a field of snow; and the third had hair the colour of fallen leaves in the dying light. They had come from the west, the east and the north.

The three queens reached Artor's encampment the day after the battle.

Queen Enid of the Otadini had not seen Artor's face since the bloody night that her son, Galahad, had been born. She had known then, in her secret heart, that her husband, Gawayne, was the queen's lover and she had wept bitter tears over the head of her baby. Now, she mourned the loss of her son, as did Gawayne, who was mired in his own nasty war of attrition against rebels who lusted after his throne. But he had yearned to stand with his uncle one last time, so Enid's duty had been clear. She must ride to give Otadini allegiance to Artor, although she was only a woman.

The three queens had met in Mamucium, as Nimue had foreseen.

As the women rode past the quiet camp, hazy with the drifting smoke of cremation, the warriors bowed in nameless superstition, for the air seemed to shiver about them with strange energy. The queens appeared to personify water, earth, and wind. Magic had come again to the west, so the whisper ran through the troops, and no sane person should speak to Otherworld queens who have come to harvest the souls of men.

Artor lay supine on his pallet, his aged face creased with pain and worry. Taliesin knelt beside his king, forcing a soporific between the dying man's teeth. Although Artor knew his strength was failing, his mind and eyes remained clear.

'I have come to the end of my time on this earth,' he murmured. 'And it is not so very bad.'

When he saw Enid's face, Artor smiled uncertainly.

'Is Gawayne well, my lady?' he asked. 'You may tell him that no bad blood lies between us. He must hold the Otadini lands safe during my absence.'

'Hush, my lord,' Enid said. 'Gawayne will hold firm.'

'Nimue?' Artor's face lit up as he made out her shining face in the gloom. 'You've not changed overly with the march of the years. Do you still wear my mark?'

'To the death, my lord.' The Lady of the Lake lifted her green-grey robe and Artor saw the rampant dragon coiling up her right leg.

'Odin made that tattoo.' Then his eyes darkened with the pain of grief. 'Odin is dead. He died protecting me against Modred.'

'Odin chose his own destiny many years ago,' Nimue explained gently.

'I've missed Myrddion so much, Nimue. I'd give anything to see him again.'

'He's waiting for you.'

Then Anna was beside the High King, and Gallia's gentle expression embraced him from the grave.

'My lady, you had no need to come to this place,' Artor protested weakly. 'Battlefields aren't for you.'

Anna stroked the dying man's hands with work-hardened fingers so like his own.

'Did you think you could keep me away, Father? At last, I may tell you that your long silence has not harmed me. Some matters are greater than the demands of the human heart and, like my mother, I always understood. Be at peace, Father, for your long labour is over.'

'Truly?'

'Truly, lord. Now sleep while we watch over you. Have no fear of the darkness for we've come to light your way.'

'It would be good to rest for a while, but there is still so much to do.'

Nimue smiled. 'Others can finish what you have begun. Sleep, and dream, dear Artor.'

The High King sighed and his eyes began to close. Then, abruptly, he dragged himself back from sleep and called for Bedwyr. He was so distressed that Nimue ordered that the Cornovii should be found immediately.

Bedwyr had led a cavalry charge on the right horn of the army crescent during the battle, a position Artor had insisted on, in order to keep the Arden Knife safe. Even so, Bedwyr had reaped a bitter harvest of Brigante souls as the traitors tried to flee back across the river and on to Bremetennacum. He had hunted the fleeing warriors down like vermin.

Now, in response to Artor's call, he came running. He paused outside the king's tent to straighten his hair and jerkin, and then entered the presence of the High King.

He bowed low.

'Bedwyr, my friend, you must ensure that Caliburn goes to

Lady Nimue. She will know what to do with my sword. Protect her, and keep your word to me.'

Shock, loss and pain struggled for mastery in Bedwyr's eyes.

Artor fell back on the pillows. 'What has been done with Odin?'

'He lies with the other dead from your personal guard, my king. They will be burned in the morning. Do you wish any special arrangements to be made for your friend?'

Artor shook his head. 'Odin was a warrior and I'll not dishonour him by sending him to his gods unaccompanied. Let his ashes mingle with the remains of my sons. Those of my guard who still live belong to Ector now. Their oaths to me belong to the son of King Bran. Give him my scrolls as well . . . and my maps.'

Anna's lips trembled but her eyes remained dry. Exhausted, Artor closed his eyes.

'He should rest now, Mother.' Taliesin knuckled his eyes like an unhappy child. 'I cannot tell how long he will endure.'

The three queens left Artor's tent, and stood amidst the organized bustle of a successful army. A huge tower of bodies had been built on rafts of tree logs near the riverbank, some distance from the Celtic encampment. Closer, and more poignant, a smaller tower of timber and dead warriors rose, ready for incineration, with Odin lying in state at the apex.

'Ah, brave heart,' Nimue whispered. 'Asgaad awaits you.'

'He'll not go there.' Bedwyr's voice was thick with unshed tears. 'Not if Artor chooses the Underworld of the Romans. King and servant are hand-fasted forever, and Odin would happily give up his heaven for his master.'

A troop of Celtic cavalry rode across the river and added

more weapons and shields to an ever-growing pile of captured arms that had been collected from the battlefield. When the warriors saw Bedwyr with the queens, they nodded respectfully and addressed the Cornovii king.

'The hunting is good, my lord. Not a single Pict will return to their highlands and the Brigante are crushed. Our king has won a great victory.'

'Aye, men. Aye,' Bedwyr said quietly.

When the warriors had ridden past, he turned back to the queens; his face was streaked with tears.

'But who'll hold back the Saxons from Lavatrae and fair Melandra? It will all be lost now – all of the loveliness that he created.'

'Look around you, Bedwyr.' Anna pointed at the churned earth, the smoke rising from the burning corpses of horses, and the huge store of weapons, armour and shields that spoke mutely of violent death. A wagon was already stacked with precious objects that had been looted from the dead, ready for the long journey to Cadbury.

'What loveliness exists here, except the brotherhood of men? And who can see loyalty, or love, or duty with human eyes? But these qualities live in this place of death, even though the earth has run with blood and corruption scents the soft air with the reek of carrion. Feel it, Bedwyr. The land goes on. We are the ones who decay and die.'

'Artor must not die here,' Enid said quietly. 'His reputation will keep the west free from invasion for a little space until the Saxons discover that he has died and passed into the shadows. We must take him back to Glastonbury so we can perform the necessary rites.'

'No!' Bedwyr exclaimed. 'You mustn't move him. The army could easily lose heart, and Artor's life might still be saved if we care for him properly.'

'We must move him,' Nimue replied firmly. 'The continued safety of the west demands that King Artor departs this field in the manner of a High King. Gather the army together, friend Bedwyr, so we may speak to them. Meanwhile, you must prepare a cart with all the necessary comforts to ensure that Artor does not suffer during his journey. Taliesin will know what has to be done.'

Nimue turned to Bors and Pelles Minor, who had come to Artor's tent in Bedwyr's wake, and both men shifted nervously from foot to foot. Neither man was particularly superstitious, but they sensed that legends would come into being from this strange evening.

'You, Bors, in company with Pelles, are in charge of returning our warriors to their homes,' Nimue instructed. 'You must then secure Cadbury Tor until Artor recovers or a successor assumes the throne as the new High King of the Britons. You must not fail in this!'

The two captains bowed. If they found anything odd in obeying orders issued by a woman, they did not show it. Privately, they wondered if these queens were even mortal.

The following dawn, Odin was consigned to the fire with Artor's personal guard, and departed for his final meeting with his gods. Artor was present, propped upright on his campaign stool, his pain dulled by poppy juice. Throughout the ceremony, his face remained composed, but some warriors swore that he wept as Odin's corpse blackened and burned.

Throughout the day, preparations were made for departure

and, as the long dusk lengthened, torches and campfires were lit and the army gathered on the banks of the river. Mounted on their steeds, the three queens rode forward to address the warriors, while Gareth and Taliesin ministered to their master in a hide-covered cart in preparation for the journey. Bedwyr held the reins of the carthorse loosely in his hands, awaiting his orders.

When Nimue addressed the warriors, her words rose over the murmurs of the men in a clear, pure voice that resembled the striking of silver bells.

'Men of the west! Brave hearts of the king! You have laboured here on these nameless fields to free your lands from a deadly danger. Now is the time for you to rest. Artor, the High King of the Britons, has been sorely wounded while killing the Matricide, Modred, and we have come to take our lord to Glastonbury to be healed. You must fear no danger. And you should not despair, for know you that when his people have most need of him, the High King will return. I, Nimue, the Lady of the Lake, do swear that what I say is true.'

Anna spoke next. Men looked at her, and could see the resemblance to their beloved King in the noble lines and bones of her face, and they accepted completely her right to address them.

'You know of me, men of the west, I am Anna, King Artor's kin, and I do not lie. I bore the twins, Balyn and Balan, who fought with you in our last Saxon summer, and who gave up their young lives for the west. When next you embrace your women and children, the High King will be with you; when you march to fight during another Saxon summer, Artor will ride with you and, when you face the last darkness, he will intercede for you with your gods to ease your journey. I swear that Artor will not die, because he is more than mere mortal flesh. You have only to call and he will be there, in your hearts, when you act with valour and honour.'

The crowd's fear and anxiety rose up in a flurry of cries and prayers. Queen Enid spoke so quietly that men were forced to pass her words back through the body of the army.

'People of the west, I bear the promise of King Gawayne that safe harbour will exist for any Celt beyond the Wall in our lands and he will endeavour to honour his promises to the High King should another Saxon summer come upon us. So, take heart, men of the west. You are not alone, though the winds of sorrow scar our hearts. I promise in my king's name, and over the body of my son, the hero Galahad.'

A few ragged cheers rose from the ranks.

'Fear no evil, people of the west.' Nimue lifted Caliburn with surprising ease. 'The sword of the High King is with you, regardless of the troubles, or the loneliness, that are yet to come. No other hand but Artor's will ever wield it, so keep faith with Artor and honour the Warrior of the West.'

At first, the crowd mumbled their doubts, but then a firm resolve entered their hearts and they roared their approval. Whether the king lived or died, he was theirs forever.

Nimue nodded to Bedwyr and the cart pulled away with the three queens riding before it.

And so Artor left the battlefield where he had risked and lost so much. His departure should have been ignominious, for he was borne away in a cart and placed on soft furs to ease the agony of his wounds. But something of his spirit invested the warriors of his guard with courage and dignity, and they held their heads high and their horses pranced with pride.

The army formed a pathway of honour and the warriors raised their weapons in tribute, while their voices stirred the sweet air of dusk in farewell.

'*Ave*, Artor, Warrior of the West!'

Artor heard the words repeated over and over as the cart took him away from all he had known and loved as a man, and tears snaked down his face.

The High King departed from the kingdom of the Celts, and was seen no more.

POSTSCRIPT

On a slate-grey day, flushed with the first autumnal fall of russet leaves, Taliesin and Lady Nimue returned again to the lake that lay in the fold near Caer Gai. Their mood was sombre, now that their separate duties were almost done.

Nimue wept at the recollection of how she, Enid and Anna had washed Artor's aged body, reduced to heavy bones covered with flaccid skin that no longer retained even a memory of youth. The long road to Glastonbury stretched ahead of them, but time must be stolen to serve these last devotions to their king.

Anna had kissed his calloused, sun browned hands that still retained a fragment of beauty in their length and delicacy, while Enid had washed his feet and dried them with her hair, much as the harlot Mary had done for Jesus five hundred years before. The Otadini queen recognized no blasphemy in her actions.

Nimue had closed the king's fatal wound and pressed a gold coin into Artor's mouth to pay the Ferryman, knowing that the Roman way had been close to the High King. The coin itself was minted with the head of Octavian, and Nimue knew that

Artor would have found some comfort in her gift.

On the long journey to Glastonbury, traders and pilgrims stepped aside from the cavalcade with superstitious dread, for who could look upon these faces of marbled beauty and not understand that something strange walked these dusty roads?

At Glastonbury, the monks sent up prayers, begging God to intercede and save the soul of Artor, the fabled son of Uther Pendragon.

'Perhaps their prayers will shorten his path to paradise,' Bishop Mark said reflectively, as a group of priests dug Artor's grave beside those of churchmen who had served Glastonbury, and Artor, so well.

'He'll only enter paradise if your god also shelters Targo, Myrddion, Odin and all of his pagan friends,' Nimue answered simply. 'My king will not consent to cross the portals to heaven without them.'

Bishop Mark had led a requiem Mass in the small church at Glastonbury for the salvation of Artor's soul. It was attended by the three queens, Taliesin, Bedwyr and Artor's surviving guard. Ector, with chin upraised to hide the tears that threatened to expose his weakness, stood beside his grandmother and gripped her hand tightly.

Finally, Mark spoke for the High King, for he had heard Artor's first, and last, confession, and he knew the depth and breadth of Artor's spirit.

'I will not speak of sins, for King Artor's faults are forgiven under the seal of the confessional. I will not speak of guilts, for King Artor carried shame for deeds that weren't of his own making, because he was a man with a conscience. But I will speak of what he did, for those exploits are what will endure down the wide, dark river of time.

'For a space, Artor saved our world. While he ruled the west, no Saxon set foot within the borders that he decided were part of his kingdom. No churches were burned, for the High King used his own body and brain to protect us from the barbarians. He gave up everything that less noble men hold dear to ensure that ordinary men and women possessed what he did not – a peaceful fireside and a quiet life.

'Do not bother with foolish regrets if, at the end, Artor's legacy fails. Without Artor, the Saxons would have destroyed the west thirty years ago, just as I know that they will come to Glastonbury's doors in time. But Artor has given us breathing space which will serve to civilize the Saxon enemy, so that the land will not be wholly destroyed. The Modreds of these isles are as nothing, mere huff and puff that will be used to frighten children in our future. But Artor will become everything that we aspire to be, while the man he was will be forgotten. Perhaps that is a pity, for Artor was good, strong and true. But so are many men. What he taught us is what will last. You did not lie, Nimue, when you promised the High King's army that Artor will come, again and again, whenever we have need of him. We will draw on his memory, and become all the stronger and better for it. So pray with me for the true king, under the legend that will be, for we will not see another warrior fit to take his place.'

Glastonbury's new bishop prayed long and hard when Artor was laid to rest under a great slab of stone that had been destined for his own grave. Mark hoped that his prayers would open the gates to heaven to Artor. Mark also prayed that God would show mercy to this wayward, well-intentioned son.

Nimue, irreverent to the end, hoped earnestly that the Christian god had sufficient sense of humour to cope with one such as her beloved Artor.

'Why do you weep, Mother?'

Taliesin's voice recalled Nimue to the fold in the hills where the tarn sat like a silver mirror, without ripples or obvious life.

'I believe that Artor was glad to die, for he was confident that he'd won a future for his people. In time, he will become a symbol of their struggle against extinction. We should rejoice, Taliesin, for Artor is at peace at last.'

'Platitudes. You weep, Mother, you do not rejoice.'

'I mourn for you, for myself and for our people. Artor is gone and, for all my promises to his warriors, he will never come again. Yet, as Bishop Mark suggested, our lord will bolster our courage in the future, so I suppose in that sense he is immortal. No one can kill an idea.'

Two days later, Bedwyr joined Nimue and Taliesin in a small boat in the centre of the lake. Here they would complete their final act of loyalty to Artor, king and man.

'The scroll of Artor's life is finished and will decay into dust,' Nimue intoned. 'So we must consign Artor's sword, the seal of his power, to the waters of the lake. Throw it high, Bedwyr, so that Artor may see that his orders have been obeyed and that no other hand will ever wield it.'

Bedwyr swung his arm and Caliburn flashed in the weak shafts of sunshine. At the top of his swing, he let the sword loose. It spun and turned, higher and higher until, at last, it slowed. Then, point downwards, the blade speared into the waters. Only a small circlet of ripples was left to remind the watchers that the sword of sovereignty had ever existed at all.

'Now we can leave the High King, and his works, to memory. At last we may grow old in peace.'

In the years that followed, Nimue's words remained a riddle that Bedwyr puzzled over, a complexity that he often tried to solve. In the skirmishes with Saxons that came more and more frequently during the summers, Bedwyr repelled the enemy time and time again. Eventually, the young Arthur and his brothers took Bedwyr's place as Cornovii warrior kings, and in their inevitable march into the west, the Saxons learned to bypass the inhospitable forests of Arden.

As she had predicted in her bitter youth, Morgan died in poverty and madness in Hibernia. She never saw Tintagel again, and even the memory of her beloved father, Gorlois, faltered at the last. Stripped of the power to govern the most basic actions of her body, she died without remembering who or what she had hated so well. Only the venom in her thoughts had kept her ancient blood pumping for so long.

The gods smiled on Wenhaver and she became the abbess of her order. Vain, capricious and imperious to the end, she died in a scented bed still bemoaning the loss of her precious bath. If she learned anything of value from her long years as the mother of the Britons, she never shared her insights with the quiet-footed women of her order.

Out of a strange loyalty to the beautiful woman she had been, King Gawayne moved her corpse to Glastonbury, opened Artor's grave, and placed her beside him so that she would lie with him for ever.

What Artor feared eventually came to pass. The Saxons

breached the mountain spine and poured through the west like an inexorable flood. Mile by mile, village by village, the Celts were destroyed, absorbed or driven towards the sea. The lands of the Ordovice, the kingdom of Wales, preserved the remnants of the Celtic peoples, while still more refugees crossed the Wall or the sea to the shelter of modern Scotland and Ireland. Angleland became England.

But Cadbury never fell – it decayed slowly. After decades of glory, it was deserted and, in time, dwindled to nothing but a conical hill, overlooking the countryside and surrounded by massive earthworks. All the grandeur fled, but the torn flags of its majesty still exist in the massive walls of sod and the trees that flame in the autumn below its bare summit.

Artor, the man, was eventually forgotten, except as a magical emperor who had supposedly conquered Gaul and Rome. As writers, and even the Saxon and Norman kings, sought to borrow the power of his name and the false legitimacy of kinship with him, his legend and strength grew until he rivalled the emperors of Constantinople and Rome. How Odin must have laughed in Valhalla to hear how far Artor's reach had become with time. Of Odin, the legends were silent, although Gareth and Percivale found places in the stories, as renowned knights. Odin would not have cared, for he had died protecting his master's back, exactly as he had sworn to do.

One day, nearly a thousand years later, a curious farmer found fragments of mosaic flooring buried under his fallow wheat field. The scholars came flocking to Bath, and the Villa Poppinidii found a new purpose long after its ancient walls had been destroyed by time. As the treasures were excavated, the children of another age could see the influence of Roman Britain upon their homeland.

The Stone from the Old Forest was also discovered in the archaeological dig, but all that remained of Gallia's Garden were the foundations of Artorex's house. The experts and archaeologists puzzled over the monolith's position in the forecourt of a Roman villa, and many learned papers were written about the stone. The truth was far more prosaic than any flights of fancy that historians could – and did – imagine.

Artor would have been amused, for he believed that a necessary falsehood could be more powerful than the truth.

Perhaps he was correct, for now the dreams of clever men and women scarcely scratch the surface of his fame. The High King lives more richly in the ordinary lives of a greater west than he ever did when he was alive.

So Artor comes once again, my friends. Will you know him when he calls your name?

Glossary of Place Names

The following is a list of place names in post-Roman Britain with their present-day equivalents.

Abone	Sea Mills, Avon
Abus Flood	River Humber
Anderida	Pevensey, East Sussex
Aquae	Buxton, Derbyshire
Aquae Sulis	Bath, Avon
Bravoniacum	Kirkby Thore, Cumbria
Bravonium	Leintwardine, Herefordshire
Bremenium	High Rochester, Northumbria
Bremetennacum	Ribchester, Lancashire
Burrium	Usk, Gwent
Cadbury	Cadbury, Somerset
Caer Fyrddin	Carmarthen, Wales
Caer Gai	Llanuwchllyn, Gwynedd
Calleva Atrebatum	Silchester, Northhamptonshire

Camulodunum	Colchester, Essex
Canovium	Caerhun, Gwynedd
Causennae	Saltersford, Lincolnshire
Corinium	Cirencester, Gloucestershire
Deva	Chester, Cheshire
Dinas Emrys	Ffestiniog, Snowdonia, Gwynedd
Durnovaria	Dorchester, Dorset
Durobrivae	Water Newton, Cambridgeshire
Durobrivae	Rochester, Kent
Durovernum	Canterbury, Kent
Eburacum	York, North Yorkshire
Forden	Welshpool, Powys
Glastonbury	Glastonbury, Somerset
Glevum	Gloucester, Gloucestershire
Isarium	Aldeborough, North Yorkshire
Isca	Caerleon, Gwent
Isca Dumnoniorum	Exeter, Devon
Lavatrae	Bowes, Durham
Lindinus	Ilchester, Somerset

Lindum	Lincoln, Lincolnshire
Litus Saxonicus	English Channel
Llandowery	Llandow, Glamorgan, Wales
Llanio	Bremia Llanio, Cardiganshire
Londinium	London, Greater London
Magnis	Carvoran, Northumberland
Magnis	Kenchester, Herefordshire
Mamucium	Manchester, Greater Manchester
Metaris Aest	The Wash
Mona Island	Anglesea Island, Wales
Moridunum	Carmarthen, Dyfed
Nidum	Neath, West Glamorgan
Noviomagus	Chichester, West Sussex
Onnum	Halton, Northumberland
Pennal	Machynlleth, Snowdonia, Gwynedd
Petuaria	Brough on Humber, Yorkshire
Portus Dubris	Dover, Kent
Ratae	Leicester, Leicestershire
Rutupaie	Richborough, Kent

Sabrina Aest	Severn River
Salinae	Droitwich, Worcestershire
Segontium	Caernarfon, Gwynedd
Seteia Aest	Dee and Mersey Rivers
Sorviodonum	Old Sarum, Wiltshire
Tamesis River	Thames River
Thanet Island	Eastern Kent (now part of mainland)
Tintagel	Tintagel, Cornwall
Tomen y Mur	Llyn Trawsfynydd, Gwynedd
Trimontium	Newstead, Borders
Vectis Island	The Isle of Wight
Venonae	High Cross, Leicestershire
Venta Belgarum	Winchester, Hampshire
Venta Silurum	Caerwent, Gwent
Verterae	Brough, Cumbria
Viroconium	Wroxeter, Shropshire
Verulamium	St Albans, Hertfordshire
Y Gaer	Newport, South Wales

M. K. HUME

King Arthur: Dragon's Child

THE EPIC TALE OF THE MAN DESTINED TO BECOME ARTHUR HIGH KING OF THE BRITONS.

The Dark Ages: a time of chaos and bloodshed. The Roman legions have long deserted the Isles and the despotic Uther Pendragon, High King of Celtic Britain, is nearing death, his kingdom torn apart by the jostling for his throne.

Of unknown parentage, Artorex is growing up in the household of Lord Ector. One day, three strangers arrive and arrange for Artorex to be taught the martial skills of the warrior; blade and shield, horse and fire, pain and bravery.

When they return, years later, Artorex is not only trained in the arts of battle, he is also a married man. The country is in desperate straits, its great cities falling to the menace of the Saxon hordes. Artorex becomes a war chieftain, and wins the battles that earn him the trust of his Celtic warriors and prove that he alone can unite the tribes. But, if he is to fulfil his destiny and become the High King of the Britons, Artorex must find Uther's crown and sword.

The future of Britain is at stake.

978 0 7553 4867 1

headline
review

Now you can buy any of these other bestselling
Headline books from your bookshop
or *direct from the publisher*.

FREE P&P AND UK DELIVERY
(Overseas and Ireland £3.50 per book)

King Arthur: Dragon's Child	M. K. Hume	£7.99
King Arthur: Warrior of the West	M. K. Hume	£7.99
Bequest	A. K. Shevchenko	£6.99
The Bishop Must Die	Michael Jecks	£7.99
Lost	Gregory Maguire	£7.99
Empire of the Mogul: Raiders of the North	Alex Rutherford	£6.99
From the North	David Gibbins	£6.99
The Levels	Sean Cregan	£6.99
The Gladiator	Simon Scarrow	£7.99

TO ORDER SIMPLY CALL THIS NUMBER

01235 400 414

or visit our website: www.headline.co.uk

Prices and availability subject to change without notice.